THE CRACKS BETWEEN US

A NOVEL

CAITLIN MOSS

For my husband—
Thank you for always whispering my dreams in my ear,
even when I barely remembered them myself.

PROLOGUE

Aila wrings her hands tightly as she stares across the mahogany coffee table where the woman with auburn curly hair and soft hips sits with her notebook, waiting for her to answer. She wants her to speak but Aila doesn't know how.

Her mouth is dry and there's a ball of emotion lodged in her throat making it hard to swallow. Her mind races and her fingers shake as she tries to grasp any sense of reality that would explain the world of pain she's caused. Beads of sweat form on her brow—the room suddenly feeling ten degrees warmer. Aila glances sideways at the fireplace across the room, wishing she could put out the fire. Wishing she *had* put out the fire all those months ago.

Instead, she played with it.

The devil handed her a box of matches and asked if she wanted to play. And she did it because it made her feel good. Seen. It kept her warm and made her feel safe. She wanted to light the fire.

She held each match in her hand and studied it. *What's a little flame?* She downplayed it and lit another one. Before she knew it, her entire life was on fire. She orchestrated the dancing flames on her own. She knows she

1

did even if she didn't realize the ashes it would leave in its wake.

How can she explain that? She doesn't know why she did it. And she certainly doesn't know how to come back from it.

Aila had done a terrible thing to someone she desperately loves.

Now, here she sits on the big brown leather couch in her therapist's office, where her husband sits a world away on the other end, wondering how he got there. How *they* got there.

She clears her throat to see if it will help. It doesn't. She opens her mouth to speak but nothing comes out. She doesn't know where to begin.

"I can see how this must be very difficult for you to talk about, Aila," the woman says, shifting in her chair.

Aila sniffs. "It's…I—I don't know where to begin."

"Well, then why don't we just start at the beginning?"

The beginning. The first hello. The first choice. The first touch. The first kiss. All the lines crossed after.

Aila glances at her husband, his eyes avoiding hers, and then stares at the therapist for a long, pondering moment.

The beginning.

"Which one?"

CHAPTER 1

15 Years Earlier...
THEN

"I fully expect you to loosen up tonight." Chantelle directed her comment at Aila as she handed her a drink in the kitchen of their college apartment.

"What's that supposed to mean?" Aila let out a soft laugh while raking her fingers through her long, chocolate brown hair and taking the drink from her roommate.

Chantelle narrowed her eyes playfully. "You know full well what I mean. You have been in your head, overthinking every detail of your life for the last two weeks but now that midterms are over, you need to relax."

"You know Aila doesn't consider them over until grades are posted," Chelsey chimed in, her icy blue eyes iridescent in the fluorescent lighting. The three roommates stood huddled around their kitchen counter littered with cheap liquor and plastic cups, preparing for a night with friends at their place.

"Not helping." Chantelle glared at Chelsey.

"Forgive me for caring about my grades, Chay," Aila said playfully, sipping her rum and Coke.

"Oh, girl, you can care. You just better not let it ruin

your last two years here."

Aila's mouth dropped open in mock offense. "I would never." She held her hand to her chest and turned to her other roommate. "Chelsey, help me out."

"Well…" Chelsey's response trailed off—her quiet and nonconfrontational personality hesitating. She was the exact opposite of Chantelle, who was outgoing with a boisterous sense of humor. Aila fell somewhere in the middle—typically mild, yet easy to love with a generous heart. Unless, of course, life started drifting into realms beyond her control—which she rarely allowed it to.

"Oh, come on, you guys. I haven't been *that* bad."

Chelsey and Chantelle exchanged a glance out of the corners of their eyes, making Aila's mouth drop open.

"Alright, tell me the truth," Aila said, placing her hands on her hips.

"You're just doing that thing you do when you're stressed." Chelsey practically shrugged her response, attempting to not hurt Aila's feelings.

"What thing?" she questioned even though deep down she knew exactly what they're talking about.

"That *thing* where you button up your entire personality and pretend everything is all fine and dandy even though if one more dish is left in the sink, you will lose your mind on us."

Aila let out an infectious, carefree laugh—the weight on her shoulders lifting.

"See?" Chantelle said pointing at Aila and pulling extra plastic cups out of the cupboard. "That right there. *That* is the Aila we've been missing these last few weeks. You need to let loose a bit. You are far too wound up."

"Okay, fine," Aila conceded. "You're right. But you know how my parents are—even from across the state I feel like they watch me like a hawk, making sure I don't slip."

"You don't have to be perfect all the time, Aila." Chelsey smiled at her, reassuringly.

"Yeah, that Aila is no fun." Chantelle winked at her

and nudged Aila. "Now everyone will be over soon. And you, my dear, better be nice to Derek's friend he's bringing over."

Derek was Chantelle's longtime boyfriend. Together since high school, the two had such an easy and comfortable way about them. He was practically Aila's third roommate. Especially since he lived in the apartment across the breezeway with his roommates. How convenient for Chantelle.

Aila groaned. "Can you please stop trying to set me up?"

"I'm not," Chantelle said, shrugging. "He's just a friend of his. Derek said he's kind of shy. Kind of quiet. Full of mystery and intrigue."

Chelsey buried a laugh in her drink and Aila rolled her eyes.

"Let me guess. He's tall, dark, and handsome, too?"

Chantelle shrugged again, feigning disinterest and exchanging a look with Chelsey.

"Oh, my God, you guys. Can you two please stop? I am perfectly fine being single right now."

"We're not setting you up," Chelsey said in defense. Then winked. "But you're a catch, Aila."

"And so is Derek's friend." Chantelle smiled, her eyes wide with excitement. Aila glared at her before her mouth curled into a grin. "Oh, come on, somebody has to get you over that high school sweetheart of yours. I mean, it's been over two years."

Aila swallowed hard, a surge of embarrassment rising in her cheeks. "Okay, first of all, he was not my high school sweetheart, so, second of all, there's nothing to get over."

Chelsey's head fell into her hand and she looked up at Aila, exhaustedly. "Nobody believes you, Aila."

"He was 'the one that got away,'" Chantelle mocked Aila's drunken words she uttered once during freshman year.

"That's unfair and out of context. I was an inebriated, homesick freshman." Aila laughed. "You can't keep using that against me."

"Then maybe you should move on." Chelsey gave her a smug smile. "But if not, please just have some fun tonight?"

"Fine." Aila rolled her eyes and clinked plastic cups with her roommates, as Derek and his friends rolled through their front door, each face familiar except for one. She nearly choked on her drink at the sight of him. Her hands began to sweat and she felt heat rise in her cheeks. She hung back in the kitchen, her fingers nervously drumming against the countertop while her other two roommates greeted their guests.

He was, in fact, tall, dark, and handsome—taller than she expected and even more handsome. Unbelievably handsome. His jawline was sharp and immediately softened by his smile. His eyes were dark but sparkled when they met Aila's. Even from across the apartment, her heart skipped a beat.

She gave a brief wave and looked away, afraid he'd think she was staring as the cluster of friends meandered in the living room and out on the deck.

"That's him?" Aila said, yanking Chantelle back onto the safety of the linoleum in the kitchen.

Chantelle was smug. "I told you," she said, swirling her drink with a straw. "Good looking, right?"

Aila practically gawked at him and then shook her head slightly, recovering. "I mean, he's okay."

"And he's smart, too." Chantelle gave a wry smile.

Aila glanced at him and then back at Chantelle. "Well, isn't he just perfect on paper?" She crossed her arms and leaned on the counter. "What's wrong with him?"

"Nothing. I swear. I wouldn't do that to you."

"You *have* done that to me."

"With who?"

"Todd, Anthony, Kyle, Jacob…" Aila began listing names off on her hand until Chantelle cut her off.

"Okay, fine. I don't have the greatest track record but he's in all of Derek's pre-law classes. They've been in study group together since last semester and Derek swears he's a nice guy."

"Derek has been hiding him since last semester?" Aila asked skeptically. She hated being set up: the awkward introductions highlighted by the matchmakers gawking at the potential—and completely unnatural—relationship forming.

But he was *really* handsome and it surprised Aila how she instantly felt drawn to him. Attracted in a way that made her nervous and eager to make a good impression—even from across the room.

"Do I look okay?"

Chantelle laughed triumphantly, drawing the attention to them in the kitchen.

"Take him a beer and relax." Chantelle wrapped Aila's hand around the dewy bottle and ushered her away.

Aila strode across the room to the deck, nerves pinging from her fingertips. He was seemingly oblivious to her walking toward him until she was right next to him.

"I don't think we've met yet. I'm Aila," she said holding out her hand, her voice calmer than she expected even though it felt like a million butterflies had hatched in chest.

"I'm Ben." His smile grew wider as his large hand encased hers. Aila let go quickly so he didn't feel her hands start to sweat. Tucking a few loose strands of hair behind her ear, she bit her lower lip to keep from smiling too obviously.

"Nice to meet you."

"Likewise." His eyes stayed on her—a watchful admiration that made her feel both beautiful and nervous. It was as if the stress she had pent up from midterms immediately dissipated and was replaced with a jolt of nerves and attraction for this stranger named Ben.

Chelsey ever so subtly nudged Aila's arm, their eyes met, and Chelsey gave her a knowing smile before leaving her alone on the deck with Ben.

The crickets were extra loud that night, which seemed unusual for the time of year, and the music from the apartment vibrated out on to the deck where Aila and Ben sat under a blanket and a million stars for hours, sipping rum and Cokes—their conversation never dying.

There was an instant and unexplainable chemistry between them and a steady common ground that made their paths crossing make perfect sense. They shared their favorite classes and most meaningful professors. He loved that she knew all the music he loved. And she loved that he made her believe there were real gentlemen out there. For once, she didn't feel like another college guy was being nice to her on a Friday night so he could get in her pants and tell his friends about it at baseball practice the next day.

She told him about the communication class she had to take with the quirkiest professor that had no issue failing not one but two of her papers for misspelled names, and in the same breath offered a letter of recommendation into the communications school.

He spoke of all his political science classes and how much the professors teased them for saying they were "pre-law" but only a quarter of them would actually make it to law school and even fewer would make it out.

"I think you'll make it out," Aila said.

"What makes you so sure?" The deep cadence of his voice vibrated into the night air.

"Well, you're spending the evening with a girl you just met, telling me all about your Civil Liberties class and you just drew a judicial process flow chart on a napkin for me." She smiled wide. "That takes passion."

Ben let out a laugh and blushed. His embarrassed laugh made him even more handsome and Aila reached for his arm, squeezing just slightly. She found him completely endearing.

Something about him felt like the perfect fit; the other puzzle piece she had been missing.

Eventually the two made their way back inside to play a competitive game of Flip Cup with Chantelle and Derek, and the rest of the night was filled with music, shy flirtation, and uncontrollable laughter until the night drew to a close.

As she walked him to the door, Ben grabbed her hand and laced his fingers with hers—the warmth of his touch making her heart beat faster.

"I had a good time with you tonight, Aila," Ben said, turning to face her, but not letting go of her hand.

"Me too." She smiled wide at him, hoping she knew what would happen next.

He's going to kiss me.

Her heart pounded in anticipation as he brushed a loose strand of hair behind her ear.

"I'd like to take you out sometime, if that's okay with you," he said instead of kissing her.

Aila was slightly taken aback he didn't make a move but she still nodded, unable to wipe the smile from her face. "Yeah, I'd like that very much."

"Is tomorrow night too soon?" His dark eyes were hopeful.

"Is it soon enough?" she responded flirtatiously.

Ben's face broke out into a smile before he brought her hand to his lips and kissed it softly, holding her gaze.

"Goodnight, Aila. See you tomorrow." `

The skin on her hand still tingled from his lips. She smiled to herself, feeling thankful she was able to unwind that night. As she watched him walk away, he turned around and smiled at her one last time. She held his gaze for a long moment and she instantly knew he was going to make her completely unravel.

~

Aila couldn't stop smiling or slow her heart even as it raced into the following day.

She waltzed around the apartment, still unable to keep from smiling—completely smitten with a man she barely knew. As the clock ticked closer to when Ben was due to pick her up, she grew unusually nervous. She had always felt so in control of her life and emotions until she met Ben. He captivated her. Enraptured her. She spent the entire day constantly thinking about him and checking her phone to see if he texted, wondering if she was tipping towards an unhealthy level of admiration.

Aila took one final look at herself in the full-length mirror in her bedroom before stepping out into the living room where Chantelle and Chelsey were sitting on the couch drinking spiked lemonades.

"How do I look?" She was wearing jeans with a white t-shirt and tan cardigan.

"Are you going to church?" Chantelle shot up an eyebrow as she marched across the room and into her bedroom. Aila looked down and assessed her outfit and shrugged. She had thought she was wearing a cute, classy first date outfit.

"Give her a break, she looks fine," Chelsey said as she winked at Aila.

"Lose the sweater and wear this," Chantelle said, as she emerged from her room holding a slinky red top and leather jacket.

"Saucy," Aila quipped hesitantly.

"Trust me, you'll look gorgeous."

Aila let out a sigh before reluctantly changing her top. Eyeing herself in her mirror, she smiled. The red top did look good on her even if it wasn't her typical style, and the leather jacket added an edgy touch to the outfit that made her feel sexy.

She waited on the loveseat in their living room, lost in her thoughts, and feeling overdressed and incredibly nervous as she anxiously picked at her cuticles.

When Ben arrived to pick her up, Aila rushed out the door to avoid any and all jokes that would be hurled from Chantelle. She was sometimes—well, always—too much.

Ben held open the passenger side of his car. Aila hopped in and gingerly slid the seatbelt across her chest, throwing her long brown waves over her shoulder.

"So, where are you taking me?" Aila asked playfully, trying to match her tone to her outfit. She hoped she did the right thing by taking Chantelle's fashion advice. "Saucy" wasn't exactly her style, and she felt exposed in more ways than one.

"Well," Ben began slowly, charmingly unsure of himself. "I thought we could stop over at Sella's to eat, and then I have a surprise I want to show you."

Yep. Definitely overdressed, Aila thought, but even still she was intrigued by the notion of surprise. *Has anyone ever surprised me like this before?*

She took a quick inventory of past relationships and realized no one had ever truly tried to sweep her off her feet. Until now. Even if they were headed to a family restaurant.

Everyone loved Sella's. They served up the best calzones in town but it was the kind of place a family would go after church on Sunday. The tablecloths were white and red checkered and children's attempts at art scattered the walls. When they were seated, Ben asked for two coloring pages of their own.

"Okay…" the waitress in her forties said slowly. She returned to the table with two pictures of an overweight cartoon chef with an unrealistically large mustache tossing pizza dough in the air and one Solo cup of half broken crayons. She took their orders and headed back to the kitchen.

"You didn't tell me you were such an artist, Ben," Aila teased him. He looked up and eyed her over the fake flower in the vase between them.

"I'm not an artist. I'm a competitor," he said seriously, as the waitress plopped down two beers in front of them before walking away.

Aila raised an eyebrow, confused.

"We each have until our calzones come out to color these, the best artist wins a kiss." His gaze sent her stomach into a flurry of butterflies and she felt heat rise to her cheeks.

She leaned in closer, placing her hand on her chin,

delicately. "And who says I want a kiss from you?"

Ben mirrored her body language. "Who says you'll win?"

Aila held his stare a moment longer and then grabbed a crayon.

"You're on."

They spent the next ten minutes as feverish artists, hunched over their masterpieces, trying to distract and sabotage each other's work, throwing themselves into fits of laughter. Aila began hiding crayons in her left hand and when Ben realized, he reached for her hand.

"You cheater!" he exclaimed in mock anger, obviously understanding this was a ploy to get him to hold her hand.

Aila couldn't control her laughter. The whole scenario was ridiculous and playful but unbelievably sweet and endearing. She felt giddy, like her head was full of bubbles. Her doubts about Ben bringing her to Sella's were gone.

Ben hollered "times up" when the waitress returned with their meals and Aila dropped her crayon and threw her hands up in surrender.

"Is there anything else I can get for you two?" the waitress asked.

"Just one thing," Ben said holding up the two colored pictures side by side. "Which one do you like better?"

The waitress raised a finger to her lip, looking at each picture intently. Aila held her breath, smiling as wide as a schoolgirl, in anticipation.

"Mmm…that one," she nodded, pointing to the one on Ben's right.

"Yes!" Aila shouted a bit too loudly in celebration, making the family of four sitting at the table next to them turn their heads in bewilderment. The waitress smiled, shook her head, and moved on.

"I demand a recount," Ben said.

"Uh-uh, buddy, I played by your rules and I still won." Aila grinned triumphantly as she picked up her fork and took a bite of her calzone.

Ben reached across the table with his large, caramel colored hand to shake hers and said in defeat, "Good game."

Aila mocked offense. "I think you owe me something else, sir."

She turned her head, slightly lifting her cheek in his direction and he leaned in and kissed it gently. His lips felt like warm clouds pressed against her skin and she had to fight every urge not to turn her head to return the affection, but there was no way she wanted their first kiss to be next to a couple in their thirties with two toddlers eating pizza.

When he sat back, Aila could still feel the spot on her skin where he kissed her, tingling with warmth.

"Thank you." She smiled smugly, and placed another bite of calzone in her mouth to distract herself from wanting to leap across the table and kiss him.

"You're very welcome." He looked at her like he knew exactly what he was doing. Aila couldn't believe how quickly she was falling for him.

After dinner, the pair went back to the car and pulled out on Main Street.

"Alright, *Ben*," Aila said, pretending to be far less excited about the rest of the night than she was. "Now where are you taking me?"

Ben glanced away from the road and smiled softly.

"It's a surprise."

When they arrived at a park just outside of town, Aila was confused about his intentions. She wanted to laugh.

First the family restaurant and now a playground?

"Alright, family guy," she smirked, "are you going to push me on the swings?"

"Only if you want me to," he flirted back, pulling a small bag out of the trunk.

He was a man of few words, but Aila found each word he said held depth, meaning, and a bit of mystery. Nearly everything he said hung in the air like bait she couldn't quite grab a hold of but desperately wanted.

Aila eyed him and his bag suspiciously.

"I want to show you something."

He looked even taller in that moment, his shoulders sharp around the edges and his broad chest a cage of protection around his heart. Aila followed him through a small clearing between trees and a short way down a path until the trees completely parted like a velvet curtain on a stage, making way to the most picturesque view of the Palouse. Rolling hills as far as the eye could see, cascading into each other, each one lit on fire by the setting sun. The sky was bright orange and red with hints of pink. It was the most beautiful sunset she'd ever seen.

Ben laid out a blanket on the grass and invited her to sit down with a sweeping gesture, "My lady."

Aila sat down while Ben pulled out two plastic cups and a bottle of champagne.

"Make a wish!" he said and popped the champagne open.

Aila squealed and let out an embarrassing laugh as champagne foam ran down his arms. He poured them each a cup, while he laughed at himself. His slight faux pas made him even more attractive and endearing, if that was even possible.

This would be no fun if he were completely perfect, she thought, realizing how effortlessly he put her at ease.

He made his place next to Aila. She was sitting so close to him she was sure he could hear her heart pounding as he wrapped his arm around her.

They spent the next hour talking about life, their families, their goals, their hopes, and their dreams. They talked about the towns they grew up in—just thirty minutes from each other—and where they wanted to end up themselves.

"Do you like being an only child?" she asked.

"I don't know any different so I guess I've never really thought about whether or not I liked it." Ben shrugged. "What about you?"

Aila contemplated the question for a moment. "It's okay, I guess. Sometimes I wish I had a sibling so the spotlight would fall on someone else every once in a while. I've always loved the attention but hated feeling like I'm not allowed to screw up." She leaned back. "Wouldn't want to reflect poorly on good ol' Mom and Dad."

She smiled at him, playfully.

"I'd imagine that's tough."

She nodded, contemplating her confession and choosing to broach a lighter subject.

"Alright, Ben, tell me something unusual about yourself?"

"Like what?"

"Anything. Any hidden talents or weird food preferences I should know about?"

"Well, I'm not a ketchup and scrambled eggs kind of guy if that's what you mean."

Aila made a face and laughed. "Thank goodness I don't have to worry about *that*." She gave him a playful nudge.

"But I do like potato chips on my sandwiches."

She looked at him, surprised. "No way. Me too!" She laughed. "Chantelle and Chelsey think it's so weird but I always thought everybody did that."

"Because everybody *should* do that—it's delicious." He smiled.

"Yes, they should." Aila smiled and took a sip of her champagne. She let a comfortable silence linger between them for a moment before she spoke again. "Do you ever see yourself moving away from Washington?"

"Sometimes. I think it'd be hard to leave my mom here all by herself. We're all the family we have," he said tearing a blade of grass into pieces. "But I don't necessarily feel bound to Washington so I guess it depends on the opportunity."

"Or person?" Aila asked, her tone sarcastic and playful.

She had always dreamed of working for an advertising agency in a place like Los Angeles or New York City.

"If you want me to…" Ben eyed her with a flirtatious smirk.

Aila's eyes narrowed in on him.

"You don't strike me as someone that would follow a girl across the country."

"You don't strike me as someone who judges a book by its cover," he said, as he sat back on his hands.

"Touché." Aila rubbed her lips together to hold back a grin.

It didn't work. Ben saw her dimples come through and he reached out and brushed them gently with his thumb. It was as if time froze. Aila's lips parted in a smile and she felt heat rise up in her belly and a tremble run through her veins. She pulled him closer by the nape of his neck, their noses almost touching. She could feel the heat of his lips on hers as she looked into his dark eyes. They were kind with a glint of mystery and risk.

Being with Ben felt like a calm and quiet surrender. She wanted to be swallowed whole, taken and consumed by him. He tilted her chin softly before leaning in completely and kissing her.

She never understood how people described kisses as electric until she kissed Ben. There was a jolt of energy she hadn't experienced before. It felt supernatural. Out of this world. And with just that one kiss, she knew.

I'm going to marry this man.

CHAPTER 2

15 Years Later
NOW

Aila peels her eyes open at the sound of her alarm. She had already hit snooze twice. She needs to get up or the boys will be late for school. Her room is still pitch black, which is typical of a winter morning in the Pacific Northwest, making it particularly challenging for her to rise and shine. So is the extra glass of wine she had last night. Her mouth feels dry and her eyes sticky. She rarely overdid it with alcohol but every once in a while, she felt like she deserved a few drinks. Deep regret would often follow her in the morning.

She groans and turns over to look at where Ben's side of the bed lay crumpled and empty. Typical Monday. He'd often say he likes to get an early start on the week, but truth be told he likes to get an early start on every day of the week. There were always trials to prepare for, clients to meet with, and emergency trips to their San Francisco office. When Ben started working at White & Associates, Aila catered to every dream he wanted to come true, even if it meant taking a backseat for a few years.

Ten. It has been ten years in the backseat.

When did we turn into this? she thinks, still staring at Ben's empty side of the bed and wondering if he even kissed her goodbye before he left.

She knows she's a good wife to Ben and an even better mother to their three boys, but she still finds herself simply running through the motions as a stay-at-home mom, trying to balance the monotony with the chaos. She makes sure to always plaster her face with a pretty smile and put her own needs last. She's never reckless, never forgetful—always priding herself in creating a consistent, picture-perfect family of togetherness.

Or is it an illusion? She presses her palms over her tired eyes as if to press the thoughts away.

When Aila finally trudges her way downstairs, she stands at the marble countertop in her newly remodeled kitchen while she chugs a glass of water and simultaneously pours herself a large cup of coffee, staring at the color-coded calendar hanging on the refrigerator.

She opens her phone to compare calendars, making sure they align perfectly—nothing out of place or unaccounted for. Blue, red, green, yellow, and only a couple lines of purple. She feels overwhelmed by her plain and ordinary life, wishing she could still find the beauty in it.

She takes a mental note of this week's routine and turns to her disaster of a living room and lets out a sigh.

The boys always destroyed the house over the weekend but this particular weekend brought a winter rain and windstorm beyond anything the Pacific Northwest had seen in a while. Their golden retriever Gus muddied up the entire downstairs from running in and outside. Josh, Caleb, and Isaac were holed up inside and their boyish level of stir-crazy wreaked havoc on their usually pristine home.

Aila thought she might lose her mind by the time Sunday night had arrived. She poured herself a large glass of wine instead and put on The Grammy Awards while the boys were upstairs playing video games and Ben was in the office returning emails. The one glass of wine accidentally turned into three, and Aila hesitantly stopped herself before polishing off the entire bottle. She knew she'd regret it in the morning.

Feeling slightly more relaxed and a bit drunk, Aila had been less worried about the disaster zone that was her home.

I'll take care of this after the boys are off to school tomorrow, she had thought, realizing she rarely left a household task undone. It usually made her feel out of control but last night—probably because of the wine—it made her feel carefree. Something she hadn't felt in a while.

She had sealed the night with a prayer and dipped under the covers with Ben.

It wasn't her favorite kind of lovemaking. After fifteen years of marriage, there aren't many surprises in the bedroom. It was brief and almost rehearsed—another item to cross off her to-do list. Before she knew it, her mind finally raced itself to sleep until she finally woke up and dragged herself downstairs to the coffee maker.

Aila stands there, sipping her coffee and scanning the room again. The dim winter sun is just barely peeking through the windows. She lets out a deep sigh as she fully realizes how much cleaning there will be once she ushers the boys out the door and on the bus. She partly wishes that extra glass of wine hadn't convinced her to ignore the mess last night.

Quit being ridiculous, she thinks to herself. *The kids will be off to school in an hour. It's not like I have anything else to do today.* The thought makes her heart constrict—she is constantly surrounded by little humans, but she still feels alone every day.

Aila blinks her thoughts away as she always does before waking the boys up for school and carrying on with another day in her plain and ordinary life.

~

"Shoes. Backpacks," Aila calls up the stairs, ready to send her boys off to school. She suddenly couldn't wait to get the house back in order and regain control of her thoughts and distract her from the reality that had become her life.

"Mom! Where's my poster about the Civil War?" Caleb yells from the top of the stairs.

"I don't remember how you keeping track of your work is my problem," Aila hollers back, her wine headache ringing.

"Mom, can you help me tie my shoes?" Isaac asks. He is halfway through his kindergarten year and still hasn't quite mastered the skill. His dark, pleading eyes are like saucers—reminding her how much he looks like Ben.

"Sure thing." She turns to her oldest. "Josh, did you put on deodorant?"

"Yep," Josh says. At ten, he doesn't look like he should wear deodorant but he smells like he should.

"Are you sure?" Aila questions. He's also sometimes fibs about personal hygiene. "Here, let me smell."

"Mom, stop. No, that's gross. I swear I put some on," he says, and Aila laughs as he squirms away from her, a sweet reprieve from her pounding head.

"Found it!" Caleb says at the top of the stairs, like the triumphant eight-year-old he is.

Of course, he found it. She smiles and halfway rolls her eyes.

"Alright then, put your shoes on and let's go, go, go," she says holding up Caleb's backpack for him to slip on his shoulders. As they file out the front door to walk to the bus stop, she adds, "Everyone have their lunches?"

There is a smattering of head nods as they pass by their perfectly manicured yard and Aila feels an absurd rush of pride. Her mother always said, a house is only as pretty as its front lawn. She took that advice to heart. Clearly, nothing was picture perfect on the inside. But she allows people to think that. She wants them to. It makes her feel worthy. Admired. Loved. Even if, on the inside, she feels completely and constantly passed over.

They make their way around the corner to the bus stop on Cherrywood Lane, and Aila kisses and hugs each boy she loves deeply even if they drive her crazy beyond imagination. The simplicity and consistency of the morning ritual makes her feel back in control of the day, her emotions, and her pounding head.

"Bye, sweet boys!" Aila calls as the bus door closes, blowing kisses and hoping she embarrasses them just a bit.

"Happy Monday," another mother, Janet, says with a nudge, a wink, and the toothiest smile. She always has that smile plastered on her face. The kind where you can see every single tooth, even the molars. Her hair is bigger than usual but still perfectly wavy, like a brassy ocean.

"Yes. Happy Monday, Janet," Aila replies with a brief nod before attempting to turn and walk back to the house.

"You feeling okay, Aila?" she calls, condescendingly. "You look really tired."

Thank you for reminding me I look like crap today, she wants to say. *I am* tired, *Janet.*

Aila takes in a deep breath through her nostrils and smiles instead, shoveling away her true feelings. She's good at that.

"I'm fine, thanks. Just a lot to get done after a busy weekend."

"Well, let me know if you want to grab a coffee and chat," she says, still smiling.

"Thank you for the offer. Not today," Aila says as she suppresses a deep sigh of irritation. "But soon."

Isn't that what motherhood turns you into? she thinks. *Promising to make plans soon and then never following through. Or making the plans and cancelling because you never really wanted to go in the first place.* She practically scoffs at the reality.

It's not even that Aila dislikes Janet. She can just be really irritating. She has an answer for everything. She's incredibly nosy. She and Ben refer to her as the neighborhood gossip queen—always in everyone's business.

Her hair is always done. Nails are always painted. And for the love of all things holy, she wears jeans to the bus stop every single day. Who is she even trying to impress? Everyone knows she's headed back to her house to clean up the hot breakfast she made for her only daughter, Grace.

Life would've been simpler if Aila and Ben had stopped at one. Not better but simpler. A thought she often allows to cross her mind, followed by a dump truck of guilt.

Aila lets out the sigh she was holding in, less out of irritation and more out of exhaustion…and a bit of regret for drinking that third glass of wine last night. *Of course* she looks tired. She picks up her pace a bit as she walks back to the house, feeling the sharpness of the morning's chill whip past her cheeks, all at once eager for and dreading the solitary that awaits her.

Aila shuts her front door and leans against it for a moment; the quiet deafening, broken only by the jingle coming from Gus's collar as he trots over to greet her. Once the golden retriever is back on his bed next to the fireplace, the silent house is so overwhelming she can hear the drip-drip of the faucet that was left running, most likely by Caleb. It was always Caleb.

The scent of strawberry Pop Tarts still wafts through the air making her miss the boys already. It wasn't too long ago she wanted this, couldn't wait for this quiet.

I am going to get so much done!

She'd fantasize about it often.

But now she just feels empty. Over the last year, Aila has realized being a stay-at-home mom now feels less like a job and more like a loss of purpose.

Purpose beyond this calendar, she thinks, eyeing the activities and time commitments written out in rainbow perfection—a different color for each member of the family.

"At least it's Monday," she says aloud.

It was the one day a week she never planned to do anything, which meant she could catch up from the busy weekend full of baseball and Taekwondo and prepare for the week ahead.

Although she was a stay-at-home mom, Aila never really stayed home. Not once she realized her loneliness would stare at her in the face as soon as the house was empty.

The first year, when Isaac was in half day pre-school, it was glorious. She could clean and exercise without anyone home. She found little projects to get started on around the house, like re-caulking the bathroom sinks and painting the laundry room.

By the middle of the year, she was so caught up on the housework, she started creating projects just to fill her time.

"I think the boys' bathroom needs new floors, don't you?" she had said to Ben, with her eyes wild with excitement, after he realized she'd already ripped out the old vinyl.

"Well, I guess so." He had smiled, rubbing his hand down his face in exasperation. He didn't anger easily; he preferred to sweep most things under the rug so he didn't have to deal with it. He's like Aila in that way.

Now halfway through Isaac's kindergarten year and all three kids in school, she makes sure to fill her time up enough that she still feels needed. Tuesday afternoons she volunteers in Josh's classroom—blue, Thursday afternoons in Caleb's class—red, and Friday mornings in Isaac's—green.

The boys love having their mom come to their class, and Aila loves that everyone calls her Mrs. Sorenson. It makes her feel more professional and gives her a reason to get dressed in something other than leggings.

Wednesdays, she leads a Bible study at church with her friend, Elena. She is only a few years older but Aila always gleans so much wisdom from her. She is matter of fact and sarcastic but kind. Plus, she cusses sometimes, which makes Aila blush at the naughtiness of saying the "s" word in church.

Aila relishes in the adult time with other women every Wednesday—and anything else on the calendar written in purple.

In addition to her regularly scheduled volunteer hours, there are practices and playdates she has to taxi her kids to and from and she always offers her services to fill in any and all gaps.

Halloween party at school? She'll bring cupcakes. Childcare provider at church service? Sign her up. PTO vice president? Yes, please. Organize a meal train for Cindy after she has a baby? Done.

If Aila fills her calendar enough with meaningful things to do for other people, her empty house will feel a little less lonely. At least that's the hope.

Still standing at the calendar outlining the week ahead, she pulls her ponytail a little tighter, pours herself a third cup of coffee, pops two ibuprofens, and starts running through her chore list.

After spending the next hour wiping down the counters, loading dishes, straightening the throw pillows in the living room, disinfecting doorknobs and light switches, and vacuuming and mopping the original hardwood floors, Aila switches off the fireplace and turns to Gus.

"You ready?" she says and he stands at attention immediately while she walks over and latches the leash to his collar.

Out the front door, the morning air is still piercingly cold and the fog is only just starting to dissipate but Aila can tell it's going to be a beautiful, sunny winter day. A great reprieve from yesterday's windstorm and hopefully a cure for her weird mood and quite possibly her low-key hangover.

She turns on her headphones and starts listening to music, while passing through suburbia and walking along Cherrywood Lane until she rounds the corner to Skyline hill. Her mind immediately feels calmer, her mood lighter. Her stiff, dehydrated, *I-drank-too-much-wine-last-night-muscles* begin to relax, her headache lifting.

Nothing a little dog walking and water can't fix, she thinks, letting out a soft laugh to herself.

By the time Aila reaches the top of the hill, the fog has lifted and the day is turning out to be clear and crisp. Something every Pacific Northwesterner longs for during the winter months. Aila stops with Gus to admire the view. It's the only spot in town where the view spans four cities away from the valley of fields below to the Puget Sound water glistening in the sun, and the Olympic Mountain range just beyond, dancing with snow.

"Can you believe we get to see this beauty, Gus?" But Gus is too busy smelling a particularly fragrant bush. Aila lets out a brief sigh.

What's next, Aila? she thinks, contemplating a life she chose and actively participated in building but knows there is something missing from it. She and Ben dreamt up this life, of course, but she often wonders where her piece of the dream is.

She never realized when she gave up her career in advertising to stay home with her boys it would pass so quickly. It became such an all-consuming, minute-by-minute, second-by-second marathon from the time she woke up to the time her head hit the pillow, every single day, that she forgot to plan for what comes next.

What comes now that she sent her last baby to school? Is she even a viable candidate for the current job market after ten years? Did she waste these years holed up with her children? Or is she just a little lost, waiting to found again?

Or is this it? Aila thinks. *Maybe I just run the rest of my life around everyone else's schedule—Josh's, Caleb's, Isaac's, and Ben's. Blue, red, green, yellow. They do really need me, after all.*

As she walks along the aptly named street lined with Cherrywood trees preparing to bud for the spring, Aila hears a faint calling of her name and pulls her headphones out so she can figure out what direction it's coming from.

"Aila! Aila Smith! Is that you?"

Aila's eyes narrow on the man with dark, short hair and tanned skin, running toward her. He can't be much younger than she is but the situation is so out of context, she can't place him or understand why he is calling her by her maiden name.

"It's Aila Sorenson, but once upon a time I was Aila Smith," she says as she plasters on her automatic smile.

With the last breath of the sentence, she recognizes him.

Of course, I run into someone I haven't seen in years on the one morning I'm slightly hungover. And, of course, *it's Jackson Williams.* She wants to hide behind a tree.

She hadn't seen Jackson since after high school graduation. Her breath catches in her throat as the memories of their late-night laughter and stolen kisses flood her mind. They were never an item—he was off limits because he dated one of her friends—but he did kiss her after Ethan Chase's party junior *and* senior year after prom. It was their little secret.

Or maybe she kissed him? Aila flushes at the memory even though it's been nearly two decades since she last saw him.

"Jackson?" She smiles wide, almost obnoxiously. The flood of memories writing excitement all over her face. "Jackson Williams? I can't believe it!"

He smiles, his straight white teeth highlighted by his chiseled jaw and softened by his dimples. The dimples that clearly haven't changed since high school. His hair is cut short but Aila knows if he let it grow out a little longer, it'd be thick with curls. Simply knowing that about him makes her heart beat faster. She once knew him completely, and now not at all. It's almost like knowing intimate details about a stranger. Or rather, a complete stranger knowing intimate details about her. It makes her feel vulnerable and nervous. She bites her lip.

"I thought that looked like you!" he says. "What are the chances?"

"Pretty slim," she says, *considering it's been twenty years.*

"Who's this guy?" he asks as he bends down to tousle

Gus's ears.

"Oh, this is Gus," she smiles awkwardly, "My trusty sidekick."

That was dumb. I'm such a mom.

Her once confident demeaner had somehow shifted in recent years causing her to constantly doubt herself. She lays her façade on thick so no one can break through it. But that's the thing about a façade: there are always cracks where doubt and insecurities seep through, like oil running down a driveway. She can't remember when or how she became so unsure of herself.

"He's a beauty," Jackson says as he pets Gus, who rewards him with slobbery kisses. "And friendly."

"Yeah, he loves new friends." She laughs, reaching down to scratch behind Gus's ears, her fingers accidentally brushing against Jackson's. The touch is small and innocent but feels warm and electric, sending a rush of nerves through her skin and making her heart beat faster.

Pathetic. Aila wants to laugh at herself.

"You live around here?" Jackson asks.

"I do. My husband and I have a house just around the corner." Aila nods in the direction of the house. "Do you live here now too?"

She immediately answers her own question as she registers his dirtied up Carhartt pants and landscaping trucks behind him with Williams Brothers' Landscaping, plastered across the side.

"Oh!" she says as she waves her hand toward the truck. "You and Adam then?"

She remembers his older brother Adam right away. Their silly banter made her laugh into the early hours of the morning before she snuck back into her house well past curfew. She had spent a lot of time at the Williams brothers' house during high school.

"Yeah," he says, smiling the same boyish smile she remembers. "It started as a summer business during college and took off. I'm not usually here with my guys but it's a new job so I like to make sure everyone has an understanding of what needs so to be done for the neighborhood."

"Wow. That's great. Good for you. Congratulations to you and your brother. You'll tell him for me?" She's rambling, she realizes, and presses her lips tight together.

Jackson is smooth and calm, and Aila feels herself getting nervous and she can't figure out why.

"Of course. Though, you might see him here from time to time. This neighborhood has been assigned to me but every once in a while, he fills in for me when I can't be here and I do the same for him. We like to stay present on all our job sites," he says, and with an almost wink, "Quality control."

"Right." Aila hasn't stopped smiling, making her cheeks ache and she can't help but feel foolish. "Well, I'll let you know if I catch your guys slipping," she adds playfully. *Why did I say that? He could care less about my opinion about his employees.*

"Please do," Jackson says. He cracks another smile. "What about you? How have you been? You said you live here with your husband?"

"Yes. Just me and my husband, Ben, and our three boys," she says, running her fingers through her long ponytail.

She lets out a nervous laugh.

"Three? Wow!" he says, like everyone does. "Good for you! I always knew you'd be a good mom. Especially to boys."

"Ha. Ha," Aila replies, a little unsure of how to respond to this comment. "I doubt your seventeen-year-old-self thought that but thank you anyway."

"True, I never did think that far ahead," Jackson chuckles in a boyish way, looking down at his feet. "Do you work or…"

Ah, there it is. The question no one knows how to ask if they aren't directly offered the information.

She'd thought about going back to work but after she

and Ben discussed it, they realized that would mean no more classroom volunteering, a nanny, more household duties to be split between the two, and relying on Ben to finish up at the office and be home on time now and then. Ben wasn't ready for that, the family wasn't ready for that, so Aila wasn't ready for that.

One day I'll get my turn again.

"No, I've stayed home since our oldest was born. My husband is an attorney. He works really long hours so it's just best for me to always be available to our kids," Aila says it with a well-practiced smile and confidence.

"What about you?" Aila turns the line of questioning on Jackson. "Are you married with a house full of kids too?"

"Uh, no." His smile fades a bit. "No kids. I was married for a while but now it's just me."

Aila nods sincerely, not wanting to discuss his divorce.

"Well, it's been so good to run into you," Aila says, ready to head back to the house. Her mouth feels dry and she knows her face is swollen from drinking wine the night before.

"You too, Aila," Jackson says, with a smile. A hauntingly charming smile.

"And I guess I'll be seeing you." Aila gestures toward the trucks.

"Yes, ma'am."

"See you around, Jackson."

"Same to you, Aila," he says as he leans down to give Gus one last scratch behind the ears.

Aila smiles and pats his arm as if to punctuate her departure from this awkward encounter. But Jackson reaches over and pulls her in for a hug, a bear-like squeeze, his arms encasing her shoulders. Quick enough to be appropriate, but long enough his scent wafts through her nose and her memories.

He smells like laundry detergent and earth. An odd combination, she knows, but one that feels familiar, transporting her back to the girl she was twenty years ago, making her stomach flip.

Aila smiles, quickly meeting his eyes and turns to walk away, letting out a breath she didn't realize she was holding.

That was awkward. Or was I just awkward? I really wish I put on some mascara.

Aila turns up her pace walking back to house.

I can't believe I ran into Jackson. She smiles at the thought, at the memories, at how good he looks… and then catches herself.

But it did feel good to run into someone who knew her before she was who she is now. A wife. A mom. A dogwalker. A housecleaner. A taxi driver. And not much else. Ben used to know that girl.

I wonder if he even remembers her.

CHAPTER 3

NOW

When the boys hop off the bus that afternoon, Aila feels a sense of relief over the normalcy that will return now that they'll be home.

After she ran into Jackson, she spent the rest of the day continuing to get the house back in order. Dinner was put in the slow cooker—a new recipe she found on Pinterest for Tuscan chicken—the bathrooms were given a good bleach bath, and then she headed out to run errands.

Once she got home, after spotting the Williams Brothers Landscaping truck still in the neighborhood, Aila couldn't stop thinking about Jackson.

It wasn't so much who she ran into—or that he turned out to be incredibly handsome—but simply that she ran into anyone she knew before marriage. And children. And her thirties. Someone she knew a lifetime ago.

Was she too awkward? Did she look like one of those people from high school that had a bunch of kids and gained thirty pounds and nothing else to show for her life but her offspring? Is he calling Adam now and telling him what happened to that one chick from high school? The athletic one that was unexpectedly hilarious but now she's just a suburban housewife with a gaggle of children?

Why is she obsessing? Why does she feel a tinge of embarrassment? She shouldn't care what he thinks. She has a great life she loves and a family she adores.

Aila attempts to shrug off her feelings of inadequacy when she spots Isaac, Caleb, and Josh practically run off the bus. Her breath of fresh air in the flesh.

"Hey, sweet babies" she calls as they each greet her. "How was your day?"

"Mine was fantastic!" Isaac says, practically skipping as he reaches for her hand with marker smeared fingers and bitten down nails. "Mrs. Johnson loved my picture I drew. She called it 'unik!'"

"You mean *unique,*" Aila says and leans in to kiss the top of his head. "And I'll bet she did."

"Can I play Fortnite with Brody tonight?" Caleb asks.

"It's Monday, so no." She only let the kids play video games on the weekends. He knows that but loves to test her to see if she'll bend. Because sometimes she did.

"But he's going to be gone this weekend and we really want to team up!"

"I get it, bud, but no," Aila says. "You have swim tonight anyway and the sun is out for once this winter so we are going to take advantage of it."

Caleb's eyes fall in disappointment.

"Whether you like it or not," Aila adds with a wink.

Caleb's eyes turn up and he takes off running back to the house with Isaac and Gus. Aila turns to her oldest, most serious boy of the bunch.

"And my dearest, Joshua. Take those ear buds out and tell your mama about your day," Aila says.

"It was good." Josh smiles, his brown hair slightly messed up, probably from playing basketball at recess. Aila wraps her arm around him. A boy of few words. Like Ben.

Back at the house the boys take care of their backpacks and paper work, clean out their lunch boxes and grab something quick to snack on. Before they grab their second and third snacks, Aila ushers them outside to enjoy the clear skies before the rain hits again tomorrow.

Evenings on days like today are always the same. Everyone in the neighborhood flocks to their driveways with bikes and basketballs and skateboards and scooters and chalk. Not too far in the distance, Aila spots Janet walking a few paces behind her daughter, Grace, who's riding her bike toward Aila's house.

She gives Janet a reluctant wave and turns to Grace.

"Well, hi, Miss Grace," Aila says. "How was school today?"

"It was great! I got to paint a heart out of magic fluffy paint Mrs. Johnson made! I covered it in glitter and had cookies for snack."

Her blonde curls bounced from underneath her unicorn helmet with every word she said before bending over to grab some chalk from the bucket beside Aila.

"Well, kindergarten sounds like a lot of fun." Her eyes linger on the chalk scribbles dancing across the pavement before looking back up to Janet approaching her in a huff.

"Hey, Aila, I hate to do this to you but I really need to start dinner and it's hard to do with a house full of kids. Can you keep an eye on Grace while I head back to the house?"

Aila smiles at Janet and nods.

You have one kid to cook for. "Sure. No problem."

It was never a problem. The kids always congregated at Aila's driveway anyway. She finally made it a rule no one could come inside, not every day at least. And certainly not on days in February where the sun shone like this. The interesting thing is though, the more she said it's not a problem, the more the parents in the neighborhood assumed she'd want to take care of everyone else's kids all of the time.

"Hey, boys!" she hollers up the street. "Too far, please. You know you aren't supposed to go past the mailboxes."

"Sorry, Mom," Caleb and Josh call back in unison.

They know the rules. They aren't supposed to ride

past the mailboxes where the turn onto Cherrywood Lane is because every so often a car will come tearing around the corner. It's usually a careless teenager or a grumpy empty nester, but Aila knows it'd only take a blink in the wrong direction for a kid to get hit on their bike. With the exception of the busy corner, it is otherwise a safe and pleasant neighborhood with tree lined streets and freshly edged sidewalks, full of families with children.

And the neighborhood children love Aila. She runs races with them and rides scooters. She is an excellent sidewalk chalk artist and a great shot with Nerf guns. She actually has a lot of fun with the kids. Kids are simple. They just want to laugh and play. They're brutally honest and live life by the rules, and painstakingly point out if the rules are broken.

But that doesn't mean Aila doesn't want to feel like an adult every once in a while.

"Car!" the kids yell as a black sedan pulls around the corner.

It's the time of night all the nine to fivers are trickling home for the night. This car belongs to Ben, who seems to be home from work a couple hours earlier than usual.

Awesome. He can play outside with the kids while I go cook dinner.

This almost never happens, Aila knows the kids are so excited to see him and they immediately flock to his car before he even parks hollering, "Hey Dad!" and "Watch this!"

Even though he works long hours, Ben is always good at putting on a happy face for the kids when he gets home, even if he escapes to his office soon after.

"You're home early." Aila approaches him with a wide, college girl smile he could still bring out in her.

Ben fully emerges from the car, his suit jacket in the passenger seat and his tie already loosened around his neck, the top button of his shirt already undone and his five o'clock shadow coming in strong.

"I have an early morning tomorrow and told Carla I'd rather go over the case tonight after the kids go to bed," he says and then pulls her in for a hug and quick kiss, his large, strong hands resting on the small of her back. His arms hang there perfectly as if they are meant to be there, a sweet claim of possession. Aila doesn't mind that word either. Possession. She wants to be desired and claimed. She feels that longing every day.

"How was your day?"

"Very exciting," she says, still lingering in his arms. "I can't wait to tell you all about it."

She's being partly sarcastic but there's a thought prickling in the back of her mind. She should probably mention running into her friend from high school, but she doesn't even get the chance to elaborate on any part of her day before his attention gets drawn elsewhere.

"Hey there, neighbor."

Aila spots Joel, who lives just across the street, walking toward Ben as if he'd been waiting all day for him to get home. The sound of his voice makes Aila want to roll her eyes.

Joel could be very polite but was often dismissive of Aila. It didn't matter his two kids were constantly over at their house playing while he tinkered around in his garage, he was always badgering Ben for legal advice about a plethora of different subjects. That's the funny thing about being an attorney, people get so excited to meet one they think they can pester them with any and all their legal problems. Who knew any one person could need so much legal advice all the time?

"Tell me later," Ben whispers to Aila as he kisses her forehead. She wonders if she'll even get a chance.

Joel nods at Aila. *You're dismissed,* she mocks in her head.

She shakes off the thought and instead says, "Good evening, Joel." And she makes sure she says it so sweet you'd think it was covered in sugar.

"I've been wanting to ask you about my cousin, you won't believe…." Joel is saying to Ben when Aila feels a quick tug on her sleeve.

"Ms. Aila, can you draw me a mermaid?" Grace says through her messy curls, holding a broken piece of yellow chalk.

"My mom draws the best mermaids," Isaac says with his big brown eyes and missing bottom teeth.

"Darn right, I do," Aila says taking the chalk from Grace and getting to work.

And just like that, Aila turns back to tending to the kids. *Just like a good little wife.*

The kids are the ones who care about what she's capable of, whether it be opening a string cheese or drawing a mermaid in sidewalk chalk.

No one wants her professional opinion. No one cares about her day. No one cares about her talents. Her hopes. Her goals. Her dreams. Her desires.

Well, Ben cares, she assumes. But she can't help but wonder if he'll remember to ask tonight before he gets wrapped up in his work or falls asleep.

CHAPTER 4

THEN

B y the time the campus was covered in a thick white blanket of snow, the two were a known item. Ben and Aila. Aila and Ben. It just rolled off everyone's tongue. They were always together—irritatingly inseparable.

Their classes were in different buildings but they always found each other in between to sneak hungry kisses before heading back to their next class. They were obnoxious. Aila usually hated displays of affection. And yet, there she was counting down the minutes until Ben's hands would be wrapped around her waist again.

As the school year progressed, Aila and Ben rarely spent a night alone, always at either of their apartments. They spent more time together than Chantelle and Derek and it drove their roommates crazy.

Chelsey and Chantelle missed being able to walk to the bathroom in their underwear without worrying about bumping into Ben in the hallway. On the other hand, Ben's roommate, Toby, grew irritated every time Aila would clean up after him in the kitchen. Not so much that she cleaned up but she cleaned up the things he had left out on purpose. A glass he planned to use later or a butter knife smeared in peanut butter, resting on the sink's edge, clearly indicating a second sandwich was in the near future.

"Why don't you two just move in together?" Chantelle would ask.

But she already knew the reason. Aila's parents were too religious and too involved in their church to explain the living situation of their "wild" college-aged daughter. Her parents would kill her.

Bob and Tina were great parents even if they were slightly hypocritical. Aila merely got eye rolls when she came in late for curfew and her mom always gushed over whichever boy she had a crush on. Tina longed to be the cool mom. She showered Aila with designer purses and spa days even though Aila would have rather been playing soccer. Tina would even let her try a few sips of her wine after dinner and made Aila promise not to tell Bob.

Despite that, there were rules and expectations; images to protect. Aila knew how to play that game. She had learned from the best.

Ben, on the other hand, was raised by his widowed mother. His dad died of a heart attack when he was in eighth grade. Ben had found him. The images of rushing to his lifeless father were forever ingrained in his mind. He was only thirteen, his voice was still squeaky and scratchy from puberty, but his spirit aged ten-fold in just that moment.

His mom, Sharon, raised him up strong, kind, and extremely straight edged. She blamed herself for letting Ben's father's health slip through the cracks, forever punishing herself for not encouraging him to take his blood pressure medication or go to his annual appointments. Because of this, she was going to be damn sure she protected her son. She would've been happy if he and Aila moved in together.

"Sure, the Bible tells you not to," she'd said when they went home for a visit. "But someone needs to keep a close watch on my boy."

And she'd laugh and laugh, while stirring a giant pot of gumbo for the three of them.

Aila would often dream of making her own choices and not worrying about her parents' approval. But even well into her thirties, they'd cross her mind when making a big decision. And at twenty-one, Aila certainly knew the answer to premarital co-habitation.

Still, she and Ben couldn't get enough of each other. They laughed off everyone else's insecurities and irritations with them, smacked on a jealousy label to their objections, and moved on with their relationship.

As the year rolled on, Ben was accepted into law school at the University of Washington and not Gonzaga, which meant he would be on the other side of the state during her senior year.

"This changes things for us," Ben said, as he looked deep into her chestnut eyes in a way that made her feel raw and vulnerable. "Doesn't it?"

Aila cleared her throat and swallowed her tears. This felt like an unexpected bump in their relationship but she didn't want him to feel like she wasn't happy for him.

"No, no, babe, this is great news. Incredible!" She wrapped her arms around him and kissed him like she meant it. And she did mean it even if she selfishly didn't want him to live on the other side of the state. "I am so very proud of you!"

She cradled his face in her palm and looked into his eyes. She could tell he was worried. She felt the lump in her throat grow. But she smiled.

"But…" He drew it out like a question.

"But it's really unfortunate you're going to be a Husky." She grinned playfully to hide her emotions.

"Aila…" He smiled but his eyes begged her to tell the truth. Ben always knew when she was saying what she was supposed to say, not what was really on her mind.

He saw right through her, and she burst into tears. "I'm just going to miss you."

Without a response, Ben swooped Aila in his arms and held her. He didn't have to say he was going to miss her.

She knew. She always knew what he was thinking. He was always a man of few words and she loved he rarely had to explain himself to her. As a result, it meant they rarely argued.

Everything about their relationship was easy. Comfortable. Even when the next school year rolled around, when they thought they'd most definitely start having issues, they didn't. Ben stuck to the books. The first year of law school was the year that supposedly scared law students to death, but Ben was unmoved. He kept his head down and studied.

Meanwhile, Aila was soaring through her senior year, on track to graduate top ten in the communications school. Without Ben around as eye candy, she cared very little about her Friday and Saturday night plans. Aside from the occasional night out with Chantelle and Chelsey to Valhalla, everyone's favorite basement bar, she had become more of a recluse, ticking down the days until graduation.

Aila could tell her roommates had missed their friend. The previous year had been spent with Aila tangled up with Ben. This year forced Aila and Ben apart in a way that only made their relationship grow stronger roots, but also strengthened her friendships with Chantelle and Chelsey.

When April of Aila's senior year rolled around, she was studying for her last two finals and completing her final paper due at the end of the month while waiting for Ben to arrive for a visit. It had been over a month since they'd seen each other and she knew this would his last visit before her graduation.

It felt surreal. This was it? How was she ready to have a bachelor's degree? She thought it'd make her feel different, but it didn't. She wasn't stressed or scared. She was just letting the days pass, counting them down until she could move back across the mountain range to be near Ben.

She tapped her pencil against her notebook, distracted from the subject she was studying and feeling anxious to see Ben.

When he finally knocked on the apartment door, Aila

rushed over to open it. He looked five years older than he did at the beginning of the year. His dark eyes seemed even deeper if that were possible, as if they held more wisdom, but at the corners Aila saw he was more tired, too.

"Hey, stranger," she said leaning against the door frame.

He smiled a dark, sexy, grown up smile.

"Let's get away."

The simple suggestion made her smile. She packed a quick bag and he took her to a surprise visit to Leavenworth just a few hours west.

Leavenworth was one of Washington's most charming towns. It was also called the Bavarian town, known for its German architecture, quaint restaurants, hiking, skiing, and festivals.

They spent the evening at one of the pubs with outdoor seating sheltered in string lights; laughing, dancing, and drinking.

When an accordion player came around wearing traditional lederhosen attire, Ben grabbed Aila's hand and swooped her around in a circle effortlessly. They clapped and danced until Ben pulled her close and kissed her softly, his lips smooth, making hers tingle with electricity.

"Marry me, Aila," he said when he pulled away.

She playfully placed a hand on his chest, "Stop, you're making me blush."

It all happened so quickly, Aila could barely register it. Ben dropped to a knee and pulled out a small black, velvety box filled with a ring that sparkled under the string lights.

"Marry me," he repeated breathlessly.

Aila couldn't imagine a better thing to do than say yes.

CHAPTER 5

NOW

Aila wakes up with an unexpected and unusual desire to start her day.

After letting Gus outside to do his business and grabbing a cup of coffee, Aila makes her way back up the restored craftsmen staircase, careful to skip the creaking third step so as not to wake the boys. They still could sleep another ten minutes.

Gus loyally follows Aila into the master bathroom, the cold white tile floors waking up her senses as she pads over to the sink. She takes the opportunity her early wakeup allots her to add a little more effort in her appearance than usual. She blows out her long hair instead of throwing it in her usual top knot, making her long hair cascade down her back, like waves of chocolate. She dabs cover up under her tired eyes and adds two layers of mascara to make her chestnut eyes look wider and brighter against her glowing olive skin. She doesn't wear much make up, so when she does put on a little extra, she stands out and it tends to get noticed.

Aila stands back to admire her enhanced look and then turns to Gus, "Let's go wake 'em up."

The retriever immediately pops up from his corner on

the cold tile and trots diligently to each boys' room. First is Isaac and Caleb's room, and he jumps up on each twin bed, attacking the boys' faces with slobbery kisses before Aila flips on the light.

"Rise and shine, my dears!" she nearly sings, feeling genuinely cheerful.

"Wake up! Wake up, my love!" she continues across the hall to Josh's room, flipping on the light.

He groans.

You are only ten; don't go all rogue teenager on me yet.

She takes his groan as a request for a kiss from his mama smack dab on the forehead, which is almost immediately interrupted by his fifty-pound fur brother.

"Ugh, Gus!" Josh, rises from his pillow.

His bed head is making him look about eight years younger and pulling at Aila's mama heart muscles. She swallows the tears before she chokes on them, realizing how quickly the years go by.

"We love you too," she says, while rubbing his already messed up hair. "Now go get ready."

For years she was spending her mornings helping everyone brush their teeth, singing the Lion King's opening song so they'd keep their mouth open long enough to brush the molars, making breakfast, hearing complaints about the wrong color cup, experiencing a mutiny, giving timeouts, helping the boys put on their pants, changing a diaper, wiping a booty, hearing wails from the kitchen, kissing a boo-boo, tying shoes, negotiating the importance of jackets, changing another diaper, putting jackets back on, until finally, heading out the door to toddler gym or preschool or the grocery store. She often found herself sweaty and exhausted by the time she actually got in the car. Sometimes tearful. Being a mom of little kids was hard.

She was good at it though. She was thorough and dedicated to her little clients—an ongoing joke she created after stopping work at the advertising agency. She never let anything slip through the cracks. Everyone was cared for, meals were always made, and everyone adored her. All of her boys—including Ben—even though she was exhausted.

Her three children were now able to get themselves ready and make their own breakfasts—an odd relief she never thought would come. As the boys toast their bagels and dump cereal into their bowls, Aila returns to her bathroom and stares at her freshly made up face in the mirror while sipping coffee and deciding to plug in her curling iron to give her hair some wave.

Who am I? Janet?

She chuckles to herself, while wondering when the last time she got all dolled up was.

When her hair is perfectly wavy, she heads downstairs to make sure everyone is eating a decent breakfast and looks sufficiently dressed.

"Where are you going?" Caleb asks, looking at Aila quizzically.

"Yeah, Mom. You look really pretty," Isaac chimes in.

"It's not Sunday, is it?" Josh adds while standing at the sink with the last of his bagel half chewed in his mouth, making Aila laugh—realizing the extra effort she put in her appearance is usually saved for church service and date nights.

Haven't had one of those in a while, she thinks.

"No, it's not Sunday." Aila shrugs. "Just felt like doing my hair today. Josh, did you put on deodorant today?"

Josh nods, but runs upstairs to put on deodorant. It's such a small and important task for a preteen, and yet, it's often forgotten.

"Mom, my stomach hurts right here," Caleb says while pointing at his belly button after clearing his plate from the table.

"Did you poop today or yesterday?" Aila asks.

Somehow whether or not they pooped was always the answer.

"No."

"Well, I'm sure you just need to go to the bathroom.

Why don't you just try before we leave?"

He nods obediently and walks to the bathroom.

Thankfully, last night while Ben was finishing up work in the office, Aila and the boys had time to double-check school calendars to ensure there wasn't any forgotten papers to be signed or Civil War posters to be found. This makes the tail end of their morning run without a hitch as they trot to the bus stop with Gus in tow.

"Wow! Where are you off to?" Janet says giddily with that same big toothy smile.

"Yeah, Ms. Aila, you look really beautiful," Grace adds.

It's almost embarrassing the amount of attention she's getting for throwing in a little extra care in her appearance today.

Then again, she isn't hungover this morning.

"Just decided to do my hair today." Aila smiles, partly satisfied her efforts are getting some notice, partly embarrassed.

After her boys, Grace, and the five other kids at the stop load up single file on the bus, Aila smiles at Janet. "Well, have a good day!" she says while putting in her headphones.

"Coffee later?" Janet suggests.

"Yeah, I could do that after I walk Gus," she replies. "I'm volunteering in Josh's class later though. Would ten work?"

Aila secretly loves she has a time limit with her visit with Janet. Not because she doesn't enjoy her longwinded chats, but they went on forever, often until the kids were home from the bus, leaving the laundry and house uncleaned and bills unpaid at Aila's own house.

"Sounds awesome!" Janet says rather eagerly, "I'll make muffins."

Of course, you will, Janet. Bless.

"Great. See you in a bit!"

As Aila heads down Cherrywood Lane and turns around the corner to head toward Skyline hill, she feels her heart skip a beat when she sees the Williams Brothers Landscaping trucks dutifully beautifying the common grounds in the neighborhood.

Aila catches herself staring and scanning every face of each man in dirty Carhartt pants and navy long sleeved shirts. *Okay, stalker. He's the owner. He won't be here every day they're here.*

Which, Aila assumes, would be often. There are so many common areas and parks in the neighborhood, which is really a fish bowl of several neighborhoods at the bottom of Skyline hill. Some are new builds with contemporary exteriors. Aila imagines their interiors look like they belong in a sky rise apartment in Seattle. Then there are the traditional homes that pull craftsman details, some new and some older, a few neighborhoods of cookie cutter townhomes and row houses, and then the rare lots of original farm houses that have been restored when the land was purchased and divvied up for the new builds.

One of which, is Aila's home.

The neighborhood is enchanting and picturesque. They even have their own country club. There is also a ton of people living in close proximity so gossip can easily leak out to the masses. This never so much as bothers Aila but there isn't any ambiguity in who she is: the wife of the handsome attorney that stays home to care for their three boys.

Here, everyone knows the Sorensons. She sometimes dreams of moving cross-country and not telling anyone who they are.

By the time Aila reaches the top of the hill where she is looking out at the Olympic Mountain range, she has said hello to ten neighbors she knows personally, shared meals with, and thrown baby showers for. It is a town like any other, full of people from all walks of life but a bit out in the country with stellar views of Mount Rainier, the Olympic Mountains, and the valley down below. Plus, they have a Target. Aila can't live without that luxury nor does she know any other mother who could.

As she sits on the rail at the top of the hill, Gus pants happily next to her while she rubs his ears. She can't shake this bizarre feeling she has. Why did she feel excited when she saw the landscaping trucks? And why was she scanning each landscaper like a lion picking out its prey? Why does she care if she sees Jackson again?

Aila laughs to herself. *Why am I acting like such a teenager? This is dumb. I'm married. I'm a mom…with three kids!*

Oddly, that's it though. Running into Jackson made her feel like a teenager again. He had clearly aged—and well, she might add—but that didn't mean it didn't stir up memories and feelings from years past.

It didn't help that Jackson's eyes are exactly the same. Full of mischief, laughter, determination and shy flirtation. Aila shudders at every memory she has of him.

Why was seeing him so intoxicating?

This feeling has been running through her veins since yesterday and she keeps questioning her behavior while she spoke to him. And now the day after, the very idea of possibly running into him again even has her worrying about her personal presentation. Because, in all honesty, hungover in a top knot is not a good look on anyone, let alone a mother.

The truth is, she realizes, she's obsessing because she's embarrassed. She wants a do-over.

Aila stands at the top of the hill as the clouds roll in from the Sound, blocking the view of the mountain range and muddying up the sunny sky. Back to the normal Pacific Northwest winter. As the sky darkens, she walks away feeling resolved. She had a flashback of being a carefree teenager yesterday that had her feeling confused, but it passed. Back to the normal Aila. Wife of the handsome attorney, mom of three boys.

Just a good little wife.

Back at the bottom of the hill, Aila turns the corner and passes the landscaping trucks without a single glance, until she hears her name.

"Aila! Hi there!"

She turns and politely crosses the street to where she sees Jackson in dark denim jeans and a navy winter coat with the Williams Brothers Landscaping logo on the right breast of the coat. His hazel eyes lock in on hers as a genuine and kind smile spreads across his face.

Of course, I see you after *I have my come-to-Jesus moment.* She sighs, but puts on a smile as she closes the distance between them.

"Hi, stranger," Aila says, feeling more confident and less frazzled than yesterday.

Aila finds it haunting a divorced man in his thirties that owns his own business doesn't seem to carry a worry in the world behind his eyes. Jackson's eyes are clear and kind. His smile is magnetic…even after all these years. But now his jaw is much more chiseled and it's clear by his stubble he has no issues growing a beard.

When did Jackson become such a man?

Aila wants to laugh but holds back. Her high school love interests always seemed to stay teenagers in her mind. Probably to protect herself from realizing the hot baseball player from high school with boyish charm and a smart wit that smelled like laundry detergent, didn't get fat and bald after high school. But instead, grew another four inches, stands taller with square shoulders, a strong jawline, and a handsome smile.

Oh, and now he owns his own business and still smells like laundry detergent, but with a hint of something masculine, like cedar or applewood.

The scent takes Aila back to the night junior year they sat out on Ethan's back patio porch swing laughing at Gerald's dance moves at the prom earlier and joking about how they'd somehow lost their dates during the course of Ethan's after party.

He had a shyness about him then, though. Aila knew he wasn't shy and yet he seemed nervous, anxiously rubbing the palms of his hands over his knees. It was cold, which is typical for midnight in May in Washington, so Aila was wearing a hoodie over her sequin boustierre and till skirt.

"We should probably head back inside," she'd said. "I have to be home at one and I should probably find my ride."

"I could probably give you a ride if you want." He looked down, unsure, when she felt like he had no reason to be. "Well, I mean, if you can't find Evan."

"I'd like that." She smiled. She'd always had a tiny crush on him, but so did Ashley so she'd never told anyone. But there she was, 17 years old and alone with a boy that made her laugh and gave her butterflies, and he'd offered her a ride home.

Now or never, she thought and leaned in to kiss him. Harder than she anticipated and the force behind her lunge for him made him go, hmmph, but the kiss landed softly and square on his lips.

They were softer and fuller than she expected. Like stuffed pillows, that tasted like strawberry lip balm and spearmint gum.

The kiss was everything she'd hoped it would be. There was no teeth-clinking or questioning of what goes where. They were in sync in a way two teenagers rarely are.

That is until Aila shifted her position so she could press her body closer to him, making the swing jerk quickly, disrupting the momentum of the moment and they burst out laughing. Simultaneously, the back door opened and Evan emerged saying, "There you are! I gotta get you home, Aila, or your dad is going to kill me."

Jackson and Aila met eyes and he smiled at her, his dimples showing. "See you around, Aila."

Aila left the party feeling giddy, like she had just made out with the coolest boy in school.

She shakes the thoughts and memories that coursed through her brain more quickly than she could stop them, and places herself back on Cherrywood Lane staring at Jackson Williams twenty years later.

"Guess I *will* be seeing you around here more often." She smiles.

"The neighborhood is just too beautiful to resist," he jokes. "No really, I just stopped by really quick to drop off some equipment left at the office. I won't usually be here every day," he assures her.

"I see."

"Where are you headed today? Your hair looks different than yesterday."

Aila fights the flush rising in her cheeks, knowing her hair and makeup is taking notice. But who is she kidding? She didn't just *feel* like doing her hair today, she was secretly wondering if she might run into him again.

"Oh," Aila waves off the underlying compliment. "I'm just headed to the kid's school later to volunteer."

"Could've fooled me. I thought you were off to some fancy luncheon of sorts," he quips.

"No, unfortunately, staying home isn't that glamorous," she says. "I'm understaffed."

He smiles slowly before breaking out in a full grin, making sure she's joking. "Well, the homes around here are probably big enough for staff."

"Not all of them. We live around the corner in the blue craftsman with white trim." She offers the information without being prompted. "It's large for its era but not large in comparison to the new builds across the way."

"Are you talking about the original one? That was the tree farm house?" he asks, knowing his history of the land.

"That's the one." She nods. "The builders updated quite a bit but we were able to restore some of the hidden gems inside the walls and do some renovations of our own."

"That's great, I'd love to see it one day," he says.

"I'd be happy to show you some time," she says. *This is harmless, right?*

He nods as if agreeing.

"Gosh, it is surreal seeing you," he says. "You are exactly the same."

"My wrinkle cream would argue with you." She crosses her arms and smiles wryly.

Jackson laughs like he's charmed by her every word.

"No, you look great. Beautiful as always," he says, raising his eyes from the pavement. He isn't being inappropriate or even crossing a line, just more or less being polite and yet, Aila's chest twists and she can feel her heart beating in her ears.

I need to calm down.

"Thank you. You aged quite nicely yourself." She lets out a breath. Better. And then adds, "You know, I'd love it if you were able to meet my husband, Ben, one of these days. He doesn't get to meet many people from my childhood years. I think he'd love it."

"Yeah? Sure. That'd be great." He shoves his hands in his pockets nodding and smiling.

He's about to say something when Aila's phone starts to ring.

"Excuse me, it's my children's school." Aila looks at him apologetically and he waves her off. After a brief conversation with the school nurse, she turns back to Jackson. "I'm sorry about that. My second grader just tossed his cookies in music class so I have to run." She gazes at Jackson apologetically. "I would really love to catch up another time though."

"Oh, no worries. Poor guy. Duty calls. I hope he feels better."

"Thank you," Aila says as she turns on her heels to rush home.

His hazel, sparkling-with-charm eyes meet hers. "See you around, Aila."

No, Jackson, you *are exactly the same.*

She smiles, biting her lower lip and rushes home to the car so she can head to the school to pick up Caleb, pushing down the flood of emotions and memories she feels rising in her chest.

She remembers her coffee date with Janet and texts her quickly.

Caleb just threw up in class. Have to cancel our coffee date. Next time!

And a few moments later...

I'm so sorry. Hope he feels better. I send my love...oregano oil!

Aila lets her eyes roll slightly out of irritation but is grateful for the intention behind it. There isn't much that's going to bring her down today—not Caleb blowing chunks in class, not Janet's essential oil solutions, and certainly not Ben's text that just rolled in saying he's going to be home after bedtime tonight.

Expected.

Something about running into Jackson makes her feel alive. She's not sure why or how but just the few encounters with him are stirring up something inside of her—waking up a dormant part of herself she hasn't felt in a long time.

CHAPTER 6

THEN

Aila and Ben were married on New Year's Eve at the Westin in Seattle in one of their banquet halls overlooking the Space Needle. There was champagne, dancing, and, of course, fireworks. Bob and Tina spared no expense for their only daughter. As always, they had an image to uphold.

The night was full of glitter, toasts, and the "Cha-Cha Slide." Aila and Ben decided not to have a send-off and danced until the early hours of the morning when the DJ was finally tearing down his equipment.

They loved a celebration. Aila was working at an advertising agency in the city, Ben was halfway through his second year of law school, and tonight, they were married.

"Want to get a room?" Aila whispered playfully into Ben's ear as the janitorial staff started to enter the banquet hall with vacuums and garbage bags.

His eyes were drunk with love and whiskey, and Aila tottered around happily with a half-full glass of champagne, her lipstick faded from kisses and her neck damp with sweat.

"I thought you'd never ask." He smiled into her mouth before kissing her.

The elevator ride to their room was all hands and lips until they finally reached their room, stumbling over their overnight bags, and making their way to the bed to make love for the first time as husband and wife.

It was euphoric and surreal, leaving them both breathless when they finished, their legs and arms tangled around each other.

"Tell me something, Aila May," Ben said.

"What's that, Benjamin Lee?" she responded, her eyes still closed, her dimples smiling.

"This is it," he said.

At his words, Aila rolled over and perched her head up resting her chin on her hand. She looked at him quizzically.

"Me and you. We're it. We picked each other. No matter what happens in the years to come, it's me and you. Forever. No matter what comes up. We work it out," he continued seriously.

"Babe, I'm pretty sure we already said our vows tonight." She gave him a wry smile.

"No, I mean it. There is nothing we can't work through. Nothing. Come hell or high water. Me and you. Forever."

His dark eyes pierced Aila's soul and she knew he was serious. She knew the words they were exchanging in that moment under twisted hotel sheets were far more important than the rehearsed vows they said earlier in the evening.

Aila grabbed his hand and held it to her mouth, pressing her lips to his knuckles.

"Me and you. Forever," she promised.

And she meant it.

CHAPTER 7

NOW

"I'll go pull the car around while you collect the boys," Ben whispers in Aila's ear, his hand on her lower back, as they walk out of service the Sunday after puke-pocolypse.

It was a typical ritual so Ben could avoid the legal advice seekers. Poor guy. He really was so bad at cutting people off from those kinds of conversations so he practiced avoidance. In the office, he was the tough attorney. At church, he was a softy.

"Sure," Aila says giving him a brief kiss before they part ways.

"There you are!" Aila's attention turns to an overly cheery, high-pitched singsong voice, and she is greeted by a sea of brown curls and jingling bracelets. "We missed you so much on Wednesday!"

"Gretchen. Hi." Aila smiles and returns the overbearing hug briefly before pulling away.

Gretchen provided refreshments every Wednesday during the women's Bible study like it was her dream job. Homemade pastries and fruit platters decorated the tabletops each week, a kind and unnecessary gesture, and each compliment was always met with, "I will spare no effort doing the Lord's work."

Aila didn't chime in when Elena, her co-leader at Bible study, gave her a Mary versus Martha lesson, because surely, Jesus loves pastries too.

"Now, where in tarnation is the rest of your catalog family?" Gretchen lets out a laugh at her own joke.

Aila smiles politely. She gets this often. Many people thought the Sorensons were the picture perfect, too good looking to be real, catalog family. It was a well-meaning compliment but each time she hears it, it feels like a crack to her ribs. Another jab of pain she hides with her smile. She often worries the glass house she's living in will shatter if she doesn't smile wide enough.

It's funny how much people care about the image of the perfect family, and how little they actually know about what goes on in anyone else's marriage.

Aila hardly knows what is going on in hers anymore. Most of the time, she and Ben are just going through their rehearsed roles—he's the one who brings the popsicle sticks to build their perfect home, and she's the glue holding everything together, hoping nothing will shift before the glue dries. She often wonders how much longer she can hold it together before anyone starts to notice everything is slipping.

"I'm headed over to grab the boys and Ben is grabbing the car so I don't have to walk across the parking lot." Aila gestures to her black too-tall for church pumps, implying Ben is being thoughtful.

"Ah, what a man. Listen, honey, we were just lifting y'all up in prayer this week. How retched of an illness to hit your family. Bless your heart."

Gretchen is the type of person that speaks with a Southern accent even though she isn't from the south.

"Thank you, I'm happy to have gotten through the week." Aila smiles.

Always smiling.

Stand there, act happy, look pretty. Like a good little wife.

She gives Gretchen a squeeze on the arm, letting her know the conversation is over, and turns to head toward the children's wing of the church, nodding pleasantries to other parishioners as she goes, until she gets another tug on the arm.

"Hey you!" It's Chantelle. *Thank God.* She hasn't seen her in weeks which is typical of their relationship since growing older and having kids. Though, they always pick up right where they left off—just a couple of college roommates. Lifelong friends. Sisters by choice.

Aila hugs her friend tightly. "Girl, we have got to do a girls' night soon. I miss you! We have so much to catch up on."

Aila finds herself begging for these girls' nights more and more often.

"Yes, we do," Chantelle agrees. "I *just* talked to Chelsey yesterday."

"You did? She has been so hard to get a hold of. I haven't talked to her in months. How is she?"

"Still living the dream in New York City." Chantelle smiles almost covetously and adjusts her purse. Chelsey is the one out of the three roommates that decided not to settle down and eventually moved to New York working as a writer for The Times. Aila lives vicariously through their phone calls every few months.

"I'm so happy for her." Aila smiles and holds her hand to her chest delicately. "I wish she would visit soon. It's been years since the three of us got together."

"Me too," Chantelle says as she nudges Aila. "Guess it's just me and you for a girls' night. This week is packed but Derek has the girls next weekend."

It still stings every time she thinks of Chantelle and Derek's divorce, even though it has been two years since it became official. They were one of those couples no one expected would get a divorce. Ever. They'd been together for so long their names were synonymous with each other. You rarely mentioned one without the other. A Branjelina of sorts.

Or maybe more of a Bennifer. People rooted for them and never worried about them.

Until Alia received that one phone call in the middle of Isaac and Caleb's nap time that changed everything.

"Derek's having an affair."

"No, Chantelle, he wouldn't."

But he would, and he did.

The divorce put Ben and Aila in a difficult spot. Loving both of them, being best friends with both of them, and being so utterly disappointed in a man they trusted and had made their children's godfather.

And then choosing to forgive him.

It took Aila longer to forgive him than it did Ben. Aila needed more of an explanation, more repentance, more punishment. After all, she had been the one holding Chantelle while she cried herself to sleep after finding out.

Derek ultimately married his mistress, Cara. And as it turns out, she was wonderful. Aila hated that she liked her and got along with her instantly. It felt like such a betrayal to Chantelle.

But as time went on, the wounds, still open but not as fresh, began to throb less and Chantelle started to view things from a logical perspective. This was going to be her girls' stepmom. Chantelle knew making nice would be better for everyone involved. Derek and Cara have been married now nearly a year, and Aila is ninety-eight percent sure she's pregnant. It makes birthday parties more awkward but as time has gone on, the awkwardness has become the new normal.

"Okay, next weekend then. I'm available." Aila is always available. She hasn't written anything on the calendar in purple in weeks.

Chantelle pulls out her phone and flips to her calendar.

"Saturday would be better for me because I will most likely be working late Friday since I told Chloe's teacher I would help out in the class Friday morning." Chantelle takes a deep breath. "I really need to cut back to just once a week."

"I can't believe you volunteer in each of their classes twice a week. I only volunteer once a week and—"

"Yeah, but you stay home so you have the time," she cuts in. It was a dig. Unintentional, but a dig. "I have to rearrange my schedule to make it happen. It's important to Chloe and Emma, especially Chloe, so I have to make it work. It's hard though. I'm doing this all on my own. My kids. My house. My work. It's a lot."

Chantelle needs to unload, Aila can tell. She doesn't doubt her friend. Being a single mom sounds like the hardest job in the universe.

But what about feeling like a single mom when you're married? The thought dances across her mind but she shoves it away even though a part of her wants to talk to Chantelle about it.

"Well, I'm sure their teachers appreciate you. Even just going once a week, I know I volunteer more than most other moms."

"Thank you," Chantelle says letting out a deep breath. "You're right. I need boundaries."

Aila smiles thoughtfully at her friend, unsure of where this conversation is going. She feels an urge to tell her about running into Jackson—she had told Chantelle about him years ago in college—but she certainly doesn't want to talk about it in the middle of the church foyer.

She clears her throat. "Girls' night, then? Saturday?"

"Yes! Oh, I can't wait."

Once they collectively pick up their kids from kids' church, they wave to one another and go their separate ways.

Back at the waiting car, Aila slides into the passenger seat saying, "Sorry for the wait, I ran into Gretchen and Chantelle—"

But Ben is clearly on a work call and holds up a finger while giving a well-meaning but dismissive nod.

Aila tells the boys to be quiet while their dad is on the phone, lets out a quick sigh, swallows her irritation, and stares quietly ahead on the drive home.

Just like a good little wife.

CHAPTER 8

NOW

By the time Saturday rolls around, Aila feels slightly embarrassed about all the daydreaming she did about Jackson the week prior.

He is simply a nice guy from high school that turned into a handsome and successful man.

She still thinks about the excitement she felt when they'd first kissed all those years ago, but that's just it: it was all those years ago. So much time has passed since then, it feels ridiculous seeing Jackson again shook up every memory she had with him, making them feel fresh and new. When in reality, they are old and decrepit. A generation ago.

I don't even think I'll tell Chantelle about running into him. She'll laugh at me.

She would, but she'd also want all the juicy details and lecture her on boundaries for the next time she bumps into him. Aila wouldn't blame Chantelle, especially after what she'd gone through with Derek. She needs boundaries with Jackson.

For one, that's what a good wife does with anyone of the opposite sex: boundaries and friendly, but distant, pleasantries. And two, she turned into a pubescent sixteen-year-old girl after he simply said hello to her. And three…

What was *three?*

She needs to get a hold of herself. She is obsessing and it is getting embarrassing yet again.

She decides not to tell Chantelle about it. No need to bring attention to something that doesn't need attention drawn to it. Plus, this is all in Aila's head. She simply ran into an old high school friend, there is no story *to* tell. She already felt stupid about it. Time to leave it alone and let sleeping dogs lie.

Always early, Aila arrives first. The restaurant sits right on the water's edge on the Sound and has a sleek but rustic design. The bar has a metal top and is wrapped in subway tile with bright orange, modern chairs. They serve everything from burgers to fresh fish—one of the many perks of living in the Pacific Northwest.

Aila always orders a heavy pour of pinot grigio and fish tacos. On special caloric intake occasions, she'll order the lobster mac and cheese. Considering she doesn't get out much, girls' night is her night to indulge.

She opts for a small table in the bar area and orders herself a glass of wine while eyeing the menu, even though she knows what she'll get.

Chantelle arrives moments later, bursting through the glass doors as if she's late to an important meeting. Aila holds up a hand and smiles, waving her over.

"Sorry I'm late." Chantelle sighs long and deep while plopping herself on the bench across from her. "Newish babysitter so I had to run through the bed time routine with her again."

"Seriously, Chantelle, I just sat down. Don't worry about it." Aila waves off her apology. "I thought you said Derek had the girls this weekend."

Chantelle rolls her eyes. "He was supposed to, but he had to fly to San Francisco to interview a client for one of his cases. Cara said she'd take the girls anyway but, honestly, if it's *his* weekend, I want him to actually be there."

"That's understandable." Aila nods, knowing all too well what it's like to have a husband with a job that whisks him away at a moment's notice, leaving her to fend for herself in house full of children while he dines with fancy clients in Armani suits. "But I'm glad you were still able to come out tonight."

Chantelle smiles and leans in slightly. "Me too."

"Can I get you something to drink, ma'am?" their server asks. He's tall, with caramel colored skin, short black hair and endearing green eyes. Chantelle notices.

"A whiskey sour, please," Chantelle replies with a flirty smile. He takes a mental note of her drink order and walks away.

Fifteen years ago, the two would have spent a good fifteen minutes looking over the drink menu deciding what to order. Now fully immersed in their thirties, they don't even look at the fruity cocktails. Aila always orders a pinot grigio, unless she's upset, then she drinks merlot. While Chantelle always drinks a whiskey sour—whiskey straight up if she's had a rough day. The whiskey sour let's Aila know it's been a good week.

Aila smiles at her friend's drink order.

"Did he just call me 'ma'am'?" Chantelle looks at Aila, aghast.

Aila lets out a laugh. "He did. And to him, you are a ma'am."

"He is not that young. I'd date him." She tosses her black curly hair over her shoulder and raises her eyebrows, knowingly, at Aila.

"Uh, he's at least ten years younger than you. Maybe even fifteen. Plus, I thought you were really liking Tyler."

Aila is both genuinely interested in her friend's love life and secretly thankful the conversation is moving so rapidly she doesn't feel the urge to bring up Jackson.

"Relax. I won't hit on him." Chantelle smirks. "Yet...."

They both laugh like the two college girls they used to be and immediately blush when their handsome, but young, server returns with Chantelle's drink.

"Ready to order?"

Oh yes, he is cute. Aila thinks, now looking at him with a different lens, hiding her blush by taking a sip of wine.

The two don't even look at the menu. They order a charcuterie board with brie and cranberry goat cheese as an appetizer and each get fish tacos with a side of sweet potato fries. The server collects their menus and heads back to the bar.

"No carb left behind," Chantelle says, raising her glass.

"Amen, sister," Aila replies, clinking glasses. "So, tell me about Tyler."

Aila clasps her hands on the wooden tabletop and leans in.

Chantelle sighs, while contemplating her response. For someone who is rarely unsure of herself or at a loss for words, the reality of being a single mom dating after her husband cheated has taken a toll on her. She's more careful about her feelings, whereas in college, she felt them just to feel them. Now love seems so calculated and thought out.

"Well…it's his son's mom," she begins.

Aila nods grabbing her glass of wine and taking a sip, letting her know to continue.

"She's just…too involved. I understand boundaries and waiting to meet each other's kids but she still has too much say in what he does with his own son, and it's not okay."

"Like?" Aila furrows her brow, confused.

"Like, I invited him to church last Sunday. His ex said he couldn't go because he had their son. They go to church on a regular basis, but she just didn't want him going to *my* church." Chantelle rubs her lips together, smearing her plum lip gloss. "We even had a plan to not make it obvious to our kids we were friends outside of church but it didn't matter to her. And for Tyler, what she says, goes."

"I don't know, Chay, I kind of get that. I wouldn't want Ben to take our kids to random churches if I hadn't checked it out first. Churches can be weird." Aila realizes this might be an odd thing for her to say considering she's been a church member her entire life. She helps lead the Bible study for goodness sake. Still, she has spent her whole life walking the fine line between grace and judgment, and some churches pour heavy on the latter.

Chantelle purses her lips and narrows in on Aila. "And then I found out he still pays her cell phone bill."

Aila's mouth drops. "I thought you said they were never married. Why would he still pay her cell phone bill?"

"Right, Aila? Why would he still pay his ex-girlfriend slash baby momma's cell phone bill?" Chantelle is letting her frustration show now. "I'll tell you why? They don't have a parenting plan. They've done it all outside of court. He provides and does what he needs to do and pays a few of her bills to keep her quiet so he doesn't have court appointed child care payments. And I just can't. She controls his life. We're grown now, bud, figure it out." Chantelle throws up her hands in surrender. "I'm out."

Aila's face is frozen in a cringe when the server drops off the food.

"I'm sorry, Chantelle. He seemed like a catch."

"Yeah, I'll be okay." Chantelle winks and reaches into her purse retrieving her buzzing phone. "Hold on, this is the new sitter."

Aila takes this as a cue to dig into her tacos and then squirts ketchup on the plate for her fries, while the tone of Chantelle's voice changes from cheerful to concerned.

"Everything okay?" Aila asks, her mouth still half-full, when Chantelle hangs up.

"Aila, I'm so sorry. Chloe just threw up, I got to get back to the house to relieve the sitter," Chantelle lets out a sigh and seems genuinely upset but Aila knows it's more from exhaustion. It's hard doing everything on her own. Sick kids can feel like the straw that breaks the camel's back.

"Oh, poor baby. Please. Don't worry about this. I got it. You go home and take care of your little girl," Aila says as she rises to get Chantelle a box from a bartender for her freshly served food. She packs up her meal like a mother tending to her child, gives her friend a hug and says, "Text me if you need reinforcements tomorrow."

"I will. Thank you," Chantelle says while taking the to-go box from Aila and then turning to leave.

Aila sits back down at the table and takes her time polishing off two tacos. She is nibbling at her fries when the server returns to ask if there's anything else she'd like to order.

"I'm good, thank you. Just the check."

Aila shoves the plate from her just a few inches as if it will help her resist the urge to keep eating and caresses her fingers around her almost empty wine glass. It's been a while since she had a meal alone. It's kind of nice. She even finds it a bit sexy—mysterious woman, eating alone in silence. She runs her fingers through her long hair smiling at her own imagination.

Surely no one else sees the same thing.

She lets out a small laugh to herself and raises her eyes from her wine glass, scanning the bar when she spots him.

Jackson. You have got to be kidding me.

Their eyes lock and Aila can see he clearly had already spotted her. He smiles at her. A sparkly, charming, up-to-no-good smile with those breathtaking dimples.

Aila is in a bit of disbelief but feels excitement rise up in her chest.

She smiles and waves at him, gesturing to the empty half of her table. He holds up a finger and then signs his check before making his way over, beer in hand.

"Hey, Aila." Up close she can smell him. His fresh scent of laundry detergent, spearmint, and earth wafts toward her, cutting through the smell of stale beer in the bar. It's oddly intoxicating.

"Hey, Jackson," she says. "Fancy seeing you here." She's being cute even though she doesn't mean to be. "Have you been following me? Last I checked I lived around here first."

He laughs as he slides into the chair. "Yes, that's exactly what I'm doing."

Aila swallows hard, unsure if he's being serious or not.

"I'm kidding. I just met my buddy, Zach, for a drink." She lets out a breath and smiles.

"Nice. I was having a drink with my friend but she had to head home to her sick kids. They seem to have the plague that hit us last week."

Jackson's scrunches nose. "That's no fun."

"No, it's not. Thank you, by the way, for the saltines and ginger ale you left on the porch," she says, remembering the incredibly thoughtful but mildly inappropriate gesture.

Aila couldn't believe it when she picked it up off the porch on Tuesday evening before Ben even got home from work. When was the last time anyone helped her out like this? Normally she was the one making the emergency supply drop offs.

Either way she was grateful for Jackson's gesture, but she didn't tell Ben.

"No problem, they're my favorite snacks and I keep them at the office," he says genuinely but also downplaying the favor.

Aila narrows her eyes on him, she doesn't believe him. Only moms have ginger ale and saltines just lying around. Still, she is flattered by the thoughtfulness.

"Would you like another glass of wine? On me." He smiles at her and his dimples are on full display making her heart flutter.

Aila hesitates.

She can't remember the last time another man bought her a drink. It feels like a crime. An old married hag's crime.

Is this allowed?

Jackson can sense her hesitation. "Only if you want. No pressure." He shrugs boyishly, reminding her of the Jackson she knew a long time ago.

She bites her lip; she knows she shouldn't but she still wants to anyway. Ben isn't expecting her home just yet anyway.

The server returns with her check just as she makes up her mind.

"On second thought, can I get another glass of wine please?" she asks and Jackson slides the check over to himself.

"My treat." His hazel eyes are not just charming, they're hypnotic. Aila feels a strong pull looking into them as if she could stare long enough he'd swallow her whole, taking control of her, mind, body, and spirit.

Aila shakes off the thought.

"I appreciate that, thank you," she says.

I'm just being polite to an old friend.

The pair spends the night laughing and reminiscing about high school. They speak about old friends, like Jeremiah and how he ran off and married Candace, and now they have five kids in Arizona. Or how Timmy never did clean up his act and ended up in prison for eight years and now lives in a halfway house. Or even Evan, and how he moved to DC—"the wrong Washington" they quip simultaneously—to work for a congressman and how he still hopes to become president one day.

"I'd vote for him," Jackson says.

"Me too." They clink their glasses together with a wink, and then laugh like a couple of blushing high schoolers with harmless crushes. Only, a crush when she's married isn't harmless. No matter how many times she tries to convince herself nothing is going on.

"So…" Aila leans over the table placing one hand around the back of her neck and the other on her wine glass, her fingers delicately dancing up and down the stem. "Who'd you end up with? And how'd you end up…" Aila realizes she doesn't want to point out he's divorced and catches herself, instead lifting her hand from her glass and waving it aimlessly, "…here?" She finishes with a smile.

He doesn't bat an eye, telling Aila he clearly isn't holding on to any shame or resentment. He picks up his beer and takes a sip then begins to tell his story.

After high school, Jackson stayed around and went to the local community college. He received his Associate's degree and was able to go right into the fire academy and became a firefighter.

"Like you always said you would." Aila feels a rush of pride. He used to always talk about wanting to become a firefighter. "What happened with that?"

Jackson takes in a deep breath and lets it out slowly. His eyes turn down to his beer and his brow furrows for a half second. Aila can tell this is one of life's disappointments for him. Everyone has them. Life takes the plan sideways and you have to figure out how to handle the change of directions. Sometimes it's hard to tell whether or not it was God's plan or the devil's handiwork.

"Well, after about four years, I hurt my shoulder rock climbing. Needed surgery on my rotator cuff and then physical therapy and then it was just never the same again." He shrugs. "The job kept aggravating the injury to the point where I didn't trust myself to be able to lift, move, and wear the things I needed to do the job how it needed to be done."

"So, you chose manual labor instead. Smart." She smiles at him over the top of her glass. She's teasing him. *Flirting some might say.* She swallows hard at the realization.

Jackson lets out a sharp laugh.

"I'm sorry, it's hard when your dream falls flat," she says empathetically. She knows all too well how it feels to have your dream within its grasp and then watch it slip away—by fate or by choice.

I chose my fate.

"Don't be. I met some great people and had a blast doing it," he takes another swig of his drink before continuing.

"A year before my injury, Adam I had started the landscaping business. Adam ran it full time and I would come in on my days off. As a firefighter, my schedule ran twenty-four hours on and seventy-two hours off, so I had plenty of days in between to help get the business going. With all the new construction neighborhoods popping up all over the Puget Sound area, business grew faster than expected and at exactly the right time. Then once the economy started to make a turn back up after the recession, new fancy neighborhoods in need of landscapers were also on the rise, so we just rode the wave and it all worked out. Apparently upper-middle class folks are desperate for green grass."

"Well, you're not wrong." Aila laughs as he smiles and takes a sip of beer.

She notices he doesn't mention his ex-wife even though she must be woven in the very threads of each year passed since she last saw Jackson. She doesn't know why he clearly left her out intentionally, but for the first time, Aila can see a glint of sadness buried behind his eyes.

She finds her second glass of wine emptied much faster than the first, until she checks the time and realizes time has simply moved more quickly.

"Another round?" he asks.

Aila leans over her elbows like she's about to tell a dirty secret. "How about dessert instead?"

Jackson grins at her.

The two share a mudslide with two spoons. Aila feels giddy and alive—like Jackson just flipped open a release valve she didn't know was closed.

If this isn't right, why does it feel right?

Aila gazes over the top of the chocolate monstrosity at Jackson, studying him. He holds her gaze and Aila lets her heart smile. She hadn't realized how much she missed her friend, but still, she feels warning signs going off in the darkest parts of her mind.

When they leave the restaurant, Jackson walks Aila to her car in the parking garage, claiming he didn't want her to walk alone at night. Aila thinks he just wants to spend a few extra minutes with her, and she doesn't mind. When they reach her SUV, she fumbles with her keys, not wanting to say goodnight but knowing the night can't go any further.

"Goodnight, Jackson. Thanks for the meal and the drinks" She smiles at him genuinely, feeling unexpectedly happy about spending the evening with him.

"No problem," he says, leaning in to hug her. As soon as one arm is around her, his lips brush against her cheek sending an electric shock down her spine. The kiss is air soft and tender, fleeting almost, but it was a kiss.

Aila pulls back in surprise and presses her fingers to her cheek. A dazed and hesitant smile dancing across her face.

Jackson smiles back and lets out an embarrassed laugh.

"I'm sorry. That was inappropriate. I didn't mean to do that."

Aila recovers with a laugh and flashes him a flirtatious smile. "Careful there, buddy. I'm married."

He dips his head and smiles, nodding.

"Goodnight, Aila. Drive safe."

Aila slips into the driver's seat and shuts the door, her fingers again touching her cheek. Her heart is pounding, her ears are ringing, and her cheek still tingled where his lips touched her skin.

I shouldn't be doing this.

CHAPTER 9

THEN

"What did you make? It smells so good in here," Aila said, discarding her heels and unzipping the back of her pencil skirt to let her waistline breathe after making her way through the front door after work.

"Roasted potatoes with bacon and steak," Ben answered, pulling the potatoes doused with crispy bacon out of the oven. The air smelled rich with garlic and butter, making Aila's stomach growl.

"Mmm, I should work late more often," she said as she kissed him. "You are too good to me."

"How was work?"

Aila let out a quick breath as she poured them each a glass of water and made her way over to the couch. "Really good, actually—just long. But I think I finally have a handle on the Chambliss account, which means I will have happy clients after I meet with them on Thursday." She turned to Ben. "How was your day?"

"Fantastic," Ben said, grinning from ear to ear as he walked over and placed two plates of food in front of Aila on the coffee table—she dug into hers right away. "Billy called me by the correct name today."

Billy White was the owner of the law firm Ben worked at—he was tough and hard to please but once an associate crossed the threshold into his good graces, their career became solid.

Aila raised her eyebrows and smiled back, her mouth half-full. "Well, look at you, moving up in the world at White & Associates."

Ben nodded sheepishly. "It took nearly a year but Danny said I should expect my workload to double and my opinion to start mattering." He let out a small laugh.

"Really? That's so great, babe. I'm so proud of you," Aila said earnestly without realizing just how many more hours Ben would be spending at the office. She sat back on the couch, letting the food she just consumed digest. She propped her tired feet up on the coffee table. "It's been a crazy year, hasn't it?"

They'd been married for three years, had just bought their house near Cherrywood Lane, and Ben was coming up on his one-year anniversary at White & Associates.

He sat back on the couch next to Aila and put his arm around her, pulling her close. "It really has."

"And pretty soon we'll have a little Ben waddling around here while we try to eat dinner. You ready for that?" She looked up at him, smiling—her young, ambitious eyes sparkling against her glowing skin.

Ben placed a hand on her barely swollen belly. "What makes you so sure it's not a little Aila?"

"Mother's intuition, I guess." She grinned at him. "Look at us: making the life we always dreamed of come true—the house, the careers, the family—all of it."

"You and this little one in here are the only part of the dream that matter," Ben said with his hand still on her belly and gazing into her eyes.

"Yeah?"

"Yeah," he agreed, biting his lip like he could barely contain his love for his wife and their unborn child.

She kissed him deeply before pulling back slightly. "And don't you forget it."

CHAPTER 10

NOW

By Wednesday morning, life for Aila carried on as usual—a smorgasbord of running around, getting kids to and from places, feeding them, doing laundry, paying the bills, and cleaning dried up pee off the floor next to the toilet...again.

Why can't those boys learn to aim?

After she drops the boys off at school, Aila makes her way over to Starbucks, grabbing Americanos for herself, Elena, and Gretchen before heading over to the church, arriving ten minutes before Bible study would be getting started.

As usual, Gretchen had already arrived with a feast fit for a king—homemade chocolate croissants, sausage egg bites, fresh fruit, bagels with onion and chive cream cheese—the room looks and smells delicious. The spread is overcompensating but Aila's stomach growls, and she grabs a croissant before the wave of women in their thirties and forties sweep through and devour it.

Aila takes a bite and examines the croissant in her hand. She can't remember the last time she ate sweets on a weekday.

"It's good, right?" Elena says coming in behind her and swooping up her coffee order from the table where Aila's Bible and study guide lay.

Aila nods through her mouthful of buttery pastry and warm, salted dark chocolate.

Elena raises her coffee cup before taking a sip. "Thanks, by the way."

"You bet." Aila smiles softly and turns toward the jingle walking through the door.

"Good morning! Oh, Aila, you are such a *doll* for bringing me coffee each week." Gretchen emphasizes the word doll like she's thankful to her for saving her puppy, instead of referring to sixteen ounces of espresso.

"No problem, Gretchen. Thank you for the delicious spread you bring each week even if it has caused me to gain five pounds this year." She winks at her playfully.

Gretchen hoots out a laugh. "Ah, you girls keep me young!" She's only forty-three but loves to point out the age gap. "I just have to tell y'all, the scripture this week just absolutely *moved* me. I cannot wait to discuss it."

Aila and Elena exchange a knowing look. Gretchen said this every week.

A few minutes later, fifteen women trickle through the chapel doors, some in hoodies and yoga pants and others in their Sunday best. They ritualistically place their Bibles at their spot at the table, staking claim of their territory week after week.

They fill their plates and indulge in Gretchen's pastries and talk about how the kids are driving them crazy or how their husbands are losing their jobs or how they've been offered an opportunity they don't know if God wants them to take. They talk, they laugh, some cry, and then they pray.

It's practically the same week after week but Aila finds comfort in the consistency of Bible study, from the women to the food. It is her safe place. People respect her there. They look to her for wisdom and guidance. They call her throughout the week and ask her to pray for them, as if she's an appointed intercessor to the pagans and sinners.

"Alright, ladies," Elena calls the room to attention. "Let's get started. We're continuing our study on David. And this week…dun, dun, dun," she says while thumbing through her Bible to the correct passage. "2 Samuel, chapter 11. David and Bathsheba."

There's a hushed chuckle that carries through the women; some purse their lips, others blush or shake their heads in disapproval. Everyone knows this story in the Bible and if they didn't, they wouldn't forget it now.

Aila remembers the first time she heard this story. It's not one taught in Sunday school. This is a story she didn't catch wind of until her early twenties.

David, the one that killed the giant, ended up becoming a great king for God. Then one day, his eye caught Bathsheba bathing. Naked, most likely. And he wanted her. And because he was king, he called her to his room and had his way with her.

The problem was? Bathsheba was married. Long story short, she became pregnant. David sent her husband to battle so he would die, and then David could legally take her as his wife. And with the snap of his fingers all his sins and infidelities were swept under a rug. And they lived happily ever after. The end.

It is definitely not a story for children's church.

"What was everyone's takeaway from this passage? How could you relate to the situation?" Elena prompts the group.

"I honestly couldn't. You know? I love Dan so much, I just fully could not relate to this story and I have trouble finding God in it," the petite blond, Lexi, says. "Sorry, just being honest."

Elena and Aila nod, they've learned to do this. Let the masses figure out the message for themselves first.

A few others add to Lexi's response.

"I actually do. I mean, at the end of the chapter it

says, God was not happy," the tall woman with brown skin and red lipstick, Anita, says. "David became a rock star after his stunt with Goliath and he thought he could do whatever he wanted without repercussions, but God could see him manipulating the situation."

"Absolutely," Aila says, as if patting her pupil on the back. "God sees whatever we do in secret and even if he doesn't approve, he loves us anyway."

The masses nod and smile.

Well done, Aila.

"But," Gretchen chimes in. "What about Bathsheba? Everyone always focuses on David in this but isn't Bathsheba at fault here somehow? Or did she not have a say in this?"

"Well, during this time and culture. Probably no. If you were told to be taken as a wife, you followed suit. If the king wanted to take you to bed, you did. Sad, but unfortunately, true," Elena answers briefly.

"Or maybe she was lonely."

The chattering room falls instantly silent and Aila can feel the stares from everyone practically prickling at her skin.

Did I say that out loud?

Aila clears her throat.

"All I meant was, maybe Bathsheba was seeking it out a bit," Aila offers. "Maybe her husband didn't really see her anymore—who she was, what she loved. Maybe he ignored her and just expected her to do her wifely duties and she just wanted to feel desired again. So, she let herself be seen by someone and he noticed her. Maybe this was God helping her see her way out of her sad and lonely marriage."

Half the room looks confused and the other half have narrowed their eyes on Aila. She can feel her neck and cheeks flush.

This was not the right thing to say. I must have been misunderstood.

Aila looks toward Elena for the assist but when she meets her eyes, they are narrowed and concerned.

Across the room, a woman named Sarah is nodding

while biting her cheek. "I get what you're saying."

Oh, thank God.

"I think more people live in lonely marriages than we know. It's so easy to get there, too. I mean ever since I had my two kids and started staying home, I feel desperate for adult interaction. Don't get me wrong, I'm so fortunate to not have to work but it's so alarming how being surrounded by tiny humans can still make you feel *alone* at the end of the day."

"Preach," Anita says while nodding. "I remember when my daughters were as young as yours, Sarah. I was working part-time so I was fortunate enough to have that outlet, but even still, I don't know how John and I stayed afloat. We went days without having any real conversations. By the time they were in school full-time, I remember looking at my husband and feeling like, *there* you are, I missed you."

Exactly. Aila's eyes fill with tears and she can't help but wonder if Ben ever misses her the way she misses him.

"I remember feeling like God was the only person I talked to," another woman named April chimes in. "Even during play dates when I'd get to see other moms, we only ever had half conversations. I remember thinking at times, my new mom friends—" she holds up air quotes around the last two words "—don't really even know who I am. They just knew my son got three timeouts while we were together and I bribed him with fruit snacks so I didn't have to wrestle him into his car seat."

The room laughs, everyone remembering trying to strap their unwilling two-year-old children into a harness.

Aila lets out a breath, comforted by the thought she's not alone in her feelings and realizing maybe she never has been.

"Still, I don't really think that God was handing Bathsheba David on a silver platter so she could get out of her lonely marriage," Gretchen adds.

"Maybe not. But maybe," Elena adds. "Sometimes I think God offers us a way out. But we have to make sure we aren't twisting the scripture. I also think God wants us to do the work, whatever that may look like. I think it's important for all of us to remember that whatever we're feeling, no matter where we are, God sees us. He already knows if we're lonely or stressed or anxious and I think it's necessary we voice those feelings. Not only in prayer but to our friends and our spouses also. We weren't meant to handle our problems alone. And when we try to do it alone and let our problems fester in the dark, they're only going to grow and then we'll find ourselves in a lot more trouble than we anticipated." Elena's eyebrows shoot up as she meets eyes with Aila, like they are punctuating her statement.

Aila feels hot and her armpits begin to heavily perspire, but she smiles anyway.

At the end of group, everyone trickles out of the room and heads off to pick up children from childcare or to the gym or back to work or maybe home to mop the floors. Aila busies herself with cleaning up the picked over pastries and placing them in Gretchen's cooler until she feels a strong presence to her left. She smells like plumeria and concern.

"Is everything okay, Aila?"

Elena. She always sees right through people. Today she sees through Aila.

"What do you mean?" Aila whips around wistfully, her fingers fiddling with her hair.

"All that chatter about loneliness in Bathsheba's marriage."

Because it could be true. Who says she didn't have feelings? Or want a better marriage? Who says she didn't feel forgotten or undesirable? Maybe all she wanted was love and affection from her husband, the one who was supposed to be the sole provider of that, and he wasn't there for her.

Aila presses her eyelids down and gives her head a small shake.

"It was just a thought I had—didn't mean to vocalize it."

"Well, you did and I just wanted to make sure

everything's okay. Those are some deep feelings to have."

"It was nothing, honestly. I just wanted to offer a different aspect to the study, that's all," she waves off Elena's concern and smiles wide and reassuringly, grabbing her Bible off the table indicating she's ready to leave the conversation and the building.

"Alright," Elena says, eyeing Aila. "Well, you can always come to me if you need to talk, you know that, right?"

"Of course," Aila says before flashing a smile and walking out the door, feeling Elena's curious eyes burn through her back. Aila never understood how Elena did it. She had an eye for the broken birds in the group and always swooped in for the rescue. Aila can't believe she let her guard slip. Even though she feels validated by the other women in the group, this is not a discussion she wants to have.

As soon as her feet hit the pavement in the parking lot, Aila's phone buzzes.

Heading to your neighborhood this afternoon. Can I grab you a coffee?

Aila bites her lip and smiles, giddy and thankful she and Jackson exchanged numbers after dessert on Saturday. They had texted with each other throughout the week—mostly sending each other funny jokes that made one think of the other. Harmless.

That'd be great. See you in a bit!

Aila lets out a breath she didn't realize she was holding and rushes home. Her friendship with Jackson is merely chipping away at the lonely parts of her life.

Maybe this is God offering me a way out.

CHAPTER 11

THEN

The sky was completely blue that day in July. A heat wave was passing through the Pacific Northwest and the evening air was warm and smelled like salt and sunshine. Aila loved days like this with the family when Ben had the day off, especially since he left his phone at home.

"What a tragic accident," Aila said while eyeing him playfully.

"You didn't." Ben froze mid-pat down, realizing Aila had, in fact, hid his phone in the junk drawer so he'd forget it.

She would often joke she'd do this. Any time they went out, as a family or even on a date, his phone was constantly buzzing and he always had to take the call because it was important. The calls were *always* important, which, in turn, made her feel less than. Aila struggled between the balance of supporting him and his growth at the law firm and needing a piece of him for herself and the boys.

He had been at the law firm in Seattle for five years now and he was well respected already. Everyone knew he was a hard worker with an intelligent mind that could build a hell of a case for his clients. It was his dream. And Aila always told him to reach for the stars.

She loved him in the most wholly and unchangeable way. Aila adored Ben. She did everything and anything for him.

She gladly gave up her career at the advertising agency to stay home when Josh was born. The recession hit soon after so she was bound to have gotten laid off anyway. When Caleb tumbled along a couple years later, her title as a stay-at-home mom solidified and she found herself relishing in the position. There was something so admirable and selfless about being a mother, even if it was painfully humbling.

She loved the image they projected.

Look at my fancy husband with the fancy job and the fancy suits in the fancy city. Oh, yes, and look at how adorable our offspring are.

She was obsessed with their family unit. The butterflies. The chemistry. Nothing had changed since that first night in college. Well, except for the fact he wasn't around as much.

Her mom and Chantelle had voiced concerns about the amount of time Ben spent at work and she at home alone with the boys, but she always shrugged it off. *It's just a season,* she'd say.

She always knew they'd be fine. He'd come home after the kids were tucked in bed, which meant they had a few hours to share about their days over a bottle of red wine. He knew how to turn off work when he was in the mood. And if he didn't know how, Aila would just do it for him.

Hence, she hid his phone before they took the boys to the beach, or rather where the water from the Sound hits the rocky shore.

Four-year-old Josh was crouched over a tide pool inspecting baby crabs and sea urchins with Gus running back and forth while Caleb, who was almost two, hobbled unsteadily over the rocks to where Aila sat underneath Ben's arm.

"Mama! Dada! Look!" Caleb said, holding his arms outstretched with two baby crabs in his palm.

Just as Aila was about to admire his bravery and accomplishment, a tidal wave of golden retriever swooped over and took one of the crabs right out of Caleb's hand. Aila screamed in laughter, while Gus shook his head and pawed at his nose, unaware the specimen he put in his mouth would pinch him.

"Uh oh!" Caleb said, his eyes becoming saucers.

Ben jumped up in a rush to grab the dog, cursing under his breath, and to inspect Gus's mouth.

Aila rolled her eyes at Ben's overreaction and tucked Caleb into her arms and said, "Don't you worry, my Caleb boy, Gus is just a puppy. We'll find more crabs." She kissed his palm. "Let's go do it."

She crinkled her nose at Caleb and his pouty lip instantly turned into a giant grin. Together they walked hand in hand over to Josh's tide pool to flip over more rocks and find more baby crabs.

"Gus, come!" Aila said cheerfully, pulling a small dog treat out of her jean shorts pocket, and Gus ran over, stumbling over his too big paws and she latched the leash to his collar.

Ben trailed behind him.

"That damn dog," Ben whispered to Aila through his teeth.

He did this sometimes. It was one of the cracks between them. She didn't sweat the small stuff and the small stuff drove him crazy. It frustrated Aila, and she couldn't quite understand it.

Who cared if the dog snuck out of the fence and they had to have the neighbors help lure him back in? Who cared if the kids spilled milk on the floor or ice cream in the car? Who cared if the dog tried to eat a crab?

None of it was worth a second blink to Aila. For Ben, it usually frustrated him to no end. Was it because Ben was stressed at work so life's little mishaps made him snap? Was he just so far removed from the messiness of toddlers and puppies and home life he didn't understand how small of a deal this was?

Josh and Caleb would probably talk about it the next day at breakfast because it was so funny they're new puppy ate a baby crab.

Aila swallowed her thoughts and reached for Ben's forearm and held him tightly, looking deep into his squinting brown eyes.

"Hey," she said softly. "It's nothing."

She smiled tenderly and rubbed her thumb gently from his temple to his jaw.

Ben rubbed his lips together and dipped his head away, still irritated by something so small. Too small and unimportant.

Aila silently pulled him in, wrapping her arm around his waist and leaning her head on his chest while delicately rubbing his back, coaxing him out of his irritation. Josh and Caleb were completely unaware of the annoyance seeping out of their dad's pores.

The two boys continued on, scavenging through the shallow water for more sea creatures to touch and explore.

Aila smiled and admired their boys' discoveries until suddenly and softly, Ben tipped his head down and pressed his lips to the top of her head. Her sign he was over it.

She'd never get an apology for his overreaction and he'd never see that way. But they'd sweep it under the rug and move on to happier moments. And that was all that mattered to Aila.

Even if it left a small crack between them.

Soon they made their way up the rocks, the four of them hand in hand, and over to the Daily Catch for fish and chips and ice cream cones. They laughed and joked and danced while Aila gazed over at her boys in awe and adoration.

They're all mine, she thought.

She looked over at Ben and he was staring at her intently. Not the boys and their antics that warranted far more attention. Just her. She returned the gaze, and his chiseled jaw and steely cheekbones cracked into a smile.

He adores me, she thought her lips pulling into a smile. She was right.

Later that night after tucking the boys into bed, Aila made her way back downstairs where Ben was opening a bottle of wine. Two glasses were set out on the counter.

Aila grabbed an empty one and pulled it toward her.

"I'm not drinking tonight," she said.

Ben's eyebrows furrowed and then relaxed just as quickly.

"Because…" he said, looking for an answer but his eyes were already smiling.

Aila bit her lip and broke out in a smile.

"I'm pregnant."

Ben set down his glass of wine and walked around the kitchen island to his bride, slowly but confidently. Encasing her face in his hands, Ben bent his head down slowly to kiss her. A fire began to burn in her belly as Ben laid her down on the couch, his hands melting into her bare skin and his lips lingering over every inch of her. He gently caressed her body—slow at first then strong and passionate until she could barely breathe and had no strength left.

"Congratulations, Mrs. Sorenson," he said.

Aila smiled.

Me and You. Forever.

CHAPTER 12

NOW

"**A**lright, boys, look here!" Aila says while grinning and looking into her phone to take the picture.

The three boys are lined up on the railing for a breather and a picture after making the trek up to the top of Skyline hill after dinner. The sun is setting over the hills in the distance lighting the sky on fire. It burns bright orange and red, with hints of pink.

"Cheese!" The boys yell in unison, out of redundant practice.

"Look at our handsome boys!" She lets out a laugh and tussles the tops of each of their heads.

Aila holds her phone to her chest while looking out into the sunset. The fields below are aglow with early springtime blooms. The rolling hills in the distance are lit with life and homes and happiness, while the water on the Sound sparkles as if it's full of glitter in the distance. She presses her eyes closed and smiles, relishing in the moment as a family, basking in the beauty.

"Hey, Mom, let me take one of you and Dad," Josh says.

When and how was he turning into such a teenager? He is only ten. A baby, in her mind and yet Aila could already hear his voice squeak and see the sheepish smiles of a pubescent young man.

She loves watching her boys become who they are but she misses when they were young and in diapers. Life was simpler back then. Not easier—babies and toddlers are utterly exhausting—but simpler.

Aila lets a deep breath out.

"That'd be great, sweetie," she says and turns to Ben to invite him over for a posed sunset picture.

Ben holds up a finger to her, his phone on his ear.

Aila blinks quickly, swallowing an unexpected lump in her throat. She crinkles her nose and softly taps her forehead to Josh's.

"Next time. Thanks, bud."

Aila throws her arm around Josh and gives him a squeeze while motioning for Caleb and Isaac to start heading down the hill with them.

She clears her throat and smiles.

This is something she's been doing often lately. Clear her throat and smile. Clear her thought and smile. Clear her frustration and smile. Clear her concern and smile.

She is tired of it. Exhausted from it. But she keeps clearing away her exhaustion, and smiling.

Why is she the only one that seemed to enjoy an evening walk with the boys? Why is she the only one that understands their jokes and references to video games? Why doesn't she have a partner as fully enamored by the people they created together as she is all the time?

Aila feels something rise in her chest and she breathes it out and forces a smile. How many times can she swallow her irritation? Over and over she has stuffed it down and then plastered her face with a pretty smile next to her handsome yet remiss husband. She is bound to explode.

It's like she has a long wick smoldering just below the surface slowly making its way to an explosion.

As they turn the corner at the bottom of the hill, Ben hangs up the phone and Aila sees an unexpected surprise.

Two Williams Brothers trucks are parked near one of the common areas with a few men huddled around for a water break of sorts. Aila narrows her eyes on the four men and spots Jackson instantly. She swallows hard and feels her heart skip a quick beat.

"Ow, Mom."

She's holding Isaac's hand far too tight.

"Oh, sorry, buddy." Her cheeks flush as she realizes the nerves escaping through her fingertips in Jackson's presence.

When he stopped by with a coffee a few weeks ago the visit was no more than an hour, but only because Aila had to run to the bus stop to get the boys. Otherwise, she could have spent the rest of the day with Jackson. She had appreciated the afternoon pick-me-up in the form of brown, caffeinated liquid and in the laughter and warmth from an old friend.

That's all he is, right? An old friend.

The afternoon had passed in a blink, and Aila felt herself being flirtatious in a way she hadn't been in years. She'd catch herself though and swallow it back while simultaneously running her fingers through her long hair. He was so easy to be around. The conversation was always fluid and always made her look forward to the next time she'd see him.

Jackson is kind and charming. His sense of humor matches hers and his dimples send Aila's hormones in a tailspin. It's as if they haven't spent the last two decades apart. Aila failed to mention this coffee date to Ben, not because of lack of intention but lack of opportunity. Now seeing him with her whole family in tow, she feels a surge of nervous energy.

Jackson has clearly spotted her too and flashes his wide smile with perfect teeth and irresistible dimples. He holds up a hand to greet the family. After all their encounters over the last month, Aila realizes he had never seen her with her family.

"Hey, there," she says, casting a friendly smile while tucking her long chocolate brown hair behind her ear as the boys run ahead. "Isn't it a little late for your crew to be here?"

"Somebody accidentally mowed over a sprinkler head." Jackson presses his lips together and closes his eyes, withholding a bit of a laugh. "So here I am with a new sprinkler head to replace it."

"Ah, I see." Aila feels another rush of nerves and excitement.

Ben, trailing a few steps behind the group with Gus, jogs up to where Aila and Jackson are standing.

"This is my husband, Ben," she says placing a hand on his elbow.

"Pleasure to meet you," Ben says extending his hand to Jackson, who takes it.

His forearm flexes and Aila blinks her eyes away.

"Jackson is the guy I went to high school with that I told you about," Aila says, hoping Ben remembers the conversation they had a few weeks ago while Ben clicked away on his laptop.

"Oh yes, that's right. I heard so much about you," Ben says.

He's lying. Aila can tell. He doesn't remember her mentioning it. She smiles but it cuts through her face like a sneer before she recovers.

"Anyway, it was such a fun coincidence to have Jackson's company in charge of our neighborhood's landscaping maintenance. After…what? Fifteen, twenty years? I couldn't believe it."

Jackson ducks his head in a nod, smiling.

"Good for you, man. That's awesome." Ben has his schmoozing voice on. "We'd love to have you over for dinner one of these nights."

Aila jerks her head in Ben's direction, her eyebrows furrowing quickly and then she forces them to relax just as quick.

"Yes. Please, that'd be great, Jackson," she adds.

She means it but she also knows Ben is unaware of their night at the restaurant a few weeks ago or coffee at the house the week after. She feels a rise of panic in her head but quickly swallows it and smiles, like she does best.

"Really? That sounds like fun," Jackson says.

Aila can tell he's genuinely surprised and excited by the offer.

"How about tomorrow?" Aila hears herself say. She looks at Ben and he half nods, half shrugs in approval.

"Tomorrow? Yeah, sure, I can be there," Jackson smiles and nods, stuffing his hands in his pockets.

"Great! Six-thirty, okay?" Aila asks.

"Sure." Jackson nods.

"We live in the original craftsmen around the corner," Ben says, picking up his ringing cell phone.

Aila and Jackson both give one solemn nod, catching each other's eye briefly. She can tell Jackson is realizing how unaware Ben has been of Aila's interactions with him.

"Great, I'll see all of you tomorrow then," Jackson says and gives Aila an imperceptible wink.

Or did he? *I think I just imagined that.* Aila's face goes hot.

"See you then," Aila says in farewell, and she begins the last leg of their walk back to the house while Ben talks on the phone.

Back inside, after the boys have showered, put on their pajamas, brushed their teeth, and cozied up in their beds to read, Aila heads downstairs to find Ben in the office with a glass of whiskey on the rocks next to his laptop.

"The boys would love it if you tucked them in tonight," she says, her way of acknowledging he hasn't tucked them in for two weeks.

"Hmm?" he says, raising his eyebrows and taking a sip of whiskey.

"The boys. Your children have requested your presence to tuck them in." Aila's trying to make light of it, but her frustrations from the night and weeks past make her come off as sarcastic.

"Sure. No problem." He says it in a way that makes it seem like he's all over it but he keeps clicking away at the laptop, not meeting her eyes.

"So…" Aila draws it out like a question.

Are you going to tuck in the boys or would you rather I just do it?

"So," Ben says matter-of-factly. "Hey, did you get that landscaper guy's number so he can be sure to find the right house? Tomorrow you said, right?"

Aila is surprised he even remembered that detail. She clears her throat.

"You mean Jackson?" she corrects him. "Uh, yes, tomorrow. We had already exchanged numbers a few weeks ago."

Ben nods and keeps clicking away at his keyboard, not even flinching. He takes another sip of whiskey.

He doesn't even care. She walks back into the kitchen without another word.

Aila finishes loading the dishwasher and puts the clean pots in the cupboard before pouring herself a glass of wine. She takes a long swig and the cold, golden liquid hits the back of her throat with a pungent kick. She glances in the office where Ben is still clicking away at his computer incessantly.

Another crack between us.

More often than not, Aila will cook the food, clean the kitchen, tuck the kids in, and Ben will just be consumed by his work. He has moments of clarity with the family, but those moments are just getting spaced out farther and farther from each other. Aila longs for them to the point where she sometimes wonders if they'll cease completely.

Aila throws the Clorox wipe she's using to disinfect the counter into the trash and makes her way to the entry of the office.

"Ben?" she asks as tentatively as she can without becoming full blown irrational. "Are you still going to tuck the boys in?"

She's being generous. It has now been thirty minutes since she asked him.

"Uh...yes," he says barely glancing up from the computer.

Aila twists her lips. Irritated.

"Never mind," she says. "I'll do it."

"No, no, I'm coming," Ben says. "I said I'd do. I'll do it."

"I asked you to do it thirty minutes ago. They needed to have lights off twenty minutes ago. They have school tomorrow." Aila's tone only scratches the surface of her frustration.

"Just stop," Ben says, cutting his hand through the air as if cutting the throat of an enemy. "I'll do it."

Aila doesn't accept his finality in the discussion.

It's bullshit, she thinks. *He has no regard for anything but work.*

"Forget it," she says, barely over her breath and turning to head upstairs to kiss each of their boys goodnight.

Once everyone is tucked in, she heads back downstairs to her now room temperature glass of wine and takes another long sip. As she finishes the rest of her glass, she feels Ben's large, warm hands slide over her hips from behind her.

"Are you kidding me?" Aila turns around more aggressively than she anticipated.

Ben's eyes go wide, like a puppy's.

"Hey," he says, his voice deep and raspy in the evening's quiet air. "What's the matter with you?"

"What's the matter with me?" Aila scoffs, narrowing her eyes. She runs her fingers over her forehead. "Ben, I don't ask you for much. Ever. The boys don't ask you for much either but somehow it always seems whenever I ask you to do something as simple as tell them goodnight and turn out the light, it is a *major inconvenience* for you. And I'm sick of it. It's ridiculous."

She throws up her hands, exasperated.

"I'm *working,* Aila. I have an important case that needed to be dealt with before I go into work tomorrow."

"I'm sure," Aila says smugly. "I'm sure it was so important you couldn't spare ten minutes to say goodnight to your three kids. Who asked for you, by the way. It's bullshit, Ben, and you know it."

"It's not bullshit, Aila. You know I'm on track to make partner and I work my ass off every day to make ends meet for us."

Aila throws her head back to mock him. "Make ends meet. Don't flatter yourself. We aren't some poor family that can't pay our bills, Ben. Last I checked, I still take care of the finances and we are just fine. So fine, in fact, you should be able to spare a walk with your family without a phone call or tucking your children into bed without emails."

"Don't, Aila. Don't do this. You know the pressure I'm under. That I've always been under since you stopped working."

Ben's dark brown eyes sear into her soul. Aila feels her heart pound in her ears. Her eyes fill with tears but she doesn't allow herself to cry.

"That's so unfair for you to say," Aila shakes her head slowly and turns away from the kitchen to the living room. "That is so fucking unfair. We always agreed." Her voice breaks into a soft sob. "We always agreed that if I stopped working, you wouldn't hold it against me. How dare you?"

"No. Don't even play that," Ben says, following her into the living room. "You're right. We agreed. But I'm the one going to work so how dare you hold it against me?"

Ben's face has turned to stone. He is clearly frustrated and incapable of finding a balance in this argument. But in Aila's mind, he's already lost this case. Her tears instantly stop halfway down her cheeks.

She raises her eyes to meet his.

"I never. Not even once, have I ever held it against you for providing the life you have given me and the boys.

But it does not excuse you from being present when you are with us. It doesn't excuse you from sunset pictures, holding hands on walks, mopping the floors, or tucking the boys into bed at night. You are our provider, but I am not your nanny or your fucking maid."

Aila wipes the last tear falling down her cheek and turns around to head upstairs to bed, leaving Ben stunned and angry in the kitchen.

But just as she puts her foot on the first stair of the staircase she yells over her shoulder, "Don't forget to start the fucking dishwasher."

CHAPTER 13

THEN

"OH, ELEPHAAAANT!" Thump, thump, thump, thump. Aila was sitting cross-legged, pounding on the kitchen floor with Josh and Caleb while spaghetti sauce simmered on the stove.

The boys laughed and clapped. This was their favorite song to sing and it was the witching hour between naps and dinnertime. Aila was hanging on by a thread, so she gladly sat on the floor to sing a silly song with her children.

She was so exhausted. Josh was four and Caleb was two, barely potty-trained and had four accidents that day. She was up to her eyeballs in toddler pee, nursery rhymes, Play-doh, and tantrums. She was also eight weeks pregnant with baby number three. So, in between the timeouts and flashcards, Aila was worshipping the porcelain god or sniffing peppermint to keep from gagging.

Ben would be home soon though, and he'd be able to take over so she could lay on the couch with minimal movement and minimal scents.

Aila sang and gestured through the third verse of the song when her phone began to ring.

"Hold on, babes. Joshie, you take the lead," she said

while dragging herself to her feet and making her way to her phone.

"Hey," she said. It was Ben. Her reprieve. Her breath of fresh air.

"Hey, baby, I just wanted you to know I'm running thirty minutes late," Ben said, and Aila felt herself grow more tired and nauseous. "Go ahead and start dinner without me. I'm so sorry, honey."

"No, no. It's fine. I'll see you when you get here," Aila said, irritated some but mostly tired. "Love you."

"Love you too," he replied before the line went dead.

Aila sighed and smiled with effort before turning toward the boys on the floor.

"Who's hungry?"

"Me!" A chorus of children's voices echoed through the kitchen and Aila transitioned to plating dinners and devouring a bowl of spaghetti herself.

The rest of the night was a blur of bath time, jammies, and books. Aila constantly checked the time, wondering when her turn to clock out would come. But Ben's thirty minutes late soon turned into an hour which turned into two hours. The boys were safely and soundly tucked in their beds when Ben finally walked through the door. He looked dapper and energized and sexy.

Aila wanted to punch him in the face.

Instead she kissed him, told him there's more spaghetti in the fridge, and then collapsed on the couch again in her three-day old sweatpants, mindlessly clicking through their DVR.

Ben told her about his day: the depositions, the clients, the interviews, the snags in the case. Aila tried to be interested but her eyelids were heavy and the smell of the room made her queasy.

"Babe," she interrupted. "Can you look under the couch? I think there's an old milk sippy cup."

There was. It had gone rancid. Aila tried not to gag but found herself racing toward the bathroom anyway.

After several minutes hovered over the toilet, Aila waved her white flag and surrendered to her pregnancy exhaustion.

"I'm just going to go to bed. I'm done with today," she said before making her way upstairs.

A few minutes later, Ben came into the room and tucked himself under the covers next to her.

"Is tomorrow your appointment for the baby?" Ben asked.

"At ten o'clock," Aila nodded, half asleep.

"I have an 8:30 meeting so I'll try to make sure I'm out of there in time to make it," he said. "Are you bringing the boys or is my mom coming over to watch them?"

"I'm just going to bring them this time and bring the tablet," she said, smiling and anxiously thinking about hearing their baby's heartbeat for the first time tomorrow.

She already knew this one was going to give them a run for their money.

~

At the appointment the next day, Aila went through the routine she had become accustomed to with the last two boys: check in, questionnaire, blood work, wait, doctor, heartbeat.

By the time she was in an exam room with Josh and Caleb sitting quietly in the chairs watching *Monsters, Inc.*, Aila was laying on the examination table with her gown on, and she checked her phone. A text from Ben.

Running late.

She closed her eyes, smiled, and shook her head. Typical. It was almost endearing to her. Almost.

Dr. Chu came into the room after a few quick taps on the door.

"Hello, Aila," she said, extra buttery. "How are you

feeling?"

"Tired." Aila laughed at her own response.

Dr. Chu pressed her lips together in a solidarity smile. She set the chart on the desk, clasped her hands together, and leaned forward. Her expression was serious.

Aila swallowed hard and sat up—the mood in the room shifting.

"Aila." Dr. Chu said it softly, like she was about to console a child.

"Yes," she responded, frowning and unsure of what her doctor was about to say. She anticipated it wasn't good.

"According to your blood work, you are not pregnant."

Aila felt the air immediately get sucked out of her lungs.

"I'm sorry?" It was a question. Aila didn't understand.

Dr. Chu cleared her throat. "The blood sample we took thirty minutes ago indicates you are not pregnant."

Aila's mouth fell open.

"When did you take the at-home pregnancy test?" Dr. Chu asked while grabbing the fetal doppler to search for the baby's heartbeat. She squirted the cold lubricant on Aila's abdomen.

"Three weeks ago but I was already two weeks late at that point." Aila was numb.

"Okay, let's just see if we're able to find a heartbeat, just in case."

She pressed the doppler down on her belly and gently slid it around, searching for the baby that was surely just hiding in there.

An eternity seemed to pass, but there was nothing. No pitter-patter, no pulse.

"Okay," Dr. Chu said softly, wiping off the excess lubricant and sitting back down. She nodded at the paperwork on the desk. "So, what I've decided to do is go ahead and schedule an ultrasound for tomorrow so we can see what is going on. Have you had any spotting or bleeding during the last few days?"

Aila swallowed back the shock.

"No," she shook her head. "No, I've been terribly nauseous all morning. I threw up last night before bed, and I napped yesterday when the boys did. I've had every symptom I did before." She choked on her words. "Every symptom, I swear."

Dr. Chu smiled empathetically. "I believe you, Aila. We have a history." She set her hand on Aila's arm. "So, what I'm going to tell you is to go home and rest. Throw Disney Junior on for these boys and don't get off the couch. Drink plenty of water. Order takeout. Don't lift a finger. We'll check in tomorrow after the ultrasound. And if anything happens before then, call the nurse line, okay?"

Aila nodded and waited for the paperwork needed before grabbing Josh and Caleb by the hand and marching them out to the car in a mere trance.

In the car, Aila immediately dialed Ben, who picked up on the second ring.

"Aila, honey, I'm so sorry. I'm stuck on the 167 in traffic. I'm almost there, I swear."

Aila cleared her throat.

"The tests say I'm not pregnant," she said and her voiced cracked. "I'm not pregnant, Ben." She instantly began sobbing.

"Oh, honey, I am so sorry. Don't worry, I'm on my way," he said. "Where are you right now?"

"In the car with the boys." She tried to take a deep breath through broken tears. "About to drive home."

"Okay. I'll meet you at the house as soon as I can," he said, and he hung up the line.

Somehow, she made it back to the house, unloaded the boys, and turned on Disney Junior as instructed. Aila laid on the couch in a fetal position, at war with her emotions, the news she heard today, and how she felt for the last month.

She heard the ping of the garage door opening and knew Ben had come home for her. He rushed to her side and knelt next to her, brushing her hair away from her face.

"How are you feeling?" he asked.

"Terrible," she muttered and instantly felt a sharp pain in her stomach, as if the baby was waiting for its father to get home. Aila pressed down on her womb and instantly felt something wasn't right. She soon found herself sitting on the toilet staring at her panties full of blood and clots and mucus.

While she stared, she wept.

She wept because their baby was gone. She couldn't fix it. She couldn't control it. There was nothing she could do to stop them from losing their baby.

Aila walked out of the bathroom in an emotional trance and tucked herself under the covers in the master bedroom before calling the nurse line. She felt stunned and angry as she stared at the bedroom wall while the phone rang.

The nurse picked up. Her name was Amy. Aila could never forget the nurse on a call like that. How could anyone? She explained what was happening, how far along she thought she was supposed to be, and explained the blood work fiasco from the morning.

She felt like her story was broken, that it didn't make sense, and she struggled to explain the situation through her tears.

"I'm sorry. I'm just having a really hard time with this," she said through her sobs.

"It's okay," the nurse on the other line said. Her voice was calm but Aila could sense she was biting back her own emotions. "This is a very hard thing."

It was. A very hard thing indeed.

The ultrasound the next morning confirmed the suspicion: Aila had miscarried their baby.

Even with two vibrant and healthy boys at home, even with a full heart and a happy life, Aila felt like the rug had been pulled from beneath her. Or rather, something had been ripped from inside her.

She was devastated and in pain, both emotionally and

physically.

After Josh and Caleb had gone to bed on the fourth day after the miscarriage, Aila went straight to bed with Gus curled at her feet. The blankets encased Aila like an envelope—a letter she had no intention of opening—when Ben walked in the room and placed his hand on the small of her back.

"You okay?"

"I will be," she said through a muffling of sheets and emotions.

"You sure?" Ben asked. "Because I don't want to lose you in this. I won't be okay if you're not okay."

Aila felt stunned at the statement.

The flesh and pieces of their baby were still falling out of her, and he was worried about how sad she was. She had every right to be sad. To be exhausted. To curl up under her covers and weep after their kids had gone to sleep. She had every right to mourn.

Sure, he had every right to be concerned about his wife. But what she needed was time to grieve. Instead, she felt like she was told to buck up.

"I have every right to fall apart, Ben," she said, broken with tears.

Ben kneeled at her side of the bed and brushed the tears from her cheeks with his thumb. "That isn't what I meant, Aila. I know you do. I just worry about you."

"I don't need you to worry. I need you to let me be sad." She choked on a sob. "I need you to be home at a decent hour so you can help get the boys their dinner or to put them to bed. I need you around so I can just have a minute to myself. I'm exhausted. My body still needs to heal and I need you here to help that happen. And right now…" She let out a shuddered breath. "I'm just really sad. And you need to let that be okay."

Ben stared at wife a beat longer, absorbing her words while tucking her hair behind her ear.

He nodded softly.

"I love you, Aila," he said. "I'll do better."

CHAPTER 14

NOW

Aila hit snooze on her alarm twice, wanting to keep her head buried under her pillow.

She's always so exhausted after she fights with Ben. Somehow letting her emotions out drains her more than swallowing them does.

It only happens a few times a year. That's probably the bigger issue—she bottles up every irritation until she explodes. This is a combination of her disdain for conflict mixed with the lack of opportunity to get a word in. Aila hates to continuously say it just as much as she hates to experience it: Ben works too much. Or maybe he just values his work too much, placing it above the needs of his family.

Aila can't tell anymore.

Last night, when her crying had subsided, she heard Ben's footsteps on the stairs, making her tears cease even though more wanted to fall. She blinked them back and let her body fall still, pretending she was asleep.

Ben came into the room silently, his breathing calm and his movements fluid and swift, almost undetectable. He slid under the covers next to her, but Aila could sense he wasn't laying down.

She could feel his eyes on the back of her head and then he reached out and rubbed her back tenderly. He held his hand there for a moment, willing her to say something; to move the conversation in any direction that wouldn't leave it stagnant and stale in the air.

She refused, stubbornly faking her slumber until he turned over and went to bed.

By the time her alarm goes off for the third time, Aila rolls over and shuts off her phone. Her eyes are swollen from crying and her mouth dry from the wine she drank the night before. She slips her feet onto the plush carpet, lets out a yawn, and arches her back in a stretch when she spots a note on her nightstand.

Aila eyes it curiously and picks it up carefully, as if it might explode.

I'm sorry. XO, B

Her eyebrows furrow in confusion. Ben rarely apologized anymore. Not for working too much and certainly not with an outright 'I'm sorry' at least. His apologies were always in the form of flowers or a night out together. A weekend away even. He lavished her with tangible apologies but rarely ever confessed actual remorse.

My tongue must've been sharp last night.

She tosses the note back on her nightstand and picks up her phone, checking it for messages and seeing a text from Ben.

Call me when you get the boys to school.

Ben always left for work before she was up. It was his attempt at avoiding the morning rush to Seattle. He used to wake her up and kiss her before he left but as the years went by, that happened less and less. Regardless, he never texted a request for a call.

Aila swallows hard. She wasn't ready for a fight. She didn't want to.

She pushes Ben's text to the corner of her mind and carries on with her morning until the boys are on the bus and off to school for the day.

Aila waves to the boys and then the other moms at the bus stop before walking around the corner with Gus loyally trotting at her side. She pulls out her phone and reluctantly calls Ben.

It rings five times before going to voicemail.

Aila hangs up, half expecting him to call back immediately. He doesn't but instead sends another text.

Client meeting. Sorry. See you tonight. Love you.

Aila sighs out of irritation. Did he not ask her to call him? Does he not even know when the boys go to school? She hates this. It irritates her to no end that because he provides the cash flow it meant he has no idea how to keep the wheels turning for the family. She does that for him.

Okay. Don't forget about dinner tonight with Jackson.

A few moments later he responds.

Oh yeah! I almost forgot. I'll be there.

She rolls her eyes to herself.

Of course, he *forgets even though* he *invited him.*

Aila ignores her growing frustrations. She pockets her phone and then heads back to the house where an apology bouquet of white roses is waiting on the front porch. Of course: there's Ben's signature apology calling card. She sighs while bringing them inside and plops them into water. Aila spends a minute looking at them, wondering just how many of these Ben has sent over the years.

Once the number is too high to count, she pushes down her simmering anger and leaves for Bible study. During the entire hour at the church, she's careful to keep her marital frustrations from coming out during any of their discussions. She purposefully avoids Elena's gaze and pleasantries, worried she'll see right through her again—even though deep down Aila knows she already has.

She fills the rest of her afternoon with grocery shopping for dinner tonight and chores around the house; scrubbing bathrooms and mopping floors—any chore to make sure her frustration stays swallowed and her mind stays off that desperate apology bouquet sitting on the counter.

Aila realizes she still has two hours before the boys will be home, so she goes for a quick run. Each time her feet hit the pavement it feels like the edges of her anger become blunter. By the time she returns home and showers, she has nearly forgotten about her argument with Ben and her ensuing frustrations.

After picking up the boys from school, she freshens up and even throws on some lipstick. She spends too much time overthinking her outfit, and ultimately lands on a pair of slimming dark denim jeans and a black blouse.

For dinner, she's planning on making beef bourguignon. The boys don't love the dish but she has mastered Ina Garten's recipe, and it's the most impressive thing she knows how to make. Plus, she knows if she serves it with garlic bread and bribes the boys with chocolate cake for dessert, they'll eat it right up.

She feels unexpectedly nervous and excited. She wants to impress Jackson in an effortless way. She has been enjoying her newly rekindled friendship with him and hopes Ben will like him just as much as she does.

Ben needs a friend, someone outside of work to hang out with. Aila was growing tired of Ben's work friends. They'd come over for dinner: eat, drink, and talk endlessly about their current cases, leaving Aila feeling like a third wheel. She'd nod and smile at everything they said as if she knew exactly what they were talking about. As if she cared. As if she was even paying attention.

Jackson could offer a nice reprieve from that. He owns his own business. He used to be a firefighter and a rock climber. He even climbed Mount Rainier twice. He knows a little bit about everything but not in an obnoxious, arrogant way. In a humble way.

To Aila, Jackson is a breath of fresh air. She wouldn't mind having him around more often.

Aila shakes the daydream about Jackson out of her head. She slowly stirs the stew—the gentle cadence of the motion and the sound of the wooden spoon tapping the side of the pot helps to calm her nerves. The scents of smoky bacon, caramelized onions, garlic, and butter waft through the air making the kitchen smell irresistible.

"What's that smell?" Isaac says, running in from the backyard, sweaty from jumping on the trampoline with his brothers.

"Beef bourguignon," Aila tells him with a wink.

Isaac's forehead crumples in confusion.

"Alright, well it smells good. I'm hungry," he says.

"Well, it will be ready in a bit. Go run and get your brothers. I need to have a quick chat with you boys, okay?"

Just as Isaac dutifully runs out to tell Josh and Caleb to come in, Aila's phone pings.

Emergency meeting with a client. Won't be home til late. Sorry. X

Is he serious?

Aila thinks about texting Jackson to cancel but decides not to. Dinner tonight was Ben's idea, and he offered zero help in making it happen or even remembering to show up. After last night's fight and this new disappointment, Aila decides she could really use some adult conversation that doesn't end in her feeling worthless and unimportant. Plus, she had really enjoyed spending time with Jackson lately. It was as if they'd always stayed in touch and their relationship just fell back into place after nearly two decades.

Okay. She texts back.

"What's up, mom?" Josh and Caleb poke their heads in through the back door.

"Oh." Aila sets her phone down and walks over to them. "I just wanted to let you know a friend of mine from high school is coming over for dinner tonight, so I need all of you to please be on your best behavior."

She eyes each of them and they nod.

"That means eat dinner without complaining and being polite to our guest, okay?"

"'kay," they reply in unison.

"Can we still play outside?" Caleb asks.

"Yes," she says kissing his sweaty forehead and smudging away her lipstick mark with her thumb. "I'll let you know when dinner is ready."

A few minutes later the doorbell rings, and Gus lets out a quick bark. 6:29. Jackson is right on time. Aila checks her hair and teeth in the entryway mirror and rubs a fleck of lipstick off her tooth before opening the front door.

"Jackson, hi!" she greets him, perhaps a bit too enthusiastically.

"Good evening," he says in an oddly charming way, his smile making Aila catch her breath. Jackson is holding a bottle of Johnnie Walker and holds it out to her. "You told me your husband likes whiskey."

Aila smiles and takes the bottle from him. "Wow, thank you!" she says examining the bottle. "He does. This was very thoughtful of you. Come on in."

She holds the door open for him, letting him pass through before she closes it behind him and takes a quick breath in.

"Whatever you're cooking smells incredible," he says.

Aila smiles in satisfaction. *Wait until you taste it.* Her beef bourguignon blew everyone away.

"Thank you," she says instead. "Dinner is just about done."

Jackson follows her into the kitchen. She runs her hand along the marble island and turns to him, gesturing toward the bar stools.

"Have a seat, friend, and let me get you a drink. What'll it be? I have red and white wine and, of course, some whiskey."

Jackson sits down and simply says, "Whatever you're having."

She pours each of them a glass of cabernet sauvignon and gently places it in front of him.

"So," she begins, giving him an apologetic smile, while wondering if she's really all that sorry. "I have some bad news. Ben won't make it tonight. He got stuck at work."

"Oh," Jackson drops his smile. "That's too bad. I was looking forward to getting to know him a bit."

Aila takes a sip of wine and sets it down, shrugging. "Welcome to my life. This actually happens more often than not."

"Really?"

"Really." Aila turns toward the oven and pulls out the crusty garlic bread and places it on the counter. "I'm thankful for his job, of course, but at home…" She pauses. "It's really just me and the kids."

Jackson gives a solemn nod, probably unsure of what to say.

"Who, by the way, are outside playing." Aila sets her oven mitts on the counter and starts walking over to the back door. "Let me grab them to come say hello properly. You know, in comparison to last night's running straight past you."

Jackson laughs as Aila steps out on the back deck, the air is surprisingly warm for March, and calls to the boys playing "popcorn" on the trampoline. "Hey boys! Come here. There's someone I want you to meet."

Much to Aila's surprise, Jackson had followed her to

the deck instead of staying in the kitchen, so the boys run up to him with sweaty faces and dirty hands to meet his acquaintance. They run through the line of introductions, each shaking Jackson's hand and looking him in the eye like they were told. Isaac even ends his introduction with a salute.

Jackson laughs and his dimples shine through, sending ripples through Aila's heart.

"Pleasure to officially meet all of you," he says, holding his gaze at the boys. "Were you guys playing 'popcorn' on the trampoline?"

They all nod and give Jackson a wide grin. Aila stands back, smiling with pride at her sweet, sweaty, polite, little boys.

"That is one of my favorite games to play on a trampoline," he says. "If it's okay with your mom, maybe I can play a few rounds with you guys after dinner?"

The three boys look at her in unison and she raises her eyebrows and says, "If you eat your dinner. Now go wash up and then meet us at the table."

They rush through the house to the bathroom and Aila already knows when she goes back in there, her sparkling clean bathroom will be a splattering of soap and muddy water. She suddenly doesn't care. Jackson is so at ease in her home and with her kids she instantly feels relaxed.

Jackson offers his help setting the table, while Aila places the Dutch oven in the middle, along with a bowl of crusty garlic bread, a salad, the rest of the bottle of wine, and lemonade for the boys. Within minutes the five of them are seated at the table, Isaac says grace, and everyone dishes up their plates.

"So, Mr. Jackson, how do you know my mom again?" Caleb asks with a mouthful of beef stew and garlic bread.

"Chew your food first, please," Aila chides softly.

"Well, I first met your mom in…" He pauses to think. "Sixth grade, I think." He looks over at Aila for confirmation but she feels shocked by his response. She doesn't remember him in sixth grade, only high school.

Jackson gives her a half smile and meets her eyes, nodding. "Yep. Me and your mom were at the same school in sixth grade but in different classes. I was in Mr. Bennett's class and she was in Mrs. Kendrick's class."

Aila's heart begins to flutter. She doesn't remember him from then and she feels slightly embarrassed. She takes a sip of wine to settle herself.

"Then how'd you meet?" Josh asks.

"We met at recess," Jackson says. "You see when I was ten, I was a really little guy. Not big and strong like you boys." The boys chuckle through sips of lemonade. Aila eyes him and sits back in her chair, intrigued. "I was new to the school—I had just moved to Washington from Virginia—and I really wanted to play kickball, but the teams were already set. And Danny—he was the big, cool kid—took one look at me and told me I couldn't play. He said to try again tomorrow. And everyone laughed at me. So, I kind of just started walking away when I heard a voice from a girl on the other team."

The boys shoot their eyes at their mom, who gives them a quick raise of the eyebrows and a smile.

"And I hear her yell, 'Danny! Quit being such a jerk-wod and let the new kid play!'"

The boys laugh, holding their hands up to the mouth.

"And then she turned to me and said, 'What's your name, new kid?' And I told her and she said, 'I'm Aila. You can be on my team. You're up sixth, okay?' So, I just kind of jumped into the game and got to play. Your mom is the reason I had a good first day of school."

He gives a satisfied smile of his retelling of this memory and takes another bite of beef.

"Did you kick a home run?" Isaac asks, in awe of this piece of his mama's history.

Jackson laughs.

"Not even close. I hadn't quite grown into my paws yet." He sets down his fork and leans over. "But your mom did, she scored three."

"You can't possibly remember that." Aila shakes her head, smiling.

"Three?!" Isaac and Caleb say in unison, Josh just looks inquisitively at his mom.

"Yeah, three. Your mom beat all the boys at everything—kickball, tetherball, foursquare, soccer, you name it." He turns his gaze to her, his dimples still on full display. "She ruled recess."

Aila laughs, thankful for the quip to ease her mind from not remembering Jackson in grade school.

"Yeah, I can see it," Josh says looking at his mom and then back at Jackson. "She still beats me when we run races in the street. And you should see her do a flip on a trampoline."

"Impressive." Jackson grins, his gaze flitting up at Aila.

"And she draws really good mermaids with chalk!" Isaac adds.

They all chuckle. Aila feels her face flush. It has been a long time since she sat at a table full of people telling her how great she is. She feels a surge of gratefulness and swallows the embarrassing lump in her throat.

"Well," she says with a slight clearing of the throat. "If you boys are done, you can clear your plates and I'll get dessert ready."

"Hey, Mr. Jackson," Caleb says. "Want to play 'popcorn' after you clear your plate?"

"Absolutely."

Aila smiles and gently grasps his arm, mouthing the words, *You're the best.*

"Nobody's allowed to break any bones though, got it?" she says to the boys, Jackson included.

He smiles and heads out back with the boys after placing his plate in the sink. Aila finishes clearing the table and storing the leftover food, and then pulls out plates and forks for the chocolate cake and ice cream, setting them on the counter. She follows the sounds of squeals and laughter on the trampoline in the backyard and calls out from the deck that dessert is ready.

"Wait, Mom!" Isaac calls back breathlessly. "Show Mr. Jackson your flip."

Aila gives an exasperated laugh. "Now?" She waves off their insistencies. "No, no. Let's go have dessert. It's almost bedtime. You already know I can do it."

"Prove it!" Jackson heckles at her, teasingly.

Aila's mouth falls open in mock offense.

"Alight, fine. Get out of my way, youngin's."

With the trampoline to herself, Aila gives herself a few bounces and then flips—the wine and food juggling in her stomach—and lands it with an Olympic pose.

The crowd of four cheers and applauds. Aila laughs with a slight buzz reaching her head from the combination of wine and the sudden movement.

"Woo! Now, let's eat cake." She laughs as the boys run inside.

"Well done, Aila Smith," Jackson says, holding out his hand to hers, helping her hop down from the trampoline like a gentleman.

Aila flushes at his touch and the sound of her maiden name coming off his lips. She doesn't correct him.

"Thank you. Now, how many scoops of ice cream do you want?"

Jackson smiles at her, his eyes a blanket of adoration. A part of her thinks maybe he is just being polite to her and the butterflies she keeps feeling are because she's being slightly delusional. But she decides not to meddle in her doubts and simply enjoy his company.

As they finish their cake on the back deck, through fits of laughter and stories from Jackson, Aila loses track of time.

"Oh, no. Boys you have to get to bed. It's thirty minutes past lights out," she says to their dismay and groans. "I know, I know. Now say goodnight to Mr. Jackson and get ready for bed."

The boys rush upstairs to brush teeth while Aila and Jackson bring in the dishes from outside and load the dishwasher. Jackson begins wiping up the melted ice cream smears on the counter.

"Oh, Jackson, you don't have to do that."

"I don't mind." Jackson shrugs, continuing.

"Hey, Mom! We're out of toothpaste," Caleb hollers from the top of the stairs.

Aila gives an apologetic smile to Jackson. "Excuse me."

She heads upstairs to get the boys an extra tube of toothpaste and tucks them into bed quickly.

"Hey, Mom." Josh yawns, the last child to tuck in for the night. "Tonight was a lot of fun."

Aila smiles.

"It really was. Good night, bud."

After shutting off the lights, Aila makes her way back downstairs to where Jackson sits at the kitchen island with his wine glass; the clean kitchen accentuated by the soft glow of the pendant lights.

She shakes her head and smiles. "Thank you for waiting…and cleaning. Really, you are far too kind."

Jackson swats away at the compliment. "It's nothing. You have your hands full."

"That I do," Aila takes in a deep breath.

"No, I don't mean it like that. But you definitely have a very full life." He looks down at his hands as they gently caressing his wine glass. "Your boys are great. They're a ton of fun. I haven't jumped on a trampoline in ages."

"Ah, I haven't jumped on a trampoline since…yesterday." She laughs, dropping her head and making her long hair fall forward. She brushes it back and looks at Jackson. He is looking at her intently, smiling meaningfully, like he has a secret he's keeping from her.

"Tonight was great," he says. "I really have had a nice time."

"I'm so glad you came." Aila lets out another deep

breath. "Sorry Ben couldn't make it."

"I actually figured he'd be back by now. What time does he usually get home?"

Aila twists her wine glass in her hand and shrugs.

"Depends. He *should* be home by six, but sometimes it's just easier for him to get ahead of things at the office, or there's an emergency client meeting, or unexpected evidence pops up in the discovery and he stays late. Which means he'll usually be home around eleven or so." Aila shrugs again and sips her wine, the red liquid making her feel bold and honest.

"Oh wow. That's a lot later than I thought." Jackson glances at his watch. It's 9:20.

"Yeah, well, his loss," she says with a smile. "Want another drink?"

"Only if you do."

Aila cocks her head to the side, giving Jackson a flirtatious smile. "Should we crack open the whiskey?"

Jackson's face breaks into a smile, his hazel eyes shining under the pendant lights. "Let's do it."

Aila pours them each a glass of whiskey on the rocks and sits down on a barstool next to him. "Cheers."

They meet eyes and clink glasses. Aila feels the pungent sting of the whiskey as it runs down her throat and warms in her belly.

"You know what, Jackson?"

"What's that?"

"I don't remember you from sixth grade."

"Really?"

"Really," Aila confesses. "That story you told completely escapes me."

Jackson takes a sip of whiskey and nods his head, smiling. He is always smiling, making Aila's heart feel like she is a teenage girl again.

"I know," he says.

"Really?" Aila is surprised. "You *know*? Did you make it up?" Aila pulls back with a half-smile, examining Jackson's expression.

Jackson dips his head sheepishly. "No. I didn't make it up. You just didn't really notice me until junior year of high school."

"I'm sorry. I didn't realize I was such a terrible person." Aila pouts her lip and then laughs.

Jackson does too.

"No, no. I don't mean it like that," he says, reaching out a hand and placing it on hers. "You were amazing. The coolest girl I'd ever seen. I had been in awe of you since sixth grade. You kicked everyone's ass at everything and I always thought, it doesn't get any cooler than Aila Smith."

Aila finds herself genuinely laughing and her cheeks flushing. "Gosh, I was such a tomboy…and a late bloomer. I didn't give anyone a second look until junior year." She stands up, grabbing their glasses and making her way over to the whiskey bottle for a refill on the other side of the kitchen.

"Really?"

Aila nods, her cheeks aching from the unprecedented amount of smiling happening this evening.

"We had some really good times as kids, didn't we?" she says, letting the memory of them rush through her mind. "Bonfires on the beach?"

"Saturdays at Denny's," he replies.

"TP'ing Chelsey's house."

"Saran wrapping Jake's car."

They burst into laughter.

"After the football games at your place?"

He runs his hand across his face, as if he's holding back a laugh. He stands and comes to the other side of the island, leaning against the counter next to her. "Parties at Ethan's?"

Aila flushes at this. She turns away slightly and bites her lip.

"We really did have some good times." Aila gazes into her whiskey glass, swirling the ice cubes around. "I'm so glad we've been able to hang out again. I really feel like you've been reminding me of the person I forgot I was for a long time."

She pauses and looks into his hazel eyes. He is studying her and she can see the longing he's so obviously feeling for her, but she can also see his determination to hold back.

She feels it too. She finally realizes the nervous energy she's been experiencing is really just the undeniable chemistry she and Jackson have always had—she remembers feeling the same thing when they were just teenagers.

Still holding his gaze, Aila reaches out to him hesitantly, but pulls her trembling hand back quickly. Her head feels fuzzy with reluctance and desire. Jackson shifts his body an inch closer and before she realizes it, she moves her hand out again and pulls Jackson closer to her by the nape of his neck. Their lips touch, igniting a fire between them until all she feels is heat. The heat of his hands on her hips, running up and down her back and cradling her face; the heat of his muscles as she grips his back, hungry for his affection. His kiss is tender and eager and awakens a fire in her belly she hasn't felt in years.

Is this what it used to feel like?

The kiss is an unleashing of every nerve. Every desire. Every lost memory she wants back until she pulls away softly, even though she desperately wants more. She places her shaking fingers to her lips and meets his gaze. Her heart is pounding so hard she can hear it in her ears.

Jackson's eyes are wide with astonishment and lust. He is captivated by her. He is looking at her like she is all he can see; all he can think about. Aila can't remember the last time anyone looked at her like that. Thinking of her sleeping boys upstairs, she places her hand on his chest and takes a small step back.

"Thank you for this evening." She looks up to meet his eye. "We should probably call it a night though. Okay?"

Jackson gently grabs a strand of her hair and tucks it back from her face, his eyes still focused on her.

"Okay." He nods, the trance breaking.

As she walks him to the door, he turns around just before opening it. She pauses a step away from him, giving him a small smile. "Goodnight, Jackson."

His smile reminds her of the Jackson she knew when they were young and carefree.

"You are exactly the same, Aila Smith," he says quietly, using her maiden name for the second time that evening.

And once again, she doesn't correct him.

Aila's mind is spinning when she closes the door. She can't believe what had just happened. What she had just done.

It was intoxicating. Thrilling.

It was so unlike her.

Aila was always a good wife. Never reckless. Always faithful.

Until she wasn't.

CHAPTER 15

THEN

"What happened in here?" Ben asked, as he walked into the kitchen after getting home from work.

Aila whipped around to survey the room, Isaac, just six months old, hoisted on her hip. Pots and pans were in the sink, sippy cups littered the countertops along with more dishes, snack bowls, small piles of Goldfish crackers and Puffs laying here and there, and stacking rings and blocks were scattered on the floor near the sink.

"What?" Aila said, half irritated, half triumphant. He really had no idea what went on in their house while he was at work in his fancy suits.

Ben held out his hands, rotating his body and scanning the small disasters, slowly, as if something might detonate. He let out a small laugh.

"Rough day? It looks crazy in here."

She could tell he was trying to make light of his reaction, probably because he didn't want Aila to get angry. She desperately wanted a third baby and after her miscarriage, she felt broken and unsure it was even in the cards for them. But a few months later, she was late. She ignored it for another week or two. Nervous and anxious, wanting to shield her heart from another devastation. But when Ben's mom poured her a glass of wine at Thanksgiving, she took a small sip, swallowed and then just stared at it. She felt a surge of guilt and didn't touch the wine glass for the rest of the night.

Seven months later, their sweet Isaac made his debut—their rainbow baby. Aila was thrilled and overjoyed to add a fifth member to their family. "Now we're a whole hand!" Josh would say, holding up all five fingers. Being a mom of three proved to be more challenging than she expected. She had a four-year-old, a two-year-old, and now, a baby. All boys. All full of energy and wrestling and words. She loved it. But she was also more exhausted than she could have ever imagined.

Ben didn't always make it home for dinner so he didn't usually get to witness the explosions in the kitchen and living room. Aila would usually clean up the kitchen and bathe all three boys, tucking them into bed just before Ben was home to admire his pleasant, perfect, sleeping little family.

He'd be there in time to read books and kiss the boys goodnight but not to witness the messy, chaotic, exhausting reality of life with little children.

Aila was a good cover up. She'd clean the kitchen messes between bites of dinner and toss toys in to their respective bins while hauling the boys up the stairs, making the crazy disappear. She'd often joke to her girlfriends she and her little boys were a traveling circus—set up during the day and gone by evening, when Ben arrived home.

Aila stood up straighter, propping Isaac up on her waist a little higher.

"No, I had a great day *actually*," she said. *Until you came home and criticized it.* "This is just life, Ben."

She breathed in through her nostrils, letting it out slowly, suppressing a sigh.

Ben held his hands up in surrender.

"Okay, okay." His eyes were wide when they landed

on Gus licking the spilled plate on the floor.

Like clockwork, Josh and Caleb ran through the room wearing superhero capes and wielding plastic swords, screaming their heroics.

"Daddy!" They yelled in unison.

"Hey, hey," he said, holding their spaghetti plastered faces back from his Kenneth Cole slacks. He smiled, almost nervously. "Let's, uh, go upstairs to get you boys in the bath."

Aila stood in the kitchen, her smile frozen and eyebrows raised at Ben, blinking at him like an irritated mannequin.

Great. Please, do something helpful when you walk in and see the chaos that is our *life.*

She set Isaac on the floor next to his toys and threw down a few Cheerios for good measure and spent the next fifteen minutes cleaning up the kitchen. She then moved to the living room to give it a clean sweep before heading upstairs to give Isaac a quick bath, clean jammies, and nurse him to sleep.

After laying him down—Aila knew she only had four hours until he was up again. She headed to Josh and Caleb's room to see them snuggled up while Ben read them *The Gruffalo*, fighting yawns in between fits of giggles. Aila smiled and breathed out a sigh of relief and peace. She made it through another busy, chaotic day with her three little boys.

Thank God Ben is here.

She shook her head to herself before heading downstairs to pour half a glass of wine and then collapsed on the couch with *The Real Housewives of Beverly Hills*. Her eyes had surely glazed over by the time Ben came down in clean sweatpants and a smug look on his face.

"The big boys are asleep," he said.

"Thanks." Aila smiled and took a sip of wine. "There's a plate for you on the counter. You'll want to heat it up though."

Ben just stood there, staring at her, wanting more from her but Aila wasn't sure what. Scratch that. She knew.

She just didn't want to right then.

In that moment she just wanted to veg out on the couch with a mindless show and her last few sips of wine. Then she'd head up to sleep for a couple of hours before waking up with Isaac, who would want to nurse, rock, and sing before she could get him back down. Which, in turn, meant she could finally go back to bed, where Ben would surely be lying there snoring and unaware of any midnight events that took place for Aila.

She looked up and plastered a fake smile on her face. "What?"

"What do you mean 'what'?" Ben wasn't angry but he was irritated with her. "I haven't seen my wife all day and I can't get more than five words out of her."

"Actually, I just said sixteen words to you," she snarked back. "Be thankful, honey. I'm exhausted."

Ben turned away to the kitchen. Aila sensed he was holding back his frustrations.

Aila took this opportunity to dig a little deeper.

"Would've been nice if you came home and started pitching in instead of criticizing me. Because you know I had it handled. I always do. No help from you."

Aila heard the microwave door slam shut.

"I'm sorry, but I was at work all day, which happened to be incredibly stressful, but you didn't ask. You just looked at me when I walked in the door like I was another burden. Another chore for you to *do.*"

Ben was clearly angry and took his hot plate of food into the office to finish whatever work it was he brought home this time.

Aila sighed and picked up her glass of wine. She didn't want to finish this fight. She didn't have the energy. She wanted to finish her wine and her show, and go to bed.

By the end of the episode her wine was drained and she realized she'd been biting at her lip and picking at her cuticles until they bled. She hated being the first to apologize. She hated unfinished conversations lingering in the air even more.

Without saying a word, Aila slipped into the office and grabbed Ben's empty plate off the desk. He mumbled a quick thank you and she responded with a, "mm-hmm."

Back in the kitchen she loaded her wine glass and his plate in the dishwasher and started it. She gave her hands one last wring and then went back to the doorway of the office.

She cleared her throat.

"I'm sorry I was rude to you," Aila said, slightly reluctant, but eager to make nice.

Ben turned in the chair slowly and placed his elbows on his knees, leaning his prominent chin on his clasped hands. His posture was expectant, as if he'd been waiting for her to come in and apologize.

Aila didn't always realize it, but he rarely apologized first. No matter the incident. He had a stubborn streak a mile wide and she was really good at putting Band-Aids on all of their cracks.

"Thank you," Ben said, standing up and making his way over to her, sliding his hands over her hips. "I love you, and I'm so sorry life is hard and chaotic right now. But we've got this. I've got you."

He dipped down to gently kiss her forehead.

Aila cleared her throat slightly.

So, you're sorry life is hard, not that you were a jerk about me trying to relax for five minutes and not helpful tonight. Got it.

"I know," she said instead. "It's just when you get home, I never know what time it's going to be which means I never know what you're going to walk into. So, when you get home, it'd be nice if you just jumped in, instead of criticizing me."

Ben pulled back. "Isn't that what I did? I came in the door and grabbed the big boys and gave them a bath and got them ready for bed, so I'm not sure what you're implying."

He was right. Sort of.

But did that make Aila wrong? Her heart raced.

Maybe I imagined his reaction. Or did I?

"I had a really hard day at work. Carla didn't get me the deposition or the evidence that was in discovery for my case on Thursday and then she called in sick so I spent the entire day scrambling, when all I wanted was to get home to see you and the boys. And when I did sneak away early to come kiss your face…" he was searching for words. "Let's just say, you weren't the most pleasant person to come home to."

Aila bit her lip, and nodded, like a child being chastised by her father.

"You're right. I'm sorry."

"You know how hard I work for us, for you, and the boys."

There it was. The work guilt trip she was waiting for. As if Aila didn't work hard all day for Ben and the boys.

"All of the hours I spend away from home are for all of you—for the family we've built."

Ben brushed her hair behind her ear and ran his finger under her chin, tilting her face toward his. His eyes were the same dark, chocolate brown eyes she fell in love with. She still got lost in them, but only if she looked hard enough.

Ben bent his head down and kissed her softly sending a shiver down her spine. His kisses became harder and more eager until they fell to the office floor. Ben kicked the door closed and made love to her right there. It was intense and passionate, like they both were unleashing their frustrations and blame until they lay there quietly, satisfied and breathless.

Only Aila wasn't. Not completely. She still felt a little unseen. A little unheard. Even still.

CHAPTER 16

NOW

Aila's entire body feels electric after Jackson leaves. The shock of his kiss pinged from her lips and surged through her veins. She can still feel it in her fingertips and all the way down to her toes.

She spends the night begging for sleep, for her mind to turn off her thoughts and emotions. The images of kissing Jackson replay over and over in her mind. She feels a level of euphoria mixed with disbelief and shock at her own actions. Her brain will not shut off. Her bones ache for him. She had gotten a taste and now she wants more, even as she begs herself not to.

What would this mean for my family if anyone found out? Where can this even go?

She hadn't kissed Jackson since she was seventeen. It was nostalgic and smothering. It made her feel wanted, desired, and seen in a way she hadn't in years.

In the last few weeks, he had become a breath of fresh air to her monotonous life. She constantly thought of ways to run into him or made up reasons to text him. Often times she'd roll out of bed and peak out her balcony window, where she could view Cherrywood Lane, just to see if his truck was there, like a schoolgirl with a crush. She, in a way, had become obsessed.

And now they had kissed. A line she didn't mean to cross but knew she couldn't take back now.

~

Aila's eyes shoot open the next morning before her alarm. Ben had gotten home and to bed sometime past midnight, after Aila had finally fallen asleep. She woke briefly to feel him slide quietly into bed, but he didn't try to wake her. Now as she wakes up this morning, she notices his side of the bed is already empty—a reminder of his frequent absence. Though this time she looks at the crumpled-up sheets with relief instead of longing.

She feels a rush of nervous energy as she goes through her morning routine of brushing her teeth and washing her face. After putting on some light makeup to liven up her already glowing skin, Aila sprays dry shampoo in last night's waves. As she's running her hand through her hair to make sure the kinks are out, a memory of the night before flashes in her mind. Aila grabs a strand of her long brown hair and pulls it toward her face and up to her nose. She can still smell Jackson. She can still feel his hands running through her hair and up and down her back.

She holds the strand of hair delicately between two fingers. Rubbing it gently while she stares up at the reflection of a woman staring back at her. A *married* woman staring back at her. A married woman who kissed someone that wasn't her husband last night. She led Bible study a mere twelve hours before she her lips were pressed against Jackson's in a frenzy of passion and hunger for something she had been missing for years. A kiss that only lasted a few moments but was enough to break every illusion she had created. She feels her chest constrict with guilt and then tries to shrug it away.

It was just a kiss and she'd kissed him before. What did it matter?

Aila takes a few deep breaths before walking out of her bathroom to calm her pounding heart, but her breath catches at the sound of Ben clearing his throat and she pauses mid-step before heading down the staircase.

She suddenly feels out of place. Like she doesn't belong in her own home. An imposter. A fraud.

She shakes the accusations in her head and clears her throat as she strides in the kitchen and over to the coffee pot.

"You're leaving late today," she says, as she pulls down a mug from the cupboard and pours herself a cup of coffee.

See? I belong here. Just act normal.

Ben's eyes lock on her. Her hair. Her makeup. Her matching Athleta outfit and perky disposition. They've been married for nearly fifteen years—Ben knows she isn't a morning person. His look is almost accusatory, sending Aila's heart racing into her throat.

She had never lied to Ben. She'd kept things from him sometimes. But nothing like this.

"You look pretty today," he says, standing up from the bar stool.

His phone is open to a news article and he turns it away gently, running his hand across the marble as he meets Aila by the coffee pot and kisses her on the cheek.

"Thank you," she responds, smiling nervously.

She turns around, cupping the mug of coffee near her chest and rests the small of her back on the counter. Ben is facing her squarely now. His body a shield of slacks and button-ups, his tie not quite done yet.

He smiles at her, his dark eyes piercing hers. She searches his eyes and wonders if he can read her mind. She looks away, suddenly uncomfortable, and turns her attention to unloading the dishwasher.

"So, you had a late night last night then?"

Ben holds a hand to his forehead, looking slightly rejected.

"Uh, yeah. I'm sorry about that. Danny and I just

figured if we stayed late last night, we could get a few more hours of sleep before our flight leaves this afternoon."

Aila nearly drops the wine glass she's pulling out of the dishwasher as she whips her body into an about face.

"I'm sorry. Flight?"

"Aila. You're kidding, right?" Ben takes a sip of his coffee. "It's been on the calendar for months. The AAJ Annual Convention?" He nods at the calendar hanging on the refrigerator—the entire weekend is painted yellow.

Aila lets out the breath she was holding in. "Oh, right. Washington, DC? Yeah. I'm sorry I forgot."

Ben laughs but it comes like condescending snicker, as if to mock her forgetfulness, making her feel inadequate.

"It's the reason I've been working so many late nights. We had to get ahead of the Jefferson McCleary trial before heading out of town for four days."

Aila swallows hard and closes her eyes hard.

"You always work late, Ben. This week hasn't felt any different. I just forgot."

She feels both genuinely sorry and genuinely irritated.

Ben rubs his lips together and nods, likes he's punctuating her statement and her feelings. "Look, I hear you. I work long hours and the workload the last few months —" *More like ten years.* "—has been insane but you know every moment I'm away is for our family. Our life. The one we've built."

"Ben, our life and your career don't feel the like they fit in the same basket anymore."

"I'm sorry?" It's a question and an accusation.

Aila blinks back her tears. She isn't feeling sad but she does feel frustrated he doesn't understand, that he can't see it with his own eyes.

"Sometimes it feels like *I've* been building our life at home. *You've* been building a career. They aren't the same life any more. You aren't around enough to see that."

"That's unfair. And it's uncalled for." Ben's voice

raises an octave. His courtroom voice.

Oh, you object, do you?

"Last night the boys didn't even ask why you weren't home for dinner. Or at bedtime. Your absence is their normal." She's cutting him down now and she knows it, but she doesn't know how else to make him see her reality.

"Oh, so now I'm a bad father." He leans on the counter and crosses his arms. Waiting. Expecting her to go too far. She reels in what she wants to say, knowing words are far more powerful than they seem because they cut into memories, leaving scars for years to come.

"I never said that, Ben. But you invited my friend—" she stutters over the mention of his name, "J-Jackson over for dinner and you weren't even here. You still haven't even acknowledged you missed it. Do you know how embarrassing that is for me?"

Not that embarrassing—she quite enjoyed the ending of last night—but she needed a punch to his gut and a reason for herself to believe it wasn't her fault she kissed someone else.

Ben hated to be an embarrassment. The color washes from his face. He didn't even remember.

Aila feels just as triumphant as she feels unimportant. Her eyes drop passed Ben's shoulder as the three boys walk in from upstairs, ready for breakfast.

They sit at the island, shoveling cereal in their mouths while Ben tells them about flying to "the other Washington" for the rest of the week.

They nod and mumble okays. Aila can tell it's not quite the goodbye he was expecting.

Ben looks at Aila, who eyes him over her coffee mug. Ben is a phenomenal dad when he's around. She knows that. Ben knows that. The kids know that. But the truth is, he isn't around often enough for a four-day business trip to throw a wrench in their week.

"Alright, boys, finish up and go brush your teeth," Aila says.

"I already did," Caleb says.

"You just ate a bowl full of sugar and chocolate," she chides, kissing his brown messy hair. "Brush them again."

While they stampede upstairs, Ben grabs bowls off the counter to put them in the dishwasher. His presence is making her uncomfortable. She's become so used to him not being around for their morning routine, that when he is, she feels like he's in the way.

"Thank you for doing that," she simply says instead, then grabs Gus's leash and puts on her tennis shoes.

While sitting on the bench by the front door, tying her shoes, she hears Ben's footsteps draw closer and she glances up at him.

"I think I'll walk the boys to the bus stop with you before heading to the office," he says.

"Sure." Aila nods, as the herd heads back downstairs to cause a tornado of shoes, backpacks, and jackets in the entryway.

Aila and Ben stand on the front porch, waiting for the boys, a palpable distance between them—thick with frustration and unsaid apologies. Gus whines and wags his tail in anticipation of his morning walk as the boys head out single file and off to the bus stop.

Ben promises them gifts upon his return from DC and gives each of them a hug and kiss before they trot onto the bus, hollering, "Bye Dad! Bye Mom!"

The other moms at the stop wave their goodbyes while Janet says, "Wow, what a sweet surprise to have Daddy at the bus stop too. You're such a great parent, Ben. I wish my husband would come to the bus stop every once in a while." She nudges and winks at Aila. "You really do have it all."

Aila crinkles her nose when Janet calls her husband 'Daddy.' She has always had the sneaking suspicion Janet is attracted to Ben. It doesn't make her jealous. It makes her laugh.

Ben tells her thank you and goodbye while flashing a

wicked smile. He knows he's charming.

"What time are you heading up to Seattle?" Aila asks before she turns to start walking around the corner with Gus.

"Soon." His hands are in his pockets and he's staring at his feet, like a little boy in trouble with his mom. He thinks he's being endearing but it is only irritating Aila more.

"And your flight leaves when?"

"One o'clock. It's on the calendar." Now he's being smart.

"Don't be like that. Dammit, Ben. I can't memorize every aspect of your life. I'm already memorizing all three of your children's."

His jaw is clenching. He's holding back, desperately trying not to pick another fight and not add any more gasoline to the flames.

"Can I walk with you?" he offers instead.

Aila looks down at his Oxford shoes then back at his eyes and reluctantly concedes. "Sure."

They walk toward Cherrywood Lane a good two feet apart, in an irritated silence. He doesn't want to apologize even if he knew how to. Aila can feel him begging her to say sorry, to make nice before he flies across the country. Part of her wants to. The other part wants to scream.

As they round the corner, Aila sees the Williams Brother Landscaping trucks, Jackson's gray truck, and then Jackson. Aila feels her heart leap into her throat and she swallows it down.

Why is he here? Why could he possibly need to be onsite today? Even though she'd grown accustomed to seeing his trucks in the neighborhood, he wasn't usually with them as much as she sometimes wanted him to be.

Aila's heart is fiercely beating, feeling like it might fly out of her chest.

Ben spots him too and gives him a wave.

"Hey there! Jackson, right?" He starts trotting over to him. Like a politician. Or maybe a concerned citizen.

Though Jackson is the one that seems concerned. His

eyes dart from Ben to Aila and back to Ben. Aila never envisioned them interacting again. The words they exchanged at the start of the week seem like a world away and even then, the words were in passing. Distracted. Now here they are. All three of them, face to face. One of them having no clue what happened the night before.

Aila's cheeks feel hot.

"Hey, man, I just wanted to apologize for last night." Ben shoots out a hand. Jackson shakes it. "I had every intention of getting home early and then work just got out of hand. You understand? Duty calls."

He's doing that nervous thing he does where he snaps his fingers and then one hand slaps the other fist. Over and over. Aila is staring at his hands, dazed.

I can't believe this is happening.

"No worries," Jackson says. He's smiling, his dimples prominent. Aila can hardly breathe; her heart is beating so hard she feels like she might suffocate. "I understand. Life happens."

Jackson shoots a look at Aila. She holds it as long as she can before he looks away. The chemistry between them is thick and electric. Aila worries Ben can see the surges of attraction shooting between her and Jackson. She always believed chemistry was not only obvious but tangible. Something to be held and witnessed by others.

"Anyway," Ben continues. "It won't happen again. After my trip this weekend, my schedule will resume back to its regular programming. So, we'll have to reschedule and have you over again."

Jackson is nodding slowly, understanding Ben has no clue he kissed his wife but unsure of how to handle this situation himself.

"Sure thing." His voice is deep and steady, like he just drank honey.

"Alright. See you around then. Take care," Ben says and he salutes. Aila is mortified.

This can't be happening.

She feels awkward and unsure. Ben was usually her steady, the one that calms her nerves and eases her insecurities but, in this moment, he's the cause.

Jackson salutes back. Aila wants to laugh, mostly so she doesn't panic.

"Bye, Jackson," she says, making sure to meet his gaze. His eyes are questioning but his body language is calm and confident.

Aila doesn't know what to make of his demeanor or the interaction that took place. She needs to call him, to explain. She glances over her shoulder as she and Ben walk back to the house but Jackson has already turned his attention to his employees.

Aila and Ben walk back in silence.

At the house, Ben grabs his carry-on and briefcase and sets it by the front door.

"Well, I'm out of here."

Aila is standing in the kitchen nursing her second cup of coffee. She gives him a half smile and nods, waiting for him to leave. Her fingers are itching to text Jackson, to tell him she didn't know Ben would be with her at the bus stop and that she hasn't stopped thinking about him since last night.

"Call me when you land?"

"Will do." He leans in to kiss her briefly and then he's out the door.

Aila immediately grabs her phone and texts Jackson.

Can we talk?

Aila sees three dots appear and pokes her head out the front window to ensure Ben's car has left the driveway.

I'm heading into a meeting in 15.

Okay. Come over later?

133

...

Be there at one.

Aila lets out a breath she had been holding since the bus stop. She feels a rush of adrenaline or maybe excitement. She can't quite pinpoint exactly what she's feeling. All she knows is she can't wait for one o'clock to roll around.

She cancels with Caleb's teacher, letting her know she won't be in to volunteer in the afternoon and gives her apologies. Then, alone in the house with her thoughts and a tired Gus, Aila decides she should probably eat something.

She scrambles some eggs but she can hardly taste them so she settles on a slice of toast, hoping it will calm her stomach.

Her phone pings.

Derek has the girls this weekend. Drinks?

Can't. Ben is out of town.

Lame. Call me soon. Need to fill you in.

Aila stares at Chantelle's texts. How easy it was for a friend to miss out on the last month of her life. How does that even happen? Chantelle would have more than a few cents to add to the predicament Aila has found herself in.

She feels a surge of guilt, but ignores it.

At 12:59, Jackson is on her doorstep with soup and sandwiches. He holds the bag out with a shrug, like an offering.

"Is French onion still your favorite?" he asks.

Aila's face breaks into a smile, her worry and apprehension melting away immediately.

"It is."

She guides him into the kitchen and notices his eyes flicker to the spot in the corner where he pinned her against the countertop and kissed her the night before. It haunted him too. It had been less than twenty-four hours, but even still.

"Look, Aila, I just…" Jackson sets the food down and turns to her, eager to get his rehearsed apology out. "I'm really sorry about last night. I never intended to cross a line with you. I didn't mean to step on your toes or—"

She cuts him off.

"No, no, don't apologize. That's just it, Jackson." Her hands are shaking and her belly is on fire. "I want you to…"

He looks up at her questioningly but with a glimmer of hope and desire.

"I want you to step on my toes. I want you hold me and kiss me. I want you around all the time. And when you aren't around, I think about the next time I get to see you or talk to you or…hell, touch you. I'm constantly thinking about you. And it's stupid and insane…"

She's standing right next to him now, practically breathing in the same air. Her voice is near tears and unable to articulate the rush of emotions she's been feeling.

"And it's exactly how I've felt for the last twenty years," Jackson says as he looks down at Aila.

His hazel eyes meet hers, like a stormy sky, searching and looking for her soul. Aila reaches out timidly at first, like she doesn't want to get burned, but she also wants to feel the heat.

Jackson grabs her waist and pulls her into his body. She can feel the curve of every muscle and the warmth coming off his skin. The heat acts as a magnet until they are kissing in the same spot as the night before. Just like last night, but only this time, they know exactly what they're doing. The kiss is passionate, intense, and enchanting.

And they can't stop. They don't stop. His lips run along her jaw and down her neck as her hands pull him closer.

Aila leads him to the bedroom, their clothes falling to the floor along the way. Jackson lays her down on the bed tenderly, running his fingertips along her bare skin making her body tremble with anticipation until finally their bodies collide.

It is gentle and playful, but also eager and hungry.

It isn't until it's over, and Aila is breathless and sweaty next to Jackson, she realizes exactly what they've done. What she's done.

She had never done a single reckless thing in her life. She always put everyone before herself. Her parents. Her friends. Her children. Her husband. She was the selfless, dedicated housewife who never stepped out of line.

No one knew what she wanted or desired. No one cared if she felt lost or used. But Jackson did, and he wanted her. He took the risk to have her just as she did.

Jackson props himself up on his elbows and gently brushes a few wild strands of Aila's hair from her face. He bites his lip as if he's biting back years of unspoken words.

He smiles in a boyish way that reminds Aila of their teenage love affair that never quite finished.

CHAPTER 17

THEN

"Y̶ou coming to practice, Aila?" Olivia called to her as she walked to the student parking lot where her gray '94 Honda Civic waited for her.

"I just have to grab something really quick," Aila hollered over her shoulder. When she got to her car, she noticed something stuck under the windshield wiper. A note, a single rose, and a bag of peanut M&Ms—her favorite.

Aila blushed.

Who would leave this?

In high school, leaving a note and flowers on someone's windshield was the equivalent to holding a boom box outside of their window, making a declaration of love. She unfolded the piece of paper anxious to see who signed it.

> *I can't stop thinking about Saturday.*
>
> *J*

"Jackson," she said under her breath, biting back a smile.

It was the Monday after senior prom, just two days

after he kissed her at Ethan's party. Again. The year before when they kissed on Ethan's back patio, it had felt silly and accidental. The year since then they never talked about it, but they'd often make eyes at each other like they had this big secret no one else could know. It was their inside joke.

Can you believe we kissed that one time? Aila would think and laugh.

Jackson had become one of her favorite friends. She'd stay out past curfew at his house playing cards or Two Truths and a Lie or watching reruns of *Friends*. He and his brother, Adam, were practically brothers to her. Their mom worked the night shift as a nurse so their house was always free for them to hang out like dumb teenagers do—watching MTV and making peanut and jelly sandwiches at midnight.

Sometimes Aila's mom would catch her sneaking back in to the house near 2 a.m. and she'd be livid until she realized she was "only at Jackson's."

Jackson was harmless. Too boyish to sweep Aila off her feet. Too polite to get her pregnant. These were the things Aila's mom worried about. She needed to go off to college and get a good head on her shoulders before settling down, and it surely couldn't be with her buddy, Jackson.

They continued to run in the same circles. They had the same friends, the same interests, the same hobbies. But they had this naughty little secret that, in actuality, wasn't that naughty. After a year of conversations with their eyes and hanging out with their favorite third wheel, Adam, Aila could feel the weird chemistry forming between them.

Maybe I like him, like him, she started thinking, but would brush the thought off just as quickly. *We could never.*

It wasn't just that they were friends but Jackson had also dated her friend Ashley from the track team for a few months in the fall. It was the whole girl code thing that couldn't be broken in high school. No one knew she had already kissed him so no one knew she had already broken it.

By the time senior prom rolled around, they didn't go together yet again. Jackson went with Olivia and Aila went with Jeremy. They were all a part of the same crowd though—they went to the same restaurant beforehand and the same after party at Ethan's. They both went with safe, platonic relationships like it was an unspoken rule between them.

Only by the time they were at the dance it was clear Aila's date wanted to be anything but platonic. He was handsy and a little drunk. Aila was growing uncomfortable.

At some point during the night, she had come out of the restroom and Jeremy cornered her at the end of the hallway. What started as a playful joke became less funny when her date wouldn't let her leave. She could smell the vodka on his breath and his funny *let's-get-drunk-at-senior-prom* charade became a serious problem as he pressed his forearm against her chest, pinning her between the wall and the water fountain, while sliding his hand down her thigh and up her dress.

She kicked his clammy hands away but he was relentless. "Jeremy, stop! It's not funny!"

She was trying to be serious but couldn't help but second-guess her reaction.

Is he joking? He wouldn't really do anything to hurt me, right? Am I over reacting?

Despite her struggle, Jeremy's hand pulled on her panty line and she froze. Her eyes filled with tears. *Stop. Please, stop.* She began pushing and kicking again, to no avail.

Suddenly the men's restroom door opened and there he was.

Jackson.

The expression on his face told her she wasn't overreacting. Jackson's eyes grew stormy and angry as he lunged at Jeremy, slamming him against a wall.

"Get off her, man!" he yelled. "What the hell is wrong with you?"

Jeremy licked his bloody lip and swiped a hand across his cheek. His eyes were glossy and drunk. Jackson turned to Aila and swooped his arms around her. They felt stronger than she remembered.

"Are you okay?"

"I-I-I'm fine," Aila blinked away her tears and grabbed Jackson's jacket sleeves to keep her hands from shaking. "He just tried to kiss me is all."

"Are you sure?" He bent down forcing her to meet his eyes. "It looked like he was doing a lot more than trying to kiss you, Aila."

"It was just a kiss, man. Relax," Jeremy slurred, stumbling slightly as he spoke.

"Fuck off, Jeremy. Go home before I tell Coach you're drunk."

Jeremy muttered something about snitches before stumbling back down the hallway.

Jackson looked at Aila, expectant, and far more concerned than Aila wanted him to be. She was so embarrassed about something that wasn't her fault, wanting nothing more than to forget what just happened.

Aila let out a deep breath. "I promise. I'm fine." She shook off the trauma of the last few minutes, refusing to allow it to ruin her senior prom, but she still felt uneasy as the memory of Jeremy's hands where she didn't want them replayed in her mind.

"Want to get out of here?" Jackson asked, clearly noticing she was not fine.

"Please."

Jackson let Olivia know he'd meet up with her later at Ethan's. She was happy to get a ride to the party in the limo Tony's parents had paid for instead of Jackson's mom's Ford Explorer.

After they grabbed their coats and left the dance, Jackson took her to the drive-through at Dairy Queen and ordered two peanut butter Oreo Blizzards. He didn't ask her what she wanted because he already knew.

Aila turned her head toward him and met his eyes. "Thank you."

He nodded and brushed off her gratitude.

"This is what you do for friends. You love them when they're hurting, you keep their secrets, and you feed them ice cream when they're sad," he said with a small smile.

She smiled back.

She loved he knew her so well. They didn't have any pretenses or expectations around each other. Aila didn't worry about her hair or her outfit or whether or not she'd say the right thing around Jackson. Their comfort level together had grown so close over the last year, she couldn't imagine sitting in a car eating ice cream on prom night with anyone else.

Jackson pulled up outside of Ethan's house and put the car in park, leaving it running so the music still played. Aila looked up from her Blizzard and smiled before leaning over the console and resting her head on his shoulder. Silent.

Her lips twisted while she contemplated the events of the evening. She was happy to be with Jackson but felt a pang of sadness because she knew he was still untouchable for her.

"Are you sure you're okay, Aila?" She could hear the growing concern tugging at the edges of his words. "Because if Jeremy did more than just try to kiss you, you can tell me. We could go tell—"

"No," she said abruptly, lifting her head to face him. "Please. No, it was nothing. I don't want to talk about it anymore. Jeremy's a jerk anyway."

Jackson chuckled uncomfortably. "Yeah, why'd you go to prom with him then?"

She rolled her eyes. "Act of charity, I guess."

He laughed softly and Aila flashed him a bashful smile. Their eyes met for a beat, and then suddenly, they're bodies were drawn to each other like magnets, kissing each other furiously, as if all the pent-up emotions and hormones from the last year were locked behind a dam that had just collapsed.

Aila had never kissed someone like that before. She didn't want to stop. She wanted to escape with Jackson and never come back—not to high school. Not to this town. In that moment, he was the only thing worth holding onto.

Their kiss was interrupted when a flash of limousine headlights hit their faces. Aila contemplated asking him to drive off with her but the sounds of their friends filing out of the limo and into the house made her snap back to reality.

She pulled herself back onto her seat and brushed a long brown spiral away from her face. She smiled, suddenly self-conscious. Jackson reached over and grabbed her hand, squeezing it. His hand was warm and strong over her delicate fingers, and he reached up to gently touch her flushed cheeks.

Aila found him both breathtakingly irresistible and devastatingly unavailable.

"Hey," he said. "It's just me."

Aila grabbed his hand from her face, met his gaze, and pressed her lips into a small smile, but she didn't say a word.

For the rest of the night, the two kept a safe distance between themselves but Jackson's eyes protectively followed her wherever she went around Ethan's house. At the end of the night, he drove her home and walked her to the door.

Her mother was waiting up, of course, so Aila didn't dare kiss him again. She gave him a hug and whispered in his ear, "Thanks for everything tonight."

"Goodnight, Aila," he had said, like a proper gentleman.

Now, as she stood at her car with the note, candy, and flowers from Jackson, Aila felt suddenly nervous. A mix of young desire and hesitation because of his stint with Ashley. She didn't know what to do. She wanted to follow her heart but she didn't want to disappoint her friends either.

Aila threw the note on the passenger side floor and looked for her spikes for track practice. When she closed the door, she was surprised to see Ashley and Olivia walking toward her in their practice uniforms.

"Girl, what's taking you so long?" Ashley asked.

Aila felt like she was caught naked in public. "Nothing. Just…nothing. I'm coming." She grabbed her spikes and walked with her friends to the practice field.

Track practice ended just after baseball, and Jackson was waiting patiently by her car when she made her way over to the lot with Olivia.

"Hey," both girls said in unison, but Jackson practically ignored Olivia's greeting.

"Aila, can we talk for a second?" he asked.

Olivia studied him and then looked back at Aila. Aila shrugged in response.

"Okay…" Olivia said slowly. "Catch you later, Aila."

Aila stood there, pressing her lips together, her arms crossed as if on guard, which didn't make sense. It was just Jackson. He's just a friend. He needed to cool it and so did she.

"Did you get my note?" he asked.

She nodded. "Look, Jackson, it doesn't have to turn into this."

"But it could. I mean, what if it did? Aila, I like you a lot. I've always liked you. And we're such good friends."

"Right," she cut him off. "We're such good friends. I don't want to mess that up. And you dated Ashley–"

"For two months," he said. "It doesn't even matter."

"It does matter. She's my friend, Jackson," she said. "Look. You made Saturday a great senior prom for me and I'll always remember it but I just don't think we need to make this something more. Not right now at least."

Aila's eyes darted to the edges of the parking lot to track any movement from fellow students that may be in earshot.

And that did it for him. She could see the understanding his eyes—that was the final nail in the coffin.

Jackson ducked his head in disappointment without another word. He walked to his car and drove off.

They finished the year as friends—their secret kisses stayed only theirs. They saw each other less and less after graduation and went their separate ways in the fall. They stayed in touch for a while but slowly drifted apart as friends from high school often do.

By junior year of college when Aila met Ben, Jackson had all but disappeared from her mind. Even if somewhere, deep down inside her, she knew there was something still unfinished between them.

CHAPTER 18

NOW

The night after Aila had sex with Jackson, she can hardly sleep. Every nerve ending in her body buzzes with an odd combination of desire and anxiety. The events of the afternoon play over and over in her mind. The way he smelled. The way his hands felt on her bare skin. The playful way he made her laugh and feel like the most beautiful woman in the world.

Before Jackson, she never imagined being with anyone except Ben. Not simply because they were married, but because her body had changed so much since having three children. Her skin sags here and ripples more than she wants it to there. She did all the things they say to do to "get your body back" after having a baby, but Aila still never felt quite the same. No one really gets their body back. Not all the way at least. Her old body would always belong to someone else Aila no longer is.

Aila is content with her curvier hips and softer stomach because her legs are long and her smile is still pretty. Yet, her self-image is still laced with a layer of self-consciousness.

It's only for Ben, what does it matter?

But then came Jackson. With the afternoon sunshine piercing through the blinds, Aila released every inhibition she was holding on to. She felt alive and beautiful and wanted. All elements of insecurities walked out the door when Jackson walked in. The way he looked at her. The way he touched her.

He had waited twenty years for Aila to let him love her. She could feel it in every touch, every kiss.

The wait was worth it.

She feels relieved when her alarm finally goes off in the morning so she can get moving with the distractions of her day. And slightly in shock about the events that took place the day before.

I can't believe that happened. I can't believe I want it to happen again.

Aila heads downstairs to busy herself making coffee and pancakes for the boys—a fun Friday morning surprise since Ben is out of town—in an attempt to drown out her drumming heart. After she flips the last flapjack, Josh hops off the bottom step.

"What's that smell?" he says.

"Pancakes," Aila says with a smile and a wink. "You're welcome."

Josh pulls up to the kitchen island and forks a couple pancakes on his plate and begins smearing them with butter.

"Will you help Isaac dish himself when he gets down here?"

Josh nods with a mouthful of pancakes and syrup, already devouring his stack.

Aila heads back upstairs to get ready. While she does her makeup, she starts brainstorming reasons to text Jackson that day. She doesn't want to seem too eager. Or desperate. But she is counting down the seconds until she gets to hear from him again.

She throws on real clothes today—dark skinny jeans and a white sweater. She'll be volunteering in Isaac's class so she decides to drive the boys to school today instead of taking the bus, a great opportunity to avoid Janet.

After they load in her SUV to head to the school, Aila eyes each of them through the rearview mirror.

"Since Dad is gone for the weekend, what you boy boys like to do?"

"Sleepover at Gammy and Gampa's!" Isaac yells.

"Oh, that could be fun. I'll call Gammy today." Aila smiles at the idea of a night alone.

"Hey, maybe your friend Jack could come over to jump on the trampoline with us!" Caleb suggests. A jolt of heat from her heart hits her face. She feels taken aback by the mention of his name coming from one of her children.

"You mean Jackson?" Aila asks.

"Yeah, Jackson. He was fun. Can he play before we go to Gammy's?"

There it is.

A reason to text Jackson.

"You know what, honey? I will ask him and we'll see," she says, feeling as hopeful and excited at the prospect of it. Caleb grins at her through the rearview mirror.

Walking into the school, Aila simultaneously sends texts to her mom and Jackson.

Can the kids have a sleepover tomorrow night?

Boys want to play with you. You made quite an impression. Lunch tomorrow?

...

Aila's breath catches at the three dots while she signs in and grabs her volunteer badge.

Sure, honey! We've been long over-do for a grandkid weekend. Yay! Pick them up tomorrow at 3?

147

Aila lets out a breath. Just her mom. She needs to get a hold of herself.

Great! Thank you. Boys can't wait.

Aila's phone burns in her back pocket the entire time she helps the kindergarteners in Isaac's class sprinkle glitter over glue to make springtime rainbows.

By lunchtime, she kisses the top of Isaac's head while he shoves his peanut butter and jelly sandwich into his face, telling him goodbye and checking for missed messages.

Nothing.

Hmmph.

Maybe Jackson regrets what happened yesterday. Maybe his fantasy of Aila didn't live up to the reality. The thought stings.

By the time she hops in her SUV in the school parking lot, her nerves are shot with emotion. She's nervous and unsure. In her mind, yesterday was amazing.

Wasn't it? Maybe it was a mistake. I should have never let it go that far.

When she turns down Cherrywood Lane, there's no sign of his truck or his landscapers. This is typical for a Friday but his absence shoots a hole in her stomach, making her feel nauseous. She thinks she might throw up.

At home, she busies herself with laundry, straightening throw pillows, and disinfecting countertops. She considers making a pot of coffee but decides against it—the caffeine will only make her nerves worse.

Her phone pings and she lunges for it.

Still at the conference. Call you and the boys before dinner at 6.

Ben.

In what world does she get disappointed by a text

from Ben? She replies with an 'Okay' and runs upstairs to throw on some workout clothes before heading out the front door with Gus to run to the top of Skyline hill.

By the time she reaches the top, she is out of breath but her nerves are calming. The sky is clear but still a light shade of gray. Aila can barely make out the Olympic Mountain range and wonders how long she'd have to run to reach those peaks. She daydreams her escape from the life and the mess she's made of it when her phone vibrates in her thigh pocket.

Sorry for the late response. Stuck in meetings. Would love to come for lunch. Just say when.

Jackson's response is a relief and she lets the air she's been holding in escape from her lungs, just before she overanalyzes every word he sent.

Is he excited? Does he feel obligated? Does he remember Ben won't be there?

Sounds great. See you at 12 tomorrow?

She presses her lips together and sprints the rest of the way back to the house with a sudden burst of energy.

Aila is enamored by him. Every memory from when they were sixteen until now. Every thought she has ever had of him. Every joke, every game, every regret. Aila knows every single time he has ever touched her. She is obsessing over it and calculating ways to make it happen again.

~

Saturday morning, after Caleb's baseball game, Aila and the boys ran to pick up some fried chicken and sides for lunch. It won't be as impressive as her beef bourguignon, but no one ever complains about deep-fried take out.

By noon, Caleb opens the front door to Jackson holding a bouquet of wildflowers. From the kitchen Aila can hear their greetings. As she peeks around the corner, she sees Jackson bend down to hand Caleb the flowers.

"Here. Give these to your mom. Say they're from you." He winks.

Caleb nods enthusiastically and runs into the kitchen. "Mom, I got you flowers!"

"Oh, wow, they're beautiful!" Aila holds them to her nose to smell them and looks over at Jackson high-fiving the boys.

She sets the food out buffet style with paper plates and tells everyone to dish up while she reaches for a vase from the upper cabinet to put the flowers in.

"Here, let me grab that for you," Jackson says as he effortlessly grabs the vase just out of her reach and hands it to her.

"Thank you," she says and smiles at him. She feels a flash of excitement and appreciation for Jackson. It feels oddly right having him in her home. She loves how comfortable he is—grabbing the vase from the shelf like he knew where it was all along, helping the boys dish up their food, and listening when he hears Josh only likes the wings and Isaac doesn't like mashed potatoes.

Which makes him laugh.

"Who doesn't like mashed potatoes?" he asks.

"Crazy, right?" Caleb concurs, with a mouthful.

Aila finds herself standing back to admire the situation. The boys love him. *Love* him.

When was the last time they all sat around having lunch after baseball with their dad? Ben was usually running off after the game to tend to some emails or paperwork. Sometimes he'd just escape on his phone on the couch or head out to the gym. He wasn't around all that much so it infuriated Aila that when he was, he was hardly present.

Not like Jackson.

Jackson spends the afternoon jumping on the

trampoline with the boys and then they move on to playing catch. He tells Caleb about how he played shortstop and left fielder in high school but shortstop was his favorite.

When a spring shower begins to fall, the four of them migrate to the table on the covered deck where Aila has set a pitcher of lemonade and five glasses. She turns on the built-in fireplace and joins them when Josh comes out of the house with Uno cards.

"Who wants to play?"

Aila and Jackson's eyes meet and he smiles at her.

His smile is sincere and warm and makes her stomach fill with butterflies. She has to pry her eyes away from his.

As the game goes on the banter between the boys and Jackson makes her mind daydream about all the possibilities of having Jackson in their life. What that could mean for the boys. What that could mean for her. She smiles inwardly to herself, her heart growing more excited and hopeful as the afternoon progresses.

The sound of the doorbell ringing snaps Aila from her daydream.

Aila looks at Jackson, slightly startled. She had lost track of time. Her mom is there to pick the boys up for their sleepover.

She breaks her eye contact with Jackson and looks at the boys, "That's Gammy!" She turns her attention to Jackson, lifting her eyebrows, "My mom."

"No way, I get to see Ms. Tina," he says, smiling genuinely.

"The one and only," she eyes him playfully.

"Wait. You know my Gammy?" Josh asks.

"I do." He smiles. "But I haven't seen her since me and your mom were in high school."

The boys make their way to the front door with Gus trotting behind them barking, and open the door to their Gammy.

"Hello!" she hollers, her voice always an octave higher than necessary when greeting the boys. "You boys ready for a sleepover?"

"Yep!" Isaac says.

"Go grab your bags from upstairs," Aila says, while gesturing for her mom to come in. "Mom, do you remember Jackson from high school?"

Tina's bright blue eyes land on Jackson, who is waiting patiently at the end of the entryway.

He reaches out his hand to her, smiling and says, "Ms. Tina. It's so good to see you."

She takes his hand in surprise and pulls him in for a hug. "Oh my word. Jackson! Little Jackson? What in the world? You look like such a grown-up!"

Jackson laughs and Tina squeezes his cheeks between both her hands.

Her mom is always a little handsy, especially with people she thinks fondly of. "Ah, but you still have those babyface dimples! Aila, doesn't he?"

Aila covers up her blush with a laugh as if she hadn't noticed until her mother pointed it out.

"He sure does."

"Oh my. What brings you around here?"

Aila answers for him. "Well, he owns the landscaping company for the neighborhood and I ran into him one day when I was walking Gus. Small world, huh?"

Tina is looking Jackson over, like he's an original art piece that has been recently discovered after being buried for centuries.

"Small world indeed." Tina smiles but Aila can sense her mother's wheels are turning a bit, processing this unlikely encounter.

Jackson throws Aila a toothless grin. She looks away quickly and back at her mom.

"Ben had invited him over for dinner the other night and he really hit it off with the boys. They wanted to play with him before you came to pick them up for a sleepover."

She makes sure to mention Ben so her mother's internal questioning ceases and she doesn't concern herself with wondering why her daughter is spending time with another man that isn't her husband. Her mom is old fashioned that way. *Married women shouldn't be friends with men,* she'd say. *The line gets too blurry so you can't see if you've crossed it.*

Aila clears the memory of her mother's words from her mind, knowing she had already crossed the line.

"Is that so?" Her eyes shoot from Aila to Jackson again. "So, you said you're a landscaper in the neighborhood then."

Jackson nods politely.

"Well, it's his company that's in charge of our landscaping. His employees are here more than he is." Aila is sure to mention that it's his company. Tina is always kind and polite but she often turns her nose up at blue-collar work.

"I see. Well, that's fantastic. Good for you, Jackson."

"Thank you, Ms. Tina."

"And where is my son-in-law this afternoon? Do I get a hug from him as well?"

"No, he's in DC for the convention," Aila says plainly.

"Ah, I see," she says and then smiles thoughtfully at Jackson. Aila can tell she feels like a mom of a teenager again—gently questioning the boy's intentions until she determines her daughter is safe in his presence.

The boys barrel down the staircase with backpacks and stuffed animals, interrupting Tina's line of questioning.

"Ready," Caleb declares.

"Alright then. Shall we?" Tina says grabbing his hand.

"I should probably get going too," Jackson says and Aila feels her shoulders sag. She doesn't want him to leave but she doesn't want to say it in front of her mother, so she simply nods.

Aila, Jackson, Tina, and the boys walk out the front door to the driveway. Tina pauses a moment and glances at the front yard while her grandkids load into her sedan.

"The lawn looks good," she says, smiling pretentiously and looking at Aila.

"Thanks, Mom," Aila responds, echoing her mother's advice in her head as usual. *A house is only as pretty as its front lawn.*

"Don't forget to cut back that clematis," Tina adds.

Aila wants to roll her eyes but instead she and Jackson exchange a brief, knowing glance. His smile slowly grows wide. He knows exactly how her mother used to be when they were teenagers: kind, image-conscious, and slightly critical. Clearly, she hasn't changed much.

Aila turns to the car to kiss her boys on their foreheads and makes them promise to be good.

"Later fellas," Jackson says giving them each a quick fist bump.

"Will you come play again?" Isaac asks.

"You bet," he says, flashing a smile. Aila's knees feel weak. His charm is undeniable even when he's talking to her children.

"Good to see you again, Ms. Tina."

"You too. Take care now. Give Ben my love, Aila," her mother says as she slips into the driver's seat, sending Aila a look that says, *Be careful, little girl. You're playing with fire.*

Aila looks away and directs her attention to the backseat as she waves enthusiastically at the boys heading off to their adventure at Gammy and Gampa's. When her mother's car rounds the corner, Aila turns to Jackson, who stands calmly next to the driver's side of his truck, waiting for his farewell.

"You know," Aila says, making her way closer to him. "You don't have to leave right away."

"Yeah, but I probably should." He lifts his eyes from staring at the asphalt between them.

Aila nods and looks down, rejected.

"But what we should do and what we want to do are probably two different things, huh?" he asks.

Aila raises her eyes to meet his. They are intense as they gaze into hers. His dark eyelashes making his hazel eyes even lighter in the daylight.

"Why don't you come over to my place tonight? I'll make you dinner. Return the favor." His smile is boyish and eager.

"That'd be great," Aila says, feeling a rush of excitement.

She has been spending so much time picturing Jackson in her life she forgot he has a life of his own too.

"Give me a couple hours?" He grabs her hand, his touch electric. "I'll text you the address." And he kisses the back of her hand and slips away in his truck.

The place on her skin where his lips had touched still feels warm and tingly when she holds it up to her chest. The kiss was sweet and innocent but the fact it happened in broad daylight in the open air of the neighborhood made it feel dangerous.

Aila suddenly doesn't care.

~

On the way over to Jackson's house, Ben calls. The very sound of the ringer makes Aila's heart race. She takes a deep breath to calm her nerves before answering.

"Just wanted to check-in since I didn't get a chance to talk last night," he says.

"That's okay." *It was more of a relief.* "Everything is fine. The boys are at my parents' house for the night," she answers plainly.

"Oh really." He's surprised. "What are your plans then?"

"I think I'll just stay home. Watch a movie. Take a bath, maybe," she lies.

"Alright," Ben is distracted and Aila can hear the chatter in the restaurant in the background. Or did he say he was in the hotel lobby? She can't remember. She wasn't paying attention. "I guess I'll give you a call tomorrow afternoon before my flight leaves. Love you."

"Love you too," she says, feeling a sudden pang of

guilt shoot through her chest. She can't believe how quickly her life is spinning out of her control.

She had already gone too far, but she still wants to go farther.

She ignores her spiraling thoughts and excuses her exchange with Ben as habitual. Just something people say when they've been together for so long. It not only felt empty coming off her lips but it was also hollow coming from Ben too. She pushes the conversation to the corners of her mind and continues her drive to Jackson's house.

By the time she pulls up to the address he sent her, it is close to six. His house is a sleek and modern remodeled mid-century house near the Puget Sound, about thirty minutes from her neighborhood.

As she pulls into his driveway, she can tell his house suits him—clean-cut and charming, with an air of masculinity and warmth. She rings the doorbell once. The massive black, wrought iron door opens, revealing sleek concrete floors, mid-century modern décor, and a breathtaking Jackson in dark denim jeans and a gray t-shirt.

"Welcome," he says, kissing her cheek. His facial expression is foreshadowing a night Aila anticipated would be full of excitement, wonder, and romance. The air smells like garlic, butter, and charcoal from the grill. A breeze wafts from the back of the house where the slider is open and a wall of windows offers a panoramic view of the water.

"Wow. Your home is stunning, Jackson," she smiles, breathlessly as she follows him to the kitchen.

Jackson is pouring two glasses of white wine. "Thank you," he says with a modest smile. "So are you."

Aila never really tried to imagine Jackson's house before. Whenever she was with him, she was simply wrapped up in who he was to his core, how he treated her, and how he was with the kids. She always characterized him as kind, thoughtful, charming, and easy-going. Now she will clearly have to add successful to the list.

She takes the wine glass he hands her; his fingers

gently brush against hers and stir up feelings of longing and lust.

She knows deep down she is feeding the beast. She knows it is wrong and out of order. She knows she will disappoint a lot of people.

Somewhere along the line, after making small choice after small choice in the direction that landed her here, she stopped caring about disappointing everyone else. She had decided she is going to put herself first for a change—to do what she feels is right for her life. She decided to finally choose her own happiness, ignoring the consequences.

Jackson grabs onto her hand and holds it up to his lips. He looks into Aila's eyes as if asking for permission to go further. She bites her lip softly in response and allows him to pull her into an embrace.

His fingers drum along her back like he is playing piano until they reach the nape of her neck. She arches her back at his touch, while his fingers run through her hair, kissing her gently and pulling back to look into her eyes. His kisses are seductive and teasing. Kissing her just long enough to make her surrender and then pulling back and staring into her eyes, making her ache for him.

"I can't believe you're here," he whispers softly and so close his lips are brushing against hers.

Aila smiles into his kiss and suddenly they are completely entangled in each other's arms. She allows Jackson to completely consume her. There is a push and pull of passion, a give and take, back and forth.

Everything about what they are doing is wrong. She knows it. But there is something right about it too. Something familiar. Something that feels like it should have been this way all along.

Lying on the couch, Aila lays her head on his chest and traces her finger along the scar on his right shoulder. He got it the summer after junior year when he flipped into the lake. He hadn't jumped out far enough as he tucked his chin to his chest, his body curling into a ball, and his shoulder snagged on the dock before he hit the water's glassy surface. She was the one that held a t-shirt to the gash as the blood turned the white shirt a deep crimson.

"Fourteen stitches," she whispers, wondering how she even remembers the number.

"Saved my life that day," he teases, as if reading her thoughts.

She laughs. "Well, you could've bled out on the dock if it weren't for me," she teases back. There were a million memories made between them, even if they were a lifetime ago.

"I'm not sure how I've survived all these years without you." His words are laced in sarcasm but there is an underlying truth buried beneath them. A truth that's buried inside her as well.

Aila looks up into his sleepy eyes, filled with euphoria and satisfaction. She presses her lips to his bare chest. His skin is still hot to the touch as her lips travel to his collar bone, then his neck, then his jaw, until landing on his lips. He closes his eyes and smiles, a deep hum rumbling from his chest. His fingers dance along her spine and Aila feels an odd satisfaction wash over her.

If this is wrong, why does it feel so easy?

"You hungry?" he asks, breaking the spell.

Aila releases a smile. "Starving."

She pulls his t-shirt over her head as Jackson sits up. He pulls on his jeans and bends over to kiss her gently.

Out on the back patio, Aila, still in his t-shirt and wrapped in a blanket, finds a spot on the outdoor sofa next to the fire pit. Jackson throws a few pieces of firewood in the pit and they ignite, the flames quickly growing to offer immediate warmth from the chilly spring evening. Aila sits gazing into the flames, mesmerized by their dancing while Jackson finishes dinner. She lets her mind stay in the moment, refusing to think of anything outside of this house and this evening.

Jackson sets down two plates of grilled salmon, green

beans, and roasted potatoes in front of her. He leaves for a second and comes back with their unfinished glasses of wine and the rest of the bottle.

"Thank you. This looks delicious," Aila says, her cheeks aching from the constant smile spread across her face since she walked in the door.

"It sure beats my midnight PB&J's."

Aila lets out a laugh.

"I might be needing one of those later."

"You plan to hang around that long?" he says it playfully, but his eyes show hopefulness.

"Maybe," Aila says flirtatiously over her glass of wine. She swirls the wine around in her glass. "You know, I've been meaning to tell you something for a long time, even before now."

Jackson leans in. "What's that?"

"You remember what happened with Jeremy senior prom?"

Jackson nods almost imperceptibly.

"Thank you," she says earnestly and looks up at him, his hazel eyes somehow growing lighter. More vulnerable. Like every layer was stripped away and she could see all the secrets he was holding. "You saved me from what was probably going to be a very bad ending."

She has never admitted this to anyone. Not even Ben. She smiles and looks away to hide her emotions. She knows how common the memory she kept a secret is for women. She also knows the memory all too often has a different ending.

Jackson doesn't stop looking at her. "I know," he says, reaching out to tuck a strand of hair behind her ear. She looks back up into his eyes.

He leans in to kiss her. It's soft and gentle, like he's caring for a broken piece of glass.

Each time he kisses her, it sends a shock down her spine that reaches into her soul. She can't help but wonder what could have been if they hadn't spent all these years apart—if she had simply said yes that one afternoon in the parking lot after practice.

As the night progresses Aila and Jackson's conversation flows as smoothly as the wine down her throat. Their chemistry and their minds are both in sync.

Jackson tells her about his marriage to a woman named Kim, someone he met through a friend. They had stayed married for nearly ten years before they split up, stating they just weren't right for each other. There were no hard feelings when they divorced, just two very different people wanting different things out of life. He wanted a family. She didn't.

There is peace in his eyes when he speaks about his marriage, but something else too—pain, regret. Aila wonders if there's a piece of the story he isn't telling her. She can't imagine what it would be like to want a family and not have one. Life without her boys is unfathomable.

Jackson asks about her children and what it's like to be their mother. Aila tells him all of it. How it's chaotic and demanding, but also hysterical and fulfilling.

"It's hard some days. Harder than I ever could have imagined it'd be," she says. "But life without them would be so boring."

She catches Jackson staring at her, his dimples showing.

"What?"

"You get very animated when you talk about your boys," he says. "Everything about you. Your demeanor, your voice. It all changes when you bring them up. You can tell they make you feel…I don't know—alive."

Aila smiles thoughtfully. "Well, they're all I've got."

"Well, they aren't all you've got."

Aila doesn't know if she's talking about himself or Ben so she bites her lip and forces a smile. They're quiet for a couple of minutes before Jackson clears the awkward silence she had created.

"You seem unhappy about something, Aila."

It's a statement, not a question.

Aila stares at the flames in the fire pit, not meeting his eyes. "I'm not unhappy, really. Life just turns out differently than you expect sometimes."

"How do you mean?"

"We just get older and we change. Our focuses shift. We spend all this time raising little humans, trying to stay afloat that by the time we lift our heads out of the sand, everything's different."

Jackson nods, realizing she's talking about Ben.

"I always thought we'd get it back. That somehow, his focus would shift back to me or even the kids but it just…hasn't. It's getting worse."

Aila feels Jackson brush a small tear from her cheek and she lifts her head to look at him.

"When I'm with you, I feel like all you see is me. No matter what distractions are around us. It's always been like that, even when we were teenagers. The way you'd look at me from across the room or across the street. You make me feel like your whole world. I didn't know anyone could make me feel like that again."

Jackson wordlessly takes her wine glass and sets it down next to his on the fire pit's edge before gently taking her face in his hands. He leans in to kiss her, laying her down as he slowly moves his body over hers while the flames crackle next to them. Without saying another word, Jackson knew exactly what she wanted.

CHAPTER 19

THEN

Aila closed her eyes as she sat in a lounge chair in the backyard, feeling the sun beat down on her skin. It wasn't usually this warm in April so when Chantelle brought her lunch, they opted to eat it on the back deck in the sunlight.

Chloe and Isaac were only three and they were covered in sand from their snotty little faces to in between their toes.

"Chloe is going to need a bath before I head to pick up Emma." Chantelle laughed. She had taken a half-day to bring Aila and Isaac lunch and enjoy the sunshine.

"When do you need to go get her?"

Chantelle checked her phone for the time. "I think I'll pick her up at four-thirty today but usually by six."

"Well, thank you for taking time off work to bring us lunch. This was really nice." Aila smiled at her best friend.

"Girl, you deserve it. The work of being a stay-at-home is not lost on me." Chantelle raised her wine glass filled with sparkling water.

"Thanks, Chay." Aila was both flattered and in awe of her friend. Her and Derek's divorce was finalized the month before and there she was, sitting in the backyard making Aila feel special.

"It's nothing," Chantelle said and winked. "Now. It is probably time I run to the bus stop and grab those boys, yes?"

"Oh Chantelle, you don't have to do that. I'll go grab them so you can run and get Emma."

"Please. It will only take me a few minutes. Can I leave Chloe here with you?"

"Of course. If you don't mind bringing home a sandy baby." Aila laughed.

"For you. I will." Chantelle held a playful hand to her heart and then walked into the kitchen. She returned a moment later with a bottle of chardonnay.

"Oh, no. I can't drink that right now," Aila objected as Chantelle poured the wine in her empty water glass.

"Girl, shhh. You only turn thirty-five once," she said as she kissed Aila on the cheek, and turned on her heel to go pick up Josh and Caleb.

Aila sipped her chardonnay and smiled.

This is shaping up to be one of my favorite birthdays.

Fifteen minutes later, Josh and Caleb thundered through the house to where Aila sat watching Isaac and Chloe play in the sandbox. They latched onto their mom, nearly knocking her chair over and making her spill her wine down her arm. She didn't care and laughed at their boisterous greeting.

"Happy birthday!" they yelled in unison.

"Thank you, sweetie pies," she said as she kissed each of their foreheads. "How was your day at school?"

"Good," Josh smiled.

"Fine. Mom, I made you a card during art today. Want to see?" Caleb asked.

"Yes, of course, I do."

Caleb pulled out a piece of red construction paper folded in half with a picture of a dragon on it with a makeshift spelling of 'happy birthday, Mom' underneath. The inside was filled with hearts and signed, Caleb, at the bottom.

"Oh, Caleb, this is great. Thank you, buddy," she said pulling him in for a hug.

Josh stood quietly behind his brother holding a white piece of notebook paper, smiling.

"I have something too," he said softly. It was a letter.

I luv u MOM. U R the best! Hapy b-day.

Josh

It was misspelled and jumbled, but Josh was her boy of few words, so when he did say them, it meant something. He was like Ben in that way. Caleb, on the other hand, was her boy that brought the color and excitement. And her dear sweet Isaac brought the wonder and hope of each new day.

Her eyes stung with tears as she hugged Josh and gazed at each of her boys.

How'd I get so lucky?

Chantelle smiled from the doorway.

"Oh, Mama. You deserve all the love today." She walked over and leaned down to hug Aila. "Happy birthday, Aila," she said before turning to her daughter. "Chloe, come on, sweet girl, it's time to go get Emma."

After Chantelle and Chloe left, the boys kept playing in the backyard while Aila sipped her wine. It felt both indulgent and decadent.

The boys were happy, the sun was shining, and Nana Sharon was on her way to watch the boys for the night. Which reminded Aila she needed to head upstairs to get ready.

She didn't know what Ben had planned for her tonight. He always surprised her on her birthday. Sometimes he'd take the day off but he always at least got home early on her birthday, usually with flowers and chocolates, or some other thoughtful gift, and he'd whisk her off to a fancy dinner or a sunset picnic.

Ben knew how to carry her away and make her feel special. He knew her life was spent waist deep in children and chicken nuggets, and he always made sure her birthday was an escape from that.

When the doorbell rang, the boys flocked to the front door.

"Nana's here!"

The boys loved Ben's mom. She always let them eat whatever they wanted and often made cookies or ice cream sundaes while she and Ben were out.

"Hi Sharon," Aila said, holding open the door. Aila had changed into a sleek black dress, a dainty gold necklace, and a bold red lipstick. Her hair was curled into waves and hung down the middle of her back.

"Oh my, Aila, thirty-five looks good on you!" Sharon said with a laugh and brought her in for a hug. "Happy birthday!"

"Thank you," she responded with a smile and grabbed the gift bag Sharon was holding out to her. "You really don't need to bring me a gift. You watching the boys is a gift enough."

Sharon brushed off Aila's humility. "It's just a little something I thought you might like."

Sharon took a seat on the couch and the boys piled on top of her soft lap, showing her toys and tricks and asking what they'll be making after they eat the pizza Aila just popped in the oven.

Aila opened her gift and smelled the vanilla lavender candle, then saw a small prayer journal at the bottom of the bag. She removed it gently, admiring how delicate it looked. It was a soft pink and had Aila's initials, "AS", engraved on the front.

"Oh, Sharon, this is beautiful. And so thoughtful. Thank you," she said and walked over making her way through a crowd of boys to hug her mother-in-law again.

"I'm glad you like it, dear. Now, tell me," she directed this at the boys but looked at Aila out of the corner of her eye, "Where is your daddy taking your mama tonight?"

They all shrugged and muttered, I-don't-knows, so Sharon looked straight at Aila, expectant.

"I actually have no idea. He hasn't hinted at anything," Aila said and looked down. "I sure hope I'm not overdressed."

Sharon and Aila laughed.

When Sharon turned her attention back to her grandboys, Aila's phone pinged.

Start dinner without me. Meeting is running late.

Aila's heart sunk. He couldn't be serious. This wasn't Ben. Not her Ben.

Are you serious? I thought you would be getting off early.

Why? Trial is in three days.

This was definitely not her Ben.

Ben never forgot a birthday or an anniversary. He always rode in on a white horse and saved any occasion. How could he forget an important one? Aila checked her phone to make sure it was actually her birthday, thinking maybe she was confused.

It was, indeed, her birthday.

Aila's heart constricted.

Maybe he's kidding. Maybe it's all a ruse to keep me guessing and he's waiting in the driveway to take me to a fancy dinner in Seattle.

She peered out the front window, hopeful, but deep down she knew he had forgotten her birthday.

She set her phone on the entryway table, took a deep breath and exhaled every emotion she wanted to feel, before she walked back into the living room to where Nana was taking turns doing giddy-up-horsey with the boys.

"Hey, kiddos." She hated the word 'kiddos' but it always came out when she was hiding her emotions. "Mind if I have pizza with you guys for my birthday dinner? Daddy's running late."

Sharon shot Aila a sympathetic look. She looked half embarrassed and half heartbroken, like Aila just said her puppy died.

Aila looked away and focused her response on the three excited boys that wanted to eat frozen pizza with their mom on her birthday.

In the kitchen, Aila pulled out five plates and sliced up the pizza. She gave the boys cut up strawberries and cucumbers and quickly threw together a salad for herself and her mother-in-law.

"Can I help you with anything, Aila?" Sharon asked, standing just on the edge of the kitchen.

"Oh, no, Sharon, you're fine. Everything is just about ready," Aila said, throwing a fraudulent smile her way.

Her smile was masking her hurt and frustration. Sharon knew this but let it slide.

After dinner, Sharon made ice cream sundaes and found a candle in the pantry to throw in Aila's. She and the boys sang the "Happy Birthday" song and afterword, Sharon took the boys upstairs to bed while Aila cleaned up the kitchen.

She was still dressed in her black cocktail dress but only the outline of her lipstick remained at this point.

Aila went into the bathroom and washed the remainder of the lipstick off of her mouth with water and dried her lips with toilet paper. She stared at her reflection. When she had gotten ready for the evening, she felt vibrant and sexy. Now the face looking back at her just looked tired.

She knew this had to be a big mistake. Maybe her birthday surprise was coming this weekend. Maybe it was actually going to be a getaway this summer. Just the two of them. Or maybe...

He just forgot.

Aila had been feeling misplaced and unseen in their marriage for a while now, but to actually be completely forgotten on her birthday cut deeper than she could have ever imagined. When she returned to the kitchen, Sharon was standing at the kitchen table, collecting her things back into her purse and she glanced up at Aila.

"The boys are tuckered out. I'm sure they are already fast asleep," she said while placing her phone in her purse.

"Sharon?"

"Yes, dear."

"Would you like to have a glass of wine with me?"

Aila had spent plenty of time with her mother-in-law over the years—cooking, watching television, watching children, relaxing in the backyard—but they had never, not once, sat face-to-face over a drink.

"Got any whiskey?" she asked, causing Aila to laugh.

Like mother, like son. She pulled out the Jamison and poured two fingers into a glass for Sharon and a glass of chardonnay for herself.

They sat at the kitchen counter for the next hour over their drinks, laughing and talking about anything and everything under the sun. Aila never understood how people complained about their mothers-in-law. She couldn't live without hers. Sharon was warm and kind but gave it to you straight. She taught Aila to cook, how to burp her colicky baby, and how baking soda and vinegar will fix a stinky garbage disposal.

She was also the praying kind. Aila went to her with her deepest requests. Her deepest hurts and worries, from her dad's cancer to her miscarriage. Sharon was always there for her with a word of encouragement or a prayer to God.

Aila looked up from pouring another glass of wine while Sharon took a sip of her whiskey. "Thank you for coming over tonight, Sharon."

Sharon nodded.

"I mean it. It would have been a very lonely birthday without you," Aila said smiling to mask the knot in her throat.

Sharon held up her glass, "Anything for my favorite daughter-in-law."

Their glasses clinked and Aila took a long swig of wine, while Sharon finished off her drink.

"You know, Aila." Sharon took in a sharp breath. "I'm sorry Ben didn't come home tonight."

"Oh, no. Sharon, it's fine. He works hard." Aila waved off the concern, excusing her husband.

"That he does." Sharon nodded. "But he needs to be better at prioritizing his life. I understand that work is important for him but it shouldn't be at the expense of his family."

Aila was quiet, listening.

"You hold this family up, Aila," she said as she reached for her daughter-in-law's hand and grasped it across the island. "You're the glue. And I am so proud of you as a mother." She paused to clear her throat. "But I am also sorry."

Aila's eyes filled with tears and she blinked them away.

Sharon patted Aila on the arm and told her she needed to get going. At the door, she turned around and hugged Aila.

"Happy birthday, Aila. You deserved better today."

When Aila closed the door behind her, her face crumpled into tears. She had a great night. She loves her boys and their Nana. But she also loves her husband and that night he not only didn't show up, he simply forgot her.

Aila walked back into the kitchen, downed the rest of the wine in her glass and then started the dishwasher and went upstairs.

After discarding her dress and putting on sweatpants and an old t-shirt, Aila scrubbed her face and climbed into bed, Gus trotting closely behind her.

Thirty minutes later, Gus heard the garage door open and let out a low growl. Aila looked at the clock.

10:06 p.m.

A few moments later, Ben walked in with a smile, his tie loose around his neck, and a bouquet of roses.

"I'm so sorry I'm late today. Happy birthday, baby," he said, plopping two dozen roses on their white duvet, and kissing her softly.

"It's okay," she said.

Even though it's not.

Aila felt angry and hurt and neglected, but instead she smiled and accepted the apology.

"I promise I'll make it up to you."

Ben went to the bathroom to change, when his phone lit up on the nightstand.

Aila glanced at the bathroom door then quickly reached over and opened his phone to a text exchange between him and his mom.

9:26 p.m.: You forgot Aila's birthday today. Fix it.

9:30 p.m.: Oh shoot! Thanks for the reminder, Mom. Heading to Safeway right now for flowers.

A deep anger rose in her chest—one that feels more like sadness. Ben had completely forgotten her birthday. Aila tossed the phone back on the nightstand and stared at her Safeway roses purchased two and a half hours before her birthday was over.

Happy birthday to me. With a sigh and holding back tears, she turned over and went to sleep.

CHAPTER 20

NOW

"What's for dinner?" Ben asks over the phone while Aila drives the boys home from Caleb's baseball practice.

"Will you be home to eat with us?" Aila asks, anticipating he'll say no.

Ben was rarely home in time to eat dinner with the family, even though he swore work would slow down after his trip to DC a few weeks ago.

"I'm actually already home. I figured I could get it started," he says, throwing Aila off guard.

"Oh. Well, in that case, yes. Could you get the pasta cooking and roast some broccoli? The sauce is already in the slow cooker," she says, partly grateful he'll be cooking but also not entirely looking forward to seeing him when she gets home.

She's been feeling this way more and more recently. Ben's very presence irritates her. Either he isn't around and his neglect upsets her or he is home and his presence bothers her. Mostly because he isn't helpful—not how she wants him to be at least. He isn't around enough to know how to be, so Aila really just feels like he ends up in the way. But apparently tonight, he plans to make himself useful.

"Great," he says through the Bluetooth speaker in the car. "How do I roast broccoli?"

Aila rolls her eyes, half smiling. She always has to walk him through it step by step. That is his version of helping.

"There's a bag of broccoli florets in the freezer. Put them on a sheet pan and toss it with olive oil, salt, pepper, and garlic powder. Put it in the oven at 425 degrees for forty minutes."

Aila can tell he's writing it down.

"425?"

"Yes." Aila draws out the "s" unintentionally, growing more annoyed.

Maybe I should just tell him I'll do it when I get home.

"And how long do I boil the noodles for?"

"Are you being serious?" Aila asks letting her irritation come through.

"Kidding. See you when you get here."

Before hanging up, she can tell he's smiling on the other end of the line by the sound of his voice.

Aila's not.

She lets out a sigh, trying not to let the boys in the backseat hear her. A few months ago, Ben being home early and making dinner would have felt like a treat, but today she feels reluctant to accept his help. He probably wants something.

Sex. He wants to have sex tonight.

Aila grips the stirring wheel, a knot forming in her stomach.

Back at home, the boys cling to Ben like a moth to a flame. Aila flips through her phone while Ben sets the table and places it facedown on the counter when dinner is ready.

The dinner table is full of animated conversation and uncontrollable laughter. Aila can tell the boys are thrilled to have dad home for dinner, especially on a night they didn't expect it. Ben keeps catching Aila's eye as she sips the wine he had ready and waiting for her when they got home.

Wow, Ben. You really know how to turn it on...when you want to.

It's true. Ben *is* capable and the boys are always ecstatic when he is actually around. Aila just doesn't understand why it isn't all the time. Ben is their father. Her husband. This is his family. He should be their constant, not their once-in-a-while.

"Dad, can we jump on the trampoline after dinner?" Caleb asks.

"Ask your mom."

"Uh-uh, Dad. They asked you, not me this time." Aila stares back at Ben, his eyes are almost pleading. He doesn't want to, but parenthood is full of big and small sacrifices.

Ben rubs his brow. "Probably not tonight, bud. It's a school night and you boys need to go get ready for bed."

Aila feels a pang in her heart when she sees Caleb's face drop and Josh pushes around a rogue piece of broccoli on his plate.

Dammit, Ben. Why can't you just want *to spend time with them every once in a while?*

"Aw, you never jump with us anymore," Caleb complains. Normally she'd correct her children for whining but this time, she allows it. "Even Jackson jumps with us."

"Mr. Jackson," Aila corrects and then shoots a look at Ben.

He looks taken aback and a bit confused. "He does? When?"

"When he came over for dinner that one time," Aila replies quickly.

"Yeah, and after my baseball game too."

Isaac and Josh nod along to this confession.

Ben turns his full attention from Caleb to Aila again. "He did, did he?"

Aila stares at him. A standoff. She breaks eye contact first and starts clearing dishes from the table. Anything to avoid this confrontation in front of their children.

"Alright, boys. Dad's right. It's a school night and you all need showers. Time to head upstairs."

As the three boys trudge upstairs to wreak havoc in the bathrooms, Aila calls, "Take turns please! And wipe up the floors when you're done!"

Aila turns her attention to the sink, rinsing and loading dishes. Ben comes up behind her and places a hand on her shoulder briefly before swinging around against the counter to face her.

His hand on her shoulder feels foreign and uncomfortable. Aila cringes inwardly at the thought.

"So where was I when Jackson came over?"

Aila keeps doing dishes, the rhythm of it keeping her calm. She feels cautious of every move and sound she makes, not wanting to give herself away.

"You were in DC."

She, of course, fails to mention the other afternoons when Jackson brought her coffee, or dropped off ginger ale when the kids were sick, or brought lunch that went uneaten while they explored other things. Or the countless conversations over the phone.

She also recognizes Ben is assuming she only saw him once while he was in DC, not three times.

His face twists at this. He doesn't like it. Aila doesn't care.

"Was there a reason you didn't tell me?"

Aila places the last dish in the dishwasher and closes it. She shakes her head. "No, I guess it just never came up. My mom was actually here too."

See? Look how completely innocent and harmless it actually was. She feels somewhat shocked at her own manipulation.

"Your mom?" he asks, confused. She can see the plot thickening for him.

Yes, see, Ben? This is what you miss out on when you aren't around. This is what you don't know when you don't ask.

"Yes, honey. My mom. She knew Jackson from when I was in high school too."

"She did?"

Give it a rest. Aila wants to roll her eyes. Now she feels validated. *This just goes to show how very little you pay attention to me. How very little you inquire about my life. It hurts, doesn't it, Ben?*

"She did," she says instead and smiles at him sweetly. "We were good friends in high school, remember?"

She kisses him briefly and heads upstairs to tuck the boys into bed.

Aila makes her rounds to each of the boys' rooms, saying their nighttime prayers and turning out the light with a soft kiss on each of their heads. She then heads to the master bathroom and changes into sweatpants, washes her face, and brushes her teeth before curling under their large white, duvet cover with a book.

Ben still hasn't made it upstairs.

Aila guesses he stopped off in the office and got distracted by work so she turns back to her book. Or tries to. She can't concentrate and has found herself reading the same page over and over. She checks her phone to see if Jackson texted her. He didn't. He wouldn't at this time of night, but there's a part of her that's still hopeful.

She puts her phone back on the nightstand facedown and tries to return to her book. She feels something inside her churning.

She isn't worried Ben knows about her and Jackson. There's no way he'd leap that far ahead. But still she can't help but realize how pitiful Ben looked finding out about the goings on inside the walls of his own home. He was lost. He had no idea. Aila almost feels bad for him.

Almost. *Maybe now he'll see how little he pays attention to me.*

Soon Ben comes into the room and slips under the covers.

"Aila," Ben says. His voice is deep and if it weren't for the topic of conversation, she'd say seductive. "Why didn't you tell me about Jackson coming over again?"

Caught. That's the word that's churning inside her.

She mulls it over a bit. No, that isn't right either.

"You never really asked about our weekend when you got home from your trip." She shrugs and pretends to start reading again.

"Didn't I though?"

"Not really, Ben. You got home, you gave the kids their gifts, and you went back to work the next day. Same thing, different day."

Ben seems to ponder this, considering her words.

"I'm sorry, Aila. I'll be better. I promise."

Aila prompts herself to smile at him briefly but it's hollow.

"Goodnight, Ben," she says while turning off the lamp and turning away from him.

His hand stays on her hip while she wills herself to fall asleep, but she can't get her heartbeat to slow or her mind to relax. She tries over and over to come up with a word for what she's feeling but none fit. When she's finally on the edge of sleep, the word hits her like a punch to the gut.

Guilt.

CHAPTER 21

NOW

As the weeks push on, Aila and Jackson struggle to find ways to spend time together, even though he is always on her mind. The opportunity just never quite presents itself. She calls him after she drops the boys at the bus stop most mornings and they text nearly every single day but it isn't enough. Aila finds herself counting down the minutes until the weekend is over.

Until Ben goes back to work.

Until the kids are back at school.

Until she can talk to Jackson again.

Mondays used to signify all the loneliness and emptiness Aila felt. Now as soon as Monday hits, so do her only real opportunities to talk to the one person who makes her feel important. Even still, life isn't lining up easily for them. They have to work to talk to each other and fight to spend any kind of time together.

Aila is growing restless. Jackson consumes her thoughts. She often wakes up from her dreams afraid she said his name out loud in her sleep. Everything reminds her of him. Everything makes her want to see him again.

She can't take it anymore. As soon as the doors on

the bus screech to a close, she pulls out her phone to call Jackson.

"Aila!" Janet says, making Aila jump. "We still have not had coffee and it has been months." Janet pulls her in for an awkward side-hug.

"Has it?"

"Yes, it has. I think the last time we scheduled it was around the Grammy's and life has just marched on and not given us another opportunity."

Aila nods. "I guess it has been a while."

"I don't know what you have been up to, lady. But I miss my friend."

Are we friends though? Aila wants to say but she doesn't and looks into Janet's eyes.

She's smiling her toothy smile with her hands on her hips and her hair blowing in the wind. Aila suddenly thinks her hair must be full of secrets…and suspicions.

Instead she smiles sweetly.

"I miss you too, Janet. But you know what, I have to make this important phone call. Can I text you later?"

"Sure thing. I look forward to it." Janet waves as Aila slips away to call Jackson.

The phone rings twice before he answers. Her heart races as the excitement of her inquiry builds in her mind.

"Come over," she says as soon as he answers.

The very sight of him on her doorstep thirty minutes later makes her knees buckle. He slips inside, barely kicking the door closed before pressing her up against it and kissing her eagerly as he kicks off his shoes. Her fingers grip his belt buckle, her body aching to touch every part of him.

She pulls away from him, wanting to savor the build of passion between them.

"We've got all day," she whispers breathlessly.

A seductive smile spreads across his face and he leans in to caress her face and kiss her again as she guides him up to the bedroom.

~

The midday sun shines through the blinds on Aila's bed when she rolls over and faces Jackson.

"We can't keep doing this." A smile spreads across her face, her head still spinning.

Jackson laughs sheepishly while pulling up his jeans. "Do what exactly?"

Aila raises her eyebrows. "I'm a married woman, sir."

She wants it to come off as sexy and playful, but Jackson looks like she smacked him in the face. She can tell it makes him feel like a one-nighter, a meaningless playboy.

He bobs his head down and presses his lips together withholding a sigh. Aila senses his genuine frustration; she didn't expect it.

Did he not realize who he's been getting into bed with?

In just her robe, Aila crawls over to Jackson and grabs his face.

"Jackson, hey, we just—" Aila gets lost in his eyes, unable to figure out exactly what she needs to or wants to say, "Can we just be careful?"

Jackson looks at her before speaking, the hesitation and frustration still lingering in his eyes. "Yeah, okay."

"Okay," she says and kisses him softly, lingering at his lips. "I wish it could be like this all the time."

Jackson's eyes narrow on hers and he brushes his thumb across her brow. He's looking at her intently and his cheek twitches like he just forced back every word he wants to say and Aila notices.

"What is it?"

"It could, Aila." He presses his lips together and slides his hands down from her face to her neck. "It could be like this all the time."

Aila looks at him longingly; her hands run down his warm skin across his chest.

"You know how badly I want that. But Ben, I—"

He cuts her off.

"Jackson," he says plainly.

She looks at him, startled by confusion.

"I'm Jackson, Aila. But I think that's my cue to leave." He swallows back his humiliation while throwing on his shirt and making his way downstairs.

What just happened?

Aila follows him down the stairs.

"Jackson, wait. I'm sorry. I don't even know how that came out."

She says "that" like she said a dirty word and not her husband's name.

By the time Jackson hits the bottom of the stairs, he is slipping on his boots. His silence is steaming, his hurt seeping through his pours. Aila reaches for his arm and turns him around before he reaches for the front door.

"Jackson. Please. Stop." She's holding his face in her hands now, tears tug at the corners of her eyes. "I don't even know what I was saying. It was just a habit. I swear."

Jackson won't meet her eyes. He's embarrassed.

"Hey," she says forcing him to look at her. "It's just me." She pauses and brushes her thumb across his cheek where his dimple should be. "I love you."

Aila feels her heart skip a beat at her own words. She hadn't said that to him before. She hadn't really even thought about whether or not she did, but it came out in this moment and it feels right. It fits.

She loves Jackson.

Wholly and completely. A part of her always has. She was just too afraid to admit it all those years ago.

Jackson's face softens and he looks at her, searching her face, studying it, begging for the truth to slip out again. Slowly, his mouth breaks into a smile, showing off his dimples and he kisses her, bringing her body to his. He runs his fingers through her hair and then pulls back.

"I love you too, Aila. It's always been you."

Her breath catches at his words and she feels a fire

ignite in her chest. She leans in to kiss him again.

Love. That's what this is, isn't it? It's all-consuming and insatiable.

The two have been drawn to each other like magnets since they first saw each other two months ago. Aila can't help how she feels about him. Life has kept them a part for twenty years but fate brought them back together. She has no doubt she loves him. This is just the next chapter in their love story.

CHAPTER 22

THEN

Aila always loved the Christmas party for Ben's law firm. White & Associates would rent out an event room in a swanky Seattle hotel, and the two would get a room for the night and let loose for the evening.

This particular year the party was at Hotel Theodore in the heart of downtown, and Aila counted down the days until they would attend.

The hotel was modern and industrial with deep navy paneling and ornate molding with gold light fixtures flanking the walls. The hotel was dimly lit making the atmosphere feel moody and eccentric.

Aila stood at the vintage sink surrounded by subway tile and gazed in the round mirror, perfecting the last coat of lipstick before stepping into the hotel room where Ben sat leaned back in a leather armchair, flipping through the channels on the TV. He was wearing slacks and a button up shirt, the top two buttons still undone, and an emerald tie draped around his neck.

He stared blankly at the TV until Aila walked in with a quick spin and said, "How do I look?"

She wore an emerald-colored satin wrap dress that cut

above the knee, short enough to show off her long legs and long enough she still looked sophisticated.

He immediately stood up and walked over to where Aila was standing. Ben's brown eyes sparkled at the sight of her and he spun her around gently before wrapping her in his arms and kissing her softly.

"You are exquisite." He smiled, biting his lip like he couldn't contain his excitement. "Maybe we should just stay in this room for the night?"

"Very funny, Ben." Aila laughed. "But you know this is the one night a year where I get to get all dolled up and fancy with no crazy boys pulling at my dress, asking me for a snack."

Ben returned the laugh.

"Well, you still might have one boy pulling at your dress," he said while looking at her with bedroom eyes that almost made her want to slip out of her slinky dress and be late for the party.

"Stop." Aila smiled, remembering they had all night. She looked at the clock on the wall and delicately placed a hand on his chest. "We need to get going, Mr. Sorenson. Wouldn't want to disappoint anyone."

She winked, grabbed her clutch off the credenza, and headed out the door.

In the hallway, Ben stopped short.

"Wait. Did you grab the Christmas cards and champagne for Billy and Gloria?"

Every Christmas party, all the associates and paralegals would flood the owner of the law firm and his wife with exquisite chocolates and expensive bottles of liquor and wine—their small gestures of gratitude for their employment. And also, for their bonuses that were sure to arrive the following week.

"I filled them out and told you they were on the kitchen counter before we left but I didn't pack them."

Ben let out a frustrated sigh. "Everyone brings their gifts to the party. How could we forget them?"

Aila tilted her head to the side and raised her eyebrows, her chestnut eyes growing darker with irritation. "Babe, I signed the cards, I bought the champagne. *You* forgot. Not we. There's still a week before Christmas. Just bring it to the office on Monday."

Her mood shifted. Aila hated when Ben made her responsible for these types of things. She understood wives were often better at picking out cards and writing little notes—she didn't even mind buying the overly priced champagne—but at some point, the gesture had to come from Ben as well.

"No, no. You're right. I just—" he adjusted his tie quickly "—don't like looking unprepared."

Of course, you don't.

Aila smiled. Attorneys hate looking unprepared. She took his hand in hers and they made their way to the top floor of the hotel, where the party awaited.

The doors of the elevator opened to a stunning, panoramic view of the city, reaching past Pike Place Market to the Puget Sound beyond it. Every twinkling city light made Aila feel like all of Seattle decorated for Christmas. She loved that about the city. Whenever the sun went down, it sparkled.

The event hall had windows on every wall, so everywhere you looked was another cityscape to admire. Sleek modern chairs and cocktail tables littered one side of the room while the other side had tables draped in white tablecloths and a buffet just beyond.

"Nice set up this year, huh?" Ben whispered in her ear while gently setting his hand on her lower back.

"Breathtaking," she said as they walked to the bar for drinks.

"Well, if it isn't the lovely Aila Sorenson!"

It was Carla, Ben's long-time paralegal. She was dressed in sequins and too much blush and pulled Aila in for a plump hug.

"Hi, Carla, how are you?"

"Fine, fine." She sipped her gin and tonic. "Now,

have you run off and gotten a job yet? You haven't been to the office in ages."

Aila felt slightly taken aback by her comment and shot a glance at Ben who was more focused on his whiskey than her.

"Uh, no. Just busy with the boys." She smiled sweetly. *Like a good little wife.*

"Oh, I see. I just figured now that they're all in school, you'd get back to being a contributing member of society."

She laughed at her own joke.

Aila forced a smile again, but she didn't laugh.

"Well, Isaac is only four so he won't be in school full time until next year."

"Right, right. Well, maybe then." She slurped the last of her gin and tonic.

"Mmm. Yes, maybe then," Aila said, swallowing hard, feeling slightly embarrassed and frustrated Ben didn't come to her defense. Wasn't he the one that didn't want her to go back to work yet?

"Carla, have you seen Billy yet?" Ben asked.

"Mr. White?" Carla batted her false eyelashes at Aila's husband. "I believe he and Gloria have already found a table near the buffet."

"Thank you. Good to see you, Carla," Ben said as he patted her on the shoulder.

"Merry Christmas!" she said.

Aila nodded then turned her attention to Ben as they walked toward the dining area.

"That was rude."

"What?" Ben was oblivious.

"Her comments about me not working."

Ben shrugged. "Well, you don't."

Aila looked at him, aghast. "Because *you* don't want me to go back yet."

Ben hushed her so briefly, it was almost inaudible but Aila heard it.

"Ben…"

"Not right here, Aila. Not right now." His eyes pierced hers, almost reprimanding her and then his eyes softened. "Please."

Aila swallowed hard, biting back her frustrations and plastering her face with a smile for Ben's boss and his wife.

"Ah, well, if it's not the Sorensons," Billy greeted them, standing up from the table.

"Merry Christmas, Mr. White," Ben said, giving him and his wife a firm handshake and an irresistible smile.

Aila leaned in and air kissed Gloria on the cheek. "Merry Christmas, Gloria."

"Well, aren't you just a sight to see." Gloria stood up and held out Aila's hands, admiring her dress and probably her figure too. "I swear, Aila, you just get prettier and prettier every year I see you."

Aila blushed, slightly.

"Thank you, Gloria. I could say the same to you."

"Probably why he keeps her locked in their castle," Billy said and he let out a deep belly laugh that made his chin jiggle.

Ben and Aila laughed, though Aila didn't find it very funny. She was no longer in the mood to be Ben's trophy wife.

"Would the two of you like to sit at our table for dinner?" Gloria asked. "Billy was going to propose a toast and hand out plaques in just a bit."

It wasn't really a question; it was an honor to be invited to the boss's table and Ben wore the privilege of it all over his face.

As the night progressed, Aila enjoyed her braised lamb with shrimp risotto, and followed it with crème brûlée and tiramisu since she couldn't decide which dessert to get. Billy White toasted to his law firm and his colleagues then handed out awards and honorable mentions to his favorite employees on his payroll.

Ben received an award for "Most Dedicated

Associate" and Aila choked a laugh into her second glass of wine. She quickly caught herself and sat up a little straighter, proudly smiling at her husband while he received his award.

After the awards and speeches, the conversation became a blur of legal terms, case numbers, client names, and laws. Aila found herself with nothing to contribute. She sat there, still, smiling and nodding where appropriate but not really paying any attention.

She leaned into Ben's ear and whispered, "I'm going to head out to the terrace for some fresh air."

He nodded but didn't offer to join her. He barely even moved his eyes away from the conversation to acknowledge her when she excused herself from the table and kissed him on the cheek.

Aila stopped and grabbed another glass of wine on her way out to the terrace. There were only a few couples outside, each of them huddled near a heater. Aila walked over to the railing wrapped in white Christmas lights and fresh garland. She breathed in the scent of pine and looked out at the dancing city lights surrounding her, sipping her wine.

She was wearing a dress that made her feel beautiful in a place that made her feel extravagant with someone she loved dearly, and yet, she felt so unimportant. Invisible. Completely lost in her own skin.

She had made the shift from being a mother of little babies to a mother of young kids and suddenly the world expected her to catch up with the career she had once upon a time, to *contribute to society*.

She felt like a child standing at the edge of a diving board, nervous and afraid, while the world stood behind her yelling, *why haven't you jumped back in yet?*

Staying home and loving her family used to feel like enough. But the monotony meshed all the days together, and the love and appreciation she received in return became less and less.

She had once relished in the idea of staying home with their children—running a household, tending to the kids, taking care of the garden, and always having a home cooked meal when her husband came home from a long day at work. Now, it felt so unimportant. She no longer recognized herself when she thought of the role she had once dreamed up. It's no wonder everyone else seemed to stop understanding who she was as well.

No one enjoys feeling irrelevant and unimportant around the people that matter most. She wanted to jump back in. But for some reason, the water looked deeper than it used to be and the diving board seemed higher. She didn't know how to jump back in, not when she was so used to keeping her children and husband afloat from the side of the pool.

Aila swirled the last of her wine in her glass and tipped it back, before checking the time. She'd been on the terrace for an hour contemplating what her life currently was.

Ben didn't come out to check on her, and she was willing to bet he hadn't moved from the table with the Whites.

As she headed back inside the party, she immediately spotted Ben.

She was right.

He hadn't moved. He was laughing and animated and charming the sequins off of Mrs. White. Aila smiled at the sight of the man she loved, but followed it with a slight roll of her eyes. She headed over to the bar.

He certainly knows how to turn it on for them*, doesn't he?*

"Could I get a glass of merlot?" The bartender nodded as she slipped a twenty in the tip jar. "A heavy pour, please."

"You got it, ma'am," he said pouring the wine to just below the rim.

She thanked him and walked toward the elevator. She took a long drink so she wouldn't spill it just as the elevator arrived, and she stepped in it.

Aila knew how the rest of the night would go.

Ben would come to the hotel room in an hour or two.

Maybe even three, and tell her he's sorry for leaving her outside for so long, blame it on his boss and how chatty his wife is, and then he'll thank her for coming and tell her everyone loved her.

Who knew I made such great arm candy, she thought to herself and chuckled in the lonely elevator while she pulled out her phone to send a text to Ben.

Headed to the room. Take your time. XO

Just like a good little wife.

CHAPTER 23

NOW

Aila pulls off her dirty garden glove and wipes her hand across her shorts before answering her phone. She almost doesn't answer. She's in the middle of planting springtime blooms in their front yard garden bed and not in the mood to talk to Ben. She rarely was these days.

"Hey, you busy?"

"Not really. Just getting some gardening done," she says, anxious to make the phone call brief, the warm spring sun making the back of her neck sweat.

"It's a beautiful day out," he says, pointing out the obvious.

Aila tries not to sigh.

What do you want, Ben? "It sure is."

"Well, what do you think about going out to dinner tomorrow night?"

Aila bites her lip. She doesn't want to.

It bothers Aila it took Ben realizing Jackson has been spending more time with his family than he thought for his attentiveness to spike. Now she feels suffocated by Ben's random calls in the middle of the day to "check in" and even questions his incessant texts to say "I love you." In her mind, it's too little, too late. Aila can't get her head straight. It feels like an endless cycle of being on edge and annoyed even though this is the version of Ben she has wanted back for so many years.

"I'm not sure, Ben. I feel bad asking any of the grandparents to watch the kids since your mom watched them last week when I went out with Chantelle and my mom watched them on Monday when I was volunteering at the church."

They were both lies though. Aila wasn't with Chantelle or volunteering. She was at Jackson's house.

"No, I know but I already talked to my mom and she said she'd be happy to watch them again," Ben says. Aila can tell he's excited. "She agrees we really need to be taking more time out for one another—offered to do it every week if we'd let her."

Ben laughs at this.

Aila doesn't. She forces a smile Ben can't see through the phone.

She never lets her smile slip. Not when people see them at church or at Caleb's baseball games or Josh's Taekwondo tournaments. Not when she bashfully accepts every compliment hurled at her family. Not even when she's making nice on every extra phone call with Ben.

It feels relentless. Giving off an impression of perfection used to make Aila feel so much pride, now it sends pangs of guilt in her stomach.

Aila doesn't want to hurt Ben any more than she wants to be with Jackson.

But people change. They grow. Sometimes that growth shifts them into different people entirely, who don't want the same things from each other anymore. Sometimes they don't even want the same things from life at all. And it happens little by little, like drops of water making an imprint in stone. It just took something drastic for Aila to realize it.

Ben and Aila have become different people. Their puzzle pieces don't match up anymore. The cracks between them she desperately tried to mend with masking tape grew wider and wider, until she realized they no longer fit together.

But Ben won't let up.

"Aila? Honey? You still there?"

She clears her throat. "Uh, yeah. Yeah, I'm here. Tomorrow would be great. Where are we going?"

"You pick," he says.

Of course. Ben's valiant attempt to put effort in their marriage is falling short of an actual plan. But, hey, at least he found someone to watch their children.

~

By the next evening, the boys are thrilled to have another evening with Nana. She brings everything for ice cream sundaes and Aila makes them promise to save her some.

Aila chooses a martini bar for dinner just a few minutes from the house. She doesn't want to go far, saying she was tired, but really, she feels apprehensive about a longer car drive, knowing they'd ride in an awkward silence.

After they're seated, Aila orders a merlot and Ben orders his usual whiskey on the rocks, which is ironic considering they're at a martini bar. They've been to this particular spot many times but Aila takes the menu and studies it like there's going to be an exam next week.

"Do you know what you're getting?" Ben asks.

"Mmm, not yet," Aila says, even though she does. She's just not ready to put away the buffer between them.

"I think I'll get a Rueben," he says. "I haven't had one of those in a long time."

Aila looks up from the menu then, studying Ben as he takes a sip of whiskey and looks at their surroundings.

When did we get so boring?

All their problems seem to be glaring at them all at once now. Their disconnect is obvious. The conversation is increasingly moot. And their presence with each other is awkward.

"I'll have the shrimp scampi," she says as she puts down the menu.

"But your drinking merlot, shouldn't you be having a white wine with that dish?" he asks. Her chance to rectify her faux pas. His comment irritates her but she ignores it.

"I don't mind," she says, licking her lips while checking her phone for the fourth time since they arrived.

"Your birthday is coming up next week."

Aila looks up from her phone when Ben says this.

"Anything you want to do?"

She puts her phone back in her purse.

"Uh, not really." *See Jackson.* "Maybe just hang out as a family."

"Want me to invite Chantelle and the girls over too? Or your parents?" he asks.

"Whatever you think." As she takes a sip of her wine, she spots a couple sitting in the lounge area, their arms and hands tangled up in each other, and she stares at them longingly.

We used to be them.

Ben follows her eyes and sees them too.

"Get a room, right?"

He's trying so hard to connect, to laugh, to make this comfortable but every single interaction just isn't. Aila can't reach past the valley between them and she doesn't really even want to anymore. All she wants to do is go home and call Jackson.

"Right," she says, flashing a brief toothless smile. When the waiter brings their food, they put their heads down and finish their dinner practically in silence.

~

Back at the house, after Ben's mom goes home and Aila checks on the sleeping boys, she comes back downstairs in her robe to wipe down the counters and start the dishwasher. Ben is waiting at the island with the bottle of whiskey Jackson had brought him a couple months back and two tumblers.

"Want some?" Ben's dark eyes are soft and pleading. For a moment, Aila feels pity for him, realizing how hard he was trying and knowing how terribly she was hurting him.

"Sure." She smiles and sits across from him on a bar stool, the very sight of the whiskey bottle sends a fire in Aila's belly and her mind floods with memories of Jackson—his touch, his smell, everything about him. She blinks away the thoughts and throws the whiskey down in one gulp.

Ben smiles mischievously and pours her another.

"Are you planning on drinking me under the table tonight?"

Aila laughs.

"Maybe." She takes another sip.

Ben moves around the island and sits on the bar stool next to her, his legs encasing hers, making her feel trapped. Cornered.

"You know, Aila." He stops to clear his throat. He does this when he's reluctant to say something. "I know things have been strange between us…"

She looks at him, pretending to be confused.

"I know you feel it too. With my workload and the kids' schedules getting busier, I know there hasn't been enough time for me and you, but I want you to know I'm going to change that. I made promises to you a long time ago and I want you to know my heart hasn't changed. I just haven't been fair to you, and I'm sorry. You carry this family and you aren't supposed to do it alone."

Ben reaches out; his hand feels warm against her ice-cold fingers.

Tears sting her eyes and she isn't sure if it's because it's the apology she's wanted to hear for years, or if she's feeling it's an apology coming a little too late. Either way, it makes her cry.

Ben leans in to kiss her and she forces herself to kiss

him back. They move from the kitchen to the couch. Their connection feels almost somber and their movements are trepid. Ben is reaching for more, eager to please her in every way, and Aila is guarded and rigid but she allows him to make love to her anyway.

When it's over, Aila quietly dresses while Ben lays breathless on the couch.

"Aila," he says while she pulls her robe back on. "I love you."

She pauses, briefly, but he notices.

"I love you, too," she says with a small, forced smile. She grabs her phone and heads upstairs to the bathroom, closing the door behind her, and cries.

Locked in the water closet, Aila sees two unread text messages from Jackson.

Can't stop thinking about you.

Call me sometime tomorrow?

Aila holds the phone to her chest, feeling both longing and regret. She didn't realize sleeping with her own husband could cause such turmoil inside her.

Call you tomorrow. Promise.

Only she doesn't get a chance to. Ben keeps his word and pays far more attention to the family than he had in months. Sunday rolls through the same way. For the first time Aila can remember, Ben put work away for the full weekend and spent every moment possible with his wife and children.

By the time Monday hits, Aila's phone is burning a hole in her pocket and she can't wait for the doors of the bus to close so she can finally call Jackson and hear his voice. As the bus begins to roll away, Aila pulls her phone out, quickly fumbling in Jackson's number.

"Aila!"

Aila jumps at the sound of her name and puts a hand to her chest, nearly dropping her phone. "*Shit.* Oh, Janet, I'm sorry, you scared me." She forces a laugh.

"You okay?" Janet asks, smiling her usual toothy smile. "You seem on edge."

"I'm good, honestly. Just eager to get some exercise. We'll talk soon!" she says, dismissing Janet and leaving her looking dazed and confused at the corner of Cherrywood Lane while she makes her way up to Skyline hill, her phone to her ear.

"What a sweet surprise," Jackson says after one ring.

Aila smiles, relief washing over her. From what, she isn't sure. She just desperately needed to hear his voice.

"I am so happy to finally talk to you."

"Me too," he says. "What are you up to?"

"Walking Gus up the hill. Where are you?" She wants him to say on his way over.

"I am still at home actually. Getting a late start today." Aila can picture him drinking his coffee on the back patio overlooking the water. "How was your weekend?"

"It was okay. Ben said he wants to make an effort to be around more often, which he was, so that was different." The honesty slips from her lips faster than she can stop it.

"How so?"

"Well, for starters he took me out to dinner for the first time in ages, so that was odd. Then normally on Saturday and Sunday he would slip off into the office to get a head start on the work week or at least go to the gym, but he didn't do any of that. Hence, why I wasn't able to talk to you much this weekend."

There's a slight pause before he responds and Aila wants to eat her words.

Why did I tell him that?

"How was dinner?" His voice is plain and unemotional.

"Fine. A little awkward, to be honest," she answers

truthfully but she finds herself not wanting to elaborate. "How was your weekend?"

"It was good." His vague answer lets Aila know something is bothering him.

"Everything okay?"

"Yeah, it's all good," he says.

"Jackson. Don't. I know you and something is bothering you. Please just tell me."

He pauses again and then clears his throat.

"Do you understand what it's like to be in my position, Aila? All I wanted to do was spend every moment this weekend with you but I knew I couldn't call or text you too much because you're with your absentee husband. I just..." His voice trails off.

"What is it?"

"It'll make me crazy if I don't know. Did you sleep with him?"

"Jackson, I..." Aila's voice breaks in her throat, not wanting to answer this question.

"It's a yes or no, Aila."

She grows quiet.

"Yes," she says softly into the wind at the top of the hill, praying the breeze would make her answer less complicated.

"You know the hardest part of you saying that? It's that I can't even be mad."

Aila begins to attempt to comfort him and apologize but he cuts her off.

"No, please. Let me finish. Do you even understand what it's like for me? I have been waiting for you for longer than just this weekend, you know that. I love you, and I can't even have you. Not completely." His voice almost cracks with emotion but he clears it away.

"You have no idea how hard this is for me, Jackson. I spent the entire weekend thinking about you, waiting to see you again. It's torture being stuck in between the two of you—"

"But are you actually stuck, Aila?"

"I don't know what you mean."

"I mean are you stuck or are you choosing to be stuck? Because there are ways out, Aila."

"Jackson, I'm just not ready to—"

"Okay. Well, then maybe we should just cool it for a bit. Call me when you are ready."

And the line cuts out, leaving Aila standing at the top of the hill staring out over the valley to the same ocean water Jackson is looking into right now.

Only this time, it feels like he's a world away.

On the walk back to the house, Aila lets her tears fall silently behind her sunglasses. She has made every choice that landed her here, wanting someone just out of reach.

Or is he? God, I have made such a mess of my life. I don't know what to do. Her marriage had been cracking for years and she stomped on the broken pieces with someone that now doesn't even seem to want her anymore.

CHAPTER 24

THEN

The smell of bacon and maple syrup wafted through her bedroom door, waking up Aila's senses as the morning sun shone through the blinds.

"Happy birthday to you!" her four men sang in unison as they each made their way into their king-sized bed.

Josh was leading the parade, holding a bouquet of flowers. Isaac and Caleb followed, each had hand-made cards while Ben came in last. He placed the tray of breakfast food gently in front of Aila as she turned over and sat up.

"Happy birthday, Aila." Ben bent down and kissed her softly.

"Mmm, waffles," she said through his kiss.

"And bacon!" Isaac shouted.

"And bacon," Ben said, laughing gently.

"Well, thank you, boys. This looks delicious," she said as Josh ate a piece of her bacon, Isaac took a bite of her waffle, and Caleb chugged her orange juice.

"It is!" Isaac said with a bit of syrup running down his chin. "Here, mom! Read my card."

This was what Aila's special breakfasts in bed always turned into—family breakfast in bed, while each kid nibbled at her meal and she read their notes and admired their artwork.

By request she looked at Isaac's card first. He wouldn't be in kindergarten until the fall so he could only write his name but he also drew a picture of five potato-shaped people with stick legs and arms. Aila's potato was the only one with eyelashes. He wanted to make her look pretty.

Aila smiled at the latest family portrait.

"Thank you, Isaac," she said, giving her youngest a kiss on top of his head. She turned to Ben. "So, what's the plan?"

It was an unusually warm Saturday in late April, everybody was home, and Aila was eager to see what Ben had in store.

Since Ben forgot her birthday the year before, he made sure to make it a point he knew her birthday was coming up during the weeks and days leading up to it.

This year he had picnic lunches packed in a backpack for a family hike to Denny Creek.

Aila loved to hike. In the Pacific Northwest there were endless options of trails, all with spectacular mountain and waterfall views. Denny Creek was a family favorite. It was an easy two miles on a heavily wooded trail through an old growth forest that lead to Keekwulee Falls.

At the trailhead, the boys ran ahead, leaving Aila and Ben trailing behind, jogging slightly to catch up. Once they reached the creek, the trees opened up like a curtain on a stage revealing nearly a mile of smooth stone leading up to the waterfall.

The water running through the stone was ice-cold glacier water that ran directly from the mountain pass, but that never stopped them from taking advantage of the naturally made water slides near the waterfall.

At Keekwulee Falls, the water falls into living room-sized pools of ankle-deep water before cascading down again to a smaller but deeper pool, and then trickles into a stream that bobs and weaves down the valley of smooth stone and back to the trail.

Just to the left of the waterfall is where the best rock water slide is, or at least the fastest. Aila had been taking the boys here since Isaac was so little, they brought him in a hiking backpack, so they knew where to find it immediately.

"Be careful, boys! It's very slippery," Ben called to them, an attempt at getting them to slow down on the rocks.

At the top of the viewpoint, Ben set down his hiking backpack before perching on one of the rocks in the direct sunlight.

"We practically have the place to ourselves," Ben said to Aila.

"This was a great idea," she said, looking back at the boys sliding down and then racing back up the side of the boulder. "Thank you."

"Come on, Mom!" Josh yelled over the roar of the water falling behind him. "Your turn!"

The boys were already drenched and shaking from the bone-piercingly cold water.

"I'm coming, I'm coming," Aila said, making her way to the top of the boulder, mentally preparing herself for the sting of the cold water on her skin.

"Watch this!" Isaac called. He slid down so quickly his foot slammed against the stone and became wedged under a beachball-sized boulder at the bottom of the slides.

"Ow!" His yell quickly turned into a shriek, and then his cries of panic and pain followed right after.

Shit!

Aila thought he had no doubt broken his foot when it slammed into the rock. Her adrenaline spiked and she jumped over the slide, landing in the kiddie pool of glacier water where Isaac sat, stuck under the rock.

"Isaac? Mom!? Is he okay?" she heard Caleb and Josh call from behind her.

As soon as she reached Isaac, she pulled with her entire body weight to move the rock.

It didn't move.

She tried again.

It still didn't move.

Isaac was crying.

"Ben!" Aila yelled but she couldn't hear his response over the roar of the waterfall.

She heaved a third time and the boulder moved just enough Isaac could slip his foot out. It was then she realized how badly his leg was bleeding. She picked him up and stumbled through the rocky, freezing water with Isaac still sobbing. When Ben realized the commotion, he jumped up from his perch in the sun.

"He got cut," she said, not wanting Isaac to hear her panic or her mention how bad the wound was.

The gash was about five inches across his shin and so deep in the flesh Aila could see fatty tissue pockets and bone.

"The rock he ran into must have had a sharp edge."

Ben didn't say anything as he made his way closer to them, but he pulled off his shirt and wrapped it around Isaac's shin, as tightly as he could and then another time for good measure.

"You're alright, bud," Ben said.

His voice was calm and reassuring over the growl of the waterfall. He took Isaac from her arms and carried him to the boulder he was sitting on. Ben and Aila made eye contact and wordlessly confirmed: he definitely needed stitches.

Caleb and Josh were trailing behind Aila to check on their brother.

"You okay, Isaac? That looked like it hurt really bad," Josh said, his eyes so wide and his face pale, Aila thought he was going to pass out. He doesn't like the sight of blood, or the pool of red water Isaac left behind.

"He'll be okay," Ben said. "Here, why don't we all have a seat and eat something. Especially you Isaac, we don't want you to get woozy after an injury like that."

Ben's muscles glistened under the height of the sun and Aila felt incredibly thankful she didn't take this hike alone today, like she had in years past. Ben didn't panic. He was their calm and steady. He knew what to do and didn't even hesitate to take off his shirt for a makeshift tourniquet.

Aila stood there watching their boys inhale their sandwiches and water. Her hands felt shaky and her heart pounded. More than anything she hated seeing her kids in pain. Isaac's tears had subsided but the memory of his fleshy wound was playing over and over in her mind like a broken record.

Ben recognized the worry in his wife's face and stood, wrapping an arm around her shoulders and pulling her in to kiss her forehead.

"He's going to be fine, Aila."

"I'm just so sorry. I shouldn't have let him slide down right there," she whispered.

She always took the blame.

Always.

Even for things beyond her control.

"Babe, it was an accident," Ben whispered back. "We'll fuel them up so nobody passes out and head out. He isn't bleeding through my shirt so he'll be fine until we make it to the hospital."

On the trek back to the trailhead, the boys discussed Fortnite tactics, baseball stats, and fart jokes, letting Aila know all was well in their little worlds. About halfway down, Ben slipped Isaac on his shoulders and carried him the rest of the way.

"I want someone to carry me," Caleb whined.

"You didn't almost lose a leg, Caleb," Josh retorted.

"Who almost lost their leg?" Isaac asked, causing Ben and Aila to laugh, her nerves smoothing out around the edges.

"Nobody almost lost their leg, but you, my man, are going to have to head to the hospital to get your cut checked out," Ben said.

Aila shot a look at Ben, wishing he hadn't said hospital. Doctor, nurse, urgent care are all acceptable words to say but hospital gets Josh's nerves in a pinch. "Hospital" to him means death and dying. Or babies. And he knew the latter wasn't happening so his quiet demeanor was instantly streaked with worry and concern.

She grabbed his face softly and kissed the top of his head. "Not to worry, Josh. Your brother will be fine."

"He just needs to get stitched up really quick," Ben added.

"Stitches?!" Now it was Isaac's turn to worry.

Aila rubbed two fingers between her brow.

Ben looked up at her confused.

"We'll see, honey. Everyone, just get to the car and let's head back to town," Aila said.

Once they made it to the trailhead and loaded up the SUV, Aila slipped into the passenger seat. By the time they hit the freeway, with the music drowning out their conversation, Ben turned to her.

"Why's everyone freaking out?"

"They aren't freaking out," she defended them. "They're just sensitive. Josh doesn't like the idea of hospitals since my grandfather died. They remind him of death and sadness. And Isaac doesn't like the idea of getting stitches because needles and thread running through his skin makes him a bit nervous."

"Ah." Ben nodded in understanding.

"Can you blame him? He's only four," Aila said while pulling her long waves of hair up in a messy bun on top of her head.

"Sounds like they need to toughen up a bit."

Her chestnut eyes shot him a glare.

"Don't be rude, Ben. They're just boys."

"They need to understand accidents happen sometimes. And they land you in the hospital sometimes, with stitches or sometimes worse." His brown eyes always grew a shade darker when he was going off on a tangent. Then he added, "My mom didn't raise me to a softy."

Aila felt her lungs fill with air and she let it out quickly with a sharp sigh. He was insulting her parenting without even being remotely aware of it.

"They aren't softies, Ben."

"Just saying. At some point they're going to have to man up a bit."

"Well, then maybe the man in their life should be around more," Aila said through her teeth.

"What's that supposed to mean?" Ben's forehead became a maze of angry lines.

"Nothing." Aila shook her head, regretting her comment.

"No, really, what do you mean by that?"

"Just forget it. Please." she turned her eyes to his and he glanced away from the road to meet hers. "I didn't mean it."

Only she did.

But she didn't want to fight. Not now in front of the kids. And not later when it was just the two of them.

She hated fighting. It was exhausting and resolved next to nothing. She decided to brush this one under the rug. The rest of the drive home was quiet with the exception of music playing in the background.

Back in town, Ben decided to drop Aila, Josh, and Caleb off at the house and take Isaac to the hospital himself. He still hadn't bled through the tourniquet—Ben had made it tight enough—so he made the call the extra fifteen minutes to drop the majority of the family off wouldn't hurt.

Ben ordered pizza for Aila, Caleb, and Josh while he headed to the hospital with Isaac. After she and the older two boys ate dinner, Aila sent them up for baths and bed so she could make her way back down to the kitchen for a glass of wine.

By the time she had finished her glass, Ben walked through the door with a sleeping and bandaged Isaac hanging over his shoulder. She kissed the top of his head; his brown, messy hair smelled like dirt and little boy.

"Twenty-two stitches," Ben whispered. "He did great though."

"Oh, poor baby," she whispered back. "There's leftover pizza. Should we wake him to eat?"

Ben shook his head. "No, he just ate his Happy Meal in the car before he passed out."

Aila smiled softly at the dried ketchup on Isaac's cheek and rubbed his back.

"Okay, do you want me to go lay him down?"

"No, I got it. You go relax."

Aila returned to the kitchen and poured a second glass of wine, staring at it in a daze before taking a sip. *What a birthday.*

Ben came downstairs after showering and poured himself two fingers of whiskey, clinking glasses with his wife.

"Happy birthday, Aila May."

He unleashed a charming smile, his teeth white and sparkling. Aila smiled and took a long sip of her wine.

"Thank you," she said. "And thank you for taking Isaac tonight. Having one kid at the hospital is much easier than all three."

"No problem." He smiled, swirling his liquor around the glass.

Aila stared down at her wine, thoughtfully, contemplating her next words.

"I'm glad you were with us today. I can't imagine getting an injured kid out of there and off the trail by myself."

Ben walked around the island to where she was standing.

"Hey," he said gently, "they're my kids too. You know I'll do anything for them."

Aila did know this. He adored his family. She just wished he was around to enjoy them more often. The balance was off and she didn't know how to fix it. Instead she chose to ignore it and try to focus on the moment and the adoring man in front of her.

"I know," she said instead. "And I love you for it."

Ben moved in closer, running his fingertips along her neck, giving her a welcomed shiver. He raked his hands through her hair and then down her back and along her hips before placing her on the counter and kissing her delicately.

She wanted so badly to be in the moment but her mind kept flashing back to their conversation in the car. She wanted to ignore it, pretend it didn't happen. She pushed it back deeper in her mind, willing it to go away.

It worked long enough for her to let Ben make love to her in the kitchen.

CHAPTER 25

NOW

Aila sits next to the fireplace on the covered deck, while staring mindlessly at her margarita. The boys are playing tag in the yard with Chloe and Emma, while the hum of music and adult conversation wafts from inside the screen door out to where she's sitting. She checks her phone again.

Nothing.

Jackson hasn't called or texted since their last conversation on the hill.

While Aila took his words seriously, she hadn't expected him to just disappear. Deep down she thought they had something stronger and deeper. For the last three months, there was a steady and unexpected build between them until they were virtually inseparable. In her mind, they belong to each other even if she technically still belongs to Ben. She was sure he'd find a way or a reason to reach out to her, like a force of gravity. But after nearly a week, Jackson still hasn't called or texted. Not even today on her birthday.

Ben had ordered dozens of street tacos, filled four pitchers of margaritas, and invited both sets of grandparents and a few close friends to celebrate her turning thirty-seven.

As the party dwindles on with the house full company, Aila starts obsessing over not hearing from Jackson. Checking her phone every moment she gets a chance.

Still nothing.

She drums her fingers along the arm of the chair, impatient, as Chantelle bursts through the sliding glass door.

"I'm pretty sure this is my sixth taco." Chantelle laughs, sitting down next to Aila, paper plate in hand.

"Same," Elena says, following Chantelle out to the seating area, letting out a laugh.

The sound of Chantelle and Elena's voices startles Aila and she slips her phone back in her pocket.

Chantelle eyes her quizzically. "You okay, Aila?"

"Me? Yeah, I'm fine." Aila hides her flush by taking a sip of her margarita. "Why do you ask?"

"Because my comment about how many tacos I've eaten made you jump like a kangaroo in the Outback."

Elena snorts out a laugh mid bite of a taco and covers up the guacamole and sour cream leaking out the corners of her mouth with a hand.

"Seriously, Aila. You're acting a bit spacey. Tell us what's really going on? Do you not like your birthday present from Ben?" Elena says nodding at the new hammock in the yard and wiping her mouth with a napkin.

"At least he didn't forget this year," Chantelle says, holding up her glass and raising her eyebrows.

Aila rolls her eyes, snapping herself out of it.

"It's nothing, you guys. I promise. I think I'm just tired." She lets out an exaggerated sigh and stretches her arms above her head. "I feel so much older today, I guess. Officially late thirties," she adds sarcastically.

"Hey, now, forty is the new thirty so technically you are still twenty-seven." Chantelle looks at each of them for confirmation, landing on Elena.

"Here, here. Which makes me only thirty."

Aila smiles.

"There you go," Chantelle says. "Now get out of

whatever headspace you're in and enjoy yourself. You've still got a lot of life left to live."

"And you're one year closer to mammograms and colonoscopies. It's a hell of a good time," Elena quips taking another bite of a taco.

Aila makes a face. "Gross."

"What?" Elena says. "It's the most action I've gotten in months."

Aila laughs.

"Wait. Are you being serious?" Chantelle's face falls, reminding Aila Chantelle doesn't know her sarcastic friend as well as she does.

"No, Joe and Elena still act like a couple of wild teenagers, all hopped up on hormones and curiosity." Aila smirks while picking a piece of salt off her glass.

Elena laughs genuinely at this. "You know me well."

"Hey, girls. Cake time!" Aila's mom, Tina, says from the sliding door.

She still refers to Aila and her friends as 'girls.' It would be obnoxious, if it wasn't endearing.

Chantelle nudges Aila playfully on the way inside, "Isn't this what every lady in their late thirties wants? To have 'Happy Birthday' sung to them by candle light?"

Aila rolls her eyes and smiles.

"Hey, I'm only going inside to get another margarita."

On the kitchen island, a triple layer chocolate cake sits aflame, while 'Happy Birthday' rings through the downstairs, the kids being the most enthusiastic contributors.

"Make a wish, Mom!" Isaac says, clapping.

Aila smiles at her boys and then makes a wish that makes her heart beat a little faster.

I wish Jackson were here.

She looks up from making her wish and catches eyes with Ben.

He's looking at her with an intensity and desire that makes Aila want to crawl out of her skin.

Did I say that out loud?

Aila looks back and smiles so quickly it's more of a facial twitch. She swallows hard. She feels like Ben can read her thoughts, like he knows she has someone else on her mind. But how? Did he check her text messages? Did he hear her crying in the bathroom last weekend?

Her mind begins to race and beads of sweat form on the back of her neck before dropping down between her shoulder blades.

Before anybody can notice her panic, she excuses herself to the bathroom and splashes water on her neck, catching her breath and calming her heart. She checks her phone.

Still nothing.

She slides her phone back into her pocket and returns to the kitchen where Ben's mom hands her a slice of cake and Chantelle tops off her margarita.

"These margaritas are delicious, Ben," she says. "I'd love the recipe."

"It's Aila's recipe," he says moving behind her and kissing her shoulder. His touch feels misplaced and it makes Aila inwardly cringe. She smiles instead, taking a large sip from her glass, the tequila making the back of her throat sting.

"Premixed," she says, honestly.

Chantelle eyes her playfully. "I swear you are always putting up a front."

More than you know. Aila smiles.

"Mom, read my card!" Isaac interrupts, shoving a piece of blue construction paper in her face.

The paper is bent in half and she opens it to reveal his latest portrait drawing of their family. He's graduated from potato-shaped people to full-fledged stick figures, all five of them dressed in brightly colored pants and shirts, with Gus standing next to a house in the background. Aila's stick figure is still the only one with eyelashes.

She smiles. "Thank you, buddy," she says. "This is the best one yet."

Isaac beams with pride.

"Yep! One big happy family!" he says before tearing off running into the yard with Emma.

For the rest of the evening, Aila feels out of place in her own home. She sits on the back deck opening an assortment of gifts—gift cards from her parents and Sharon, candles from Chantelle, and bubble bath and a book from Elena—plastering a smile on her face after each one and showing an exaggerated amount of gratitude.

All eyes are on her and she doesn't like it. She feels trapped. Raw. Like her thoughts are on a scroll rolling above her head, on display for everyone to read.

Why does it feel like everyone knows what I'm thinking? What I've been doing? What I've already done.

She continues to brush the thoughts away and smiles politely, until the last guest trickles out the front door.

"Thank you for coming," Aila says, holding the door open while Elena and Joe walk down the front steps.

"Joe, will you go grab the car for us? I'll be just a second," Elena says.

"But I'm the one with the bum knee," he retorts.

"You get a new knee next month, might as well wear this one out. Now go on. I need to tell Aila something."

Aila swallows hard and looks at Elena, her smile frozen on her face.

"Aila, you need to be honest. No more bullshit," Elena says.

She plays confusion across her face but she can hear the sound of blood pumping through her ears as her heart begins to pound.

"You have been quiet all night and constantly checking your phone and giving half-assed head nods instead of actually having a conversation. What's the matter?"

"Nothing." Aila tries to let out a laugh but it comes out as a breathy smile.

"I don't believe you." Elena's eyes narrow on her.

"Well, I promise you. I'm fine," she says as Ben walks

up quietly behind her.

"Fine about what?" he asks, startling Aila.

"Oh, nothing. Church stuff." Aila lies so quickly and easily she forgot she was in front of Elena too.

She shoots her a glance.

Elena is looking at her, studying her, obviously also taking note at how quickly Aila blurted out a lie.

Her eyes dart from Aila to Ben and back again.

"Right," she says reluctantly. "Thank you for the margaritas, Ben. Aila, I'll call you tomorrow."

And she turns on a heel to where Joe has just pulled up with their car.

Closing the door behind them, Aila heads to the dining room to collect her gift bags and stack of cards from the table.

"I think I'm going to go take a bath," Aila says and Ben looks up from the pitcher he's drying with a hand towel.

"Sure. Whatever you want, birthday girl." He flashes her a seductive smile that sends a sharp pain in Aila's stomach.

Instead of wincing, she smiles and heads upstairs to their bedroom. She sets her cards on the nightstand and moves into the bathroom to draw a bath. While lying in the hot water, Aila tries and fails to shut her mind off over and over, until her phone buzzes once on the counter.

Her heart jumps and she lunges out of the bath, dripping water over the white porcelain tile as she reaches for her phone.

Happy birthday, Aila. J

Jackson.

She smiles and lets out a breath she'd been holding in since the night began. He is the one person she wanted to hear from all day. She wishes so badly he could have been there today—present in a way that wasn't just in her head.

Miss you so bad, she texts back.

She watches the three dots come and go, and a moment later his text comes through.

More than you know.

His words bring a smile to her face and a pain in her heart. Her love for him is growing and she knows it. She just needs to decide what will come of it.

CHAPTER 26

NOW

"I didn't realize how hard this week was going to be," Jackson says, a half-smile pulling at the corner of his mouth. He sits next to her on the couch, her legs draped over his as she sips the Americano he brought her while he rubs her feet.

"Me neither," she says, leaning forward stroking his neck with her finger tips. She breathes out a short sigh. "You were all I thought about yesterday."

"Yeah?"

"Yeah. I just kept thinking—dreaming about what'd it be like to spend my birthday with you and my friends…my parents." She smiles at him, the dream lingering in the air between them like a carrot on a stick.

He turns his body toward her, pulling her legs around his waist so they're face to face. "You know we could have that, right?"

Aila opens her mouth and closes it, unsure of what to say.

"Aila, I know you love me. You know I love you. I've loved you for most of our lives and I'm just asking for you to finally give me the opportunity to do that. Properly. The way you should be loved and cared for. All I'm asking is that you let me."

His hazel eyes are pleading and honest. Aila can feel the emotions rise in her throat so she grabs him by his neck and pulls him in, pressing her lips against his, silencing his plea. The kiss is intense and passionate. An insatiable hunger.

Jackson pulls back softly, running a finger down her face and landing on her lips.

"Tell me you want that, too." A request, not a demand.

She pauses, studying the storm in his eyes before getting lost in them again.

"Of course," she whispers and leads him up to the bedroom.

After, Aila falls back on the bed, reeling and breathless. A laugh escapes her throat and Jackson returns it. She leans up to kiss his lips then lingers a second longer after to stare at him. His eyes are familiar and honest and his arms feel like home.

I can't believe this is still happening.

Aila consciously participated in the building of their relationship, but also feels surprised to be sitting in the deep end of it, still wanting more.

"I should get back to work," Jackson says smiling, and Aila emits a quick groan before rolling over to the edge of the bed.

Then she sees it.

A piece of blue construction paper peeking out beneath a stack of generic birthday cards. Her euphoria collapses as she pulls out the picture Isaac had given her just the day before and holds it with shaking fingers. All five of them, holding hands in a sea of hearts and a smiling sunshine.

One big happy family, she hears Isaac's voice echo in her head.

Aila suddenly feels unsteady and nauseous and she runs to the bathroom and vomits in the toilet. She's still retching when she feels Jackson's gentle hands rub against her back.

"Are you okay?" his voice is calm and concerned.

His presence makes her feel embarrassed and ashamed, and she wants to shout at him to just go. Instead she flushes the toilet and walks to the sink to rinse out her mouth, catching a glimpse of herself in the mirror.

Her hair looks tattered and frizzy, her eyes swollen from vomiting and her skin pale from the rush of guilt that washed through her.

"I'm so sorry. I'm fine. I'm just not feeling well, all of a sudden."

"What can I get you? Some toast? Ginger ale?" Jackson's following her every move now like a lost puppy and it is making Aila feel trapped and irritated.

"No!" she shouts, unintentionally. She takes a deep breath, calming down. "Sorry. No. I'm so embarrassed. I'll be fine. I think I'll just lie down after you leave."

Aila can see Jackson swallow hard, nodding in understanding.

"You sure? I can stay a bit longer. Make sure you're okay."

He's trying so hard to please Aila. She finds it endearing and also humiliating. She smiles sweetly in an attempt to convince him to leave.

"I'm fine. Promise."

At the front door, Jackson turns around before opening it, his brow furrows briefly before he looks at her in concern.

"Are you—could you be pregnant?"

The color washes from her face.

"No. No, of course not. It's not possible."

The mere thought sends her mind in a tailspin.

"You sure?"

"I'm sure." She forces a smile. "Now, get back to work. I'll call you later."

He smiles slowly until his dimples are on full display and he leans in to kiss her.

"Bye, Aila," he says, unable to wipe the smile from his face.

She closes the door behind him, fully aware his smile stemmed from the very thought that is making her nauseous. And it terrifies her.

A love child.

A manifested sin.

A scarlet letter.

Tears sting her eyes as she runs to the bathroom to vomit again.

CHAPTER 27

THEN

"Mom, Dad cooked tonight!" Caleb said as Aila made her way through the front door, slipping her shoes off in the entryway while being greeted with a barricade of hugs.

"He did? What'd he make?" Aila asked.

"Pizza!" Isaac said, pulling his mom's hand down the entryway to the kitchen.

"Oh wow! What recipe did he use?" she asked playfully, her eyes meeting Ben's, who was wiping down the counters in the kitchen.

"Domino's," Ben said, raising his eyebrows at her and smiling.

Aila laughed.

It wasn't that Ben couldn't cook; he just never really had to anymore. So, on a night like this one, when Aila had to be at the church for a women's conference, he went straight for the takeout menu and the boys always loved it.

"You'll have to tell me your secrets, master chef," Aila said while making her way over to him. She offered him a soft kiss on his cheek and lingered under his arm for a moment before sitting down. "How were the boys tonight?"

"Great," Ben said, shrugging. "We watched a movie and ate pizza and they just got down from taking showers and putting on PJ's. I told them they could stay up 'til you got here."

"Lucky boys," she said, eyeing the clean kitchen and picked up living room.

"Now that Mom's home, you boys need to head upstairs and brush your teeth. I'll be up to tuck you in in a minute."

The boys followed commands, stumbling up the stairs as they went.

"How was your conference?" Ben turned his attention to Aila.

She swiveled the barstool she was sitting in back to him. "Oh, it was so good. The speakers were phenomenal. Their preaching was inspiring without being too...you know... 'inspirational,'" she said, giving air quotes on the last word, making Ben laugh.

He tossed the dirty rag in the sink and took a seat next to Aila. He leaned his elbows on his knees and held her hands in his.

"Good. I'm glad you went. But we missed you."

"I'm sure." She laughed.

Ben cleared his throat slightly and rubbed his lips together. Under the pendant lights, the edges of his face were sharp and seductive, his gentle smile like water breaking through chiseled rock. Between that and the clean kitchen, Aila found her husband irresistible.

She leaned in to kiss Ben, but they were quickly interrupted by stomping feet landing in the kitchen.

"Dad! Can we get a story tonight?" Caleb asked.

Aila turned her eyes from Caleb to Ben then back to Caleb. "Can I tell you guys a story tonight?"

"Maybe next time, Mom. We want Dad tonight. He tells the best stories," Caleb said, trying to reassure his mother, making her heart smile.

"Well, Dad," she turned to Ben. "Can the boys get a

story tonight?"

He looked at her, giving her a smile and a kiss on her forehead before heading upstairs to meet the boys' demands.

It was true though. He told the best stories. He'd lie in Josh's bed with all three boys piled in; they'd give him a main character and he'd turn it into something great. The stories were adventurous and outrageous and always, always funny.

Aila would stand outside the doorway listening, muffling her laughter with her hand.

She didn't understand how Ben did it. He was always all business or all romance or all stress. But for the boys, he could turn it on and be all imagination. The boys squealed with laughter until they finally settled and drifted off to sleep. Ben transported each boy to their appropriate bed, one by one.

By the time Ben made it back to their room, Aila was sitting in bed reading while wearing one of Ben's over-sized t-shirts.

"Everyone tucked in now?" she asked.

"Yep," he said, leaping on the bed and face planting on his pillow, making her bounce slightly. She smiled at his childish plop on the bed next to her.

"Thank you for taking care of everything tonight," she said, running her hand over his head and under his shirt to his bare back.

"Of course," he said. "I'm glad you were able to go the conference."

"Me too."

"Any big takeaways this year?"

Aila paused in her reading, closing her book on her lap.

"I guess you could say the theme of the whole thing was about choosing joy," she said, looking down at Ben as he turned on his back to face her. "That joy is something we feel deep down, not based on our circumstances. And if we actively choose to feel and experience the joy God has given us through whatever gets hurled at us, then our lives will be full and satisfying."

"I like that," he said, stretching his hands behind his head.

Aila set her book on the nightstand and nuzzled into the crook of his arm.

"Me too," she said, running a finger from his chest to his belly button.

"I like you too," he said, cracking another smile.

Aila laughed.

"I like you too, but only on one condition," she said.

"What's that?"

"Tell me a story," she said and he laughed and leaned over to kiss her. "It better be something great."

"Okay. Once upon a time, I met the most beautiful girl in the world…" he began, recounting the chilly autumn night they met in college.

But the rest didn't matter to Aila. The sound of his voice, the way his chest moved up and down with each breath, and the cadence of his speech comforted her to her core and brought her immense joy, until she drifted off to sleep.

CHAPTER 28

NOW

Aila makes her way to the top of Skyline hill, her running pace slower than it has been in months. She's exhausted. Emotionally. Spiritually. Physically.

It's a clear, sunny day in May but the air hangs heavy with the promise of a rainstorm. Much like Jackson over her marriage.

It's been over a week since she vomited in front of Jackson. They texted back and forth throughout the week with no concrete plans to talk or see each other again. Aila knows she is being standoffish in her attempts to avoid a conversation she doesn't want to have.

The reality is his reaction to the idea of her being pregnant frightens her. There is so much about Jackson she wants—his heart, his mind. But his child?

She doesn't want to give him a child.

The look on his face that day told her how much he wants that from her. He wants a baby of his own and he wants her to be its mother.

Does he love her kids? She thinks so.

Was he good with them? Incredibly.

Does he still want one of his own? Absolutely.

Aila isn't a fool. She had started seeing the cracks between her and Jackson, ones she isn't willing to fill. *Couldn't* fill. It had just never come up in their endless, almost daily, conversations.

When she was thirty-four weeks pregnant with Isaac, they realized he was breech. Dr. Chu was convinced he'd flip on his own like the other two pregnancies but he never did.

At thirty-eight weeks, her doctor attempted a painful and lengthy inversion procedure at the hospital where Dr. Chu and two nurses attempted to flip him by pushing and twisting her stomach from the outside.

It didn't work.

She was scheduled to have a cesarean section the next week and opted to get her tubes tied during the surgery. She and Ben agreed their family was complete and this way, Ben didn't have to get his procedure.

If Jackson wants a baby, she can't give him one. But deep down, she doesn't want to either. The look on Jackson's face when he thought maybe she was pregnant made Aila's heart hesitate. She began questioning and doubting the parts of their relationship that gave her hope for their future.

Now she just feels like she is stuck in the deep end, waiting for someone to throw her a life preserver.

When she finally reaches the top of Skyline hill, she is breathless.

She stands for a moment or two catching her breath and looking out at the very same salt water sea Jackson wakes up to each day, now with a distinct dark cloud looming over it and it is growing closer by the second.

She thinks about letting it come and consume her. Letting it pour down and wash her clean like a baptism by nature.

A roar of thunder echoes in the distance and Gus lets out a whine. The black cloud is growing darker and angrier and closer, devouring the blue sky she stands beneath.

"Let's hustle, Gus," she says, breaking away from her thoughts and then taking off in a sprint down the hill.

Once she hits the corner of Cherrywood Lane, the storm catches up to her, unleashing buckets of water and wind while Aila and Gus trudge through half-blinded by the rain to the house.

Suddenly, a shadow of gray metal pulls up next to them and Aila hears a familiar voice yell, "Want a ride?"

Jackson.

Is this her rescue? Aila nearly laughs at the irony of her thoughts to the reality of Jackson swooping in to shield her from the storm.

Without thinking or hesitating, Aila jumps in his truck with Gus, both soggy and wet from the downpour that came upon them more quickly than anticipated.

"Thank you," she says, shaking out her long brown ponytail. "That rain came out of nowhere."

Gus sits up on the console and shakes wildly.

Jackson laughs.

"Oh, I'm so sorry," Aila apologizes and pulls Gus down to the floor. "Gosh, we are soaked."

She lets out a laugh. It is relaxed and melodic and makes Jackson smile at her, his eyes slowly watching her with desire and adoration.

When he pulls up to the house, he hesitates before getting out, waiting for an invitation Aila assumes he would know he already has.

"Are you coming in?" she asks.

"Do you want me to come in?" His smile is soft and Aila sees a glimpse of a dimple that makes her smile back.

"I always want you to come in."

Inside, Aila towels off Gus and turns on the fire. He lays in his bed, soaking up the heat from the flames.

"Thanks for the rescue, Jackson," she says, pulling off her soaked sweatshirt.

"It was just good timing." He smiles. The very sight of him brings back a flood of emotions.

The way his right dimple shows more when he's genuinely happy or the way his eyes crinkle when he smiles at her. The way his stare cuts through the tension of unsaid words and the way his presence begs Aila to come closer. The smell of his skin is intoxicating and the touch of his hand sends electricity through her spine.

Aila loves Jackson.

Their parallel worlds somehow found each other and now she knows she will feel absolutely wrecked if she doesn't pursue his world further.

"I'm really glad you're here." She sits down on the couch next to him, letting out a laugh and a sigh.

"Are you?" His question is innocent, almost playful.

"I am. I've really missed you." Aila means what she's saying and now she's questioning why she had been so distant the last couple of weeks. What is she so afraid of? It's just Jackson.

My Jackson.

He licks his lips and presses them together nodding. He turns to her then.

"How have you been feeling?" he asks, referring to her episode the last time they were together. The reminder gives Aila a flash of embarrassment.

"Fine," Aila says, twisting her lips slightly. "Jackson, you know I can't get pregnant, right?"

His eyes show a flash of shock then disappointment but he masks it with questions. Why? When? How? And Aila answers him honestly.

"I never brought it up because it's not even a thing for me. That part of my life is already done," she says. "I didn't realize that was something you still wanted."

He nods, absorbing the information he was just given.

"I mean, I already have three kids," she adds.

"It's not about that, Aila." He turns to her, brushing a wet strand of hair away from her face. "It was never about that."

"I know, but you told me your marriage didn't work out because you wanted kids and she didn't so I just started assuming..." she trails off.

"No, I get it. But that wasn't the only reason my marriage failed. And honestly it doesn't even matter now, because it's you, Aila. It's always been you."

She falls into his arms and rests her head on his chest, listening to his words, running her fingers up and down his arm. A silence falls between them but it doesn't bother Aila until she feels Jackson's heart begin to beat faster.

"Seriously, Aila. What exactly are you doing with me?"

Aila doesn't like his phrasing. She sits up to face him and clears her throat.

"What exactly are *you* doing with me?"

"Aila," he says, simply. Knowingly.

Aila grabs onto her hair, pinching it softly while she searches for the right answer. Jackson grabs her hand, forcing her to stop and look at him.

"I don't really know," she says finally.

Jackson looks down. Hurt.

"I didn't plan for this to happen, Jackson. I've never done anything like this before. It's just kind of happening and I'm trying to figure it all out as it comes, I—"

"I didn't plan for this either, Aila. But when I saw you back in February…" he shakes his head trying to find the words. "When you turned the corner, you looked like an angel. Like God sent you back to me right when I needed you the most. Ever since we were kids, you were all I wanted. And I tried to move on, and I stayed married to Kim for years but there was something always missing with her. She knew it too, which is why she left."

He grabs Aila's hand and brings it to his mouth, kissing it gently.

"I have compared everyone to you ever since we were kids. No one ever held a candle to you. The truth is, it was you. You were what was missing. You never left my mind, not for the last twenty years, not once. And now that I found my way back to you, I don't want to let you go."

Aila feels like a weight is sitting on her chest. She is

unable to take a deep breath, completely caught off guard by Jackson's confession. She doesn't understand. How could someone stay in love with someone like he claims, even after years and years of not seeing each other, not even speaking? His words ring truth in her ears but a part of her is worried he's in love with the idea of her—not what they'd become after fifteen years together. People rarely change who they are, but time always changes *how* they are.

"Jackson, I—" Aila searches for words. "When I ran into you a few months ago, I had no idea the feelings that would surface as time went on. I thought it was nothing at first. You know, just two old friends reconnecting. But I guess I just really enjoy how much you see me. Know me. When I'm with you—even when you're with me and the kids—it's like you let your world revolve around us. Around me. I haven't felt that for a long time."

He nods at this and brushes a loose strand of hair behind her ear, running his fingers to her shoulder and all the way down to her hand.

"When are you going to tell Ben?"

Aila feels struck by that.

"I, I'm—I wasn't. I mean, I haven't thought about that."

Jackson's nostrils flare and he takes in a deep breath, nodding in frustration.

"This isn't a game for me, Aila. I don't do the sneaking around stuff. Either you're all in or you're not."

Aila feels a rise of anger.

"I'm sorry, Jackson, but you are doing the sneaking around stuff. That's what this is. And I'll admit it's messy and I have no idea what I'm doing but I'm not ready to tell Ben."

"But you've said you're unhappy. That he's never around." His eyes are piercing now, like lasers of truth she can't dodge. "You text me all the time. You invite me to play with your kids and to sit around for family meals when your husband isn't around. You made love to me in the very same bed he sleeps in."

Aila flinches as if his words slapped her. His last comment physically stings.

"This isn't some little break up, Jackson. If I leave Ben, it'd be a messy divorce. A custody battle. I don't know if I'm ready for that or if I even want that." Her voice is unsteady, teetering toward bursting into tears.

"I've been divorced too, Aila," he says, holding her face gently in his hands. "It was the best thing I ever did. We weren't right for each other. Once we admitted that to each other, our lives were able to move on and that decision led me to you."

Aila cups his warm hands with her own and gazes anxiously in his eyes.

"But I have my kids, Jackson. It's different."

His hands drop and he droops his head below his shoulders.

"I don't know what else I need to do to prove to you I care about your boys. I would step up to the plate and be their stepdad if you'd let me. I promise you that."

Aila's eyes well with tears.

The love this man has had for her since she was a young girl is overwhelming. And the love he already has for her boys makes her heart ache. She desperately wants to do the right thing. It isn't fair to Ben to sneak around like this. But she isn't ready to blow up their life just yet, even if the bomb has already been planted, waiting to detonate.

"Jackson." Aila grabs his face in her hands and turns him toward her. "I just need time. Please. Be fair to me."

His jaw clenches slightly and he blinks back something that looks like tears tugging at the corners of his eyes.

She kisses him and presses her forehead against his.

"Please."

"I need you to be fair to me, too," he says. "I can't...I won't stay stuck in your shadows, Aila."

Aila blinks, sending a stream of tears down to her chin. "I'm just trying to do what's best for my family."

My family.

The words tumble out of her mouth before she can stop them. Before she can package them in a way that doesn't make Jackson feel like the runner-up in her life.

Jackson doesn't say a word. He wipes the stream of tears on her cheeks with his thumb. He sighs and then gently presses his mouth to hers softly but passionately. He lays her down on the sofa while the flames crackle next to them.

It's gentler this time. Jackson moves slowly over her body, savoring it. Remembering it. Aila can tell this time it feels a lot more like goodbye.

CHAPTER 29

THEN

"Promise me something, Aila May," Ben said from behind the helm.

Aila could feel his eyes on her, admiring her.

The boat was teetering in the middle of the Sound while the sun came crashing down on a hot summer day. Pillars of light shone through the Narrows Bridge and landed on the rocks of Titlow Beach, making the water glisten in shades of gold, orange, and pastels.

She turned from the bow, where she sat peacefully with Isaac asleep in her lap while the other two boys sat across from her playing I-Spy. It was the Labor Day weekend before all three boys would be in school full-time, so she was soaking up their last few days together as a family before the hustle of a new school year stepped in.

"What's that, Benjamin Lee?" she asked, catching her loose hair running wild in the breeze and pulling it away from her face.

"That you'll only ever love sunsets more than me."

Ben flashed a breathtaking smile at her, sending a wave of warmth from her head to her toes.

"Promise." She smiled wide at him.

"Me and you forever, Aila. No matter what." He winked at her playfully.

She laughed softly before gazing back at the sunset, watching it fall deeper into the Earth, turning the sky darker shades of ember and fuchsia. The sky was on fire, smoldering until the sun dipped below the surface completely.

Me and you. Forever.

That evening her heart felt content. Happy. *No,* she thought. *This is joy.*

CHAPTER 30

NOW

After Bible study on Wednesday, Elena had asked Aila to meet at her place the next day.

"Let's walk around the lake," she'd said. "We haven't had a good walking chat in a while."

Aila agreed with some trepidation. Especially since Elena was fishing for secrets at her birthday dinner a few weeks prior.

Elena is her no-nonsense, cut-to-the-chase friend. She takes no prisoners and she doesn't tolerate half-ass answers. But she also speaks life into her unlike anyone she'd ever known.

And lately, Aila feels like the life has been sucked out of her. Sure, she still knows how to smile pretty and dot all her i's and cross all her t's, but at her core, she is worn down, her gears just barely turning.

Everything's going to be okay. Everything will sort itself out.

Of course, she barely believes what she's thinking. She feels on edge, caught up, and unsure of how to move forward.

Spring is finally in full bloom and the sun feels warm on Aila's face as she pulls into Elena's drive way, perched just across the street from the lake trail. The sun makes the lake sparkle so bright it looks like it's on fire—completely up in flames.

Much like her life. There are not enough prayers she can say to make everything right in the world again. But Aila knows it is time to start trying.

Elena is on the porch waiting for her and watering her freshly planted petunias.

"Look at your beautiful flowers!" Aila says, giving her a brief hug.

"Well, it's a start." Elena sets down the watering can and leans in a bit closer. "Now if only the damn neighbor cat will quit shitting in my flower beds."

Aila laughs, reminded of how good it is to be in the presence of her friend. She hasn't laughed in days.

"Shall we?" Elena throws out her elbow for Aila to grab onto like a couple of middle school girls as they begin their trek around the lake.

Aila loves their walking talks. They feel safer somehow. Probably because she never has to make eye contact. Aila tells Elena about the boys and how much Caleb is taking off with baseball and Josh had just earned his green belt in karate.

Then Elena tells her about how Gretchen is mad about the study they chose for next session and took it to Pastor Adam, and how her husband's knee surgery is getting pushed back to this summer.

"Which means I have a few more months of him hobbling around while he cooks me dinner and he has to wait a little longer to be waited on hand and foot. Which he can't wait for by the way." She laughs. "He wants a bell after surgery. A bell?! I told him to dream on."

"Hey, at least he cooks for you. I don't know the last time Ben cooked a single meal," Aila says, quickly realizing it was an unnecessary dig at her husband.

"But he orders some mean tacos," Elena adds playfully, defending Ben.

Aila chuckles but it's forced and shaky.

She shouldn't have said that. Why did she bring up Ben? She doesn't want to talk about Ben.

She grows quiet next to Elena, who is surely observing her change in mood. She could always see when Aila was lost in her own head. She saw it at the party and she's seeing it now.

"Aila." Elena swoops her head down, tilting it so she can see her eyes. Aila knows what she's doing. Elena knows something is up—the war inside Aila is written all over her forehead.

Aila looks square into Elena's eyes and smiles in an attempt to mask the violent struggle inside her mind.

"What's going on? You have been acting strange for weeks. You're distant and quiet, and there is something going on in that pretty little head of yours, so why don't you just spill it before I call Ben and ask him?"

"No!" she says a bit too aggressively, then immediately quiets herself down. "I mean, no, don't do that. He's got enough going on at work. He doesn't need to add anything else on his plate. To be honest, he's just not around much these days. He's at the office *a lot* and when he is home, he barricades himself in the office with more work. It's just been a lot of years of late nights and it gets lonely. I just feel like I want something for me for a change."

"Have you told him this is bothering you?"

Aila looks at her feet.

"No, it's just a season. Honestly, it'll pass."

Fake, fake, fake.

Ben hates the term, "it's just a season." Aila can feel Elena's eyes burning through her, seeing there is far more than she is letting on.

"Aila, darling." Elena stops abruptly, grabbing Aila by the shoulders turning her toward her, gently but firmly. "Cut the shit."

Aila's eyes waver as she tries and fails to maintain her composure, bursting into tears. Uncontrollable, ugly, shaking sobs. Her legs go slack and she crumbles to the pavement, head in her hands. Elena sits down next to her, holding her like an inconsolable child, not saying a word. Just waiting.

After several minutes, Aila sobs subside and her beautiful face rises, blotchy and swollen.

Elena wipes the mascara from under Aila's eyes with her thumb.

"Ben and I have been having major issues for a while now. It's getting harder every day. I can't take it anymore."

"Like what? Tell me what happened."

Not a question but a statement. Like a parent asking a child what happened at school today, knowing full well they had already discussed it with the principal.

Aila tells Elena about the arguments regarding the amount of time Ben spends working, the disagreements about responsibilities at home, the stresses of being a parent and finding time for each other, and special occasions forgotten. The culmination of each tic mark has made Aila feel like she's in the middle of a broken marriage.

Elena's eyes narrow gently.

"Aila, I don't mean to minimize your feelings about any of what you just told me, but that doesn't sound like *major* issues. That sounds like marriage. Nothing too catastrophic it can't be sorted out."

Aila lets out an exasperated breath. Exhausted from keeping her secret.

"I've also slept with someone else."

She says it plainly, no more, no less.

Elena's eyes go wide, this is clearly not what she was expecting to hear.

"I'm going to need more information than that, honey."

Aila gives her the brief synopsis of running into Jackson and how it turned into a friendship and how she hasn't felt this way in a long time and how "it just happened." She hates that phrase. Because deep down she knows it's untrue and irresponsible to say.

Affairs don't just happen. People don't just wake up one day and cheat. Affairs blossom after a million little choices in the wrong direction. One has to actively participate in the cultivation of each choice until suddenly they've crossed the line.

Aila had crossed the line months ago.

She lets out a breath. "I've made such a mess of things."

"Do you love Jackson?" Elena asks. Her expression is one of genuine concern, not judgment.

"Yes." And she does. In an unexpected, uncontrollable way.

"But do you love him enough to hurt a bunch of people who don't deserve it? Because that's what's going to happen here, Aila. It's not just between you and Ben."

That is when she knew. Her biggest fears are true. The repercussions of her actions won't just hurt Ben. It will hurt her kids. Her friends. Her family.

None of this is right. None of this is fair.

She fell for Jackson when she least expected it. Her feelings and desires met perfectly with the opportunity to pursue him. She loves him but wonders if she's more in love with the escape he's given her. Would they even be able to nurture and cultivate their love for years to come or will it get wedged in the same rut she and Ben are in? Is Jackson actually worth the destruction of her life as she knows it? And who will even be standing in the dust after it settles?

The questions flood her mind until they're back at Elena's house, after finishing the trail around the lake in silence.

"I love you," Elena says, as she grabs Aila's hand and gives it a heartfelt squeeze. "Even though I don't agree with a choice you've made. You know that, right?"

Aila purses her lips and gives her a quick nod before dipping into her SUV. She waits until Elena is safely inside her front door before she pulls out of the drive and lets her eyes well with tears.

She only lets a few teardrops fall before driving off, but soon her chin is quivering again and tears stream down her face like a flooded river. By the time she is around the corner from her house, her eyes are so wet with tears she can barely see the road so she pulls over.

They are silent tears that rush down her face and land on her chest as she stares blankly through the windshield.

What am I going to do? What have I done?

She feels so heavy—her feet like cinder blocks as she stands in the midst of rising waters.

"Yoo hoo!" There is a drummer's knock on the driver's window.

"Oh shit," Aila places her hand on her chest, startled and then rolls down the window while wiping her wet cheeks frantically. "Janet. Hi. You scared me."

"Sorry about that! I keep doing that to ya. Say, I was just wondering what you were doing all alo—" Janet's comment cuts short when she notices Aila's shiny cheeks and blotchy neck. "Are you okay?"

"I'm fine, thank you. Just a little stressed about the boys' schedules lately." She recovers a bit and masks the emotions, something she still does best. "You know…busy, busy. It's silly, honestly."

"Oh, I am just so sorry." Janet reaches for her arm but Aila shifts in her seat to let her know this is not up for discussion. "Well, I do have a really nice essential oil blend I made last night. It's a calming blend. I really think it'd help."

Her eyebrows shoot up to her hairline and her smile is so big and excited, a genius solution to Aila's catastrophic problems, obviously.

"Or better yet! Join me for yoga tomorrow morning!"

Typical Janet. If only Aila's problems could be solved by dousing them in essential oils.

"Thank you." Aila smiles tiredly. "I'll let you know. Take care."

She rolls up the window without a proper goodbye before driving off.

For fuck's sake. I've got to figure out my life.

CHAPTER 31

NOW

Aila collapses on the couch when she walks through her front door. Gus loyally trots over to her and places his head on her lap, his eyes staring up at her. Even Gus knows she's done a terrible thing.

Aila's mind spins now that Elena knows her secret. She's partly furious with herself, partly relieved.

She didn't realize how her affair with Jackson was really an ominous weight she carried around everywhere. Like a kettle bell she dragged from place to place.

The more she carried it, the heavier it got, until finally she wore herself into the ground.

God, please tell me what to do. How do I fix this? It is a Hail Mary. A prayer she knows God will not answer the way she wants him to no matter how desperately she pleads with him. *I just want this to go away.*

But it can't.

Not when real people and feelings are involved. It isn't something she can hide or sweep under the rug. It isn't a fight she and Ben had in passing that is made right with a bouquet of orchids and making love after the kids fall asleep.

This was a terrible, terrible thing.

240

And she knows it is time to tell Ben.

~

Aila drives to the bus stop that afternoon to avoid having small talk with the other moms, especially Janet.

It doesn't work though. Janet marches over to her SUV with a little gift bag full of pink lavender scented tissue paper and taps on her window.

Rolling down the window, Aila says, "Sorry about earlier, Janet, I'm just really not feeling well today."

Janet holds up her perfectly manicured hand.

"Say no more. Just that oil blend I told you about." She plops the bag delicately in Aila's lap. "Look, Aila, I know life is hectic and busy right now but I want you to know I'm here for you if you need anything. Whatever it may be. Everything happens for a reason."

She smiles her toothy smile.

Aila frowns.

"Thank you."

Aila rolls up the window, annoyed. She has no idea. She doesn't need Janet's daily quote from Pinterest. She needs a time machine. A new identity. A deep, dark hole she can crawl into until she disappears.

Everything happens for a reason, Aila mocks her in her head. *Well, sometimes you're the reason your life is falling apart and not even God will save you.*

She feels tears sting her eyes but she blinks them away.

Not now. Not in front of the boys.

The rest of the evening plays out bizarrely normal. The boys ride bikes outside while Aila draws chalk with the two neighbor girls across the street. Then, Josh runs inside and comes out with a laundry basket of Nerf guns and Aila finds herself in an all-out war.

How easy it is to forget your problems when you're playing with children.

241

Maybe it will be okay. Maybe not at first. Everyone will be upset but maybe it did happen for a reason and I'm just not meant to be married to Ben anymore. I could be happy without him, couldn't I?

Aila's mind quickly gets lost in a sea of maybes and what ifs when the sound of Isaac's voice snaps her attention back to reality.

"Dad's home!" Isaac yells yanking Aila out of her thoughts. He's early. Unusually.

Shit.

~

Aila hardly touches her dinner. She keeps the kids talking about nonsense for the entire thirty minutes, avoiding eye contact with Ben and pushing food around her plate.

"Are you going to eat any of that?" Ben, says with a smirk.

Aila offers a shaky smile.

"I am," she says taking a bite. The food has no taste in her mouth and Aila feels like she swallowed sand. Her heart races and her hands begin to shake so she gets up and busies herself with dishes in the kitchen.

After dinner, Aila is getting ready to take the boys to swim, and Ben tells her he needs to stay back to tie up some loose ends at work. There are always loose ends. Work is rarely tied up for Ben.

This is how I got myself into this.

"Oh, okay," Aila says instead, though she's partly relieved he isn't coming.

The thirty minutes alone while the boys are in the water will allow her to rehearse her delivery. She scoffs at herself. This isn't a speech. This isn't a pitch. This is her marriage and her life.

Aila knows the gravity of her words. She wonders if there is even a way to construct her confession that doesn't make her look like the villain.

She wants to tell Ben—get it over with. Like ripping

off a Band-Aid. But she is so apprehensive about the pain she knows will follow. How will they find a way to move forward and be good parents? Will he get a place in the city and she stay at the house with the boys? Will she need to move closer to her parents and leave the house to Ben?

Or will he forgive her? Will he understand how alone he'd left her while he was climbing the corporate ladder as a successful attorney? This wasn't only her fault. Was it?

Not a chance.

Aila and Ben had fought over the years about his work—he should know how underappreciated and worn out she feels and has felt on a regular basis. Still, she can't grasp how he could possibly forgive her and is positive this will be the end of them.

Nothing lasts forever, right?

By the end of the lesson, Aila feels confident in how she is going to tell Ben. Terrible, but confident.

Her mind has constructed a plan for recovery just as it always does—a backup plan, a rescue mission. There is always a plan, even though she had veered the ship off course.

"Great job, boys," she says as her shivering boys escape from the pool area to her waiting towels. "You swam hard."

They mutter thank you and then Caleb says, "Can we stay up late tonight?"

Aila thinks she smiles but it really comes across as more of a twitch.

"Nice try, straight to bed after showers. There's still school tomorrow."

And I have to figure out how to tell Dad I destroyed our marriage.

CHAPTER 32

NOW

After the boys are safely nestled in their beds, Aila makes her way to the kitchen where a single pendant light burns over the sink giving the room a warm glow. She feels tense, each nerve in her body pinging off the energy floating in the room.

"Aila, I need to talk to you."

Aila turns slowly from the pantry to where Ben sits at the kitchen island. She puts the granola bars in her shaking hand in the kids' lunchboxes, before zipping them up and placing them in the fridge.

"Okay, let's talk." She swallows hard.

"I ran into Janet at the mailboxes tonight while you were at swim with the boys."

Aila nods, confused, her nerves buzzing like a loose wire.

She told him she saw me crying, I bet. Dammit, I wish I wasn't so rude to her at the bus stop.

"It was funny," Ben runs his fingers across his jaw and clears his throat. "She asked if I had gotten a new car."

Aila's heart pounds.

"A truck actually. A dark gray truck."

She can barely hear his words over the rush of blood pumping through her ears.

"So, I, uh, of course said no and she said she was curious because she'd been seeing a gray truck at the house quite often." He pauses, studying Aila like a witness on the stand. "Usually during the day, you know, when I'm working. She asked if I knew who drove that truck and at first, I said no, and that I'd ask you about it. But then after she walked away, I remembered."

That nosy bitch. How could she know?

Aila swallows hard. It feels like cotton balls line her mouth, making her throat burn. Ben is looking at her, waiting for an explanation. She can feel her neck break out in hives.

"Aila," Ben says, as if he's talking to a child. "Want to tell me whose truck that is?"

He's giving her an out.

No, she thinks. *Not an out.* An opportunity to lie, so he can catch her.

It's now or never.

She closes her eyes and shakes her head, her hands clasped at her mouth, squeezing them tightly to keep them from shaking.

This is where everything changes.

She opens her red-rimmed eyes and meets his.

"I've done something terrible."

Ben leans over the counter so they are face to face. His expression washed with worry, his eyes hopefully searching her face for a clue, begging it not to be true. She squeezes her hands tighter until her knuckles turn white.

Aila clears her throat so she doesn't burst into tears.

"I've slept with someone else."

The silence between them becomes deafening. Only the hum of the refrigerator can be heard.

"I'm sorry, what?" he says finally—the shock washes the color from his face. He's stunned. Aila knows it had crossed his mind but he's too hopeful, too trusting to believe it could be true. "You can't be serious."

Aila doesn't say anything for a few moments, and Ben raises his body and slowly maneuvers himself in the armchair in the living room.

"I'm afraid I am." Aila bites her lip so hard she tastes blood. Tears well up in her eyes. "I made a horrible, horrible mistake."

"I really thought it was just Janet being Janet. Nosy and paranoid and trying to stir up neighborhood gossip. But this...Aila?"

Ben's face crumbles. Pure devastation washes over his face and he begins to cry. The sound he makes doesn't feel right in Aila's ears. Ben doesn't cry. He isn't supposed to cry.

There is something about seeing him cry she doesn't expect. It seems out of place. Like he'd been carrying the weight of the world on his shoulders and today it crushed him. Broke him.

I broke him.

Through fits of sobs, Aila makes her way over to him and kneels at his feet, clasping his hands in hers.

"Ben, I'm sorry—" She hardly gets the words out, choking over them sporadically like there's a hitch in her throat she can't control. "I'm so, so sorry."

"How could you do this to me? To *us*?" Ben yells. "Have you lost your damn mind?"

Ben pulls his hands from her so vehemently, Aila feels like she's been slapped.

"I-I-I don't know what to say, it ju—"

"It just happened? Things like that don't *just* happen, Aila. You know that. We know that. We've always said that."

That was true. They always said that.

Ben gets up and paces across the room, his hands on his head as if he's trying to push the information out of his head.

"It was Jackson, wasn't it? That's his gray truck, isn't it?"

Of course, he knows who. He knows his truck. And he knows Aila even when she doesn't know herself. Even though she pretended like he didn't. Aila buries her face in her hands nodding through her tears and remorse.

"Yes, it was Jackson."

"Great." He's nodding. "Right in front of my face. Like a fool. How many times did it happen?"

"I mean, Ben, please…does it matter? Do you really want to know?" Her face is awash with tears and snot and shame.

"Do I want to know how many times you consciously chose to cheat on me….and our boys? Yeah, I want to know."

"It happened but it's over. I promise you, I'll end it." Aila wants to reassure him, to rectify the situation somehow—as if ending something that should have never happened will make it hurt less. She suddenly realizes she doesn't want to lose Ben. *Can't* lose Ben.

He scoffs at this, shaking his head.

"So, you haven't even ended it yet? How many times?"

"I don't know…" Aila's voice trails off as she searches her memory for a number. Her face is wet and swollen with misery and regret.

"Great," Ben says, nodding. "That many times. For how long? When did it start?"

"It doesn't matter, Ben."

Aila didn't expect this. Ben wants details.

"Actually, it does matter, Aila," Ben retorts, shaking with anger. "I may not be the perfect husband and maybe we've had our issues but I damn sure didn't sleep with anyone else. How could you?"

"I just…I don't know! You were working all the time and I was always doing everything at home. I just… I started feeling lonely and then Jackson was always around. And it's no excuse. I promise you. I'm not going to make excuses. But I want to apologize. Sorry doesn't cut it and I know that. But I love you and I'm so terribly sorry. I just can't live with this hanging over me…us. I love you."

Aila is pleading now, suddenly desperate to not lose him.

"That's not love, Aila. That's guilt," he says. "If you loved me you would've never—"

Ben stops and stays silent. His face a mix between anger and devastation.

"I need to go. I need to get out of here," he says.

"Ben, please don't leave. Let's talk about this..." She reaches for his hand but he pulls away and is out the door.

That's the thing about coming clean. It's not as easy and refreshing as it sounds. Coming clean isn't a quick wash of the hands with soap and warm water. It's more of a scrub with a fine-tooth brush, scratching the surface until it's raw, making sure every spec of dirt and infidelity is removed. Then comes the polish. And even that takes a lot more effort and work than expected.

Coming clean is where the work begins.

CHAPTER 33

NOW

"He's gone. I told him and he's gone."

Those are the only words Aila can muster when she calls Elena, minutes after Ben stormed out of the house. Fifteen minutes later, Elena is on her doorstep dressed in plaid button-up pajamas and a bottle of wine in each hand.

"This is probably the last thing you need, but..." her voice trails off as she places each bottle on the counter. She's busying herself opening both bottles and getting glasses down from the cupboard. She's avoiding making eye contact with her and Aila knows it's because she doesn't know exactly what to say.

"Red or white?"

Aila stares at the bottles blankly; neither sound good.

"Doesn't matter," she says, turning to the living room and curling herself on the couch.

Elena comes over with a glass of red wine. Aila feels repulsed by it, like it's a goblet of blood from the sacrifice she made. She laid her marriage on the alter and gutted it, watching the blood seep out until it lay lifeless.

"Can I pray for you, Aila?"

Aila wants to laugh.

"God could not care less about my problems right now."

Elena nods slowly and reaches out a hand to touch Aila's arm. "I bet it feels that way. But you and I know as good as anybody the power of prayer and the love God has for you even when you screw every good and sacred thing up."

"Does he?"

Aila has never doubted God. She knows her belief is buried somewhere inside her but she feels so far away, so removed from God that his ability to care about her self-destructive problems seems impossible.

Elena prays anyway. Aila tries to close her eyes to focus but she ends up staring at her feet in a trance, waiting for the prayer to be over.

Aila takes a sip of the wine, hoping it will numb her emotions. It doesn't. She hasn't eaten all day so the wine just sloshes around in her stomach, making her nauseous and dizzy.

"I don't think we'll make it," Aila says, staring into her glass. "Maybe it's for the best. Maybe it's time to start over with a different life."

Elena's eyes narrow. "Is that what you want? Do you even believe that is what's best?"

Aila thinks of Ben and her boys and closes her eyes hard, pressing her eyelids down hoping when she opens them the last few months will be erased.

"This is too hard. What I've done is too terrible."

"You're right. What you did was terrible. It was real shitty. But you know what else is hard? Having a split family. Trading holidays and not seeing your kids every weekend. Divorce *is* hard, too. It'll take work from the both of you. You and Ben just have to pick your hard. No one can do that for you. But you can choose your marriage if you want, Aila. You can choose to redeem it."

"Ben already decided." Aila blankly shakes her head.

"Aila…" Elena says as if to console her and convince her there's another way out.

"Ben left, Elena," Aila says, her expression now void of color and emotion. "He's not coming back. Not to forgive me at least."

"Well, he wouldn't be a fool to leave you, Aila. But he wouldn't be a fool to come back either."

Aila's eyes swell again. "You should have seen him, Elena. He's gone."

"You don't know that."

"I do though. I know him. He won't forgive me. He'll hang this over me until the day I die."

Elena leans forward. "You've only just told him. Give him time to cool off. When he comes back, you can hash it out then. Just take small steps in the right direction."

"What is the right direction?"

Elena's shoulders slump. "I don't know." She shakes her head. "And you won't either until you start moving."

Aila tries another sip of wine. It burns down her throat and sits like a rock in her stomach. She sets the glass on the coffee table and pushes it away from her like it's poisonous.

"I need to talk to Jackson."

Elena narrows her eyes. "I'm sorry, honey, but now is not the time to go back to him."

Aila closes her eyes and shakes her head slowly. "No, he doesn't know I told Ben. I need to tell him what happened."

Elena sits back, crosses her arms and looks at Aila, questioning.

"Aila, have you even ended things with Jackson?"

Aila glances at Elena. "Not really."

"Aila."

"Well, kind of. We want different things. I told him I want what's best for my family and he, well…he wants me."

Elena lets out a sigh.

"End it, Aila. You can't keep him on the back burner

while you figure out whether or not Ben has left you for good. You're all in or all out."

Aila winces like she's been slapped. "I don't want to hurt him, Elena."

"Stringing him along is hurting him."

"He's a good person."

Elena scoffs. "Yeah, aren't we all? He slept with someone's *wife*, Aila. Knowingly. Over and over again. He pursued you, knowing he was trying to rip you away from your husband—from your children's father. It's bullshit, Aila. Do I think he might actually be a decent person in another circumstance? Sure. Would I forgive him? God willing. But he is not your cross to bear."

"We have a long history together, Elena. I have a responsibility to him," Aila says in defense.

"No. You don't," she cuts her off. "You have a responsibility to your husband. To your family. Those are the vows you made."

"I can't just abandon him."

"Fine." She holds up a hand like she's slicing through the air. "But end it. Make it clear. Don't be afraid to hurt his feelings. And when Ben comes back—"

"If…"

"*When* Ben comes back, call me. I'll take the boys for a bit to give the two of you some time."

Aila nods but doesn't get up when Elena grabs her purse and heads for the door. She pauses before opening it and turns around.

"Aila?"

She looks up from her corner on the couch.

"I love you no matter what." And she turns and walks through the front door, closing it behind her.

At the sound of the latch, Aila's throat releases and she lets out a cry. Shaking and exhausted, she grabs the still full wine glasses and walks them over to the sink and dumps them out. She stares at the red liquid as it flows down the white porcelain to the drain, all while thinking of everyone she's disappointed, everyone she's lied to.

Ben. Her boys. Her parents. Sharon. *Chantelle.* Her heart constricts when she thinks of her best friend.

So much blood has already been spilled, and the wound hasn't even gotten close to bleeding all the way out.

CHAPTER 34

NOW

Ben never comes home that night and all Aila's calls and texts go unanswered. She tosses and turns in bed between checking her phone until she finally falls asleep at 5 a.m. Her alarm goes off an hour and a half later and when she wakes up, she wonders if the night before was simply a bad dream.

Every emotion and fiber of her being feels exhausted, like she had been drugged the night before. She tries making coffee but it tastes too bitter and scalds her already raw insides as it hits her stomach.

She throws her hair in a ponytail and dons a pair of sunglasses at the bus stop, ignoring any greeting from Janet, who smiles and fluffs Grace's pigtails, oblivious to the tornado she pushed through Aila's marriage yesterday.

After the kids are safely on the bus, she gets back in her SUV and heads straight to Jackson's. She figures he's already at work but she texts him to be at his house in forty minutes.

She doesn't greet him with a kiss or a hug when he opens the door. She barely mumbles a hello and his concerned eyes study her as she sways through his house to the dining room.

It's the safe choice—they have to sit in separate chairs, the table acting as a barrier. She relays everything that had happened in the last twenty-four hours, each piece of information cascading over the table and cutting through Jackson like a knife.

"What exactly are you saying, Aila?"

Aila can't remember if they'd ever actually sat at Jackson's dining room table but here they are, face to face. A couple of feet and a whole world apart.

She looks down at the hangnail she'd been picking at since last night. It is bleeding.

"What I'm saying, Jackson, is we're over." Aila closes her eyes hard. "I can't—we can't…anymore."

She can't even bring herself to say the correct word that quantifies their relationship.

"No, Aila. I don't believe you," he says reaching for her bloody hand across the table. His touch is magnetic and she longs for it, but she forces herself to pull her hand away. "That can't be what you want. I'm no fool. I know what we have."

She's silently shaking her head at his words, hoping to shake off any ounce of truth they have.

"I never meant to hurt you. I still don't want to hurt you. I wish it were a different time—a different life. But I've made choices before you, Jackson. I have to live with them and honor them."

Jackson comes around to the other side of the table where she's sitting and kneels at her feet.

"I promise you I will never simply give you a life that you have to 'live with.' I will give you more than that—a life you want. A life that doesn't make you want to run out on the choices you've made. Let me give that to you. Please."

Aila is in his arms now, unaware of how she got there. She looks up at his eyes, they're stormy and pleading. He leans in to kiss her and she can feel the warmth of his lips draw closer.

She stops him short and pushes him away.

"Stop it, Jackson. Please," she pleads. Tears are streaming down her face now. "I've disappointed enough people already."

"Is that what this is about? Disappointing people?" He scoffs. "I'm sorry, Aila, but this is just as much your life as it is anyone else's. You get to choose how this story ends too. Be an active participant in your own life. Quit making choices that will make everyone else happy… for once."

Jackson's words cause Aila's tears to cease. She lets out a soft sigh.

"You don't get it, Jackson," she says softly, like she's nurturing a child. "My children's happiness—even Ben's happiness is my happiness. I made that vow a long time ago. Only worrying about myself did nothing for the people I love."

Jackson is shaking his head. "So not me then."

Aila's eyes jerk up toward his.

"What?"

"I'm not someone you love." He lets out a quick sigh and turns away, pain passing over his face.

"Jackson, stop. I do. I do love you. What we've had is real, it just—"

"It just isn't enough for you," he says, walking toward the front door.

"No, maybe in a different life. I just have to do what's best—"

"Enough, Aila," he cuts her off. "Just stop. Quit trying to make this better—to make me *feel* better. You told me you're done. I didn't force you to love me when we were seventeen, I sure as hell won't do it now."

He holds the door open for her to walk through, tears gleaming at the corners of his eyes.

"Jackson, I'm so sorry."

"Aila, stop." He holds up a hand to stop her apology and mutters, "Just go. Please. Go love your family."

CHAPTER 35

NOW

Aila's tears run dry by the time she turns on Cherrywood Lane. She feels numb. Depleted.

Just take small steps in the right direction, Elena's words echo in her mind.

But how does she do that when every single step has a mountain in between it? She can't see around it and she can't see through it. She has no idea what waits on the other side.

She wants someone to hold her and tell her what she did isn't as terrible and awful as it feels. There's no one she loves that will agree with that.

Except Jackson.

The thought makes her angry and embarrassed, and she shakes it away, gripping the steering wheel sitting in her SUV on the driveway.

The sharp sound of ringing pierces through the silence, making her jump and pulls her out of her spiraling train of thought.

Chantelle.

Even just thinking of Chantelle's reaction makes Aila's chest tighten, and she swallows hard. Her hand hovers over her phone, hesitantly. She lets it go to voicemail.

Her phone immediately rings again and she answers reluctantly.

"Hey, Chay. What's up?" She tries to mask her voice with cheer but it cracks.

There's a brief pause.

"Aila," Chantelle begins, taking a shaky breath after she says her name. "I'm going to need you to skip the pleasantries and tell me what the hell is going on."

Aila clears her throat. "Okay. What do you mean?" she asks more timidly.

"I talked to Ben this morning." *Shit.* "I have never—" her voice cracks "—ever heard Ben that upset. I'm going to need you tell me the truth."

It's not a question. "What did he tell you?" Aila asks hesitantly.

"Aila!" she shouts at her, then collects herself. "That you've been having an *affair*. Which sounds like the truth, I'm guessing, since you're acting so shady right now. For God's sake, I feel like I don't even know who you are. Tell me, is it true?"

"Where's Ben, Chay? Do you know where he is? He won't call me back. I don't—" Aila asks through tears.

"No, you need to answer me first."

Aila sniffs and her chin begins to quiver.

"It's true," she says, no louder than a whisper.

Chantelle is silent and then lets out a shuddered breath that sounds like she's holding back tears.

"How could you? After everything I went through with Derek? After everything my girls—" She chokes on the last word. "You watched me walk through hell for the last five years. You held my hand in court. You prayed for me the night I found out. You held me like a baby when I cried myself to sleep and you…you go and do the same damn thing to Ben."

"Chantelle, I'm so sorry," Aila chokes out the words through her own wave of tears. "I didn't…I…I messed up."

Her chest floods with emotion as she fully realizes the betrayal her best friend is experiencing.

"Aila, I know you. God, even at your birthday, I *knew* something was up and you just told me you were tired. And I believed you because we don't lie to each other. But now, I guess we do." Chantelle tries to compose herself on the other line, clearing her throat and letting out a long sigh. "You have been a sister to me. But now I feel like I don't even know who you are."

"Chay…"

"Ben's at his mom's," Chantelle says. "You should call him."

And the line goes dead.

Aila lets out a sigh before walking into the house. It's empty and quiet, and Gus stays on his bed, not getting up to greet her.

Great. Even the dog's mad at me.

She throws herself on the couch, exhausted. Hollowed out and void of any energy to feel anything anymore. Her face is dry and swollen. She can feel the trails of dried tears as she runs her fingers down her cheek.

Gus walks over to her and licks the salt from her face.

"Forgiven me, have you?" she says to him.

Aila feels a wrench of desperation shoot through her heart as she hopes Ben will do the same.

And Chantelle.

And her mom and dad.

And Sharon.

Oh, Sharon. Ben has been at her house so she must already know.

A few more tears slip from her eyes as she contemplates the list of people she has utterly disappointed.

Each time she reads the list through her head, her heart surges with guilt. It makes her want to call Jackson and tell him she's changed her mind.

He would save her from this; defend her.

That's the tricky thing about guilt though. If it's not

met with confession and restitution, escape feels like the best option.

~

"Can I put Cheetos on my sandwich, mom?"

"What?" Aila looks up at Caleb, confused.

Oh yeah, that's right. I made ham sandwiches for dinner tonight.

Aila can't even remember the last time dinner wasn't a hot meal.

"Uh, sure," she says. "But you know it's better when you use potato chips."

"Or Doritos!" Josh adds.

"Or Doritos," Aila confirms and laughs.

It's a small chuckle, barely qualifying as a laugh but the sound startles her. When was the last time she laughed? Was that even acceptable to do anymore?

Aila wrings her hands like a wet rag when she hears the ding of the garage door.

"Dad's home!" Isaac yells. Aila's heart races and she's breathless; the very idea of Ben's presence knocks the wind out of her.

Ben walks into the kitchen, wearing the same sweatpants and t-shirt he left in last night. He looks terrible.

She feels suddenly self-conscious. How must she look? She rubs her frizzy hair back toward her ponytail as if it will help; as if it even matters.

"Ben, hi," she says, smiling with relief but she doesn't go to him.

He looks at her briefly, his eyes dark and cold, and then keeps walking toward the boys at the table.

"Hey, guys," he says, smiling genuinely, the darkness melting away. "What are you eating?"

"Mom made sandwiches for dinner! I put Cheetos in mine."

Caleb is more excited about this than an actual home-cooked meal.

"Cheetos?" He laughs, the sound echoes in Aila's ears, making her chest swell. "You know that's better with potato chips, right?"

Aila's eyes fill with tears.

Ben loves chips on his sandwiches. So does she.

"I know. Mom said the same thing," Caleb says.

Ben shoots a look at Aila, no doubt remembering this commonality they discovered on their first date and the lifetime of potato chip sandwiches that followed. It's a small and unimportant detail of their life together but it causes the depth of their history to wash over her. She blinks away her tears and turns her attention to the dishes in the sink. Scrubbing at the plates from breakfast—anything to hide the fact her hands are shaking.

"If you boys are finished, can you head upstairs to get ready for bed?" she says over her shoulder.

"But Mom! It's Friday. We always stay up late on Fridays," Josh pleads.

"I know. I have a surprise for you boys."

She turns to her phone and texts Elena asking if she'd come take the boys for the night. They love sleepovers with Elena and Joe, and her promise from the night before echoes in her brain.

Elena texts her she'll be there in fifteen minutes.

"Surprise?" Ben says calmly with an inkling of irritation after the boys run up the stairs.

"Elena is going to pick the boys up for the night." She bites her lip and moves toward him. "Ben—"

He holds up a hand. "Don't. We'll talk, just…" he lets out an exasperated breath. "Not right now."

He marches upstairs to help the boys pack, and then Aila hears the shower in their bathroom turn on—the water is running down the hollow walls in the house that now feels barren of love and safety. She stands in the kitchen alone and separated from her boys in more ways than one.

Exiled. A traitor in her own home.

CHAPTER 36

NOW

Aila closes the front door and presses her back tightly against it after Elena picks up the boys. Maybe if she had kept the door closed, she could've protected her family from this disaster. Maybe the storm wouldn't have blown in and maybe, just maybe, Ben wouldn't be sitting on the couch, silently staring at the entryway, waiting to slay the villain.

She takes a few timid steps away from the door and pauses to catch her breath. Her hands are so shaky they feel numb. She makes her way to the living room, stepping around the corner to where Ben sits. His eyes are dark and piercing. He looks calmer than he should.

It alarms her to feel so misplaced in her own home. She's looking at the man she's been married to for nearly fifteen years, but his energy isn't right. She should fit right next to him. But she doesn't feel welcome anymore.

Aila isn't afraid of Ben; she's afraid of what she's done to him.

The person whose world she wrecked is the very person she wants to comfort her. The dichotomy of the situation is not lost on her.

Aila clears her throat. "Where should we start?"

Ben presses his lips together and hangs his head. He's resting his elbows on his knees and it looks like he's composing himself but Aila knows better.

He's falling apart.

She goes to him and kneels at his feet.

She can't see him cry again.

But it's too late. Tears are streaming down his face and falling into his lap. She grabs his hands and holds them, bringing them to her mouth, kissing them and covering them with her own tears.

For a few moments they cry together, mourning the loss of the sacredness of their marriage. Mourning the destruction of the loyalty and trust they once had, until Ben raises his head and meets her eyes.

"Do you love him?"

Aila recoils at the question. She presses her lips together and shakes her head slowly. She doesn't want to answer.

"Aila…" Ben says knowingly.

She closes her eyes and nods ever so slightly.

Ben lets out an exasperated sigh and runs his hand down his face and looks at her. His eyes are stony and dark.

"But it's over, Ben. I love you. I never meant to hurt you."

"I'm having a really hard time believing you right now."

Aila nods. Silenced by her own fear and hesitation.

"For months you've been sneaking around with some guy from high school that just so happened to show up in the neighborhood. It sounds like a fucking ploy to get me to believe this could accidentally happen."

"Ben, no. That's not true. I had no idea I was going to see Jackson again. I promise you. I hadn't seen him since just after high school."

Ben is quiet, his eyes darting around as if he can't fathom how this could coincidentally happen.

"Where did it happen?"

"What?" Aila looks at him with wide eyes, hoping he isn't asking what she thinks he's asking.

"Where did you have sex with him?"

Aila presses her eyelids closed tightly, willing the question to go away. "Why would you want to know those things?"

"Where, Aila?" His voice thunders in the room.

Her chin quakes and a tremble rises in her hands.

"Here," she says, quietly. "And at his place."

"Where here?" Ben is so still Aila can't tell if he's even taken a breath.

Aila's breath shakes. "Our bed," she says swallowing hard. "And there." She nods at the couch Ben is sitting on.

He stands immediately as if the couch went up in flames. He looks down at it, repulsed, and then walks across the room, rubbing his hands down his face as if he's trying to wipe away the images Aila just put in his mind.

"I'm so sorry, Ben," she says through a wave of tears.

Ben turns to look at her and slowly shakes his head as he collapses in the armchair. He's trying to be strong. He's trying to un-see his own thoughts. He's desperately trying to understand how it is they got to this place. Aila goes to him, kneeling at his feet again, wordless and desperate to undo her mistakes.

They sob together again for what feels like an eternity. Aila finally reaches up and grabs his cheeks, pulling him in to kiss her but it's one-sided. Her mouth is begging for his affection until he grows stony. Aila pulls back and stares at Ben, wiping the streams that have fallen from his eyes.

It wasn't supposed to hurt this bad.

"Ben, I wish I could explain to you how deeply sorry I am, but I can't. There aren't words enough in any language to adequately express how deep this hurts me...that I've hurt you. And I know this is such a disappointment to you and our family. My parents...your mom..."

Her voice breaks off.

"This isn't about disappointing people, Aila." His voice is cold. "You've *hurt* people. Not just me. You're a liar. A fraud. A fake. No one likes a liar, and no one trusts one, and that is exactly what you've become." His voice towers over her.

Aila feels like she just got kicked in the stomach, and it shows on her face.

"Truth hurts, doesn't it, Aila? Bet you didn't think about that when you were laid up in *our* bed with him, did you?"

"You weren't ever around, Ben!" Aila explodes at him. "It took Janet cluing you in for you to even suspect anything! We have hardly had sex in months, you work late every night, the kids practically beg you to spend time with them, and any time you go anywhere with us, you are constantly on the phone or returning emails. We haven't been your priority, Ben. *I* haven't been your priority in years."

"That's not true, Aila. Everything I do is for you and this family."

"You love to say that, don't you?" Aila scoffs, shaking her head. "Just because it brings home a paycheck doesn't mean it's all for me. Your job stopped being about providing for your family years ago."

"Me working late is still no excuse to go fuck some random guy from high school, Aila."

His voice is growing wild and his volume rises, making Aila stand on her feet and take a few steps back.

"Ben. Stop…"

"Stop?" He cinches his eyebrows together and glares at her. "You betrayed our family!"

Aila recoils at his words, not because he's shouting but because she knows it's true.

"Ben, please. You're being cruel now."

"Cruel? Oh please, Aila. How dare you? I have every right to be angry at you, and let you know how angry I am. It's bullshit for you to insinuate otherwise."

"He isn't just some random guy, Ben. I fell in love

with him," Aila says through tears, surprised by her own admission.

Ben is shocked silent and runs a hand down his face.

"And he loved me. He's loved me for years. And I didn't know that at the time but once we started spending time together, I realized everything that was missing in this marriage. Everything that I've begged you to give me for years. And he was willing to do that." Aila wipes the tears from her face and lets out an emotional sigh and throws up her hands. "And I fell for him, and now we're here."

Ben holds her gaze. His eyes are cold and rimmed with red as he turns and walks to the kitchen and fills a glass of water. After he drinks it, he throws it into the sink and it breaks off into shards of glass.

Aila jumps at the sound of the glass shattering. The action makes her skin crawl. She doesn't know this Ben. She wants *her* Ben back.

"Ben," she says without moving forward. "Why don't you just come sit down? We can talk. I'll tell you everything you want to know. I promise. Just please calm down."

He doesn't respond. He's hunched over the counter and his shoulders are shaking. At first Aila thinks he's full of rage and anger but when she moves closer, she sees he's sobbing.

She rushes to him, not knowing whether or not he'll flinch at her touch. She doesn't care and she pulls him into her arms anyway.

"Oh, Ben," she weeps into his shoulder and he cries into her hair.

What have I done?

Their legs go slack and they slide down the cabinets and sit on the floor, locked in each other's arms. Aila doesn't know what else to say—she doesn't even think there's anything she can say or do.

The longer she holds onto Ben, the more she realizes the anger and rage she just witnessed isn't that at all.

It's hurt.

It's sadness.

And she is the culprit.

She holds him close and rocks him like a child.

How could I have done this?

His arms tighten around her and she clasps his shirt, pulling him closer and aching for his touch and affection. He wants no part of it and gets up and walks into to the living room. His hands are on his head and he's breathing heavily.

"How'd we get here, Aila?" He turns and stares at her sitting on the kitchen floor with swollen eyes and a broken heart. "This wasn't supposed to happen to us."

She shakes her head and looks up at him, almost dazed. "Can we come back from this?"

He sits on the couch and stares back at her. He's out of words, and maybe out of hope.

"The way I see it, I can leave now with my dignity and I won't ever have to worry about not trusting you again." He pauses and swallows hard. "Or, I can stay so our boys don't have to grow up in a broken family."

Aila looks at him, wondering how he's going to choose, and if still loving her will fall into the equation somehow.

"For the boys, I will do anything."

Aila nods, realizing it's not about her. That his forgiveness is conditional. That it's about their family. She doesn't know if it makes her feel relieved or sad. Either way, she's willing to try.

CHAPTER 37

THEN

"Come on, Mama, join in!" Ben said, turning from the half circle of boys in the living room. Nineties hip-hop music was blaring out of the speakers and Ben was doing the Running Man while his three mini-me's attempted to copy his moves.

"You just love old school music, don't you?" Aila burst out laughing and hopped right in when they started doing the "Cupid Shuffle."

She had just spent the evening eating sushi and drinking wine with her girlfriends and came home to a full-blown dance party. She didn't know when it started but they shook their tail feathers for another twenty minutes, each Sorenson attempting to out dance the next until they were out of breath and sweaty.

"Looks like I almost missed the party," she said, pouring them each a glass of water. "Did you boys miss me at all tonight?"

Isaac's eyes shifted from left to right, looking at his older brothers for the politically correct answer to give their mother. They offered no help, staring straight into their water glasses.

"I take offense to that," she said sarcastically, then laughed and gave the top of Isaac's head a playful rub. "Alright, you crazies. Upstairs to brush your teeth. We can't stay up all night."

She collected the empty water glasses and placed them in the dishwasher as the boys went upstairs. Ben came up behind her and slid his hands down her hips, leaning in to kiss her neck. He smelled like cologne and sweat and his kiss tickled her neck, making her laugh.

"Well, I missed you," he said. "How was girls' night?"

She turned around to kiss him and then said, "It was nice. Kelly drove me crazy tonight as usual. But other than that, it was great."

"What'd she do this time?"

Aila paused and twisted her lips for a contemplative moment.

"Nothing, really. It's just incessant talking. I can't get a word in edgewise. I always feel like I need a drink after having a drink with her."

Ben laughed. "Now, Aila. Don't be a bully."

"I'm not. She's just…a lot sometimes. All the time," she said, giving a wry smile.

"Well, I'm sure Gretchen was happy you came to celebrate her birthday," he said, wiping down the counters.

"Thank you for letting me go out tonight and watching the kids," she said.

He scoffed slightly. "It's not about getting my permission, Aila. Don't be silly."

"Well, it is about fitting it into your schedule."

"Okay, that's fair." Ben nodded. "Just don't make me out to be a warden."

"Then let Rapunzel out of her tower every now and then." She smiled at him, mischievously.

He gave her a heartbreakingly handsome smile and kissed her. "But, baby, that's right where I like you."

Aila smiled. It was funny. It was flirtatious. But it also hit a nerve.

CHAPTER 38

NOW

Aila's thumb hovers over the green button on her phone, desperately wanting to answer but knowing she shouldn't. It had only been a week since their conversation at Jackson's dining room table but it felt like an eternity. She misses him. She can't help but believe he would save her from every horrible word hurled at her in the heat of the moment and every accusation thrown in her direction.

She hesitantly moves her thumb to the red button and hits it.

I can't. I shouldn't.

But she still wants to. The very desire of wanting to hear Jackson's voice makes her cry.

Oh God, I can't live like this.

The last week had felt like Aila was walking around on shattered glass. If she or Ben stepped around each other wrong, another wound would slice open, leaving them both bleeding out on the floor. Ben slept in the office most nights and left for work soon after the kids ate breakfast. The boys love having him around more but Ben and Aila have struggled to resume any kind of normalcy between them. They need help. They don't know how to heal from this or where to even start, but Aila knows answering a call from Jackson doesn't fit anywhere in the equation.

Jackson, please. Let me move on.

After she texts him, Aila walks over to the kitchen to retrieve the business card for the therapist Elena had suggested. When Elena gave it to her, she had wrapped the business card in Aila's hand and held it close to her chest, giving her a meaningful look. Aila had felt her heart beat across her knuckles.

She walks back over to her phone in the living room and dials the number. While it rings, Aila's heart pounds and her mouth goes dry. She's so nervous. The very thought of telling strangers her darkest secrets makes her want to hang up.

"Joanne Kensington's office," says the voice on the other line. Aila thinks it sounds too cheerful to handle the grotesque magnitude of her marriage's problems.

"Yes, hi, I'd like to make an appointment for marriage counseling."

"Okay." Aila can hear clicking on the other end. "Will this be for pre-marital counseling or post-marital."

"Post-marital."

"Is the nature of the appointment urgent?"

"Yes." *You have no idea how urgent.*

More clicking.

"Okay. It looks like Joanne is available to see you in a couple weeks. Is that soon enough for you?"

"Yes, I suppose so."

After Aila gives them their names and confirms the appointment, she hears a soft knock on the door and lets out a deep sigh. She doesn't want any visitors. She is exhausted from seeing people and talking about the dumpster fire that has become her life.

When she opens the door, she practically chokes on her own breath at the sight of Jackson standing on her doorstep. He looks wearisome and tired—his smile faded and his eyes swollen—but still overwhelmingly handsome.

"What the hell are you doing here?" she says grabbing him and pulling him inside while glancing down the street. "You cannot be here."

"I parked around the corner, no one will know," he says, answering her unspoken question about where his truck is.

"*I* will know, Jackson," Aila says, rubbing her temples. She is purposefully not inviting him to move past the entryway.

"I just had to talk to you."

"What could there possibly be to talk about?" *Everything. I want to tell you everything.*

Aila shakes the thought away not letting herself fall into temptation.

"This can't be how it ends, Aila." His eyes are rimmed with hurt and tears as he reaches out and grabs her hands. "I've always pictured my life with you ever since I was a kid. And now after these last four months, the dream is even more vivid. I can see everything with me and you. And your boys, too. I'm not ready to give up. I said I was, but I'm not. I'll wait for you, if that's what you want. I've waited long enough. What we have is *real.*"

Aila squeezes his hands and presses her eyes closed, desperately trying to navigate her choice of words. "I never said it wasn't real, Jackson," she says, while chewing on the side of her lip. "Saying goodbye to you was one of the hardest things I have ever done. It wasn't an easy choice."

"Then undo it," he says, drawing her closer. "You don't have to pick the harder path."

Aila lets out an exhausted laugh as tears stream down her face. "There's no easy way out right now."

"Aila, please." Jackson is pleading now and there's a part of her that wants to say yes. To hop in his truck and run away with him. To start over where no one knows her mistakes. Where no one can see the damage she's caused.

She takes in a deep breath.

"Jackson, no," she says pulling away from him and reaching for the door. "I love Ben. And I need you to go."

"Aila…"

"Go!" she practically shouts and then softens her voice. "Please."

Jackson's eyes ache for Aila as he passes over the threshold, and she wants so badly to wash the pain away, but she can't. Not without losing Ben.

She closes the door with her back pressed against it as she slides down to the floor sobbing. A part of her still loves him. A part of her still wants him. But not more than what she will stand to lose if she chooses him.

CHAPTER 39

THEN

Aila's eyes shot awake and she looked at the clock on her nightstand. It was 1 a.m. and Isaac hadn't woken up for his midnight feeding like he usually did. She felt anxiety rise in her chest. No matter how many times she did the baby phase, she always felt nervous and over-protective in the midnight hours.

She slid out of bed and padded down the hall, careful not to wake Josh and Caleb in the bedroom across the hall. When she reached Isaac's crib, it was empty and she suddenly felt panicked, not knowing where he could be. Three-month-old babies don't just get up and walk away.

When she reached the hallway, she saw a dim light coming from the staircase and a gentle hum of a melody coming from downstairs. As she drew closer, she heard Ben singing "Bye-Bye Baby" to Isaac while he gave him a bottle and swayed throughout the room.

She stopped at the edge of the living room, watching him tenderly while he rocked Isaac in his arms until his eyes grew heavy. Ben saw her and smiled. Aila made her way over to them, placing a hand on Ben's shoulder and gently cupping Isaac's head.

"I didn't even hear him wake up," she whispered to Ben.

"It's okay, I was still up going over a case and watching sports when I heard him fussing. I figured you could use a few extra uninterrupted hours of sleep, so I went ahead and gave him a bottle."

Aila kissed Isaac on the top of his head and smiled at him fondly, even though her lactating breasts ached to feed him. She didn't care. She was so grateful for the gesture.

"Thank you," she whispered to Ben.

"It's nothing. Now go back to bed before he smells you and wakes up," he said with a grin and a wink.

Aila smiled back and shook her head, holding back a laugh before kissing Ben.

"I love you so much," she said.

"I love you too."

She could feel his eyes admire her in her milk-stained t-shirt and sweatpants as she walked back up the staircase, so she gave a flirtatious shake of her backside making Ben stifle a laugh. She flashed a wide, playful smile before heading back to bed. As she drifted off to sleep, she thought of how grateful she was for the life they built. It was layered with mess and chaos, but it was beautiful and it was theirs.

CHAPTER 40

NOW

Aila didn't realize the weight of the shame she'd drag around with her from place to place from now on. Walking a half step away from her husband, who won't hold her hand. It's as if she has a Scarlet letter A plastered to her denim jacket.

Even checking in with the receptionist at their therapist's office, the young blonde with thick-rimmed glasses and a black blazer eyes her knowingly.

Ah, so you're the adulterer of the day. Why would you cheat on this guy?

Her eyes taunt Aila.

She bites her lip and holds in a breath, then takes her turn signing the HIPPA form.

"Joanne will be right with you," the blonde says.

The waiting room is small but warm. The walls are painted a deep emerald green and the reception desk is made of a deep rustic wood with succulents scattered about.

"Ben and Aila," says a plump woman in her late forties with short, curly, auburn hair and deep red lipstick as she pokes her body through the door to her office. She is wearing black pants with a white blazer. She looks too clean and tidy to handle the mess that is about to sit on her leather couch.

Obediently, the couple enters the office and the three of them exchange introductions and pleasantries. They each take a seat on opposite ends of the couch. Aila's mouth is dry and her heart is pounding through her ears. She wants to look at Ben for comfort but knows it's best not to because the very sight of him will make her burst into tears.

"Alright now, the first thing I'd like to do is open in prayer if you don't mind," Joanne says.

Aila and Ben nod though Aila doesn't see the point.

God doesn't care about the mess I've made.

She stares at her shoes in a trance until she hears, "Amen."

"So…" Joanne says, settling into her chair with a notebook in hand. "Tell me a little about what brings the two of you to see me."

"Uh," Aila can barely say the words. "I had an affair." She clears her throat.

"And what are each of you hoping to get out of this?" Joanne says, looking up from her notepad.

"We—I want our marriage back." Aila knows she has no right to speak for Ben right now.

Joanne jots something down and shifts in her chair. Ben sits still as a statue. Calm. Unmoving. Meanwhile Aila wants to tear out of her own skin. She tries to appear still and calm. As a result, every other movement in the room feels heightened.

"And Ben?" she says.

Shift, shift.

"Same," he says plainly, his deep voice is raspy with emotion.

Joanne nods as if giving them approval. She smiles gingerly.

"So, tell me a bit more about what happened?"

Aila side glances at Ben, who is stone cold clearly wanting her to admit her crimes to yet another soul.

That's what the last few weeks have entailed: Aila confessing over and over. To her parents. Her friends. Their disbelief. Her tears. Their anger. Her apologies. Repeat.

It's okay, *I deserve it.*

She wrings her hands tightly as the warmth of the room makes her sweat. Her eyes dart around the room before landing on the fire. She's captivated by it, watching it while trying to find the words to explain herself but she can't. Do words like that even exist?

She opens her mouth and closes it. She clears her throat, unable to speak.

"I can see how this must be very difficult for you to talk about, Aila," Joanne says. "Why don't we start at the beginning?"

The beginning. Aila side glances at Ben who won't meet her eyes and then holds her gaze at Joanne.

"Which one?"

Joanne stares back at her over her reading glasses and gives a noncommittal shrug. "You could tell me about your marriage and what led to your affair. Just…wherever you'd like to start."

Aila's mouth is dry and her armpits begin to perspire excessively as she recounts both their marriage—at least parts of it—and her affair. When did it start, how long did it last, how many times? Each answer a punch to the gut.

Joanne nods and shifts her plump body in her chair, directing her attention to Ben. She begins to make a quick note and pauses, her pen still touching the paper. "And Ben? What do you believe is your role in this?"

"Me?" Ben looks genuinely hurt and Aila can see the anger make its way up his neck and into his jaw. "What the hell kind of role would I have in my wife sleeping with someone else?"

Joanne eyes him over her reading glasses and clears her throat.

Aila swallows hard.

Shit. Maybe she isn't the right kind of therapist.

"I'm sorry," she shifts again. *Always shifting.* Like the chair is uncomfortable but Aila can't help but think it's the topic of conversation. "Let me rephrase this: infidelity in a marriage or any relationship isn't just about getting wooed away or actively seeking relations outside of the marriage. Infidelity has roots. And once those roots begin to sprout, the marriage will either fertilize it or nip it in the bud."

Aila feels like she can't catch her breath and gives a side-glance to Ben. He's furious even though he hides it well.

"I want you to visualize this fertilizer as issues in your marriage and the 'nipping it in the bud' so to speak as your marriage's strengths. The roots are the opportunities one has to step away from the marriage."

Aila hates this analogy. She never, not once, ever thought of cheating or even having the opportunity to cheat.

There were no roots! She wants to scream. *I created them. Made them up in my head because I ran into Jackson.*

She wants to cut Joanne off and tell her she's at fault, completely; that it's nonsense to even insinuate Ben is to blame.

She looks over at Ben.

Her Ben. Her sad and angry Ben. He wears the devastation like a mask on his face. She wants so badly to tear it off. Pretend it never happened.

But it did. A history un-erasable. Reprehensible.

I did this to him.

"Joanne, uh…" she begins before Joanne holds up a hand to silence her.

"This is only directed at Ben, Aila."

"Yes, I see that but I'm at fault…" Aila is shaking.

Joanne narrows her crystal-clear blue eyes on Aila. "I understand you want to have time to explain yourself and to take ownership of your mistakes. I applaud you for that. And that time will come. But if we do that before we strip down the layers of how this came to be, we are simply putting a Band-Aid on a much bigger problem."

Joanne uncrosses her ankles and looks between the

both of them.

"This is going to be uncomfortable. And this is going to take a lot of work. But if you want to save this marriage, if you want to truly heal from this and I believe you can, you need to play by my rules."

Aila sits back on the sofa, nodding solemnly.

Ben is resting his fist over his mouth, contemplative, the corners of his eyes glazed with tears.

"So, are we in agreement?" Joanne says as if she's lecturing two students in the principal's office.

They both nod. Aila's chin quakes with emotion.

Oh God, please let us come back from this.

It's the first prayer she has uttered in a long time she feels in the depth of her bones. She prays as hard as she can God is actually listening.

CHAPTER 41

NOW

"Hey, Ben." Aila knocks quietly on the bathroom door while Ben brushes his teeth after tucking each child in their beds. "Do you have a minute?"

Their conversations now always begin with such trepidation and it breaks Aila's heart. They were never supposed to be like this, but once they realized the hurt and betrayal that was wedged between them, their movements and interactions were no longer fluid and comfortable.

Ben rinses his mouth and dries it with a towel.

"Yeah, sure," he says turning around slowly and leaning against the bathroom counter.

Aila enters the bathroom and sits on the edge of the tub.

"I need to tell you something." She swallows hard. "And I know it's going to upset you but I also know I can't keep this from you."

"Okay," he says slowly, clearly hesitant about any other bombs she might hurl at him.

"Jackson came here a couple weeks ago." Ben's eyes narrow on her. "He had called and I didn't answer but then he stopped by anyway."

"What'd he want?"

Aila can practically see the anger rising in Ben's chest.

"He just wanted to talk and…" Aila hesitates. "That was it."

"Did you sleep with him?"

Aila closes her eyes and shakes her head. "No. I promise. He was just having a hard time but I just reiterated it is over and that I love you."

She swallows hard, anxious to hear Ben's response. But he is too tired to be angry. He stares at her for several moments before nodding slowly.

"Why'd you wait to tell me?"

Aila can tell they're both trying so hard to stay calm, to hold it together for this conversation, which in turn, means their words are hesitant and choppy.

"I thought it didn't matter because nothing happened. But then I've been thinking since therapy yesterday and I don't want to keep anything from you anymore. I'm all in, Ben. So, if anything like this comes up, I'm going to tell you. I don't want to chance ruining anything for our family because I didn't tell you the truth."

He contemplates this for a minute, rubbing his fingers over his brow. Aila knows the images he's trying to push out and it makes her heart beat faster. "Does he still want you?"

Aila nods.

"Shit, Aila…" he lets out an exasperated sigh. "How'd I let you slip away?"

Aila looks up at him sharply, unsure of how to interpret the question.

"I have something I need to tell you too." Ben sits on the tub next to her, his hands gripping the edge. "Yesterday when Joanne asked what my role in this was, it made me angry. But it also got me thinking about us and what we've become over the last several years. Our balance has been off, hasn't it?" He looks at Aila when he says this and she meets his eye and nods, her chin shaking.

"I just couldn't see it. You handled everything, Aila. Always. All the time. You made motherhood look so easy. The boys are always so happy and taken care of, and they love you so much. I've always felt so proud of you, even if you're not living the dream you thought you would be. You never let anything slip through the cracks, so I never had anything to worry about. I always thought, Aila's got it covered. We're good." He swallows hard, pushing back his emotions. "I didn't realize it was you that was slipping through the cracks."

Aila nods and squeezes her eyes shut, then begins to cry.

Ben's fingers brush hers slightly and they both stare at the white porcelain tile in a trance of exhaustion and uncertainty.

"Where do we go from here, Ben?"

He shakes his head not looking her. "I have no idea."

CHAPTER 42

NOW

The moments drag into days. The days drag into weeks until it has been a full two months since Aila told Ben about Jackson and their marriage shattered.

The last two months they have been standing around, looking at all the pieces, examining them, trying to figure out which ones are worth salvaging, which ones can find a place again, and which ones they need to sweep in the trash.

To stay married after infidelity is mind-numbing. Draining. Exasperating. Aila and Ben have been going to see their therapist, Joanne, every week for nearly six weeks. Aila thought it would feel a lot more like healing, but most days it just feels like salt in the wound—an uncovering of every issue or doubt in their entire fifteen years of marriage, a twist of the knife each time something new pops up.

Every session ends with a prayer and Joanne saying, "You did good work today, friends."

Aila wants to rip her ears off every time she hears it. Work and progress are two very different things. They have done a lot of work, but they have made zero progress. At least, that's how Aila feels.

Ben still barely makes eye contact with her, let alone

talks to her, and he's taken to sleeping in the office every night. They even threw out their old mattress that was littered with unfaithfulness and bought a new one. Anything to push the memories of the affair out of their marriage.

Aila is lost in thought, silently pushing a pea around on her dinner plate when Caleb asks, what she can only assume is the second time, "*Mom?*"

"What?" She blinks heavy and looks at her son.

"Can we have a movie night with popcorn tonight?"

She shakes her head to register his question. "Uh, ask your dad."

She feels four sets of eyes narrow on her.

"I just did. He said to ask you."

Of course, he did. Aila looks at Ben across the table.

"Oh. Well, sure. That's fine with me. Just shower and get your pajamas on after dinner."

They obediently oblige while Aila clears dishes and starts scrubbing pots and pans. Ben places his plate next to the sink. The very clink of the glass hitting the countertop infuriates her. She had been walking around on eggshells for the last two months—begging, trying, pulling for conversations and acknowledgment Ben simply would not give. He is still so stuck in his anger. He can't see over it and he can't see through it. So much so the effort he is putting into their marriage stops short of coming home earlier from work, spending more time with the kids and less time at the office—something their therapist recommended as being paramount to the success of their marriage. Unfortunately for Aila, it feels like he only wants his family to stay intact to the outside world. Whereas on the inside, Aila is still the nanny and the maid, barely acknowledged by her own husband.

"Are you going to load that?" she says, looking at him with eyes like lasers, willing him to meet her eye.

"If it's that big of a deal…"

"It *is* that big of a deal, Ben. Load your own damn dishes."

She scrubs the already clean pot harder.

He holds up his hands, indicating for her to hold her fire. "What's gotten into you?"

She drops the pot in the sink and soapy suds fly.

"I can't do this, Ben. I *can't*." She holds up her hands and dries them off with a towel. "This is complete bullshit. If you want to work it out, Ben, I need you to actually *try*."

"I'm sorry but last time I checked there isn't a time limit on getting over your wife sleeping with her ex-boyfriend," he whisper-yells at her.

She'd cry if she wasn't so angry.

"Okay. Fine. Here's what's not going to happen. You can't throw that in my face from now until...*forever*. You have to find a way to get over it, to *forgive me,* because at this point with how you treat me, how you look at me—God, we're better off splitting up."

"Oh, please," he chastises her. "You know I'm trying. I am giving you everything I have."

Aila's shoulders drop and she places her hands on her hips, "Oh, so all you have is anger, resentment, and disdain for me. Great. Fantastic way to forge through our marriage."

"Why are you acting like I'm not allowed to be upset, Aila? You *cheated*. That's not easy to just forgive and forget." He lowers his face to meet hers. "How dare you even insinuate that things should be back to normal?"

He lets out a sigh and waves a dismissive hand before she has a chance to respond, then he turns to leave.

"Ben," she says calmly enough he pauses in his tracks. "You look at me like you don't even like me. Like I disgust you. And, there's a part of me that understands that, I'm not an idiot to think you should be over it by now. But you don't even try. You don't ask how my day was or how the boys were or if you can help with dinner or clean up after the meal is over. You don't even pretend to try. You are giving me *nothing* to work with here."

Aila feels desperate.

Ben swallows hard and looks at her.

"Right now, Aila, I am doing everything I can to even

hold it together around you. That is all you deserve to *work with* right now."

His words lodge a lump in her throat and she swallows it. She wills herself not to cry. Not right now. Not tonight.

~

The movie with the boys is practically torture. The tension between them is palpable. Josh keeps sneaking glances at Ben on one couch and his mom on the other. Aila notices and smiles at him reassuringly. He smiles back but there's something else behind it. At ten, he already knows so much more than he should. Aila can sense he's picked up on more than she and Ben have let on to the kids.

When Aila takes the boys upstairs to tuck them in bed, Ben stays downstairs to clean up popcorn bowls. She lands in Josh's room last and just as she reaches to turn off his lamp, she hears a crack of a voice from his bed.

"Mom?"

Aila takes in a sharp breath. "Yeah, honey?"

"What's going on?"

Oh no.

"What do you mean?"

"You and Dad have been acting funny…like, you don't even really talk to each other, you just talk around each other," he says and fiddles with his blanket between his fingers. "And like, sometimes I hear you guys yelling—but not like real yelling, like you're trying not to yell or something. And when I hear you guys downstairs, you seem mad. Like you guys are in trouble with each other."

Aila presses her lips together.

"Well," she begins, not wanting to lie but not wanting to reveal too much. "Dad and I haven't—well, we have been upset with each other recently. Sometimes grown-ups do that, we get mad, just like kids do. But when you're a grown-up, it can be a little harder to work out our problems because we don't have anyone telling us how to do it. But we're trying hard, that's what you need to remember, okay?"

She smiles, pushing down the lump rising in her throat.

Josh nods. "But shouldn't Dad just listen to you? You always have the right answers."

"I wish that were true," she says while brushing his hair back from his forehead, wanting to laugh.

"But it is, Mom. You never mess up," he says with pleading eyes, causing a shooting a pain across Aila's chest.

"I do though, honey," she says. "I'm human. We're all human so we all mess up sometimes. Sometimes we do worse things than others. Sometimes we hurt other people. Sometimes we hurt ourselves. But it's all the same though, really—just messing up. And then we have to figure out how to fix it and ask for forgiveness."

"Why though? Why do we hurt people?"

She clears her throat and confesses a thought that has hung in the back of her mind for months. One she kept pushing away every time she made a choice in the wrong direction.

"Because we're all a little broken. Sometimes that makes us turn our back on the good things we have in life. And we just kind of let our faith slip away when we need it most."

Josh looks down briefly before meeting his mother's gaze. "I still have faith in you, Mom."

Aila's chin quivers and she swallows her tears. "Thank you, baby. You have no idea how much I needed to hear you say that."

CHAPTER 43

NOW

The fighting is incessant, the tension thick, stinging them every time either of them tries to cut through it. It makes no sense to Aila. Hadn't they agreed? Doesn't Ben want to work it out? She has apologized over and over. She hasn't even talked to Jackson since the day he stopped by.

The affair is over by all accounts, but it doesn't feel remotely close to over to Aila. Ben hangs it over her head constantly. Not always outright, but she feels it. He doesn't even love her anymore. Not like before. He can't see past it. He says he's forgiven her, but he makes it clear he isn't going to forget any time soon.

"I want out," Aila says, sitting across from Joanne in her office. It once felt warm and cozy but today it feels stuffy and suffocating.

Aila is at the end of her rope.

Joanne's eyes squint quickly before she raises her eyebrows at Aila, shifting in her chair. "What do you mean by that, Aila?"

Her eyes dart to Ben, his jaw is pulsing under his clench, and then back to Aila.

"I can't do it, Joanne. I get zero respect. Zero attention, compassion…regard. Honestly, I thought working it out would look a lot different than it does right now…because right now—" Aila takes a deep breath. "Right now, I feel like I am in a terrible marriage to someone who is cruel and doesn't love me or even like me, if we're being honest."

Joanne nods and looks at Ben. "Do you feel the same way?"

Ben takes in a deep breath and lets it out slowly.

"It has been incredibly difficult to be around Aila right now. I want to get past it. I know that's best for our boys but umm…" he swallows hard and looks up at Joanne. "I don't know."

"I don't only want to stay together for the boys. It has to be about us too." She shakes her head vehemently. "What you're saying is bullshit, Ben. Be honest. You hate me right now."

Ben's head turns sideways. "I don't hate you, Aila. It's actually the opposite. I love you. I always have. *That* is why this is so hard. And believe it or not, it sucks more being on my end than it does on yours. I didn't get to run around for months—"

"Oh, really? How long are you going to play the victim, Ben?" Aila is livid. But so is Ben.

"Victim? You made me the victim!"

"Oh, here you go again." Aila rolls her eyes.

"We wouldn't be in this mess if you hadn't slept with someone else!"

"No. We wouldn't be in this mess if you didn't spend every waking minute working and ignoring the very family you helped create—"

"Enough!" Joanne takes a deep breath and leans back in her chair, studying the two of them. Her specimens in her laboratory. She leans forward, placing her elbows on her knees.

"Do you want this marriage to succeed?"

"I do." Ben speaks up faster than Aila expected, and a calmness seems to have washed over him. "I'm just struggling to…uh…get past the anger part."

He's trying to hold it together. Aila can tell and it drives her mad. He rarely says these things when they're at home actually trying to make progress, but almost always when they're in front of their therapist.

"Aila?" Joanne turns to her.

She blinks and turns her attention from Ben to Joanne, like a defiant teenager. "That is what I want. What I thought we both wanted but it's not working. I don't want to live in the same household as someone who despises me. Honestly, I think we need to take some time apart. Maybe he can stay at his mom's so I can still get the kids to school until the year is over and then during the summer…"

Her voice trails off when Joanne holds up a hand.

"Let me stop you right there. Separation wouldn't be a good idea right now. If you both have the intention of staying to together then you actually need to *be* together."

"He doesn't want me around!" Aila shouts. "He sleeps in a different room. He doesn't even say hello and if, hell forbid, I ask him to load his dishes, it turns into a blow-up fight. I'm sick of it. I need space."

Joanne contemplates this for a moment.

"The reason," she pauses briefly, "I don't think one of you leaving the home is a good choice right now is because it creates space, which creates distance, which creates opportunity. Opportunity to think life is better or more peaceful without the other. It also provides you the opportunity to slip and step out on your marriage."

Again.

Aila takes a deep breath and rolls her eyes in frustration. Ben is stoic.

"So, I can't recommend space is a good choice for you right now. However, Ben," Joanne turns her attention to him, "I understand forgiveness doesn't happen completely overnight. The memories and the questions and the thoughts aren't going to simply dissipate. But you are going to have to put forth some effort with Aila as well. She made a horrible mistake. One she has owned up to and apologized for. She hasn't only asked for forgiveness but she has said she is willing to work to make things right between the two of you. Many would say that is a right you have since she broke her vows, but it is really a gift. Because you know she could have left if she wanted to and then we'd be cleaning up an entirely different mess here, wouldn't we?"

Ben's eyes dart at Aila sitting immobilized on the other end of the couch.

"So, Ben." Joanne looks at both of them. "Aila. The two of you need to decide what mess we're dealing with. When you came in here, you both said you wanted to bring your marriage back from a horrible place but just simply being here, as admirable as that may be, is not going to cut it. This is going to be dirty and ugly much of the time, but if the both of you choose to clean it up little by little, there will be healing."

"I'm still just so angry," Ben interjects. "I look at her and I just see...I see *him.*"

He says it with such disgust Aila feels as if she's just been gutted.

"Well, then you need to remember all the things you used to see when you looked at her. Remember why you love her. What drew you to her." Joanne sets down her notebook. "I'm going to give you an assignment this week. Go on a date—not a movie—any date, where the two of you can actually talk and be reminded of who the other person is."

She directs the last statement toward Aila and it stings deep. Because as much as she thinks Ben has forgotten who she is, Aila has lost who Ben is along the way too.

CHAPTER 44

THEN

"For you, my dear," Ben said, placing a glass of crisp, cold champagne in front of Aila. She sat at a table, clad with a white table cloth, a bouquet of orchids and gardenias, and scattered with votive candles lit against the setting sun during her parents' fortieth wedding anniversary party.

"Thanks, babe," she said, toasting to his whiskey.

"You throw one hell of a party, Aila May."

"You sign one hell of a check, Benjamin Lee," she joked, and they both threw their heads back in laughter.

Ben leaned over and held Aila's face in his hands, "I love you."

Aila bit her lip and smiled. Ben still wrecked her emotionally in all the best ways, even after all these years. His lapses of attention were more frequent, but when she did catch his eye, he was completely captivated by her and she couldn't get enough of him.

She leaned in to kiss him and then said, "I need to make a toast."

Aila stood and clinked her glass of champagne with her butter knife, gathering the attention of all seventy-five guests there to celebrate the commitment of her parents.

"If I could have your attention, everyone, I'd like to make a toast to two of the most incredible human beings I have ever known." Aila cleared her throat as she waited for the chattering crowd to die down. "Their love surpasses all understanding. They have taught me the importance of laughter, of keeping your word, of forgiveness, of loving people through their darkest times, and trusting God to pull you through when times get tough. I cannot think of greater examples of love and commitment. I am so honored to be your daughter and I am so happy to celebrate your anniversary. Congratulations, Mom and Dad. Cheers!"

Aila raised her glass to toast her parents, then sat and clinked her glass with Ben before taking a sip.

Ben tucked a strand of hair behind her ear and Aila turned to smile at him. "That was perfect."

"Thank you," she said, taking another sip of her champagne just as Ben rose to add to the toast.

"Good evening, everyone. I'm so glad all of you made it out here tonight to celebrate Bob and Tina's fortieth wedding anniversary. I am so proud to be their son-in-law. As many of you may know, I lost my dad when I was thirteen. Through that, my mom always taught me to be strong. To always act with integrity. And to love people with best of your ability. Ever since I met Bob and Tina, they really took me in and have always treated me like I was a part of their family and instilled those same values in Aila and me. For that, I am forever grateful. Years ago, when I asked Bob if he'd give me permission to marry Aila, he said something I'll never forget. He said, 'Son, I don't think you know what you're asking. A lifetime of commitment to one person is going to be the hardest battle you'll ever fight. But if you are willing to do whatever it takes, I give you my blessing.'"

Ben paused and looked at Aila, whose eyes had welled with tears.

"We haven't hit anywhere near forty years yet, but I think as time goes on, I understand more and more what he meant." Ben raised his glass. "To whatever it takes. Cheers!"

He sat back down and clinked glasses with Aila again and she admired her husband as she sipped her champagne. "Thank you for being so good to my parents."

"Me and you. Forever," he said and he kissed her cheek, making her skin tingle.

When one of their favorite songs started blaring through the speakers, Aila turned to Ben.

"Did you request this?" she asked.

"Of course," he said and grabbed her hand, pulling her to the dance floor where their boys were already in a full dance-off.

They danced. They laughed. They celebrated family and love and commitment in its truest form.

Aila and Ben knew how to be a team when they wanted to be, even if they were constantly struggling to find a way to not have either one of them stuck on the bench. But on this particular summer night, throwing a spectacular anniversary party for her parents, they were a beautiful united front. The layers of their relationship are what complicated it, but it was also what made it beautiful.

It was the summer before Isaac's kindergarten year. The year their lives would change irrevocably and completely.

Even if they didn't know it yet.

CHAPTER 45

NOW

At the ring of the doorbell, Aila walks to the entryway to open the door to retrieve what she's assuming is a package being delivered.

It's not a package.

It's Chantelle with Chloe and Emma.

"Hey!" Aila says, with genuine excitement. She bends down to catch the eyes of Emma and Chloe. "The boys will be so excited you girls are here to play. And guess what? I made cookies!"

The girls squeal and tear through the house looking for their friends, while Aila gives Chantelle a hug. She returns it but it feels loose and sloppy. It makes Aila's heart drop. As does the fact Chantelle didn't just walk in to her house. She always just walked in. Ever since they were roommates. But today, she rang the doorbell.

"You don't need to ring the doorbell, Chantelle," she says.

"Don't I?" Chantelle says, setting her purse on the credenza.

"You know you can always just walk in, like you

always have." Aila gives her a smile that walks the line between hopeful and desperate.

"Aila, it's different." Chantelle lets out a breath. "I can't fully explain how, but it is."

Aila knows how. It's different because she lied to her best friend. She kept a secret from her for months. A big secret, one that held consequences and deceit. One that caused her friend to doubt who she is as a person.

So no, Chantelle doesn't just walk through the front door anymore. She knocks to make sure she's welcome first.

The realization hurts and it's something Aila wants to address later, but not right now. Not when she and Ben are supposed to head out on their homework assignment from Joanne while Chantelle watches their kids.

Aila nods instead and rubs her lips together, forcing a smile before stepping into the living room.

"So, where are you two headed tonight?" Chantelle asks, leaning against the arm of the couch.

Aila tucks her hair behind her ear. "Uh, I don't actually know. Ben said he'd plan something."

Like old Ben would. My Ben.

Ben waltzes in wearing shorts and flip flops with a t-shirt, the smell of his cologne wafting past her make her stomach flip.

"We're taking the boat out on the Sound," he says and smiles almost nervously.

Aila smiles back—though her smile is just as nervous and hesitant. They hadn't taken the boat out since last summer, and it's something they love to do together. So do the kids. Her heart begins beating faster. She feels both excited and anxious—while wondering if a ride on the boat will stir up memories that help them heal or memories that tear them further apart.

"Aw, man. Can I come?" Josh must have overheard.

"Next time," Ben says, smiling at him while grabbing his keys.

Out on the water, Aila quickly realizes Ben knew exactly what he was doing. It was a great choice. When they're on a boat, they can talk but they don't have to. They can look at each other but they don't have to. They can talk about all the beauty surrounding them, or they can just look at it and listen to the subtle sound of the waves lapping at the sides of the boat. They motor around the Puget Sound for nearly an hour before Ben cuts the engine, letting the boat rock with the tide.

They'd barely spoken during the ride, but Aila looked back a few times from the helm and was met with softer eyes than she'd seen on Ben in months.

Aila stares at the sun, willing it to set so the evening would be close to over. It still hangs in the sky, bright and robust, forcing her to look away.

"Hey, you remember that time I got stung by a jelly fish?" Ben asks, breaking the silence.

Aila smiles. "You tried so hard not to swear in front of the boys."

"Oh man, that hurt like a…" he clears his throat and looks at her, his eyebrows raised knowingly.

"I can only imagine. But, hey, I said I'd pee on it but you wouldn't let me," she says, laughing.

"Yes, and further traumatize our children." He laughs. "Good thing I know that doesn't actually help."

"You've always been the smarter one." She smiles, tossing her hair back and looking at Ben. "I knew you'd laugh about it one day."

He meets her eyes briefly but then looks away.

"Yeah, who knew."

…It'd be today.

Aila wants to finish his sentence but she doesn't. Instead she feels rescued from the awkward discussion of the memory that resurfaced by the sun finally falling into a sunset. She quickly becomes entranced and thankful for the distraction. Ben joins her on the bow of the boat—his close proximity surprising her.

They are so broken. There is so much damage between them. Pain from her infidelity. Emptiness from his neglect for years. The crack between them is painful, jagged and angry but laced with desperation. Aila desperately wants to mend them back together but she knows she can't do it alone. She needs Ben. And they both need something more.

He smiles at her and then looks at the sunset. They're sitting at least a foot a part but Aila realizes quickly this is the closest they've been to each other in over a month. At least on purpose. His presence feels comforting and Aila can feel it consume her, washing away a little bit of the guilt and shame she's been carrying around.

She reaches over the seat and grabs his hand. He doesn't look at her. Not right away at least. But he takes her hand in his and holds it tightly. The warmth from his fingertips radiates through her body and makes her heart swell.

Ben looks at her, his eyes are dark but soft. Hopeful. She sees it. It's brief but she knows it's there.

Hope.

Aila wipes a tear from her cheek and smiles.

"I love you, Ben."

He nods and hangs his head. Tears are slowly tumbling down his cheeks.

"You know that, right?" Aila says through her tears. "I never meant—this isn't how our story is supposed to go. And I'm so sorry. I don't know how to fix this one alone. I need your help."

He places the palms of his hands on his eyes and drags them down his face, letting out an exasperated sigh.

"Aila, I have loved you since the first night I met you in college. I thought to myself: I am going to give this beautiful girl a wonderful life one day. A life she deserves. A real-life fairy tale with her as my queen." He clears his throat in an attempt to gain his composure. "I thought that was what I was doing—what I did. I had no idea that wasn't what you wanted."

"You're right. It isn't what I wanted. All I wanted was you. I wanted you to be home. To love me. To love our boys. To spend time with us." Aila wipes her eyes and lets out a breath. "You were my dream. Not the house. Or the boat. Or not having to work. I just wanted you. And somewhere along the line, you just disappeared and we became this functioning, picture-perfect family where the dad got photo shopped in here and there."

Ben clasps his hands in front of his face, contemplating her words. "Why didn't you ever tell me?"

She sighs. "I did tell you."

Ben sits back quickly, surprised by that.

"This just tells me how little you heard me. Ever since the boys were little, it was a constant battle of asking you to be home at a decent hour, to help out around the house, to pay attention to *our life*. You always just nodded as if you were acknowledging what I was saying, promising better, but without changing any of your behavior."

"Well, why didn't you make me change my behavior?"

Aila shakes her head. "I shouldn't have to scream at you to get you to treat me well. That's not fair."

"Well, it's not fair for you to run off and cheat."

She scoffs. "Ben, you were already gone."

Ben closes his eyes and rubs his brow, withholding a rise of anger. "So, you think my behavior justifies your actions then?"

"No, I'm not saying that."

"Then what are you saying? Because me working too much is no excuse for you to turn into a liar."

The mood shifts quickly and he gets up to walk back to the wheel, Aila's eyes follow him.

He is partly right and it feels like a punch to the gut. Aila was so concerned about being what she thought was a good wife that she lost her voice and thought she could find it with someone else, which only destroyed every illusion she had ever created.

But she has finally found her voice and she isn't going to lose it now.

"Don't stop now, Ben," she says. "Let it out. Tell me what you really think."

Ben holds up a hand. "Aila, stop."

"No, Ben." She stands to meet him. "Let it out. I'm sick of the secrets just as much as you are. Because let's be honest, Ben, the facade and lies started long before the affair."

"That's not fair. I have always been honest with you. I never lied."

"No, you never lied. You just dismissed me. You stopped showing up. At least when it mattered to me, and I became exhausted and invisible. Until somebody actually noticed me and I realized *that* was what was missing from my life. From *our* life. And I should've told you how I was feeling because maybe things would have turned out differently. But I didn't. So right now, all I'm asking is you meet me where I'm at right now. Because we can't change what happened. I can't fix it. You can't dismiss it. But we have three beautiful boys counting on their mom and dad to quit acting like strangers...or enemies. And I am just asking you to please *try* to love me again."

Ben's gaze pierces through Aila. He's searching her eyes for honesty even though the words she just spoke are more raw and sincere than they've been in years.

He nods finally, like he's in agreement.

"I never stopped loving you, Aila," he says. "But I need something from you. I need transparency—not just with the affair but with your feelings, day in and out. Quit trying to make everything perfect all the time because you know I take things at face value. So, if something isn't right, I need you to just say it. I also need the new password to your phone."

Aila nods, agreeing.

"There's one more thing," he says, pulling in a deep breath and letting it go. "I need to talk to Jackson."

CHAPTER 46

NOW

Aila just wants Jackson to disappear. She doesn't want Ben to talk to him. That makes him even more real in their marriage and it feels humiliating.

But Ben needs answers—wants to face the problem head on, man-to-man. Aila also knows he was comparing stories between her and Jackson. As an attorney, Ben is thorough. He'd research and interview and gather information from all sides of a story, taking everything into account before making his argument.

She knows this because she knows him.

Still, giving Ben Jackson's number felt like a betrayal to Jackson and that was a really tough pill for her to swallow. Shouldn't Jackson's feelings be the least of her concerns right now?

Shouldn't I be over him?

In most ways she is. She hasn't spoken to him since the day he came to their house begging for her to change her mind. After that, she didn't even respond when he texted her his brother would be supervising her neighborhood's landscaping to "make things easier." Even though there was a part of her that wanted to.

Aila can't help but wonder if he meant easier for himself or easier for her, because truth be told, she needs the memories of him to be gone as well. Especially the good ones. How was it possible her betrayal broke her own heart just as much as it broke Jackson's and Ben's?

Aila stands at the counter opening a bottle of wine after the boys went upstairs to bed, pouring two glasses with shaky hands before heading out to the back deck where Ben sits.

His demeanor is calm and his expression is contemplative but it wanders.

He had met with Jackson earlier that day. His behavior tells her he isn't any angrier than he was before, which meant Jackson was honest and his story lined up with hers. As it should; she didn't lie to Ben once she started to tell him the truth again.

As she answered every gut-wrenching question, Aila never felt more embarrassed or humiliated. Her ego, her pride, her image, everything was stripped away while Ben took note of everything she had to say.

Then he was humiliated.

What a mess we've turned into, she had thought.

And now, they both sit and stare blankly at the fire on the back deck, mindlessly swirling their wine waiting for someone to break the silence.

"It was real for Jackson," Ben says finally, not meeting her eye.

Aila's chest constricts and she swallows back her tears.

"It was real for you too, wasn't it?" he says. This time turning to look at his wife, just as two tears roll down her face.

She doesn't move or nod or shake her head, she just looks back at Ben. Her heart is pounding so hard she can hear it throb in her ears.

"Do you really want me to respond to that?" she asks finally.

Ben gives a solemn nod.

Aila blinks back more tears and clears her throat.

"I think it could have been, if I'm being honest. I think when you go down a rabbit hole, it all feels and looks real, even when it's not the truth. I think the friendship was real. The attraction was real. But the commitment..." she trails off, shaking her head before taking a deep breath. "We weren't committed. I didn't make promises to him. So whatever attraction and relationship we had, it doesn't really matter if it was real or not. The only reason it happened was because I broke my promises to you. And if I had kept my word—if we hadn't crossed the line—it would have never happened."

She shrugs.

"But do you miss him?"

"Like I said, Ben, if I hadn't ever let this happen, there wouldn't be anyone to miss."

"Dammit, Aila. Quit speaking in what-ifs. It's not helpful. I get it, if you didn't have an affair, we wouldn't be having this conversation but you did and we are. So please, answer the question. Do you miss him?"

Aila's eyes feel swollen from all the tears. She presses her lips together before answering the question.

"Sometimes."

Ben lets out a long sigh and leans his elbows on his knees.

"But I miss us more," she says as her chin shakes and she holds back more tears. "Not just how we were before this happened but just how we used to be. Before kids and careers, we just...loved each other and supported each other and we laughed together. We were unstoppable, a force to be reckoned with. Nothing was forced or rushed. And I miss that. Because somewhere along the way, I didn't just forget who I am but we... *we* forgot who we are."

Aila lets out a shaky breath and Ben looks up at her, his eyes rimmed with silent tears.

"I am just so sorry," she adds. "And I don't know

what else to say or what else it's going to take, but I'll do it. We can get through it. I know we can. But I need the both of us to *want* to."

He stares at her a moment with exhausted and sad eyes before responding.

"I'm sorry too." There's a sincerity and regret lined in his voice and Aila can physically feel a weight lift off her chest. "I should have been around more. My absence made you vulnerable. I kept saying I'd do better but I never did. I left you unprotected and I'm sorry."

Aila's eyes well with tears as he leans over, grasping her face gently with his hand.

His palm feels warm and strong and brand new against her skin. When his lips touch hers, they feel both intoxicating and familiar, but somehow different—like a second first kiss.

When he makes love to her later that night it feels vulnerable and slow, like they each want to savor and consume each part of each other, until they finally fall away, exhausted and satisfied.

Ben gives her a sheepish grin just before he gets up to get dressed. Her watchful eyes follow him. Aila can tell there is still something off—something not quite right. But she hopes time will help and she knows tonight is exactly what they needed. The words, the tears, the confrontation, the gut-wrenching honesty, the intimacy.

It all matters.

At this point she realizes, they have the ability and the power to do what feels impossible: they can love each other back together.

CHAPTER 47

NOW

"Well, it appears things are going well for the two of you," Joanne says, shifting in her chair as she looks between Ben and Aila.

They turn their heads and exchange a glance.

"What makes you say that?" Aila asks.

"Well, if you remember, when we started this three months ago, you each sat on either ends of the couch. Today, you are merely two inches apart and you're holding hands."

Joanne raises her eyebrows at the lack of space between them.

Aila blushes but she doesn't know why. The innuendo in the eyebrow raise is about her and her husband.

Joanne smirks at them with her palm pressed gently against her chin.

"So, I take it the two of you have been intimate recently."

They both narrow their eyes on their therapist and let out a laugh simultaneously.

"Look at you two...like a couple of teenagers." Joanne takes her glasses off and leans forward to speak directly to them. "Sex is a great indicator of healing. It is not the end all, be all. Don't misunderstand. But good, healthy sex is a key indicator of a good, healthy relationship. Would you say that's what you're having?"

"Yes," Ben says, nodding.

"Aila?"

"Most of the time, yes," she says.

Why did I preface that?

"You say 'most of the time.' Why?" Joanne asks as Ben's eyes shoot through Aila like lasers.

"Uh, just sometimes I feel like I'm trying really hard to make it happen. Other times it feels like Ben is second guessing me while it's happening." She shrugs and chews on the side of her cheek. "I don't know. I'm probably overthinking it. It's nothing, honestly. Forget I said that."

"We don't need to forget it, Aila. If you said it, it's something you're feeling and we should address it," Joanne says and then turns to Ben. "Does this ring any truth in your ears?"

Ben is silent a beat too long and Aila presses her eyelids closed.

"Sometimes there's a disconnect," Ben says finally. "I get in my head a bit, I guess."

"Aila, it seems you sense that?"

Of course, I sense that. I know you, Ben.

"You're thinking about me and Jackson, aren't you?" Aila directs this at Ben.

Ben half sighs and tilts his head from side to side like he's cracking his neck.

"Aila, I don't know…"

"I knew you going to meet with him was a bad idea. He didn't tell you anything I didn't already tell you but now you have more details and confirmation. Now that you've heard from him you can't stop thinking about whatever he said or however he said it. Isn't that right?" There's a pained desperation laced in each word she speaks.

Therapy is really just a bobbing and weaving through memories and pain. Over. And over again. Each time there is any healing, the flesh pulls back more. Every time they bandage something new, an old wound resurfaces.

It is painful. It's defeating. But it's raw and vulnerable too. Aila always knew Ben, but now she truly sees him. And he sees her too, every part of her. Even the parts she always wanted to keep hidden so she could appear perfect.

"Aila, we discussed this collectively and agreed his conversation with Jackson could provide him some closure so his unanswered questions didn't make him second-guess everything," Joanne interjects.

They both ignore her.

"Aila, I needed those answers but getting them made everything more real. Your affair became tangible. Somebody else knows everything about us and that hurts." He shakes his head. "I don't know how else to say it."

"But I've given you everything. Answers to your questions, access to my phone… I've been completely transparent. What else is there?"

He presses his lips together, silent.

"What *else*, Ben?" Aila asks through tears.

Ben holds his silence until Joanne speaks up.

"Ben, maybe that's something you should consider over the next couple of weeks. With the exception of time, is there anything else you need from Aila to move forward?"

"There isn't really anything else," Ben says, finally. "It's just hard."

He's exhausted. She's exhausted. And it is written all across their faces.

"I told you this was going to take lot of hard work when we started this ascent, and I am very proud of the both you," Joanne says smiling empathically. "We did good work today, friends. Let's pray."

Out of all their therapy sessions, this is the first time Aila truly heeds each word Joanne prays. She squeezes her hands together tighter and begs God to listen. To hear them. To hear her.

She wants forgiveness. She wants redemption.

For their family.
For their marriage.
For Ben.
For herself.

The work feels too hard. Aila knows it's going to take something beyond their control to heal them. Something like a miracle.

CHAPTER 48

THEN

Aila sat in their apartment the day after Christmas, staring at the pile of wedding gifts from her bridal shower the month before. An unopened blender. A new set of wine glasses. The overly priced China they'd probably never use but her mother insisted she register for.

"Do I have to return all of these if the wedding gets called off?" Aila asked.

"One, if the wedding gets called off, returning the gifts would be the least of your concerns. And two, the wedding isn't going to get called off, drama queen."

Aila's eyes rolled in the direction of Chantelle, who was also sitting on the floor, heelless in the night's cocktail dress.

"Chay, I am so mad at him." Aila couldn't reel in the fumes coming out of her ears.

"Girl, I get it. But I honestly think it was just an oversight. He didn't realize the importance of getting this handled before the rehearsal," Chantelle said.

"With the exception of his tux measurements, the only thing he was supposed to do was order the catering for the rehearsal. Which is only like thirty people, and yet, he's acting like I asked him to plan the whole wedding. I've handled absolutely everything else. This was his only responsibility for the rehearsal or the wedding," Aila sighed and wiped a tear from her mascara smeared face. "It feels like he doesn't even care about getting married."

"Aila, he messed up. He feels terrible, I'm sure. And even Sharon was upset. I bet she's on the phone with every restaurant she can think of getting it taken care of," Chantelle said, resting her hand on Aila's arm.

"I just want it to be perfect. My family has expectations, you know?"

Chantelle smiled. "I know. But I also know you care more about marrying Ben than having croque monsieur for your rehearsal meal."

Aila laughed and wiped her runny nose, just as there was a knock on the door.

"I'll grab it," Chantelle said and then kissed Aila on the forehead.

Aila heard the muffled conversation of a distraught Ben at the door, asking if he could come in.

As if it isn't his apartment too.

Chantelle conceded and then slipped out the door to let them talk.

"Hey," Ben said, standing by the front door.

"Hey," Aila said, wiping her mascara-streaked tears on her hand.

He looked terrible. Aila knew he felt awful.

"My mom and I called Stanley & Seafort's. They can cater the rehearsal," he said, his hands in his pockets. It was his only offering.

"Great," Aila said plainly.

"I mean they don't serve croque monsieur but there will be crab and artichoke dip. I hope that helps," he said, smiling slowly.

Aila smiled back, reluctantly.

Ben approached her then and sat next to her on the

floor.

"Aila, I am so sorry I forgot about the food for the rehearsal. I know how hard you've worked at putting everything together, and I think because you've just handled everything, I forgot I had anything to do."

Aila's eyes narrowed on him.

"How long were you listening outside the door?"

Ben smiled. "Not long."

She laughed then let out a sigh. "Ben, you make me crazy."

"Crazy enough to forgive and forget?" His eyes were charming and hopeful.

"Almost," Aila said. "Look, I'm thankful you handled the catering situation with such late notice but don't you realize how that makes me feel? I have been working like crazy while you're still in law school, and planning the wedding, and I only asked you to take care of one thing. One. And you totally forgot. It makes me feel like you don't even care. Like you don't even want to get married."

Ben nodded slowly, absorbing her words.

"You're right. I dropped the ball and it was the one thing you made me carry, while you've been juggling more than you should have to. I'm so sorry. I promise you, I'll make it up to you. But I need you to understand one thing," he said, placing his arm around her.

"What's that?"

"I want to marry you more than anything in the world. I only care about the parties and the big fancy wedding because you care about it. I just want you. I want to spend a lifetime with you. Loving you. Hurting your feelings and making it up to you. There is no else in the world worth fighting with or fighting for, I promise you that."

Aila smiled at him. "That's so corny."

"Yes, it is," he said, smiling. "But love is sometimes corny. And I love you, Aila. More than anything."

Ben pulled her into his arms and she rested her head on his chest, letting out a deep sigh.

"I hope this is the biggest fight we ever have."

Ben laughed at that.

"I guarantee you it won't be. We've got a lifetime to beat this one."

And they did.

Each one a crack on the surface that was patched and repainted. Over and over again. Sometimes the same crack would resurface, other times a new crack would appear all together, but they always repaired it one way or another.

Until the day when their world shook and the walls rattled, shaking out every crack and crevice that was there. Until the day they stood next to each other looking at their ruins, both wanting to walk away, but deciding to rebuild.

CHAPTER 49

NOW

"So, who has the boys this fine afternoon? Shouldn't you have picked them up by now?" Elena asks, sitting across from Aila on the couch in her living room, after finishing an autumn walk around the lake.

"Chantelle, actually. She wanted to pick the boys up for ice cream after school with her girls." Aila rotates the hot tea in her hand and checks her watch. "They're probably back at the house, but she said to take my time—they'll just let themselves in the house to play. I really shouldn't stay too much longer though."

"Sounds like you two have made some progress?"

Aila nods. "It took a lot of talking and convincing and apologizing… but we're practically sisters. We can get through this. We still have some uncomfortable moments but we're getting there."

"I'm happy to hear that." Elena sets her tea on the table. "So, how are you and Ben right now?"

Aila lets out a long breath.

It's been six long months since she told him about her affair.

The reality is their marriage has become a mix of

contradictions. Trust and broken promises. Healing and wounds that cut deeper still. But redemption is always around the corner. The trouble with corners though is they can't see around them, which meant each day feels like they are walking around with blind hope.

But it was enough. At least most days it feels like it's enough.

"We're good mostly," she says, furrowing her brow. "Some days are harder. I can tell when Ben is thinking about it. He's moodier then. I used to give him a pass but I haven't been lately. I get I can only reassure him of my fidelity over time, but he can't hold it over me either. Therapy has been helping though. We've carved out time for weekly date nights and that's made a tremendous difference. We didn't realize how much we've missed each other."

Elena nods. "And you? How are you feeling about everything that has happened?"

Aila ponders this for a moment.

"I think if you asked me a few months ago, I would have told you I truly believed I fell in love and it was beyond my control. It was real in so many ways and probably could have become more if I chose it. But now that I'm out and Ben and I have made so much progress, I just think I was lost. Not in love."

Elena nods silently.

"Sometimes when you're lost, it doesn't matter who finds you. You cling to that person and they become your hero. Your savior. But Jackson didn't save me. He didn't ruin me either, thank God. We just both said yes to something that was off limits." She shrugs. "It's just still so difficult most days. My relationships aren't the same with anybody. Everyone wants to talk about it and ask us how we're doing. It's draining."

"I can only imagine," Elena says, placing her hand over Aila's. "You must feel so depleted at the end of every day. I know sometimes it feels like you aren't right in step with God and he seems far away, but I will keep praying for you as you navigate through the mess."

"Can you pray for it all to just disappear?" Aila half-laughs at her request.

"Well, we know that isn't going to happen, so please tell me that's not really what you want me to pray for."

Aila eyes her quizzically.

"What do you pray for, Aila?" Elena asks.

Aila stops smiling and clears her throat.

"You don't have to tell me. I know it's not my business."

"No, no. I guess I've just never been asked about my own prayers. I just pray I forgive myself. And that Ben forgives me. Like true unconditional forgiveness." Tears well up in her eyes as she thinks about it. "God, it is so hard. Some days I don't know if it's even worth it."

Elena grabs her hand and squeezes it.

"It is worth it. And I know it might feel like all eyes are on you, judging you right now—and some might be—but the eyes that matter are loving you through it. And we are so very proud of you both."

"Thank you." Aila offers a smile as she wipes her cheeks and looks at her phone. "Chantelle's calling me. Excuse me while I check on everything quickly."

"Maybe five kids at the ice cream shop was too much for her to handle," Elena says with a chuckle.

Aila smiles at Elena and answers her phone.

Within seconds her posture changes from being laid back on the couch to being perched on the cushion as if it is loaded with springs.

The color washes out of Aila's face completely when she hangs up.

"What's going on? Everything okay?"

She is already slipping her shoes on before Elena even finishes the question.

No, God, please, not my baby.

"Isaac was hit by a car."

CHAPTER 50

NOW

Ben is the first person Aila sees when she and Elena reach the hospital. He was already on his way home from work when Chantelle called so he beat them there. As he stands at the counter in the emergency room, hastily signing something that didn't matter as long as it'd get him to his son, their eyes meet and their expressions match— a mix of desperate worry and determination to find answers.

Chantelle told them Isaac was transported via ambulance to the nearest children's hospital so Elena drove Aila straight there. The rest of the kids and Chantelle are already in the waiting area a little deeper in the emergency room, which is never a good sign. Aila has a feeling this means Isaac's injuries are more serious than she hoped.

When Ben, Aila, and Elena reach the waiting room, they see the four other kids are sitting on navy chairs with coloring pages provided by the hospital staff, while Chantelle paces in front of them, biting her thumb nail.

Her face is smeared with mascara and tears, and she rushes over to Aila when she sees her, holding her tightly.

"Aila, I'm so sorry. The car just…just came out of nowhere. I didn't even really see it happen. One second he was riding his bike next to Chloe and the next—" Chantelle's voice breaks off into a cry she tries to clear away.

Aila pulls back and holds Chantelle's face in her hands.

"Where is Isaac?" Aila asks, trying to stay calm until she has more information.

"They rushed him back. I haven't seen him yet. When it happened I ran to him but he wasn't conscious so I called an ambulance and followed them with the kids. Aila, I am so sorry. It all happened so fast. I wish I had done something."

"Was he wearing a helmet?"

"Yes, of course."

She goes on to explain when they had gotten back to the house after getting ice cream, the kids asked Chantelle if they could ride bikes out front while they waited for their mom to come back. She, of course, thought it'd be a great way to burn off the extra sugar before dinner. Caleb and Emma grabbed the chalk and started drawing a town on the street, Josh took off on his skateboard, Chloe was on a scooter, and Isaac took off on his bike.

One moment he was laughing because he'd won the race. The next, he was laying on the concrete unconscious next to a blue Honda Civic with a frantic teenage driver yelling for help, just passed the mailboxes near the busy corner that turns onto Cherrywood Lane.

Unable to speak, the shock of the news washes over Aila to the point her hands begin to shake so badly she can feel it in her chest. She turns to look at Ben who was checking in with the kids.

They are doe-eyed and calm, except for Josh. His brow is furrowed.

"Is Isaac going to be alright, Dad?" Josh asks, looking up at Ben. Being the oldest, he better understood the gravity of the situation.

Ben blinks away a tear and squeezes his shoulder. "I'm sure he will be," Ben says and turns to Aila. "Let's go find someone that can tell us what's going on."

Aila looks at her boys and then looks at Elena, who has taken a seat next to Caleb.

"Go on," she says, her eyes are filled with tears but none of them fall and her smile is hopeful. "I'll help Chantelle hold it down over here."

Aila grabs Ben's hand, and they walk to the nearest nurse station to gather any more information they can find.

A short, round woman with cropped brown hair is pecking away at the keyboard for what feels like an eternity, until finally she has more information on her screen.

Aila allows her grip to ease up on Ben's hand, not realizing her nails were digging into his skin.

"Ah, here it is. Isaac Sorenson. He is still getting his CT-scan but should be done in the next thirty minutes or so. They are preparing a room for him, which someone will take you to when he's out. Okay?"

"A CT-scan?" Ben asks, the concern in his voice growing. "Can you tell us the extent of his injuries?"

"Right now, they are taking every precaution to find out the exact extent of his injuries and his doctor will explain everything to you in better detail than I can."

"Ma'am?" Aila can barely formulate words. "He's only six. He is my baby and he is alone. Can you please take me to him?"

The nurse smiles, sympathetically, and reaches out to touch Aila's arm.

"I promise you he is not alone. He is in excellent care, surrounded by nurses and doctors, and they will let you know when you can go see him."

"We understand, thank you," Ben says. He appears composed but Aila can feel the anxiety pulse through his fingertips.

He looks at her and an entire conversation passes through that one stare.

This was their child. Their baby. And they had no idea if he was okay.

The walk back to the waiting area feels long and the

white hallway seems endless. The beeping of heart monitors intermingles with announcements from the intercom and faint sounds of babies crying behind closed doors.

This is a nightmare. I need to wake up.

It wasn't more than fifteen minutes that Aila and Ben were away talking to the nurse, but when they return to the waiting room there are more people with Chantelle and Elena than when they left.

Sharon sits with Caleb, enthralled by a game of tic-tac-toe on the back of a coloring page. Aila's parents are there too, her mother holding Chantelle's hand and her father doing simultaneous thumb wars with Josh and Emma. Joe had come too. Even Derek is there with Chloe on his lap.

Each pair of eyes turn to look at Aila and Ben. That is when Aila finally starts to cry.

She looks around the room, tragedy washed across everyone's faces, but also hope and relief.

Her parents, Sharon, Elena and Joe, Chantelle, Derek, Chloe and Emma. Her sweet boys. Ben. *My Ben.*

These are the most important people in her life. These are the people that show up regardless of her mistakes. They are the strength and bones of the village they've built around their marriage. She needs them. And she had failed them.

Her mom reaches her first and pulls her and Ben in for a desperate hug, like she is trying to take a bullet for them. The kind of hugs only moms can give.

Then Sharon. Her dad. Chantelle. Elena. Derek. Until each person in the room, even the kids, come together wrapped in each other's arms in the middle of sterile walls and they pray.

Aila cries, her body shaking with hope.

By the time Elena says amen, a woman in purple scrubs is standing near them. She is taller than the first nurse they spoke with. Her hair is pulled back in a tight bun and the smattering of freckles across her nose makes Aila think she looks too young to be a nurse.

"Mr. and Mrs. Sorenson?"

"That's us," Ben says, pulling Aila gently under his arm.

"Isaac is ready to see you, if you'll follow me. I will warn you though, he's a bit groggy from the pain medication." She reads the room. "But maybe most of you should wait until Mom and Dad have seen him."

"That's fine, honey, we'll all wait here with the kids," Sharon says.

When they reach his hospital room, Isaac's appearance nearly brings Aila to her knees. She clings to Ben to keep her up, but she can tell he's wavering too.

Isaac's head is bandaged and the left side of his face is swollen and purple. He has an IV in his right arm and a telemetry monitor on his finger. His left arm is bandaged and braced.

"Hey, baby," Aila says, rushing to his side and lightly kissing his forehead. "It's Mom and Dad. We're here, sweet boy."

Isaac turns his head toward them and offers a soft, swollen smile.

"I went past the mailboxes, Mom. I'm sorry."

He's conscious.

Ben and Aila exchange a look of relief.

"Oh, don't you worry about that. We are just going to worry about getting you better, okay?" Aila sniffs and gently pats his leg.

She wants to pick him up and rock him like an infant but she doesn't want to break him anymore than he already is.

"You feeling okay, buddy?" Ben's voice is low and raspy.

Isaac doesn't have time to answer because they're interrupted by two swift knocks on the doorframe. They turn to see a man standing in a white coat with rolled up sleeves and short brown hair that's going gray on the sides.

"Hi there, I'm Dr. Panzer," he says, reaching out a hand.

"Ben." He takes Dr. Panzer's hand and shakes it.

"Aila," she says, likewise shaking the doctor's hand.

"Well, let's take a look at what we have going on here." He sits at the computer, clicking around a few times to pull up Isaac's scans. "Now, he was brought here via ambulance, correct?"

They nod.

"Was he with you when he was struck by the vehicle?"

"No, he was with a friend," Ben says.

The doctor nods.

They had already given this information in the waiting room to someone else on staff. So did Chantelle. So did the EMTs. Aila knows they are just confirming the events to protect Isaac but the repetition of the trauma makes her feel like she is going to throw up.

"So, because he was reported unconscious at the scene—even though it was less than a minute—it is standard to do a CT-scan. And if you look here," he points to a black and white image of Isaac's brain on the screen, "we can tell there isn't any bleeding or trauma to the brain or brain stem."

Ben and Aila nod solemnly, anticipating the "but..."

Dr. Panzer smiles, his teeth are shinier than they should be and his breath smiles like coffee.

Too close.

Aila takes a half step back. She hadn't realized she was hovering over the doctor's shoulder.

"This is good news then?" she asks.

"Yes, great news. Good job wearing you're helmet, bud," he says, winking in Isaac's direction. "He definitely has a concussion and a mean headache, which could potentially last through the month. If any longer than that then he'll need to have another follow-up appointment with his physician."

They nod again.

"Now, it appears the car hit him on his right side, so he has a large hematoma on his right thigh. This will be tender until it heals over the next several weeks."

"And his arm?"

He clicks to another image.

"This here is his left arm. As you can see here, his ulna is broken. This most likely happened when he tried to brace his fall when he got hit." He swivels in his chair away from the computer. "Now, his arm will most likely need surgery to set the bone in place before casting. I'm going to have Dr. Jacobson from orthopedics come take a look—she's excellent. And then we'll know for sure."

"When can we go home?"

"I'd like to keep Isaac here overnight for observation. And that's out of an abundance of caution since he lost consciousness upon impact. But honestly," Dr. Panzer logs out of the computer and turns back to Aila and Ben, "your son is very lucky to escape with bruises and a broken bone. And he has a great attitude to boot—he must have great parents."

Aila wants to crumble to the ground. She feels exhausted with relief and gives the doctor a small smile of thanks. She turns back to Isaac on the bed and curls beside him, careful not to press against his bruised leg.

"Thank you, Dr. Panzer," Ben says, shaking his hand.

"Of course. Here's my card, if you have any more questions. Dr. Jacobson will be down to check his arm shortly and I'll be back tomorrow to do one final check before we send you home."

Aila and Ben nod their gratitude and the doctor slips outside the door.

Ben lets out a deep sigh and looks at Isaac.

"You scared us, buddy."

Isaac's chin quivers and a tear falls down his bruised cheek.

"I'm sorry, Dad. I didn't mean to go past the mailboxes, I was just going so fast I couldn't slow down to turn around."

Ben smiles and sits down on the end of the bed,

holding on to Isaac's hand that isn't braced and bandaged.

"No, you don't need to apologize. This was just an accident. You are all that matters right now."

Aila feels like she's looking at Ben through a whole new lens, even though this was always who he was.

Her Ben.

He loves and provides. He's their protector. Their calm during the storm.

"Dad's right, sweet boy. And when we get home, we're ordering you a cape because you definitely earned your superhero status today."

Isaac smiles and winces at the same time.

"I'm going to go get your brothers really quick. I'm sure they'd like to see their real-life superhero brother," Ben says with a smile, as he gets up and heads out of the room.

Minutes later, Ben returns with everyone from the waiting room. In the small and crowded room, they all flock to Isaac's bed and tell him how brave and strong he is, though they all say it with tears in their eyes and a quake in their voice. A six-year-old should never be as bruised and battered as Isaac is regardless of the miracle that protected him from the car.

Chantelle is shaking with relief, even though she can't stop crying. Aila holds her as she would a child and pulls into the hallway.

"He's okay, Chantelle," she says. "You did what any of us would have or should have done. I will never be able to repay you for taking care of our boy."

Chantelle wipes her face.

"I just wish it never happened."

Aila presses her lips together and smiles with tear-filled eyes.

"But it did and you did the right thing and I'm so thankful you were there. Look at him." She peers through the door. "He's going to be okay."

Chantelle nods and shudders in relief.

Everyone visits a few more minutes before trickling

home. Elena promises to bring back dinner before visiting hours are over.

Sharon ends up staying the longest. Her quiet presence offering a calm and peace Aila and Ben both need in the moment.

"Well," Sharon says, after Elena drops off teriyaki chicken takeout. "Now that you two are fed, I think I'd better head out too. Call me when you get an update, okay?"

"Sure. I'll walk you out, Mom," Ben says, standing from the chair next to Isaac's bed.

"No, I'd like to walk you out if that's okay?" Aila looks at her mother-in-law, hopeful and unsure.

Sharon smiles and nods once, like she has been waiting for this for months.

She probably has been.

They walk down the hall in silence for a few minutes—the sounds of their footsteps echoing as they make their way outside. Aila grabs Sharon's arm and pulls her closer, their lack of eye contact and close proximity making her braver somehow.

"Sharon, I owe you an apology."

Sharon clears her throat and nods.

"You know that though."

Sharon nods again.

This makes Aila cry.

"I am so, very sorry, Sharon. I made promises to you. To your son. And I didn't honor them." Aila's voice breaks and it takes a few moments for her to gain her composure. "I don't know how to make it up to you or regain your trust or mend our relationship. But I want you to know I still love Ben and I'm so sorry. And I'm trying."

They stop at the trunk of Sharon's car and she turns toward Aila, grabbing her by the shoulders.

"Aila, I have always loved you. I have always seen you—truly seen you. For who you are, how you love, and what you can orchestrate out of life. And as much as it's hurt me to watch the two of you battle it out over this last year; to see how broken you've made each other feel; to hear of the betrayal you promised would never come, I want you to know this: I am still on your side."

Tears fall down Aila's face and she tries to smile.

"Thank you, Sharon."

Sharon hugs Aila and whispers in her ear, "Don't stop fighting."

When she pulls away, she squeezes Aila's hands and silently slips in her car. Her words echo in her ear. She expected a reprimand or a sneery silence. Aila had cheated on her only son and Sharon responded with love.

She had feared this conversation for months; let it twist through her heart like a knife even though it hadn't even pierced her skin. And yet, Sharon responded with grace.

Unconditional, undeserved grace.

CHAPTER 51

NOW

"What time did he eat last?" Dr. Jacobson asks Aila and Ben while Isaac sleeps.

"They brought in a sandwich and apple sauce at seven but he only ate a few bites of the apple sauce. He was pretty hopped up on pain meds and in and out of sleep," Aila says.

Dr. Jacobson nods and types something in the computer. Her face frowns but her eyes smile, emitting a warmness in the room.

"Okay. So, I'll be able to reset it tomorrow morning then. He'll go into surgery at eight. I'll cast it while he's still under anesthesia and you should be able to head home a few hours later. Just be sure he doesn't eat anything before surgery tomorrow."

Aila nods.

Surgery. Anesthesia.

This day just won't end.

"I can see your mind racing," Dr. Jacobson adds, reading Aila like a book. "This is a very straight forward surgery and it won't take long. It is merely to make sure his bones heal correctly so he doesn't have any problems in the future. It is not as scary as it sounds. Our bodies were created to be resilient, in more ways than one. Trust me."

Dr. Jacobson smiles. Her words offer them both comfort but the worry of a mother lays thick below the surface, like sap in a tree.

Through the night, Aila doesn't sleep. She offers the cot to Ben but she can tell he doesn't sleep either.

Finally, he sits up and moves to the side of the narrow mattress.

"Would you like to lay with me?"

Aila nods and moves into the crest of his body. She molds into him. A perfect fit.

"I don't think I'll sleep much, but this helps. Thank you."

Ben rests his arms across her hip and nuzzles her head under his chin. "I probably won't either. But it's the thought that counts." He chuckles softly.

Aila closes her eyes and breathes in the warmth of his presence and relishes in the strength of his arms encasing her body. Ben always made her feel secure. He was her safe place, always. Her betrayal made him feel distant, but his embrace still felt familiar.

Ben kisses the top of her head and the action makes a lump rise in her throat.

"Are you worried about Isaac's surgery tomorrow?"

"No," Ben offers with a smile in his voice. "And you shouldn't be either. He'll be okay, Aila. I promise."

Aila nods imperceptibly and a tear falls down her cheek.

"I love you, Ben."

The room fills with silence except for the hum of the air flowing through the hospital vents. Aila presses her eyes closed wondering if maybe this is it; they've finally completely sunk. Maybe all hope is lost and they'll never reach the surface again.

Ben pulls in a sharp breath and Aila swallows hard

unsure she wants to hear what he's about to say.

"I love you too, Aila."

Aila turns to face him, their tear-soaked faces just a few breaths apart. She looks at Ben. He's looking at her intently. They don't say a word but continue to lock eyes with tears drifting down to the pillow wrapped in over starched white hospital sheets. Aila grabs his hand and holds it up to her lips, kissing his fingers softly and pressing her eyes closed, willing her tears away.

"I'm sorry, Aila," he says, the very words making her bones crumble on impact. "The weight of this whole thing has fallen on you and that's not completely fair. As angry and hurt as I've been, I let you slip away. I didn't love you properly. Not the way I promised to anyway, and I'm sorry."

"I'm sorry, too. For everything that should have never happened," she says, her chin quivering with emotion. "Are we going to be okay?"

Ben takes a breath and pulls Aila in even closer.

"Yeah, Aila. We're going to be okay. Everything is going to be okay."

EPILOGUE

6 Months Later

Aila wishes it didn't take an accident and their son in the hospital for them to come together. It shouldn't have. But it did.

The world told them to be afraid. To fall apart. But Ben and Aila decided to stand together for the same love and the same cause. To lock away the hurt and the blame. To repair the cracks, and remember every promise they made to each other.

Aila knew this wouldn't be the magic wand waved to make everything as it should be. But it would be the reminder of all that could be, if they both decide every day, moment by moment, to choose each other and their family over every doubt. Every fear.

They were so unsure of what came next. They didn't quite know how to put one foot in front of the other but they decided to do it anyway. It was messy and sloppy, and they stumbled more than they stood, but they knew it was time to clean up the rest of the ashes.

They didn't arrive at the decision lightly or all at once but when faced with tragedy, they realized just how deep their love ran. It was as if the car that crashed into their son also wrecked any illusion of them being better off without each other.

They could have chosen to walk away and no one would have blamed them. But out of the ashes of Aila's affair, they chose to build something even more beautiful.

The year after the affair was torturous. It was destructive and transforming. It was filthy and cleansing—as if their marriage was being baptized. They let the water rush in and clean out the cracks, and together they rebuilt the marriage that was the foundation of their family.

Aila used to think she couldn't help who she loved. That it was fate: an unexpected and uncontrollable series of events that led one person to another. It made it easier to let the blame linger between her and Ben. That is until she realized that was a lie. She can choose who she loves. Love is an active and conscious choice she makes every single day.

Aila chose to be unfaithful.

Not in one specific moment. But little by little, like hopping from tiny stepping-stones sitting in the waves until she was out too deep, and she could no longer see the bottom of the ocean. Each moment was a choice to walk farther away from the life she built with Ben. Now, each moment was a conscious choice to put it back together again.

There were days when Ben wanted to walk away. There were days when Aila wanted to quit. But something always brought them back together, binding them tighter and stronger than they were before.

Their boys were always full of questions and suspicions, but they also became witnesses of how a husband and wife could break almost completely apart and be sewn back together again.

Marriage isn't flippant. It isn't boring or stagnant. It dances and falters. It shatters and can be rebuilt. It can be desolate but it can also be redeemed.

Some of their issues remained, and they knew more would spring up as time went on. But they stopped sweeping them under the rug.

Aila continued to pay her penance for her transgressions, and Ben paid more attention to his wife, spending more time at home and putting boundaries around work. Aila also decided to return to work a few days a week as a freelance advertising consultant.

Their love story isn't perfect. It never was. But they were choosing each other every day. Over and over again.

As Aila stands at the top of Skyline hill, looking out through the crystal-clear blue sky to the snowcapped Olympic Mountains glimmering in the spring sun, she ponders a life she almost chose instead and feels immensely grateful she didn't.

Ben sweeps Aila's hair to the side and kisses her neck softly.

"We've come a long way this year."

Aila breathes in his words and the scent of Cherrywood trees blossoming, knowing they still have so far to go.

She feels the warmth of the sun hitting her face as she leans her head back onto his shoulder, savoring the safety, beauty, and forgiveness in his arms. She turns around slowly, holding his face in her hands, gently caressing his jaw with her fingers.

She kisses him softly and smiles.

"Me and you. Forever."

THE CRACKS BETWEEN US

DISCUSSION QUESTIONS

1. Who do you identify with in the story and why?
2. In Ben and Aila's marriage there were several "cracks" that led to her affair. Which one do you think was the most problematic and why?
3. Looking at your own relationships, how could you relate to their marriage?
4. What do you think Ben's Love Language is? What do you think Aila's is?
5. Do you think Aila fell in love or lust with Jackson? Why or why not?
6. The narrator says that love is a choice. Do you agree or disagree? Why or why not?
7. Do you agree with Ben's decision in the end? If not, why would you have chosen differently?
8. Do you agree with Aila's decision in the end? If not, why would you have chosen differently?
9. Do you think faith played a factor in their decisions? Why or why not?
10. What do you think happens to Jackson?

 Caitlin Moss is a graduate of the Edward R. Murrow School of Communication at Washington State University. She has been published in *North Park News,* and *the San Diego Metropolitan Magazine.* She is a writer turned stay-at-home mom turned author and currently resides in the Pacific Northwest with her husband, three children, and goldendoodle. She loves connecting with her readers on Instagram.

The Cracks Between Us is her first novel.

ACKNOWLEDGMENTS

"I think it's going to be a late night with my laptop, babe," my husband heard me say repeatedly for months, while he effortlessly put the kids to sleep and let me click away at a key board until I created this story. Darren, you have always believed in my dreams even when I stopped talking about them. Thank you for all the support, encouragement, and love over the years. I love our life and I love you.

To Amy, Angelique, Kristen, Trisha, Samantha, Kelsey, Riley, and Teresa, for reading my early drafts and picking apart my writing without completely breaking my spirit. I have grown as a writer and this story has evolved because of your input. Thank you, sweet friends.

To my editor, Annie: you ran through this novel with a fine-tooth comb. I appreciate your eye for literary detail and your brilliant suggestions that completely altered the introduction of Aila and Ben's story. I couldn't have polished this novel without you.

To one of my favorite cheerleaders, Katie: you have always introduced me to people as a writer—even when I hadn't written anything but a meal prepping blog in years. Sometimes the best encouragement is having friends like you in my corner always believing in me.

To every teacher, professor, and editor that has ever pulled me aside and asked, "You wrote this?" Thank you for believing in me, teaching me, and steering me toward writing.

And to all you writer moms out there for being an incredible village of support: let's keep dreaming outside of the pages.

Printed in Great Britain
by Amazon